MARY E. LOWD

THE ENTROPY FOUNTAIN

THE ENTROPY FOUNTAIN
©2020 MARY E. LOWD

Aethon Books
www.aethonbooks.com

Print and eBook formatting, and cover design by Steve Beaulieu. Artwork provided by Luciano Fleitas

Published by Aethon Books LLC.

ALSO IN SERIES

ENTANGLEMENT BOUND

THE ENTROPY FOUNTAIN

STARWHAL IN FLIGHT

1. CIRCLING THE DEVIL'S RADIO

Saving the universe is hungry work.

And a team of heroes who have risked everything—life, limbs if they have them—deserves a moment to rest, recoup, and hopefully feast before moving on. But the edge of a black hole isn't the best place to rest. Nonetheless, two ships orbited the black hole known as the Devil's Radio, lazily circling the deep gravity well. One mechanical and one organic.

The mechanical ship, shining with bronze metal, released a slow stream of space dust into the clear space around the Devil's Radio, and the organic ship, a cybernetically upgraded starwhal, followed along, hungrily devouring the nutrient-rich particles. The stream of space dust was heavy and dense, thick like chocolate cheesecake, when the starwhal was used to subsisting on lighter puffs of dust that spread across space like smears of fluffy whipping cream. Delicious but insubstantial.

The thick space dust filled Cassie's stomach, leaving her feeling full and drowsy, even though her vein-like corridors were emptier than usual. Most of Cassie's crew was aboard the traditional, mechanical spaceship that she was following around the Devil's Radio in lazy loops.

The bronze spaceship was called *The Warren*, and an extended family of lapine aliens lived aboard it. Cassie's crew was a more eclectic assortment of creatures, drawn together by circumstance to save the universe. Now that it was saved, they were taking their moment in the sunlight—or in this case, the dark shadow of a black hole—to revel and reward themselves, celebrating with the several dozen lapines who'd saved them.

Yes, saving the universe was hungry work, but it's also dangerous work, and the intrepid band of adventurers had barely survived.

Clarity kept looking out the wide window of *The Warren*'s mess hall, watching Cassie drift peacefully through space behind them. She missed traditional windows when she was aboard Cassie. The starwhal's blubbery purple body didn't have windows, so the only way to see the stars was through video screens connected to external sensors. It wasn't the same. Even so, she had already come to love the gentle thrumming sound of Cassie's heartbeat. The engines aboard *The Warren* felt cold, clinical, and relentlessly constant in comparison. A single mechanical whine, instead of the rhythmic thudding of life surrounding her.

Of course, the whine of the engine was drowned out by the padding of bare lapine feet dancing across the floor and the musical chaos of panpipes, whistles, flutes, and timpani. All of the tables had been pushed to the sides of the mess hall to make room for the revelry. Most of them were piled high with delicious foods—honeyed croissants, baked tubers, crunchy carrot salads, and molasses-soaked nut breads.

Half the lapines danced; the other half played the music, making for a very large and disorganized band, tapping their feet or twirling in place. Long ears flopped and whirled. The lapines might be short compared to humans, like Clarity, but their fuzzy feet and ears were long.

Clarity's long-term traveling companion, Irohann, danced among them in the best spirits she'd seen him in for a long time. He stood out among the lapines like a red wolf among a sea of brown and gray rabbits, but without any sense of menace. His wolfish grin was all joy today. He'd been freed, at long last, from his fear of his old lover, Queen Doripauli, a sentient tangle of flowers who ruled over an entire sector of the western spiral arm of their galaxy. She had made a formidable enemy in Irohann's previous life, before he gene-modded himself on the black market into an entirely new identity. Fortunately, Cassie's crew had made a formidable, if elusive, ally through saving the universe—an AI named Wisper, who promised to keep Irohann's new identity secret by digitally scrubbing any connection made between him and his old self.

It lifted Clarity's heart to see Irohann so happy.

Irohann stopped dancing and stood in the center of the bouncing lapines, nearly twice their height, simply grinning at Clarity. He gestured toward her, beckoning, inviting her to dance. But Clarity shook her head. Her whole body ached still from floating in space, nearly freezing to death inside her spacesuit after escaping a Doraspian spaceship as it was torn apart. She didn't know how Irohann and Roscoe, the lapine member of Cassie's crew, had recovered so fast.

Irohann's eyes twinkled, like he had an idea, and his tail swished behind him as he turned away. He made his way through the crowd toward Roscoe. The elderly lapine was father, uncle, grandfather, or granduncle to most of the other lapines here, and he'd been dancing with one of his younger grandbunnies balanced on his long feet.

Irohann leaned down and spoke, his muzzle close to Roscoe's ear. The grandbunny on Roscoe's feet seemed to overhear, because the child jumped up and down, excitedly clapping her paws, then scurried off away from the crowd. Roscoe and Irohann followed her.

Clarity's interest was piqued, but she turned her gaze back to the eerily split darkness outside the window. On one side, the blackness was so thick it seemed like swallowing up the fabric of space-time wasn't enough, and the Devil's Radio wanted to reach out and scoop out Clarity's eyes as well. On the other side, starlight blurred, streaming around the edge of the Devil's Radio brightly.

The Warren and Cassie were firmly on the starlit side of the Devil's Radio's event horizon. There would be no revelry if they weren't. Only a long, frozen moment of time, stretching out to infinity. Clarity would have been trapped, floating in space for eternity with nothing but a spacesuit between her and the vacuum, unsure of whether the universe had even been saved.

Instead, dancing. On the edge of a black hole.

Why not?

Clarity blinked as she saw an impossible spark of light on the dark side of the window. It had to have been a neuron misfiring in her brain, or a fleck of something in her eye. Maybe a reflection on the window from a light inside the mess hall.

There could be no light coming from the darkness on the other side of the event horizon. Nothing could escape the Devil's Radio. What she'd seen couldn't have been real.

The jangled, disjointed music changed tone, thinning as many of the instruments stopped playing. The fluting, whistling, and rhythmic chiming were replaced with a confusion of rushed lapine voices, murmuring and arguing. Clarity didn't speak the lapine language, but she'd started studying it since she and Roscoe were co-pilots aboard Cassie. She had picked up enough so far to catch the words "where" and "trouble" coming from several lapines on the dance floor. She'd certainly heard Roscoe say "trouble" plenty of times during their tenure aboard Cassie. It was probably the lapine word she knew best.

Clarity watched the lapines scurrying and rearranging. They seemed to be looking for something. Or someone.

Someone had gone missing.

Clarity got up from her seat on the window ledge and approached the crowd. She might not speak lapine, but some of the lapines probably spoke Solanese. So, she said, "What happened? Is someone missing?"

One of the older lapine women, probably one of Roscoe's

daughters or nieces, turned toward Clarity. Her long ear had twitched when Clarity spoke, and her eyes gleamed with recognition now. She approached the much taller human woman and said, "The eldest young'un and her two friends." The lapine woman's nose twitched furiously. She looked agitated and anxious. "They're always causing trouble, and now they're gone."

"Gone?" Clarity asked. It wasn't easy for someone to be "gone" on a spaceship. "Like they're hiding somewhere?"

The lapine woman shook her head, long ears sagging. "I hope so."

Clarity wasn't sure what the alternative could be. "I can help look for them," she said. "Can you tell me what they look like?"

The lapine woman held out a paw, a little below the height of her head. "Teya is this tall. Gray fur. One ear always lopped. Her friends are an avian and an ungulate." She didn't describe them any further. She didn't really have to—onboard this ship of lapines, an ungulate and an avian would stand out as much as Clarity and Irohann did. Since Clarity hadn't seen either of them, they must not have been in the group that welcomed her and the others aboard. Or at the party.

The lapines divided up—some of them went back to playing music and dancing, but a crew of a half dozen, including the woman Clarity had been talking to, left the mess hall. Once they were in the corridor, the woman spoke rapidly in lapine, gesturing at the other five bunnies and then down the different hallways. They loped away, one by one. When they were gone, the woman said to Clarity in Solanese, "They're checking the most likely places she could hide."

"What can I do?" Clarity didn't know the layout of the ship, and she was realizing that she was out of her depth. Maybe she should just go back into the feast and keep feeling like a third wheel on a jet-board for surfing the oceans of a gas giant. Totally useless, kind of awkward, and a little bit in the way.

The woman said, "Roscoe told me about you and your friend, the Heffen."

Clarity lifted an eyebrow. "Oh?"

"I didn't tell the others this, but..." She shook her head again, both ears flopping forward. "Look, just, come with me, okay?"

Clarity nodded, and the bunny woman led the way, walking down the hall with a characteristic hop-step. She led Clarity back toward the airlock where she and others had entered *The Warren*. She opened a closet beside the airlock door and began rifling through the spacesuits hanging there. All of them were lapine-sized, far too small for Clarity or Irohann. Though, spacesuits these days were built to be stretchy, made out of smart fabric, just in case. It would be miserable, but if Clarity had been forced to squeeze into a lapine suit to save her life, it would be possible. Really uncomfortable, but possible.

With a deep sigh, the lapine woman stopped pawing through the suits. Her head fell forward, and she stared sullenly down at the ship's deck and her long fuzzy feet. "I thought so," she said. "Both Oksana and Kwah's suits are gone."

"You mean... They went out the airlock?" Clarity was stunned. "A young one? Left the ship and went outside here? Beside a black hole?"

"They're daredevils," the lapine woman said. Her long ears had turned backward. "Always urging each other into worse and worse stunts. Causing trouble. I told Teya's mum that it was a bad idea to let her friends come along. They're gonna get her killed."

Or frozen in time. For infinity. But Clarity knew better than to quibble. The difference between death and frozen at the edge of a black hole forever was not something a worried family member would find reassuring.

"So, what do you want me to do?"

The rabbit looked up, nose twitching slowly. "You have experience..." Her paws fluttered, like she was looking for the right words and hoped that churning the air in front of her would make them turn up. "You know, zipping around in the vacuum of space, doing dangerous things."

Clarity took a deep breath. "Yes, I have." Sometimes for fun.

Lately, though, because she'd been stranded in dead space when her own spaceship, Cassie, had knocked the enemy vessel she'd been aboard into the Devil's Radio. She'd barely escaped, not knowing if she would be rescued or left to freeze and die in space.

The vacuum of space wasn't the most appealing environment to her right now. Clarity was much more in the mood to get back to Crossroads Station and surround herself with the busy chaos of countless travelers of more different species than she could keep track of crossing paths.

"Would you like me to go out looking for them?" Clarity asked, already pulling up the sleeves of the jumpsuit that had been tied around her waist. She hadn't felt comfortable taking her spacesuit off when they came aboard *The Warren*. Not yet.

Clarity zipped her spacesuit up to her chin, then flipped the hood with the faceplate of transparent cloth over her head. She pulled the attached gloves out of their pockets on her wrists and put her hands into them. Once the suit had sealed shut around her, vacuum tight, the internal computer came to life, lighting up the inside of the faceplate with translucent streams of information.

"Damn," Clarity said. "My built-in jetpack is fried from..." Words failed Clarity as she thought back on the catastrophic events of the last few days. Instead, she simply stuttered, "I... I haven't had time to fix it."

"We have some external ones," the lapine woman offered gently.

"Alright, grab me a jetpack," Clarity said, "and I'll go out looking for your missing young'uns." Clarity's own voice sounded weary, but, truth be told, she was glad of something real and momentous to do. Perhaps being a hero is addictive. Save the universe once, and you'll find yourself needing to help every stray alien with a problem that you run across, just for another hit of that sense of perfect clarity and purpose.

The lapine woman pulled a stand-alone jetpack out of the far side of the closet and handed it to Clarity. It looked like a backpack and was a little smaller than one designed for humans.

The rabbit woman helped extend the jetpack's straps as far out as they would go, and Clarity shouldered her way into it. The pack was tight, but that meant secure. As long as her arms didn't go numb from the straps cutting off circulation. She'd just have to make sure that she wasn't out there for too long.

Once the pack was settled firmly in the middle of Clarity's back, and the hand controls were readily and comfortably available at her sides, she said, "Okay, I'm ready."

"I'll be here, monitoring any radio waves you broadcast back."

"Wait—what are their names?"

"Teya's my cousin's daughter. Her friends are Oksana, the ungulate, and Kwah, the avian," the lapine woman answered.

Clarity nodded.

Under the lapine woman's command, the door to the airlock slid open. Clarity stepped inside, and the door slid shut behind her. The gravity shut off. The air cycled out. The door in front of her opened. With a soft kick against the airlock floor, Clarity rotated herself enough to get her feet on the door that had closed behind her. She kicked hard, launching herself into the blackness of space.

2. CROSSING PATHS AT THE EDGE OF FOREVER

The only landmarks in the empty void above the Devil's Radio were the boxy, bronze ship, *The Warren,* and the bulbous, purple mass of Cassie with her spiraling horn, gaping tube organs on either side, and ruffle-like belly fins. Other than that, there were distant, smeary stars, and all-consuming blackness.

Clarity fired her jetpack, steering away from both ships, and aiming as carefully as she could to keep the same distance between her and the Devil's Radio. Every impulse in her body itched, telling her to steer away from the black hole's maw. But she was looking for daring, stupid teens—gods, she hoped they were teens and not toddlers; the lapine woman hadn't been completely clear about their ages, just the one bunny's height—and daring, stupid teens wouldn't be flying away from danger.

No, they'd fly right towards it.

Clarity used her short-range scanners, and spiraled around *The Warren* and Cassie, getting incrementally farther away with each orbit of them. She flipped on her radio and used the short-range frequencies to broadcast: "Teya, Oksana, Kwah, this is a fellow adventurer, please answer." The kids might not answer broadcasts from the ship, but maybe they would answer her.

Clarity repeated the message several times, with no response, then switched to saying, "Come on, guys, I just want in on the fun."

The radio sputtered in Clarity's ear, like someone had started sending a message and then thought better of it. Or maybe had been talked out of it—or blocked—by one of their friends.

"I've surfed the gas oceans of New Jupiter and daisy-chained through asteroid fields in a dozen different sectors," Clarity said, trying to sound as imperious and nonchalant as she could. She needed these kids to think she was a thrill-seeker, not a babysitter sent to gather them back up. "I can show you tricks you've never dreamed of." She put a slight taunting tone in her voice, and maybe that made the difference, because her radio crackled to life, and this time, it didn't shut off right away.

"You're too high," the voice in her helmet radio said. "Much higher than us. And... I think we need help."

Clarity's blood ran cold. If these kids had gotten too close to the event horizon, she wasn't sacrificing herself for them.

Nonetheless, Clarity re-aimed herself, firing only her left jets while bending forward until she was aimed directly at the dead void of the Devil's Radio. Against every impulse in her body, she tapped the controls, firing both jets on her pack for the briefest fraction of a second. And she began falling forward.

Clarity watched the display on her faceplate flash yellow, then orange. She cringed when the warnings changed to red, but she didn't turn herself around and jet away. Not just yet. Finally, a blip showed up on her short-range scanners. Then another. Then two more.

Four? The three trouble-makers must have lured another young lapine along with them. Or brought along an empty spacesuit for some kind of stunt? Maybe they wanted to watch it fall into the blackhole. A waste, for sure, but Clarity had to admit she'd have wanted to do the same when she was younger and less tired. It's like skipping stones across a pond—you may not want to jump in, get soaked, and swim yourself, but you want a piece of you—something you'd just been holding—to fly across the surface of the lake and then plunge into its mysterious depths for you.

Except, if you fall into a pond, you get wet.

If you fall into a black hole, game over.

"Can you guys turn your spacesuit lights on?" Clarity asked. She was still edging toward them, and she turned her own headlight on, aimed in the right direction.

Three standard spacesuits caught the light of her headlamp; the beam shined especially brightly off their faceplates. One had wider arms, perhaps the avian's. Another had a larger head, causing Clarity to wonder if the ungulate had horns to fit inside its helmet. But otherwise standard.

The fourth object caught in the beam of light.

Clarity had to squint and stare, puzzling out what she was seeing. A hemispherical dome with seams in it, like it had been built from metal plates, glinted dimly. It was a little larger than herself and made from a dark metal. Around its edges, tendrils... flailed. Well, they waved, like seaweed underwater. There was a lifelike quality to their movement, but Clarity didn't see how they could be alive, trailing out from the edges of the metal dome holding them.

Clarity tapped the controls on her jets, aiming them forward. The effect was to slow her already low speed approach to an agonizing crawl. A moment later, two of the three spacesuits honored her request, and their own helmet lights flashed on, along with smaller lines of light sewn into the suits' seams. Clarity was surprised to see that the two suits doing what she'd asked were the ones that she'd pegged as belonging to Oksana and Kwah. The unaltered lapine suit stayed stubbornly dark.

"So, uh, what have you guys got there?" Clarity asked, hoping these kids had a better idea of what that metallic dome with waving tentacles was than she did. It sure didn't look like something they'd brought out here with them.

The same voice as before crackled to life over Clarity's helmet radio: "It zoomed past us, so fast."

Another voice added, "Like a shooting star."

Based on the sound of the voices and the movement of the suits as they spoke, Clarity was pretty sure the first voice came from the ungulate, Oksana, and the second voice was the avian, Kwah.

Finally, a third, different and defiant, voice spoke, "Then it bounced back. Almost like it teleported."

Clarity could hear the similarity in timbre to the other lapine voices, but she'd never heard a lapine sound so strident before.

"Bounced back?" Clarity asked. She remembered the flicker of light that she'd seen inside the Devil's Radio event horizon. But she'd imagined that. Surely.

Clarity tapped her jetpack controls again, bumping to a stop in the middle of the spacesuits congregated at the sloping edge the Devil's Radio gravity field. This was a terrible place for a group of unruly children and a mystery. "Here," Clarity said, pulling a retractable tether out of utility belt around the middle of her spacesuit. It had a clip on the end. "Let me hook you guys in, and I can guide you back to *The Warren*."

This close, she could see the faces inside the spacesuit helmets. She'd been right—the ungulate had some kind of horns inside her helmet; the avian was the one with broader, more wing-like arms; and the lapine girl looked furious.

"You said you were gonna teach us tricks like we've never seen," Teya said.

"True," Clarity said, holding the clip end of the tether out. "The best trick you'll ever learn is staying alive."

"That sounds good to me," Oksana said. "But what about... this thing?"

"We can scan it when we get back to the ship," Clarity suggested.

"I think it's alive," Oksana said, reaching a gloved spacesuit hand toward one of the gently writhing tentacles. "And I think it's hurt. We can't leave it here. It's too dangerous out here."

Now that Clarity was closer, she thought she could see leaves and buds on the slender appendage. Not a tentacle, then. A branch. Clarity wasn't sure about the metal dome, but the branches looked like the limbs of a Doraspian, one of the sentient tumbleweed-like aliens who had almost killed her and the rest of Cassie's crew, all in the process of trying to destroy the universe. She hadn't realized their limbs were resistant to the tortures of vacuum.

Clarity wasn't sure she wanted to tow it back to *The Warren* with them.

"And we can fly back to *The Warren* ourselves," Kwah said, beak clacking behind her suit's curved faceplate. "We don't need you to tow us. We have jetpacks, and we're not hatchlings."

"Yeah, we don't need help," Teya added imperiously. Her long ears were squashed against the sides of her face inside her helmet, giving her a rumpled look that undercut her arrogant tone. "We didn't need help getting out here, did we? We'll come back when we're ready."

"I'm ready," Kwah squawked.

When it came down to it, Clarity couldn't leave a living creature floating in the dead space beside a black hole. Even an enemy. She slipped the clip at the end of her tether into one of the seams around the edge of the hemispherical metal dome, where the Doraspian branches reached out. The clip spread into a small grappling hook with the press of a button.

The Doraspian's metal shell was tethered to her. Clarity would simply have to hope that if she led Teya's more cooperative friends back to *The Warren*, the petulant bunny would follow.

Clarity jetted upward, slowly and carefully. Kwah and Oksana zoomed past her, towards the starry side of the sky and away from the void, so black it hurt Clarity's eyes. The tether went taut and tugged on Clarity's utility belt, but it held. Cautiously, she increased her speed, tapping on the jetpack's controls in short bursts. To her relief, she saw on her short-range scanners that the bunny was following. Thank the stars for that.

The trip down toward the Devil's Radio had passed quickly,

but the flight upward seemed to drag on forever. At first, Clarity thought the difference was simply her fear that the Doraspian's branches would climb along the tether and grab her from behind. Tear her suit. Rip off her helmet. Murder her.

Her jetpack struggled to overcome the powerful gravity, flying away from the Devil's Radio instead of toward it. And towing a Doraspian in a big metal shell wasn't helping. It took more thrust to get the same change in velocity. She hoped this jetpack held enough fuel.

If it didn't, Cassie would come for her.

Or Irohann would make *The Warren* fly down and save her. She could see them ahead. They looked the same size as they had before. Toy ships, out of reach. Was she getting any closer at all? Or just treading water?

Clarity wasn't ready for the depths of space again. This was too soon. She could feel the darkness closing in on her. And also expanding out... leaving her unmoored, disconnected from everything. Anchorless in a sea of space-time.

She started to panic. Her heart pounded in her ears, and she couldn't breathe fast enough.

The radio flickered on, and she heard Irohann's voice: "What are you, a moth drawn to the incandescent flames of black holes?"

Clarity laughed in spite of herself. A short, nervous yet relieved, laugh. "I'm gone a few minutes, and you have to mock me?"

There was a pause that lasted a little too long. "It's been more than a few minutes, Clarity."

Oh gods, she'd fallen into the event horizon, and time was passing faster for *The Warren*. Irohann would come and check on her, every few years for the rest of his life, and to her, it would seem like he spoke to her every few hours. He'd tell her about entire adventures that he'd had without her. His life would pass, and she'd listen. Then maybe, after he'd died, he'd choose an emissary to take his place, coming to visit and tell her stories while she floated here until her air ran out and she died.

"No," she said. "No, no, no, no, no."

"Whoa, now, whoa. You're not trapped forever," Irohann said, presumably realizing his mistake. "It's been hours, but Oksana and Kwah made it back twenty minutes ago. They said you and Teya were right behind. The numbers that we've run through the computer show that you'll make it."

Clarity squinted at the scene ahead. She could still see Oksana and Kwah, in their spacesuits, flying toward *The Warren*. "They're inside? You're sure?"

"Safely inside and thoroughly lectured," Irohann said. "I didn't know Roscoe could yell like that. He always seemed so quiet."

"Then why can I see them out here?" Clarity wondered how long it had been from Irohann's perspective since their last interchange. Relativity made her head hurt.

"Time dilation."

Clarity could hear the shrug in Irohann's voice. She wished she could see it. His thick, red mane always tumbled so nicely over his shoulders when he shrugged. He made her feel safe. For now, his voice would have to do. Time-delayed as it was. He must be hovering beside the radio, waiting for each message from her. Or maybe he wandered off and danced at the party, and one of the lapines summoned him to respond each time she spoke. That seemed more like him, and given the condensed time on her end, she wouldn't know the difference. Except... belatedly, Clarity realized the party must be long over.

Damn, she'd been hoping to grab a few more of the pecan puffs. Maybe there'd be leftovers.

"The kids found a Doraspian in some kind of metal shell, floating above the event horizon. I'm towing it back with me. It..." Clarity hesitated before continuing; she didn't see how the Doraspian could really be alive with its branches exposed to space, and she didn't want to sound like a fool. "It seems to be alive. I think."

Maybe the metal shell was an escape pod. Although, it didn't look like any escape pod that Clarity had seen before. Of course, she had never really interacted with Doraspian technology before, except for her brief imprisonment on their ship that Cassie had knocked into the Devil's Radio.

Ahead of her, Clarity finally saw *The Warren*'s airlock doors slide open, and the two spacesuit-clad kids jetted inside. The doors slid shut behind them. Time was very weird and confusing on the edge of a black hole.

"I'm not sure if we should bring a Doraspian survivor aboard *The Warren*," Irohann said.

"You think it's better to bring it aboard Cassie?" Clarity asked.

"There are families aboard *The Warren*," Irohann countered.

Clarity didn't respond. Irohann was right. But... Cassie was Clarity's family now. Twelve of one; half a dozen of the other—or rather, dozens of bunnies versus one big, child-like starwhal.

"We can keep it trapped in *The Warren*'s airlock until we all head back to Cassie," Clarity suggested. She didn't want the Doraspian released on Cassie unmonitored, but if she, Irohann, and Roscoe were there, hopefully they could keep an injured Doraspian under control. She wasn't sure how much help Mazillion would be; the swarm alien was still recovering from losing more than half of their insect bodies during the battle with the Doraspians. And, of course, Roscoe generally hopped along with a walking stick in one paw, in spite of his earlier dancing. Though, she supposed, even if that meant he wasn't physically strong, he did have a decent weapon always at paw in the form of his staff-like walking stick.

After a pause, Irohann said, "That works."

Clarity knew her companion didn't feel the deep connection to Cassie that she did. He hadn't felt as connected to their previous spaceship either. Although, that one had just been a lump of metal, not a living being. Clarity was almost too good at connecting to inanimate objects, anthropomorphizing them and becoming emotionally attached. Irohann wasn't. He kept her balanced.

With a satisfying thump, Clarity rammed into the airlock's closed doors on the side of *The Warren*. She was grateful for the solid feel of a metal hull under her gloved hands. She was less grateful for the whump of the Doraspian's metal shell slamming into her from behind.

Teya didn't slam into the hull. She gracefully slowed herself with precise blasts of her jetpack, twirling as she stopped. She was showing off, pirouetting like that. At least, that's what Clarity thought. She got the sense that Teya had been showing off for her friends before, acting tough. Now she was showing off for Clarity, flying fancy, instead of simply being relieved to get home alive.

She was a rabbit with a lot of spirit. Clarity liked that. She could also see that it could cause a lot of trouble, especially aboard a craft filled with her elders who expected her to still be a young one, under all of their thumbs. That was a lot of thumbs. Clarity could understand feeling stifled and acting out.

Even so, stunt jetting around the lip of a black hole was just plain stupid. Clarity was half-tempted to invite Teya and her friends to come aboard Cassie and get away from too many stifling family expectations. But only half-tempted. She wasn't sure she needed that kind of reckless stupidity around.

That was her role. And Clarity didn't need any help with it.

The airlock door slid open, and Clarity pulled herself inside, dragging the metal dome after her. None of the branches had grabbed onto her, which was a relief. Though she wasn't sure how they'd react when the atmosphere poured in and the artificial gravity kicked on.

3. SAYING GOODBYE TO THE WARREN

The atmosphere poured into *The Warren*'s airlock, and the artificial gravity kicked on, settling Clarity's feet firmly on the floor. She had managed to wedge the metal dome against the side of the airlock and the floor, curved side to the wall, before the gravity turned on, so it didn't do anything annoying like smash her foot or tumble into Teya.

The tendrils extruding from the hemispherical dome's edges froze, stock still at the feel of the atmosphere. As if the Doraspian were startled. Although, all of the branches' movements could be simple autonomic responses. Clarity still didn't see how it could be alive, let alone conscious.

She unsealed her spacesuit and pulled the hooded helmet off her head. Teya had done the same with her spacesuit and was already removing the gloves from her paws. She looked smug, and Clarity was awfully tempted to chew her out for causing so much trouble. But she didn't get the chance before the inner airlock door slid open. Clarity placed a hand on Teya's back and hurried the young lapine through the door. She followed.

If the Doraspian woke up, Clarity wanted a solid door between it and any of these bunnies. She felt better the moment that the airlock re-sealed behind her.

Irohann, Roscoe with his walking stick, and a crowd of other lapines welcomed them back aboard. Well, they welcomed Clarity. Warmly. Teya's reception was much more chilly.

While grown lapines thanked Clarity, embracing her and grasping her hands with their paws, Teya received nothing but icy glares and an order to return to her quarters and stay there. She didn't even get the lectures or shouting that Clarity had expected. Maybe those would happen later. Maybe Teya's adults were too angry to talk to her at all.

With a shrinking feeling inside, Clarity remembered being treated that way—she'd been too much trouble for her parents to even bother reprimanding her by the time she ran away from the isolated, isolationist dirtball of a planet where she'd been raised. She'd never looked back.

Teya stomped away down the corridor, long fuzzy feet slapping against the metal floor with echoic, clanking thuds.

Roscoe shook his head and stuffed a paw in one of the pockets of his brown jumpsuit. "She's a troublesome one."

"Or a troubled one," Clarity murmured.

She didn't feel right leaving Teya here. It could lead to rifts that might never heal, when a little space might prevent them. Before Clarity could say anything though, a young bunny, much shorter than the others, hopped up to her.

The young lapine had fuzzy, dappled fur instead of a sleek, glossy coat like the adults. (Or Teya. That troublemaker was clearly much closer to adulthood than her elders liked to admit.)

The young one's nose twitched as she looked up at Clarity; her paws were clasped behind her back, seemingly holding something and hiding it from Clarity's view.

The human knelt down on the deck, placing herself at the young lapine's height. She realized this was the grandbunny she'd seen dancing with Roscoe earlier; the one who'd left the party with him and Irohann.

"Hello," Clarity said. She didn't know if such a young lapine would speak Solanese, but she figured an adult could translate for her if necessary. "You look like you have something to show me?"

The young lapine bounced up and down, nose twitching even faster. She was practically vibrating with excitement as she pulled a floppy, plush doll out from behind her back. It was a rendering of a lapine, with long ears lined in a shiny, pink satin and eyes made from dark, glass beads. In a sing-song rush, the young lapine intoned, "You saved the universe, and I like the universe, and your big Heffen friend says you like dolls and that most of your dolls got lost when your spaceship got destroyed, and that sounds so sad! And so, I want to give you a doll, because I don't want this doll anymore, and I want to say thank you for saving the universe!"

Well, then, that answered the question of whether the young lapine could speak Solanese. She thrust the doll toward Clarity, a little too close to her face, and jangled it, causing its limbs to swing about like it was dancing. Clarity leaned back, trying to avoid any of the plush limbs swinging into her face and smacking her.

"Uh, thank you," Clarity said. She let the young lapine force the plush doll into her hands. Its fabric was worn, thin in places, like it had been well-loved. Up close, the shiny pink fabric inside the ears had complicated patterns sewn into it. Swirls and stripes in shades of coral and rose thread, carefully hand-stitched, as a synthesizer couldn't replicate a pattern so delicate and detailed.

Clarity didn't feel right taking this toy from a child. "But, you don't have to give me your doll. It looks like you love it a lot."

"I told you," the young lapine said with a sniff, "I don't want it anymore!"

Irohann leaned down until the end of his long muzzle was close to Clarity's ear and whispered, "I believe the child has been promised a new one, but she won't get it unless you take this one."

Clarity turned to Irohann and looked at the big red wolf quizzically. "Did you engineer that?"

Irohann shrugged, and his long auburn fur around his neck and shoulders made the gesture glorious.

Clarity shook her head. "Fine. Thank you." She clasped the young lapine's paw, and the child grinned before hopping away, having already lost interest in her.

Looking at the raggedy, threadbare doll, Clarity was unsure whether she'd been given a precious gift or had a piece of rubbish offloaded on her. And yet...

There was something deeply precious about being given a well-loved doll to commemorate her heroic brush with death at the edge of a black hole. Clarity hugged the bunny doll, squeezing it to herself, and it squished soothingly in her arms.

Save the universe, get a toy, Clarity thought. Heh, well, Irohann knew her well. She closed her eyes and pressed her face into the plush doll's satiny ears. It smelled like dry reeds and flowers. She loved it.

Lapine voices began arguing around her, pulling Clarity from her reverie. Her moment of peace. She opened her eyes to see them clustered around the airlock door, twitchy noses and whiskers pressed against the porthole window so they could see the mysterious metal dome that she'd towed back from the black hole. Most of their ears were flat back in consternation.

Roscoe said, "They want to know what our plan is for..." He gestured at the airlock. "That."

"I don't know yet," Clarity said. "It seems to be a Doraspian that survived the crash in an escape pod."

"It looks like it's waking up," Irohann observed. He was staring over the bunnies' heads, looking at the Doraspian with the strangest expression. He'd been terrified of the Doraspians—or rather, the agents of Queen Doripauli—finding him for so long. Now that he didn't have to be afraid, he looked... almost as if he was enjoying having a Doraspian under his power. He looked more wolfish than usual, and Clarity wasn't sure she liked it.

"Is there anything we could use to knock it out? A gas we could release into the airlock?" Clarity tucked the plush lapine doll under her arm. It was time for her to be serious now, not playing with toys. "We'd be safer getting aboard Cassie if we knew the Doraspian was unconscious before we entered the airlock."

"Flash ultraviolet lights at it," Irohann said. Again, looking a little too fierce.

"Won't that hurt it?" Clarity asked.

"Long term exposure, yes." Irohann shrugged. "But a couple of quick flashes will just make her sleepy."

"Her?" Clarity asked.

Irohann pointed at the porthole into the airlock. "She has little purple, bell-shaped flowers with yellow stamens, and there are clusters of white tendrils at the base of her buds. So, yes, probably 'she'."

Clarity stepped closer. She saw leaves and flowers littering the floor around the metal dome. The Doraspian was shedding pieces of herself at an alarming rate. She could not be healthy. "Roscoe, can you get them to flash UV lights in the airlock?"

The lapine elder nodded and relayed the request in his own language, and one of the other lapines adjusted the external controls on the airlock. Roscoe seemed to be the only lapine in the corridor who spoke Solanese at the moment. The woman who had entreated Clarity to risk her life chasing after the young'uns must have left, sometime during the hours that had passed aboard *The Warren* and the interminable, terrifying minutes that had passed for Clarity in the dark shadow of the Devil's Radio.

Clarity couldn't blame her for leaving the post she'd promised to keep beside the airlock, monitoring the radio. Not really.

Not... really.

Clarity's neck tightened, and she gave the plush lapine under her arm a surreptitious squeeze.

When the UV light flashed inside the airlock, Clarity didn't see anything different through the porthole, but she felt the pulses of short spectrum light in her hair. She didn't have any smart-ink tattoos, but she had gotten one gene-mod after entering the more cosmopolitan societies of deep space where species from dozens of worlds entangled their cultures with each other: Clarity had gotten photosynthetic cells in her hair. She liked the emerald, pine color that the mod had given her hair, and sometimes bright lights gave her a boost in energy. A little like drinking coffee.

The UV flashes fizzed against her scalp, a little ticklish, and they left her with a giddy, fluttery feeling in her chest.

"I suppose this means we should be on our way," Roscoe said. He sounded regretful. He'd be leaving a whole spaceship of his family behind, and Clarity knew that he had reservations about both Cassie and the rest of her crew. But he also felt a responsibility to the young starwhal. Cassie had fixated on him, and he didn't feel like he could abandon her. He was her pilot, like it or not.

Maybe he would appreciate the suggestion Clarity was about to make: "I think we should invite Teya and her friends to join us on Cassie." Then Roscoe wouldn't be the only lapine aboard. He'd have family with him. "There's an empty room, and there'll be another one soon, since Am-lei's leaving with *The Warren*. I'm sure the three of them could sort out sharing two rooms between them."

Roscoe's ears shot up, tall as they went, like someone had pulled his puff of a tail, assuming he had one. It was hard tell given the jumpsuits that most of the lapines wore. "What! That troublemaker and her gang?"

Another lapine voice spoke behind Clarity: "That troublemaker is more like you, Pops, than any of your other grandbunnies. And she could use your firm paw guiding her."

Roscoe grumbled.

When Clarity turned to see the lapine behind her, she saw the woman from earlier, looking bashful, almost stricken. "I'm sorry that I didn't stay by the airlock like I promised, but I made sure your friend was here." She glanced up at Irohann. "And I brought you this..." She held forward a bundle wrapped up in cloth. "Leftovers from the party—there's a little of each kind of nut bread in here. I know you had to miss the rest of the celebration."

Clarity grinned and said, "Thank you!" Free leftovers from a party were better than treats eaten while actually at a party. She took the bundle. She'd have snacks for days in there. Between the lumpy bundle of leftovers and the plush doll under her arm, she was starting to feel kind of weighed down. It was time to say goodbye to these bunnies and get back home to Cassie.

And if it weren't for the Doraspian in the airlock, when she got home, she could go straight to her room, put her lapine doll on the shelf beside her butterfly-like lepidopteran doll made from wicker and her fluffy, gray Woaoo doll. Perhaps she'd sit on her bed and eat leftover nut breads or play a video on her pocket computer. Maybe she'd just sit there, staring at the video without really watching it. That sounded good... resting and not saving the universe. And not talking to anyone about saving the universe.

"We all appreciate what you've done so much!" the lapine woman said. "And offering to take in Teya and her friends. That's so generous! Traveling with Grandpop Roscoe is exactly what they need."

Roscoe sighed deeply. "Fine," he said. "I'll go talk to the young'uns." He shot a meaningful glance at Clarity, then Irohann. "You two deal with whatever that nonsense is!" He rapped his paw against the airlock porthole. "And if I'm bringing more grandbunnies aboard that whippersnapper of a spaceship, then you'd better have this nonsense actually under control. I'm not bringing any grandbunnies aboard to have them strangled by an irate plant."

The way Roscoe said "grandbunnies," Clarity suspected he was already including Teya's ungulate and avian friends in the category. She'd heard him call Cassie a grandbunny more than once, and if the term could stretch far enough to encompass a star-whal outfitted with tech-rigging to turn her into a spaceship, then an ungulate and avian were no stretch at all.

Clarity watched Roscoe amble down the corridor, leaning on his walking stick, the same direction Teya had stomped away. He was a crusty fellow, and Clarity had mixed feelings about having a patriarchal figure around. She'd never gotten along with her own father, a human who didn't want to believe in all the profusion of diversity in the universe. He was happier pretending that humans had never encountered other species at all and keeping his life small. He'd tried to keep Clarity's life small too, and escaping his rule had been the driving motivation of her entire childhood.

Roscoe wasn't anything like Clarity's father, but she sometimes rankled at a father-like figure in her life at all, especially since the power hierarchy on Cassie wasn't at all clear yet. Other times, it felt kind of warm and, well, fuzzy having a surrogate father-type around. Like she was still a young girl on a dirtball world, wishing her father would just listen to her, instead of a grown woman who had long ago accepted that he never would. And moved on.

And moved away.

"Shall we do this?" Irohann asked. His paw was hovering over the control panel for the airlock, ready to open the door.

"Is Cassie ready?" Clarity asked, trying to shift her bundle of leftovers into a less awkward grip.

"I summoned her as soon as you were onboard. She's latched on and waiting."

Clarity nodded.

Irohann pressed his paw to the control, and the airlock door slid open.

Clarity and Irohann stepped inside, and one of the lapines in the corridor must have activated the controls again, because the door slid shut behind them. As soon as they were locked away, sound sealed in by closed door, Irohann said, "I didn't want to say anything before, but that's not a Doraspian escape pod. In fact, it doesn't look like Doraspian technology at all."

Irohann knelt down and picked up a dried, curled up leaf from the floor. He turned it over, examining it, then picked up a wilted flower petal. The detritus of leaves and petals were all around the metal dome, littering the airlock floor. "I don't even think it's an escape pod."

"If it is," Clarity said, "it sure wasn't doing a good job of keeping its occupant... well, healthy, I guess. It did seem to be alive. Though, I didn't know Doraspian limbs were vacuum proof."

Irohann shook his head. "They're not. This is all very strange."

Clarity worked the controls to cycle the atmosphere of *The Warren*'s airlock, synching it with atmosphere of the airlock on the other side. The air grew warmer and more humid. There was a familiar, almost coppery smell. When the light turned green on the control panel, showing it was safe to open the door, she pressed the control to open it.

The external door of *The Warren*'s airlock slid open, revealing a very different kind of room, ready and waiting for them on the other side. Instead of smooth, bronzed, metal walls with angular corners made out of right angles, the other airlock was all lumpy curves, organic, purple, and glistening. Sure, the bronze walls of *The Warren* sparkled a little at certain angles, but mostly it was a single, uniform shade lit by a harsh, yellow ceiling light. Cassie's purples, on the other hand, ranged from warm, pink fuchsia to cool, blue violet, with plenty of mauve, mulberry, and orchid along the way, and her flesh glowed with soft, pink bioluminescent patches.

Clarity could already hear the comforting thrum of Cassie's heartbeat. Sometimes, it seemed like Cassie was one big heart, flying through space.

Clarity carried her bundle of leftovers and plush doll into Cassie's airlock, appreciating the springy feel of the starwhal under her feet, much more forgiving than the unyielding metal of *The Warren*. She stowed the wrapped-up leftovers against the curved side of Cassie's vesicle-like airlock, and after placing the lapine doll carefully on top, she went back over to *The Warren* side and helped Irohann lift the metal dome with the sleeping Doraspian inside.

The metal was cool against Clarity's hands, but it had deep, swirling engravings etched into the surface that bit into her skin.

She shifted her position, lowering her body and getting her arms under the curved side.

Irohann grunted. "This is much heavier than it should be."

"What do you mean?" Clarity gritted her teeth. It was heavy. Fallen leaves crunched under Clarity's feet, and she slipped. But Irohann kept ahold of his side, giving her the chance to get her footing again.

"If this shell is hollow, and it has one Doraspian inside, it shouldn't weigh this much. Doraspians weigh almost nothing. They're just flowers, vines, and leaves."

"Maybe the shell is really thick," Clarity suggested. "Or maybe it's just a really dense, heavy metal."

It only took a few steps to get from the metal closet of *The Warren*'s airlock into the purple vesicle of Cassie, but Clarity's arms were already fatigued, and the shell was leaning dangerously toward her. Irohann was a lot bigger and stronger than her, and she was struggling to hold her side up. It was a relief to put the heavy metal shell down.

The big red-furred Heffen looked unfazed. He went over to the mechanical control console embedded incongruously in Cassie's purple flesh and used it to seal the airlock. A nictitating membrane slid shut between the two airlocks, enclosing them inside Cassie.

Clarity looked at her hands. The etched patterns from the metal shell were mirrored in her skin. She rubbed her hands together, trying to rub the dents away. "I don't know how far I can carry this thing. Maybe we should crack it open and just bring in the unconscious Doraspian."

Irohann rolled his eyes. "Your answer to everything heavy is to just leave it blocking up the airlock." He worked the controls, and the inner nictitating membrane slid open. "But some of us like to keep the airlock clear so that we're not always tripping over things when we come aboard."

Clarity returned his eye roll. "Fine." Except, it wasn't fine. She was going to hurt herself if she had to help Irohann haul the metal shell very far. If they were still aboard *The Warren*, maybe they could have rolled it, but Cassie's lumpy, fleshy floor was unlikely to make that easy. "We need to pick up an anti-grav cart when we get back to Crossroads Station."

"Among other things," Irohann said wryly. He had to be referring to Cassie's communications system. The Wespirtech scientists who'd wired her up to be a spaceship—without asking her permission—had given her a rather unusual and difficult to use communications array.

"Let me get us some help," Clarity said. She picked up her bundle of leftovers and plush lapine, so they wouldn't continue cluttering up the airlock, and set off to find Mazillion and Am-lei.

Mazillion was a swarm composed of insect bodies, a hive mind. Most of their gnat-like bodies were clustered in the scullery, a wide room with a large viewscreen affixed to the flattest part of the curving wall, in lieu of a window. There were no windows aboard Cassie, just viewscreens wired up to her brain and a bunch of small exterior cameras embedded in Cassie's blubbery skin.

The Wespirtech scientists had really done a number on her. Clarity shuddered to think of how much pain there must have been. Of course, Cassie had no way of communicating that pain before they'd wired her up with all the fancy tech to turn her into a spaceship, but nobody had bothered learning to communicate with her before then.

Why ask a starwhal for permission to turn her into a spaceship when you can, instead, ask her for forgiveness later?

Or, better yet, not even bother asking for forgiveness.

The same AI who had promised to keep Irohann's identity secret from the Doraspian empire had also promised to free the remaining starwhals that Wespirtech was still experimenting upon. Clarity had no idea if Wisper had followed through on that promise yet.

Clarity spoke to the largest cluster of Mazillion's insectile bodies, hovering like a cloud in the corner of the scullery with the mechanical food synthesizer and strange udder-like organs of

Cassie's that released a golden liquid into a trough-like trench along her wall. "I know you're still weak from losing so many bodies in the vacuum, but we have something heavy in the airlock. Could some of you come and help carry it?"

Clarity still felt weird talking to an amorphous cloud of tiny bodies. Mazillion remained one of the most alien creatures she'd encountered since leaving her isolated dirt ball home world, and she'd encountered quite a few unusual aliens. Am-lei was still aboard Cassie, packing and preparing to leave with *The Warren*, and she was a giant insectile alien from a race, the Lepidopterans, who ceremonially cut off their beautiful butterfly-like wings after metamorphosing into their adult form. That was pretty strange. But when it came down to it, Am-lei was one being—one centralized brain, six jointed limbs.

Mazillion's personality and intelligence was so distributed throughout their ever re-populating bodies that they'd experienced a schizoid personality split during the chaos of the conflict with the Doraspians, dividing them into two wholly separate beings because they couldn't decide whose side they were on.

The remaining Mazillion was, of course, the one who had sided with Cassie's crew. The other half had perished with the Doraspians. What was left of Mazillion had become a diminished being, further diminished by the time they spent in the punishing vacuum of space, clustered tightly in a ball, their outer bodies sacrificing themselves to protect the inner bodies.

Since then, Mazillion had been in the scullery, eating the golden cantaloupe-flavored liquid from Cassie's udders, clustering around them like beards of bees, and re-growing.

The amorphous cluster hovering in the corner pulled together more tightly, forming a constellation that Clarity had come to think of as Mazillion's mouth—an orb of insectile bodies who fluttered their tiny wings together, manipulating the air into recognizable speech.

Mazillion's mouth said in its droning, buzzing voice: "Our

scouts are already examining the unconscious S'rellick and Doraspians."

"The what now?" Clarity said. S'rellicks were reptilian aliens; she'd known many of them on Crossroads Station and had visited a few planets in the loosely organized S'rellick Mercenary Syndicate. "Are you saying there's a S'rellick curled up inside that metal shell, along with... more than one Doraspian?"

Mazillion's orb mouth stretched out, widening into a nimbus cloud of insectile bodies. It looked like their version of a shrug. They tightened back into an orb and said, "This is what our scouts report. Am-lei is already on her way to the airlock to assist with moving the shell."

"Thanks," Clarity said. Apparently, it was crowded inside that escape pod. She wondered what a S'rellick had been doing aboard a Dorspian military vessel. And she wondered how quickly Mazillion had sent scouts into the airlock to examine the shell. Had it been before Clarity came to ask them for help? Or had they simply done their scouting very quickly?

It was disconcerting sometimes to have a crew member who could be present in a room with you, without your knowing it. Mazillion at their full size was very strong, and by distributing themselves out—a few gnat-like bodies here, a few there, never enough to be noticed—was an ideal spy.

Mazillion had sacrificed a great deal, proving their loyalty to Cassie's crew... and yet, Clarity could feel herself still doubting them, questioning them and their motives. If they'd turned on her before—even half of them, even though that half was now gone—what would stop that from happening again?

4. OPENING THE SHELL

Clarity put her leftover nut breads and plush lapine doll away in her quarters, carefully leaning the lapine doll against her wicker lepidopteran one, with one of the lepidopteran's colorful velvet wings tucked behind the lapine's back, so they looked like friends. The lepidopteran doll's other wing was tucked behind the fluffy gray Woaoo—koala, butterfly, bunny. They looked cute together, sitting on a shelf above a synth-wood bureau, beside a bed covered in an anachronistic patchwork quilt.

The Wespirtech scientists had outfitted Cassie's alien, pinkly glowing interior with both cutting-edge technology—including wide viewscreen in most rooms, to make up for the lack of windows—and oddly homestead-feeling furniture. The effect was disconcertingly mismatched, but Clarity had started to find it charming.

Simple, old-fashioned human-designed furniture, inside an utterly alien environment: the glistening, glowing, pink and purple internal organs of a literal space whale.

Clarity returned to the airlock to find the metal shell already held aloft by Irohann, Am-lei, and a fraction of Mazillion. Irohann held one side with his broad red-furred arms, and Am-lei held the other side with her stick-like arms. She was a giant insect, all angles and shiny black exoskeleton. Her thin arms looked like they should break under the weight of the metal shell, but she seemed to be straining less than Irohann. Insect strength. What can ya do? Most of Mazillion was probably still in the scullery, feeding and regrowing, but clusters of their tiny winged bodies coated the underside of the shell, presumably pushing it upward, making it lighter.

If the orb that spoke were Mazillion's mouth, then Clarity supposed these rivulets of insectile bodies lining the underside of the metal shell were Mazillion's arms.

Irohann, Am-lei, and Mazillion carried the metal shell down Cassie's gently curved, vein-like corridors to the large, ventricle-like room that Am-lei had been occupying. The few belongings that Am-lei had brought with her aboard Cassie were packed in a simple suitcase, already beside the valve-like door.

When the metal shell had been settled, carefully, on the side of the room away from the bed (also covered in a homely patchwork quilt), most of Mazillion's bodies flitted away, flying out of the room in a stream of speckles dotting the air. Some of them clearly flew out of the seams around the edge of the metal shell and had been inside of it.

A small orb of Mazillion stayed, hovering, and said, "They're all still sleeping inside. You one-brains are so strange. Sleeping with your whole selves all at once."

"We should crack it open," Irohann said. "See if they need medical care."

Am-lei spoke with a fluting voice, formed by her long, curling proboscis, and said, "There's a toolkit in the bottom drawer of that bureau." Her antennae waved like a pair of orchestra batons, and the collection of finger-like mouth parts at the base of her small mandibles wriggled. "Good luck. I'll miss all of you, but I don't think I'll miss these constant adventures."

"Wait," Clarity said. She wasn't ready to say goodbye. She'd known Am-lei would leave as soon as the party on *The Warren* was over—and the party was long over—but now that it was actually happening, it felt too sudden.

"We'll stay in touch," Am-lei said. Her multi-faceted eyes—silver like disco balls—gleamed in the soft pink light. "You mammalian species like hugs, yes?" Am-lei's wife, who she would be returning to, was an elephantine alien. So, she was used to the squishier, cuddlier qualities of mammals.

Irohann accepted a quick embrace from Am-lei before kneeling down to fetch the toolkit. Clarity held her embrace—angular and uncomfortable though it was—for longer. Hugging Am-lei felt a little like hugging a Swiss Army coat rack. You don't want to hug too tight, or all the sharp angles will hurt you.

As Am-lei left, Clarity reminded herself that Roscoe would return soon, most likely with three new, potentially long-term inhabitants for Cassie. Possibly, crew members, if they decided they liked it here and found ways to be useful.

Then Clarity marveled at herself: it wasn't that long ago that she had been traveling the universe with only Irohann by her side, disgruntled by the idea of having to take on passengers. Now her living spaceship felt like it would be empty without Am-lei aboard.

How quickly we can adjust to new life situations and expect them to last us forever.

Irohann found a light emitter in the toolkit and handed it to Clarity; she tucked it into a pocket where she could easily grab it.

"Set it to UV," Irohann said. "Just in case."

"Already done." She'd adjusted the setting automatically, as soon as he handed it to her.

Irohann took a stembolt seal-spanner out of the toolkit and began unsealing the stembolts around the edge of the metal shell. Once the entire disc had been unsealed, Clarity took one side, and Irohann took the other. They pulled up and pried the disc off the hemisphere beneath it with a soft pop of atmosphere equalizing. The smell of underbrush in a forest after a rainstorm blasted into the room. Potting soil, old leaves, and the bright green smell of fresh growth. Clarity pictured new plants sparkling with dew drops.

The large metal disc was heavy, and they set it aside, laid atop the quilt covered bed. Inside the remaining metal hemisphere, there were two main compartments separated by a contoured layer of transparent aluminum. The higher compartment closer to the base of the upside-down shell, where the disc had been removed, had the S'rellick curled up inside it, looking gaunt. His blue-tipped, green scales didn't have the shine and luster of health.

The compartment beneath him, and partly to his sides, was packed tightly with an algae filter on one side, a compu-drive on the other that was wired into a display screen on the interior of the shell, and a crowded mix of dirt, dead leaves, and tangled, quivering Doraspian limbs, bright with gem-colored flowers and leaves in every shade of green. They smelled like an herb garden and looked like a trash bin outside a flower shop—filled with crushed, unwanted cuttings of gorgeously mismatched flowers and greens.

Doraspians were like tumble-weeds—a collection of tapering branches, growing from a centralized point. They didn't have faces or centralized sensory systems in the way of a bipedal creature, but their different types of flowers and leaves served specialized sensory purposes. Some sensed light like eyes or tasted chemicals in the air; others vibrated, creating sounds, and functioned as voice boxes. Some of the flowers looked like roses, others like camellias or daisies, and the leaves varied in shape from spades to ovals to serrated stars. They were beautiful creatures, even crumpled and crammed into a metal, dirt-filled shell.

Given the layers of crumpled, wilted leaves and flowers, shed and discarded, Clarity was surprised by how healthy and colorful the living leaves and flowers of these two Doraspians seemed to be.

"I've heard of this..." Irohann said. "Going turtle."

Clarity had heard of "going turtle" too. It was something S'rellick did sometimes—build a space-worthy shell and take off into the unknown, no spaceship, nothing. Just a reptilian alien, gone turtle, flying through the darkness between stars. Clarity wasn't sure if it was a migration instinct or some kind of pilgrimage. She'd never studied the phenomenon, only heard it mentioned briefly in passing. Back when she was a bartender at The All Alien Cafe on Crossroads Station, occasionally a S'rellick who'd been a regular customer would stop showing up, and when she'd ask after them, the answer was "Oh, they've gone turtle."

That was all she knew. But even so, Clarity was pretty sure that "going turtle" didn't involve packing Doraspian passengers inside your shell and letting their limbs wave about in the vacuum of space.

"Maybe this S'rellick rescued these Doraspians from the ship that crashed into the Devil's Radio," Clarity suggested.

"Maybe."

"Or else they grabbed on to its shell to rescue themselves... like stowaways. Or barnacles."

Irohann didn't reply. He probably hadn't heard of barnacles. Instead, he knelt down beside the metal shell, reached into the opening and gently lifted a narrow, leafy end of one of the Doraspians' limbs.

Leaves fell from the branch, drifting back into the pile of limbs, dirt, and detritus. Only moments later, buds appeared on the branch, each one in the same place as where a leaf had been. The buds swelled, looking like the spiky tips of tiny pinecones. The spiky buds grew, stretching out, and unfurled into new leaves as Clarity and Irohann watched.

Irohann dropped the branch.

"That doesn't seem right," Clarity said. "Do they usually regrow leaves that fast?"

"No." Irohann stood up and backed away from the metal shell. "Even sproutlings who are still rooted don't grow that fast. And this one—he's old. I can tell from the speckles on his leaves. His new leaves."

"Him?" Clarity asked. "So this branch belongs to the other one?"

"Yes," Irohann said. His fluffy tail swished behind him agitatedly. "His buds were spiky like pinecones. That probably means he's male." Irohann shook his head, ears twitching as if they didn't know which direction to point in. "There's something wrong. The other Doraspian's leaves look young, almost like a sproutling, but this one... I'm surprised a Doraspian with leaves this speckled by age would regrow them at all."

The S'rellick stirred, lifting his head, and a long, blue forked tongue flicked out of his mouth several times. His eyes opened slowly, closed again, and then finally stayed open. "My Genniperri is not a sproutling," he hissed with a hoarse voice in Solanese. "Even if she looks like one. She's older than me." He laid his head down again, against the layer of transparent aluminum between him and the coiled, unconscious Doraspians, their leaves folded against their branches and their flowers closed in sleep.

But his eyes stayed open. His turquoise eyes. With pupils like crab nebulas. He looked like he'd stared into the abyss, and it had stared back at him.

"What happened to you out there?" Clarity asked. "I was watching the event horizon and I saw... I thought I saw..." She couldn't say it. She couldn't say that she'd seen a flash of light cross back from one side of the event horizon to the other. It was too far-fetched.

"You saw us," the S'rellick said. "You saw us spat back out of the mouth of the Devil's Radio."

Clarity nodded.

Irohann's triangular ears perked in surprise.

"The eternally hungry black hole didn't want us. It didn't want them," the S'rellick hissed. "What did we look like being spat out by an indiscriminately hungry black hole? A black hole who had suddenly turned picky..."

"How did that happen?" Clarity asked.

"I don't know," the S'rellick hissed, then repeated his question more urgently: "What did we look like?"

"A shooting star," Clarity said. "An impossible shooting star. I thought for sure I'd imagined the flash of light, that it was something in my eye, or a glare on the window."

"I've gotten used to the impossible," the S'rellick hissed. His eyes closed, hiding away the haunted turquoise of his irises and tiny crab nebulas of his pupils. "Oh, Genniperri." His voice got soft, sibilant, like the dying whispers of an evening wind on a desert world. "My Genni, what will you do now?"

The S'rellick reached a scaly talon behind himself, into the dirt-covered coils of Doraspian limbs. One of the branches seemed to curl around his arm, brushing its leaves gently against his scales, tightening, squeezing. Though its flowers stayed closed. Not looking. Not listening. Not tasting the air.

"The Doraspians came here with you?" Clarity asked. "They weren't... on the war vessel?"

The S'rellick opened his eyes again, wide with surprise. "War vessel?"

"If you weren't here with the vessel that attacked us," Irohann said, "then why are you here? It's a big universe. I wouldn't expect to find a pair of Doraspians on the lip of a random black hole, shortly after battling a whole vessel of Doraspians in the same location, without there being a connection." His red ears flattened against his head in consternation. "It's *statistically unlikely*," he barked.

"Everything is statistically unlikely in a universe of infinite complexity," the S'rellick hissed in response. "And I learned a long time ago that unlikely is nothing. We live side by side in this universe with the impossible. At least some of us do."

Clarity had trouble disagreeing with that. She still remembered the way that the universe had fractured around her, reflecting herself in myriad broken mirror patterns. She shuddered at the memory. "I've seen a little of the impossible," she said. And she wasn't sure that she wanted to see any more. And yet, she suggested, "Maybe that's the connection? What impossibility have you lived side-by-side with...?" She trailed off, not knowing the S'rellick's name.

"My name's T'resso," he hissed, answering the question she hadn't asked. "And the impossibility that lives beside me... it is not my secret to tell."

The leaves on the Doraspian vine twined around T'resso's arm flared. At least one of the two Doraspians was awake now, and listening. Clarity wondered if the Doraspians also spoke Solanese.

Irohann took yet another step back. He'd been afraid of the Doraspian Empire discovering his identity for so many years that the fear was deep inside him, hard to shake, even though Wisper had promised to keep his new identity separate. Even so, there were a handful of people who knew the connection—Clarity, Cassie, Roscoe, Am-lei, Jeko, and Mazillion. All of them could be trusted. But the stakes were high. Irohann's former identity was a traitor to the High Queen, and he would be executed if she ever found him.

"Fine," Irohann said. "I don't care about your secrets and impossibilities. But why are you here?"

"For my Genni," T'resso hissed, squeezing his talon tightly around the span of branch wrapping around it. "She and Paurizau—the older Doraspian whose leaves keep shedding—they tracked a... space-time anomaly to this location. We were chasing it." His voice came out in labored huffs.

Fractured mirrors, thousands of herself, stretching in every direction flashed before Clarity's eyes. "I think you arrived too late," she said. "We sealed the fracture. There was a pair of entangled particles... fracturing the universe, trying to return to each other, but one was stuck inside the Devil's Radio. We returned the other one to it, and the fracture is sealed."

T'resso's forked tongue flicked, and his turquoise nebula eyes blinked. "Too late," he hissed, mulling the words over. He didn't sound convinced. But before he could argue or ask more questions, the reptilian alien's gaunt body was wracked with a fit of coughs. He curled around himself, shaking from the coughs; his long, spiky tail was long enough to curl over his shoulder.

The Doraspian vine twining around T'resso's arm twisted farther, wrapping around his torso, and two more branches reached out as well, grabbing the S'rellick, holding him still against his wracking coughs. The branches belonged to the younger-looking female Doraspian who must be the S'rellick's seemingly beloved Genniperri. Her purple bellflowers began to quiver, and she spoke in a voice like a choir of tiny, singing fairies: "Can you help him? He needs medical treatment. Please." So, she did speak Solanese.

"I'm sorry," Clarity said. "We're being terrible hosts." Because somehow, during the conversation, their role in her mind had changed from interrogators of prisoners of war to rescuers of errant travelers. "My name is Clarity." She gestured at Irohann, whose ears were still flat and who had backed himself all the way against the wall, trying to keep distance between him and the Doraspians. "This is Irohann, and the ship we're aboard is a starwhal named Cassie."

Yellow daisy-like flowers opened on Genniperri's branches and turned toward Clarity, then Irohann. They must be light sensing flowers that functioned like eyes. The purple bellflowers quivered again, and Genniperri said, "Thank you for rescuing T'resso. He would have died if you had not come along."

Wouldn't Genniperri and Paurizau have died too? The question was so large and so obvious that Clarity was almost afraid to ask it. The answer had to involve the mysteriously impossible secret T'resso had hinted at, and Clarity wasn't sure she could handle anymore impossibilities. She was ready for a nice, quiet return trip to Crossroads Station, followed by a vacation to somewhere safe and fun, with no black holes or fractures in space-time.

Or maybe she wasn't? Clarity had practically jumped at the chance to seal her spacesuit up and dive into the vacuum around the Devil's Radio to save a young bunny she'd never even met before...

Adrenaline is a hard drug to come down from.

Irohann went back to the bureau where the toolkit had been. He replaced the seal-spanner and pulled out a standard issue medical kit. "I don't know much about S'rellick physiology or health, and we don't have extensive medical supplies. But I can inject him with some standard first aid nano-bots." He withdrew a bot-injector from the med kit. "S'rellicks are common enough in this area of space that the nano-bots should be programmed to treat them, at least minimally."

"Thank you," Genniperri said.

"We're heading to Crossroads Station," Clarity said. "We can take you there."

"Crossroads Station..." Genniperri repeated with her chorus of purple flowers. "That's in human space? A human space station?"

"And Heffen," Irohann said, looking for all the world like a Heffen refugee, defensive about his species' position in the universe after their sun had expanded, destroying their home world. Except, Clarity knew that—while physically, Irohann was a Heffen—he'd been an entirely different species when she'd met him. An amphibious woman, beloved by and betrayer of Queen Doripauli. He'd transformed into a Heffen—a much more common species in the areas of space he preferred to frequent—through black market gene-mods and would have never looked back, except for the nagging fear that Queen Doripauli would find him, which kept him always looking over his shoulder.

"I know that Crossroads Station is a long way from any Doraspian outposts—"

The other Doraspian, Paurizau, cut Clarity off before she could finish, speaking with bellflowers that were a more faded shade of purple than Genniperri's, more of a soft violet with rose-pink stamens that looked like little tongues: "Crossroads Station will be fine." His voice sounded more like a choir of pixies than a choir of fairies. Clarity wasn't entirely sure what the difference was between fairies and pixies—but those were the images that the sound of the Doraspians' voices called to mind.

Paurizau's limbs reached upward, over the lip of the metal shell, pulling himself out, and the Doraspian tumbled to the floor in a tangle. His butter-yellow daisy-like flowers turned toward Clarity and Irohann in clusters, almost creating the illusion of a face. The pile of dirt and branches left inside the shell were easier to understand, now that one Doraspian was disentangled from the other.

Genniperri's branches were thinner, more delicate than Paurizau's. They didn't thicken from twisty emerald vines with soft flesh into crusty, bark-covered branches in her middle like his branches did. Where she did have bark, it was thin and paper-like, more like a birch tree or madrone than an oak or maple. And half of her body seemed to still be buried in the rich, dark dirt.

Clarity glanced at Irohann and saw his ears had splayed and his mouth fell open. "You don't just have the *leaves* of a sproutling..." he said. His muzzle snapped shut and his ears flattened fully against his head. "I'm sorry. That was very rude. Whatever condition has caused you to stay rooted... I'm sure it's none of our business. Is there anything we can do to help you?"

Genniperri's tender green branches twined together, braiding and then unbraiding. As they did so, it became clearer to Clarity what Irohann was talking about: Genniperri wasn't a free-roaming Doraspian; her body was still rooted in the dirt. She had roots.

If she wasn't a sproutling, she must suffer from a hormonal or genetic condition—something that had stunted her growth before physical maturity. And for a Doraspian, that meant she wasn't motile. She was, essentially, a potted plant.

"Could you brighten the lights in here?" Genniperri asked, a tremulous quaver in her melodic voice. Apparently, Cassie's cozy pink glow wasn't enough for her.

"Most certainly," Irohann said.

Clarity wasn't sure if she had imagined it, but it almost looked like he subtly lowered his head in a bow to the potted plant.

Clarity removed the light emitter from where she had stowed

it in her pocket and surreptitiously changed the setting from UV to full spectrum. That was probably the tastiest blend for a Doraspian. At any rate, it was better than handing over an emitter that had clearly been set to a light range designed to zap the Doraspians to sleep.

"Here," Clarity said, holding the emitter out for the Doraspians to see. She placed it on the top of the bureau and turned it on. Clear, bright, full spectrum light poured into the ventricle-like room, making the bioluminescent patches of pink on Cassie's purple skin look like nothing more than a slightly different color. Certainly, not an actual source of light.

"This emitter has enough power to last a while," Clarity said, "at least, until we can talk to Cassie—she's our spaceship—and see if she can, uh, I guess glow a little more brightly in here."

"Thank you," Genniperri said. Her yellow daisy-like flowers had turned toward T'resso, who was still unconscious and breathing raggedly in the metal shell with her, separated only by the layer of transparent aluminum. Three of her vines still twined around him, and her leaves stroked his scales absently.

Paurizau echoed her thanks with his voice like a pixie choir and then, in the sweetest, most sing-song tones possible, politely asked them to leave. "We need our rest," he entreated.

Clarity and Irohann had little choice but to comply. Though as they were leaving, Clarity noticed several of Mazillion's gnat-like bodies perched silently, almost unnoticeably, with their wings held still, on the fleshy walls of the room.

5. EN ROUTE THROUGH THE DARKNESS BETWEEN STARS

Cassie's corridors twisted organically. The valve-like doorways to the ventricle-like rooms done up as quarters clustered together. The doors into the other rooms on the ship, however, were tucked out of sight by the gentle curves of the passages in between. Yet, when Clarity and Irohann emerged from the room where they'd left the Doraspians and their unconscious S'rellick to rest, they could immediately tell that Roscoe was back aboard and had brought the trio of young'uns with him.

Voices didn't really echo aboard Cassie; her vein-like corridors were too twisty, and her fleshy walls too dampening for that. But voices sure could carry, especially when shouted: "Don't tell me you're treating me like an adult in the same breath as ordering me to my room!"

The voice was Teya's. Clarity hadn't heard her voice before, except over a crackly spacesuit helmet radio, since she'd stomped off as soon as they were back aboard *The Warren*. But Clarity recognized the tone and timbre.

"Besides, I don't have a room anymore, remember? Since you convinced Mum and the others to kick me out." After that, Teya's shouting switched from Solanese to Lapine. Her voice grew louder as the group approached them.

When the two lapines, one avian, and one ungulate arrived in the wider part of the hall where all the doors to the quarters were clustered, Roscoe pointed sternly at the door to the remaining empty room. He glanced at Clarity and Irohann briefly, asking, "That one's free, right?"

Clarity nodded. "That one has two bunk beds." She'd checked.

"There," Roscoe declared. "You have a room. It should be big enough for all three of you. Get in it." He placed a paw on the mechanical sensor embedded in the wall beside the valve-like door, and it slid open like an eyelid.

Each of the young ones had a bag or two slung over a shoulder or clasped in their hands. Roscoe had an additional bag over his shoulder on the side without the walking cane. He went in first. Kwah and Oksana followed docilely. A moment later, Teya followed as well. If Cassie had doors that could be slammed, Clarity was pretty sure Teya would have slammed it. Instead, it slid shut silently, sealing the two angry bunnies and the avian and ungulate who were mixed up with them inside.

Irohann tilted his head as he looked down at Clarity; he was a good head taller than her, even without counting his pointed ears. "Interesting choice," he said, drily. "Inviting a group of troubled youngsters to join us in a small vessel. And here, I thought you wanted us to have a spaceship all to ourselves."

Clarity shrugged. "Things changed. That happens when your home blows up. Besides, Cassie's not that small. She's several times larger than *The Serendipity* was, and she's alive. We'd rattle around in here with too much space if it were just you and me, and I think she'd be lonely with too small of a crew."

Irohann skewed an ear. He could tell that Clarity was coming up with explanations after the fact. The truth was she'd invited *The Warren* to send their troubled youths to Cassie without thinking through the implications.

"Whatever," Clarity said, feeling judged by Irohann's skewed ear and piercing gaze. "If it's a disaster, they can get off at Crossroads Station and stay there. That's what? Only a couple of subspace hops away?"

Of course, given how little they knew about how Cassie managed to hop into and navigate subspace—and how much her health had been affected by the battle on the lip of the Devil's Radio event horizon—that could add up to anywhere from a couple of days to a month. There are disadvantages to flying an untested prototype spaceship. There are even more disadvantages when the spaceship is sentient and never asked to be a spaceship in the first place.

"I'll feel better about living aboard a cyborg starwhal masquerading as a spaceship when her systems have been checked out a little more thoroughly," Irohann said.

As Irohann spoke, the door to Teya's room slid open again, and Roscoe came hopping back into the corridor and added, "You and me both, fella."

Oksana followed Roscoe out of the room and the door closed behind her. Now that she was out of her spacesuit—which Clarity hoped was safely stowed in the vesicle-like closet beside the airlock—the color patterns of the ungulate's fur and the shape of her horns were much easier to see. Her horns curled back from her head, dark as obsidian but ridged; they spiraled slightly more than once around, ending in blunted tips at the base of her floppy ears.

Her fur was soft brown on her ears and the back of her neck and head, but tawny ecru under her chin, with a wispy tuft of a beard; the sides of her face, her forearms, and ankles beneath the lime green jumpsuit she wore were zebra striped, strikingly black and white.

Oksana's digitigrade legs bent steeply backward at the knee, and forward again into long ankles, ending in cloven hooves that Clarity hoped weren't uncomfortable for Cassie on her squishy floor. They looked sharp. Although, they probably weren't any worse than the tip of Roscoe's walking staff. Oksana also had tough, keratinous fingertips, such that when she held her hand tightly together, her fingers seemed to form hooves like her feet.

The funny part was Clarity had assumed an ungulate would

stand out from a crowd of lapines, and she realized now that Oksana could have been in the crowd of dancing bunnies, and she wouldn't have noticed at all. Sure, Oksana might have stomped a little louder with those hooves, and she stood taller than Roscoe... But he was an older lapine, a little hunched and bent from age. Overall, Oksana was much closer in height to the lapines than either Clarity or Irohann. And though her ears were wider, more oval, and a little shorter than the long lapine ears, when they perked up, they weren't obviously different, and standing tall, they drew attention away from the big difference: her horns.

"Is there anything I can do to help?" Oksana asked, addressing the question to all three of the adults in the narrow corridor.

Roscoe sniffed and suggested, "You could help talk some reason into my grandniece."

"Kwah's doing that," Oksana said. She turned her attention toward Clarity and Irohann, apparently deciding that Roscoe wasn't likely to give her any helpful directions. "Is there anything else I could do?" The ungulate's milk-white eyes had horizontal bars for pupils. They looked a little like goat eyes. To Clarity's mind, her eyes looked a little spooky, but very sincere.

"What are you good at?" Clarity asked.

Before Oksana could answer, Roscoe harrumphed and said, "What all you whippersnappers"—because even Clarity and Irohann were apparently whippersnappers to him—"need to be good at is sitting down and strapping in. I'm off to the control room to see if Cassie's ready for a jump out of here, so I can get you troublemakers home to Crossroads."

"That wasn't the plan..." Clarity trailed off, realizing that Roscoe wasn't listening. He was already hopping away. Instead, she turned to Oksana and said, "I didn't invite you three aboard so that we could kick you off at our first stop."

"Invite us aboard?" Oksana said, sounding skeptical. "Teya's grandpop said the lapines on *The Warren* were done with us, and we could either take a ride back to Crossroads with him or 'go back to our beloved black hole.'"

Clarity could hear Roscoe's inflections imitated in Oksana's deeper, bleatier voice. "I can't believe he said that to you..." And yet, she kind of could. "I'm so sorry. It was supposed to be an invitation. An option. Not something that got forced on all three of you. It just looked like," Clarity shrugged, "you were feeling kind of hemmed in there."

Oksana's long, goat-like face smiled. "Well, yeah, clearly some of us were." She had a small mouth for how long her face was, and her smile looked impish. "But some of us were happy there. Well, one of us, I guess." She shrugged and tilted her head. Her curved horns looked heavy. She must have a strong neck to handle them.

"I didn't mean to get you kicked out," Clarity said.

Oksana shrugged again. "I wasn't expecting to live aboard a lapine family ship for the rest of my life. But it was kind of nice for a while. Now what can I do to fit in here?"

"What were you doing to fit in there?" Clarity asked.

"Mostly, looking after the little ones," Oksana said. "I'm from a big family back on Crossroads, and I'm good with little ones."

Clarity raised an eyebrow, wondering what Oksana meant by a big family. She had trouble picturing that the ungulate came from a family that counted as "big" compared to the ship full of bunnies, grandbunnies, and bunnies-in-law she'd just left. "Well, we don't have any little ones here," Clarity said, eventually. Other than Oksana and her friends, of course.

"We have a sick S'rellick," Irohann offered wryly. His tail was swishing, clearly enjoying Clarity's discomfiture at the turn her philanthropy toward Teya's crew had taken.

"My big sister is a S'rellick!" Oksana exclaimed, surprising both Clarity and Irohann.

Cross-species adoption was uncommon on Crossroads Station, but not unheard of. Why, Am-lei's mother had been adopted by a human woman who hadn't known lepidopterans cut off their wings after emerging from their pupal chrysalises. She'd suffered through many years of sporting gorgeous, colorful, and extremely impractical wings before learning that her people considered them vestigial and removed them after less than a day.

Clarity wondered whether Oksana had been adopted into a S'rellick household, or whether her reptilian sister had been adopted into an ungulate household.

Oksana continued, "I know how to program a food synthesizer to make a good facsimile of snailer shell broth with crunchy crickitats that always made my sister feel better when she was sick."

Irohann's tail swished in honest happiness. He loved cooking and learning new recipes. "I'll show you where the synthesizer is," he said. It was in the scullery. He placed a paw on Oksana's shoulder as he stepped past her in the corridor, guiding her to follow him toward the large, common room in the opposite direction of the cockpit.

Clarity supposed that if they were heading to the scullery, Oksana would be meeting Mazillion soon. She was tempted to follow along and see how that introduction went—between insectile swarm and young ungulate. *Youngulate.* Clarity almost cracked up at that thought, telling her she was much too tired to be useful to anyone right now. Which meant she also shouldn't stop by the room where Teya and Kwah were sequestered and try to... She didn't even know what she'd do. They'd still be there after she got some sleep.

Though she would miss Oksana's reaction to Mazillion. Even among all the different species of aliens aboard Crossroads Station, Mazillion was unusual.

Clarity said aloud to the seemingly empty corridor, "Hey, Mazillion, if you're here, I think our new ungulate crew member is about to meet the bulk of you. Tell me about how it goes later, 'kay?" She imagined a slight buzzing, a little higher than her head and a little further down the corridor, just past a rib-like archway of bone-like material. Though it could have been her imagination or simply one of the many, countless organic sounds that come with living inside the belly of a space whale.

Clarity went to her room own room, grabbed the plush lapine she'd been gifted aboard *The Warren* from its place on the shelf, and unwrapped the bundle of leftover nut breads. After a few nibbles, she fell sound asleep on top of the patchwork quilt covering her bed, lapine doll clutched tightly against her chest.

If Clarity dreamed, the dreams were deep and dark, a black hole of the mind. She awoke, groggy, as if she'd had to climb back out of the Devil's Radio, clawing for each hand hold along the way. She was covered in sweat, and the lapine doll had fallen to the floor. But a cluster of five of Mazillion's gnat-like bodies were perched on the back of her right hand. Up close, their wings were translucent; their bodies were the glittering color of smoky topaz; and each one had a different number of many-jointed legs and lacy wings. They were beautiful. And Clarity found their almost imperceptibly light presence on her hand comforting.

"Keeping an eye on me while I sleep?" she asked.

Their wings fluttered and tiny legs stepped, nearly dancing on her hand. Clarity smiled. It was nice, not being alone. Sometimes, back when she and Irohann had traveled together on *The Serendipity,* she crept into his room at night and slept, curled up against his warm, fluffy bulk. Their friendship had never been anything but platonic, but he made the best, fuzziest pillow.

Clarity didn't think that Mazillion could speak in Solanese with so few of their bodies, but she was sure that they could listen. So, she talked to their presence as she worked her way through waking up, sharing the trivial thoughts that crossed her mind and enjoying the feeling of companionship, even if it was mostly one-sided and possibly in her imagination.

Mazillion's five bodies flew around her, hovering close beside her when she stood still and whirling farther away when she moved. She finally changed out of her spacesuit jumpsuit and into a fresh pair of clothes from her limited supply.

Most of her belongings had been destroyed with *The Serendipity,* and the only place she'd had a chance to shop for more since then was Leioneia. But Lepidopteran clothes didn't exactly fit a human body. And she wasn't very skilled at programming the synthesizer to produce clothing. She needed to buy some pre-designed clothing programs for the synthesizer when they got to Crossroads.

Clarity took her spacesuit to the vesicle-like closet beside Cassie's passenger airlock and placed it inside. She hesitated before leaving it there. Being in space, even aboard a spaceship, without a spacesuit on is an act of trust.

Clarity trusted Cassie. She trusted Cassie's intentions. She trusted Cassie's heart. But she had to also trust Cassie's health, and the basic physical integrity of her body. In this case, it helped, actually, that Cassie had no windows.

Spaceship windows tend to be built from incredibly strong materials. Even so, one of the most common nightmares among spacefaring sentients who dream is the one where all the windows start to crack, and the cracks grow, and you can put your hand against the window and feel the rough, sharp edges, but you can't do anything to stop the transparent material from blowing outward, throwing you into the vacuous depths of space.

Clarity shivered. She hated that dream.

The windows had cracked in her dreams countless times, so many times that Clarity had learned cracking windows with star-studded space behind them was the surest sign she was asleep.

There'd only been one time when the windows cracked in real life, and that was when *The Serendipity* had been destroyed. One of the worst days of her life. But also, not at all mistakeable for a dream. Her nightmares had never been clever enough to predict that the windows on *The Serendipity* would crack because an angry, aggressive starwhal impaled the entire vessel on its spiraling horn.

In her nightmares, the windows always cracked for no reason. No reason at all. And somehow, that made it even scarier. You can run from an angry starwhal, abandon ship and take refuge elsewhere. But when the fabric of the universe itself is out to get you, there's nowhere to hide.

Given the tension among Cassie's occupants when Clarity had fallen asleep, she was surprised to enter the scullery to the sound of laughter. She recognized Irohann's deep, barking laugh, from back before the life-threatening, life-altering exploits of their latest adventures, but she wasn't sure she'd ever heard Roscoe's wheezing chuckle before. And the bright, cheery, braying laughter of Oksana and Kwah's hysterical squawks of delight were entirely new.

But what surprised Clarity the most was to see Teya smiling. The expression was subtle, but the young lapine's whiskers had turned up, and her dark brown eyes shined. She looked happy, ears standing tall.

All five of them sat around one of the long tables that protruded from the floor in the middle of the large room. To the eyes of a human from an isolationist colony world, they looked a little like two bunnies—one brown and one gray—a red-and-gold feathered hawk, a goat, and of course, Clarity's beloved red wolf companion.

Sometimes, Clarity remembered how she would see the universe she lived in with the untrained eyes of her childhood, like she lived in a magical children's book. Something like the ancient Earth stories of Christopher Robin and Winnie the Pooh.

Clarity approached the table which was laid out with a feast, enhancing the surreal feeling of having woken up to a happy bedtime story. There was Irohann's famous salad, which Roscoe loved so much that he'd made it the price—jocularly—of keeping Irohann's identity secret. But around it, there was an array of dishes Clarity hadn't seen before.

"What's all this?" Clarity asked.

Oksana beamed as she pointed at one dish after another with her keratinous hoof-hand, explaining what they were and when she'd learned to make them. Apparently, she had made them all, and she had learned most of them to please an array of siblings she rattled off, too fast for Clarity to keep track of them. She hadn't been awake long enough yet for her brain to process that kind of information.

"Wow, you really do have a large family," Clarity said, taking a seat beside Irohann. She was already suitably impressed by the ungulate's industriousness, and then she took a taste of the first dish: it was a mushy mess of soggy grains, studded with dried fruits. It didn't look like much, but the texture was pleasantly complex, and it melted in Clarity's mouth, the perfect mix of savory with bursts of sweetness from the dried fruits. "That's amazing," she said.

"My mother has a heart as big and warm as a red giant star," Oksana said, "but she isn't much of a cook. I don't want to say anything against humans, but you do seem to have a weaker sense of smell than most other sentients. No offense." The ungulate looked at Clarity with her spooky goat-like eyes, seeming to expect forgiveness for being so forward.

"Um, okay," Clarity said, around a mouthful of the delicious mush. "None taken."

Was Oksana implying that her mother was a human? Or was she just insulting humans for no reason? Clarity wasn't sure. If Oksana's mother was a human, and her sister a S'rellick... What kind of family was she from?

"Anyway, since I'm the second oldest," Oksana continued without further explanation, "I kind of took over the role of feeding everyone. It's nice to have a use for that skill again."

Teya sniffed drily and said, "The elders on *The Warren* wouldn't let her cook anything. They didn't want any help from an outsider to the family."

"They didn't say that," Oksana brayed. "They just..."

"Told you that you were doing everything wrong and should watch how they did it until you got the knack of doing it *exactly the same way*." Teya's smile was gone now, and her ears had flagged to half mast. Her voice had twisted until it dripped with sarcasm: "They were real friendly and open minded."

Roscoe harrumphed. "I won't have you talking like that about your elders. They took in your friends."

The warmth in the scullery seemed to have melted away in less than the time it took for Clarity to eat three bites.

Oksana tried to deflect from the tension by offering to serve more of the dishes onto Clarity's plate.

Kwah clacked her beak shut in a way that shifted the tone of her silence from amicable to prickly. The avian's feathers fluffed, making her look a little like a gold-and-red pine cone. After a few moments of watching the two lapines stare at each other angrily, she flapped her wings, knocking some silverware to the floor, and stormed away from the table. She went straight out the scullery door without looking back.

Oksana's mouth dropped open, and her ears drooped low.

"Kwah!" she brayed after her friend, but the bird was already gone.

"Look what you've done," Teya said to the older lapine. "And here you claim to be the bastion of respect. Or does that only apply to elders? It's perfectly fine to be rude to your guests, as long as they're younger than you?"

"All I said was—" Roscoe began, but Oksana cut him off.

"You implied that she didn't have a loving home back on Crossroads and that she was only here because she *needed* somewhere to be."

Roscoe almost looked uncomfortable. "Is that not true?"

"That's the problem," Oksana said. "For her, it is true. I don't mind your callousness so much, because I know you're full of space dust and solar flares. See, I have somewhere else to be, so I know I'm here because Teya *wants* me here."

From what little Clarity had seen so far, she was pretty sure that both she and Irohann wanted Oksana aboard Cassie too. She was feeling extremely impressed with the ungulate.

Oksana seemed to be the glue that held Teya's group together and also the interface between them and the rest of the world. Conflict resolution came naturally to her. Or maybe it just seemed that way because she'd been practicing it her whole life in that big family of hers.

Oksana continued putting Roscoe in his place: "Kwah's biggest fear is that no one wants her anywhere, and you stepped right on it."

Roscoe turned away from the table. "We have two jumps left to Crossroads Station," he grumbled without looking at any of them. "I have work to do." He got up and left the scullery.

A ribbon of Mazillion streamed after Roscoe, following him into the corridor. Clarity looked to the corner where Mazillion's ribbon had come from and saw that the swarm had noticeably grown and still hovered in that corner, an amorphous, evolving cloud. They'd be large enough now to mimic the shapes of the other crew members again. They did that, sometimes, while talking with them.

"Mazillion," Clarity called out. "Would you like to join us over here?"

The cloud withdrew inward, growing denser, darker, smaller. The cloud pulsed, buzzing the words, "Thoughtful. No." They tended to be terse. And they stayed in the corner.

Maybe Mazillion didn't like social tension any better than the rest of them. Given their recent schism—arguably, an example of social tension taken to the point of a mental breakdown—perhaps they had even less tolerance for socially tense situations. Clarity would have to ask them about that later, when they were more alone.

"So what's involved in piloting this thing?" Teya asked suddenly.

Irohann said, "Why? You hoping to take your grandpop's job?"

"That's the idea," Teya agreed.

"First off," Clarity said. "Cassie's not a thing." In fact, she could have sworn that she saw the pink glow of Cassie's bioluminescent patches dim slightly when Teya called her a 'thing.'

Cassie loved bunnies. She would have instantly loved Teya as soon as she came aboard. And casual cruelty hurts the most from those you love.

Now Teya looked uncomfortable, and her body language was eerily similar to Roscoe's. "Okay, fine. So, what's involved in piloting this... uh... ship?"

"Her name's Cassie, short for Cassiopeia," Clarity said. "And you have to let her hook her brain up to yours with tentacles that latch onto your head."

Teya stared at Clarity like she was joking.

Clarity was not joking.

"Your minds kind of blend together," Clarity said.

"It's damned disconcerting," Irohann added.

"You've both done it?" Teya asked. "I thought Grandpop Roscoe was the pilot."

"Crazy stuff happens when you're saving the universe," Irohann said.

Clarity couldn't have said it better herself.

"So, if you can both pilot, uh, Cassie, then why do you even need Grandpop? I mean, I can tell he doesn't really want to be here."

It was Clarity's turn to feel uncomfortable. She had abandoned Cassie and the rest of them during their last mission, swearing she was going to buy a new ship of her own and never see the rest of them again. It had not been her best moment. She didn't want to share it with an idealistic and judgmental young lapine.

Irohann said, "He feels responsible for Cassie. She may be a spaceship, but she's also very young."

Teya rolled her eyes dramatically.

"Younger than you," Clarity said.

"By quite a bit," Irohann added. "And she's dealing with a lot more—she didn't ask to be a spaceship. She didn't ask to be trained in ways that took her fondness for cute, fuzzy animal videos and exploited it, growing the fondness into an, um," Irohann's ears twisted around, showing he was keenly aware of the fact that Cassie could be listening to the conversation currently happening in her belly, "well, an intense, compulsive desire for a lapine pilot, just because you look a little like an animal from the human home world."

"Wait..." Teya's ears shot straight up, very, very tall. "Cassie is a spaceship that loves bunnies?"

Again, Clarity felt sure that she could see the pink light in the scullery dim. Teya had better not start laughing.

"Make fun of this powerful, graceful, and *generous* spaceship at your own peril," Clarity said, teeth clenched. She felt suddenly very protective of Cassie. "She is keeping you alive, safe, warm and breathing. And she doesn't have to. She could ditch us all and go frolic in a nebula. But she's chosen to take care of us instead, because she's really kind and good."

And the pink light surged, glowing brighter than Clarity had seen it before. The surge was noticeable enough that even Teya froze, twitchy nose suddenly still.

Oksana looked up toward the ceiling of the scullery where the bioluminescent patches were thickest. "Cassie's listening to us?"

"And you never know where some of Mazillion's bodies might be perched," Clarity added, "so this isn't the best place for keeping secrets."

Irohann caught her eye. The secret of his previous identity was safe, because Wisper would scrub it from any computer systems where it popped up, and the only people who knew it were completely loyal. But now there were new people aboard Cassie, and one of them wanted to become Cassie's pilot, which meant mind-blending with her. Which meant learning Irohann's secret.

"You'd need to really prove yourself," Irohann said, "before you'd be ready to try piloting Cassie."

Teya nodded, ears folding over at their tips. She seemed to be carefully considering Irohann and Clarity's words, as well as Cassie's visual addition to the conversation. "I can do that," she said. "I can prove myself to Cassie."

Irohann's wolfy muzzle opened, but he closed it without saying anything. He had probably meant for Teya to prove herself to him, Clarity, and Roscoe. Maybe Mazillion. But Teya had seen right past all of them. And it was true: Cassie was the only one she really needed to prove herself to.

And if a young bunny decided to charm Cassie? Well, this troublemaker of a lapine could probably poach their spaceship right out from under their feet if they weren't careful.

6. HEY HO, HEY HO, TO CROSSROADS STATION WE GO

Long before Clarity had ever stepped foot in a spaceship, she'd had a bicycle. Even on the backwards, backwater planet where she'd been born, most of the kids—all human, since it was an isolationist colony—got around on hoverboards or anti-gravcycles. But no, Clarity's parents bought her a bike. It had honest-to-goodness wheels—the oldest invention imaginable—that rolled along the ground. The dirt ground.

Clarity had hated her bike. While every bump on the ground jostled her right down to her bones, she had pushed her pedals as hard as she could, straining to keep up. Other kids zoomed ahead, smoothly, effortlessly, while her muscles screamed at her until their cries became a dull ache pervading her body down to her soul.

Her parents said it built character. A few times, they claimed the old-fashioned bike had been cheaper than a hoverboard, but Clarity checked the price listings. A used hoverboard cost less than an antique bike—especially in maintenance—and when young Clarity found a collector willing to swap a new hoverboard for her bike, her parents' lie became undeniable. They refused to let her swap.

As best as Clarity had been able to tell, her parents simply didn't like any technology that reminded them that humans didn't still live on the planet where they evolved. Hoverboards were only one step above the ground, but for her parents that was too far.

Eventually, Clarity rode her bike off a five-foot drop and claimed she'd been following friends on hoverboards who hadn't realized her bike wouldn't simply float, gracefully to the ground. She'd broken both legs and an arm, but luckily she'd lived. Preteens can be really, really foolish. Her parents had been forced to let the hospital treat her with nano-bots that they didn't approve, and the looks they'd gotten from every adult who heard the story made it perfectly clear that they couldn't risk making her ride an antiquated, *dangerous* bicycle.

Clarity had been given a hoverboard as a recovery gift as soon as she was home from the hospital.

And she'd taken apart the bicycle. Well, the remains of it. Partly, she was curious and enjoyed the simple physical work of dismantling a mechanical object. Partly, she wanted to punish the bike.

When Clarity was done, and the bike lay before her in pieces, she'd taken one of the wheels and contrived a way to hang it from the ceiling of her bedroom. Hanging there, above her while she slept, the spoked metal wheel looked a little like a space station.

Eventually, Clarity painted her ceiling black and decorated it with glowing stars. She would lay on her bed at night, staring at the pretend sky and the representation of a space station, imagining what her life would be like when she finally escaped the gravity well of her home world. She'd always known she'd live on a space station someday.

That was why flying toward Crossroads Station always felt like going home to Clarity. At a practical level, her home for most of the thirty years that she'd been traveling the galaxy with Irohann had been their spaceship, *The Serendipity*. And certainly, at a deep level, her home now was Cassie.

But Crossroads Station was her home town. Her port of call.

The city where her spaceship—be it *The Serendipity* or Cassie—docked when it was time to take a break from adventuring.

Cassie's crew had spent most of the final two subspace hops to Crossroads Station divided into their own rooms, separated by differing sleep schedules. Clarity had woken up twice to find Irohann and Oksana clearing up the dishes from a big meal that the rest of them had shared.

As far as Clarity could tell, the tension between Teya and Roscoe had found a holding pattern. No less tense. But stable. Not explosive. Kwah seemed to have stayed entirely in the room she shared with her two friends. Oksana brought her food after clearing up.

Clarity found herself alone in the scullery, catching up on her pleasure reading—or trying to—while listening to Mazillion buzz mysteriously in the corner. After her recent ordeals, Clarity knew that she needed down time and actual rest, but instead, she kept finding herself struggling through articles about black holes and event horizons. She crafted a message to Am-lei, describing the blip of light she'd seen and what the S'rellick had said about his mecha-shell essentially bouncing off the Devil's Radio. Am-lei was a Wespirtech-trained physicist. If anyone could help Clarity understand what she'd seen, it would be Am-lei. Yet, while she wanted answers, she also didn't want to sound like a fool if what she'd seen didn't make any sense.

Clarity sat at the long scullery table, staring at the message she'd written and dithering over whether to send it ahead to Leioneia for a long time. There was no way to send a message directly to *The Warren* while it was en route; ships are too small and hard to find in the vastness of space while they're traveling. Sometimes a ship can call ahead to a stable port to see if there are any messages waiting for them, but Leioneia was notoriously uncooperative with alien vessels. So, it was unlikely that Am-lei would receive a message from Clarity before arriving at Leioneia anyway.

Clarity was still at the scullery table, poking at her breakfast and squinting at a screen full of quantum mechanics equations on her pocket computer when Cassie dropped out of her second subspace hop, and the beautiful spoked wheels of Crossroads Station appeared on the star-studded backdrop of the scullery's wide viewscreen embedded in the curving wall.

A bicycle wheel, turning, turning, turning in the sky.

Glossed over and enhanced by her imagination, the bicycle wheel hanging from the ceiling of her bedroom hadn't looked so different. And that's how Crossroads Station had become the home of her heart from the first moment she'd seen it, through the window of the passenger freighter she'd saved up and bought a ticket on, a one-way ticket out of the gravity well where she'd been born.

Clarity put away the synthesized bowl of crunchy grains and creamy fruit jelly that she'd been eating. She headed to the cockpit —a small room that she imagined to be nestled directly under Cassie's brain—and found Roscoe, sitting cross-legged in the scooped-out bowl chair of a throne that was centered in the constantly curving space. There were very few right angles or straight lines aboard Cassie, and almost all of them had been added to her body by overeager Wespirtech scientists.

The tentacles that hung from the bone-like spikes on the ceiling of the room, above the chair, still clung to Roscoe's furry scalp with their sucker disks. Those spikes were the only naturally straight lines that Clarity had found aboard Cassie, and even those had twisty, spiraling patterns like her giant horn if looked at closely.

Clarity knew that she was seeing some of Roscoe's thoughts reflected on the panel of rectangular video screens—a dozen screens across by a dozen down, forming a giant, pixelated display altogether—in the front of the room. His thoughts were skewed through Cassie's interpretations of them, of course, and blended with Cassie's own.

Many of the screens showed exterior views of Cassie—star fields, the asteroid belt in the Crossroads Station system, glittering like an ice field; the spinning wheel station itself, still far enough away that the spaceships surrounding it were nothing more than tiny beads of metal; and the big, red, gaseous ball of New Jupiter beyond, shining like an especially bright star—but other screens showed lapines dancing and feasting. It looked like Roscoe's memories from the party aboard *The Warren*, except wavery and dreamlike. A few screens along the bottom of the display showed scenes aboard Crossroads Station, crowded with all species from all quarters of the galaxy. Except, Clarity was fairly sure that Cassie didn't have any actual views of Crossroads Station, so those were likely Roscoe's memories too.

"You've come to check on our progress?" Roscoe asked. His eyes were closed and his ears laid back, but in a peaceful way. He looked very zen. From Clarity's experience, he had to be focusing very hard to manage to speak with his own lapine mouth while his mind was blended with Cassie's.

It's hard to even remember that you have a mouth when you're floating in space, navigating with tube organs and communicating through your spiraling horn that can pick up radio waves.

"It looks like we're only a few hours out now," Clarity said. Traveling through normal space was much slower than hopping through subspace, and it's always safer to hop into a busy star system on its fringes.

"Yes," Roscoe agreed, still peaceful. Eyes still closed. "You've slept through all the hard work."

Clarity rankled at that. What had Roscoe wanted her to do? He was the pilot. He acted like he didn't even trust her with Cassie ever since Leioneia, and yet now, he seemed to be implying that he'd wanted her to take one of the shifts hopping through subspace. "If you wanted me to take a turn piloting," Clarity said, feeling very prickly, "all you had to do was wake me up and ask."

"I'm not asking you to be a pilot, sleepyhead." Roscoe opened his eyes, and the sucker disks began popping off of his scalp. Their tentacles withdrew, drawing the disks upward toward the straw-colored spikes they hung from. The views on the screens changed. No more dancing rabbits. No more interiors of Crossroads Station. Crackling gray static instead. "But if you think you're the captain hereabouts—"

Clarity opened her mouth to object, but Roscoe held up a paw, stopping her.

"—and *you do* think you're the captain, then it might be to your benefit to be awake and paying attention to the tension among your crew."

Clarity felt a confusing mix of feelings. Pride that Roscoe thought of her as the captain, but also umbrage that he was pinning the responsibility for the tension between him and his grandniece and her friends on her. Also, uncertainty—maybe Roscoe wasn't saying he thought she was the captain, just that she was an upstart who saw herself that way?

But also... shame. Maybe she should have been awake and paying attention, hanging out in the scullery when everyone else was there.

"We don't have an established day-night cycle," Clarity said, weakly defending herself.

"Maybe we should," Roscoe said, hopping down from the fleshy mound that was Cassie's pilot seat.

"Maybe." Clarity wasn't sure that it was a good idea to have everyone aboard a spaceship on the same sleep cycle anyway. Although, she'd never managed a spaceship like Cassie before—alive and big enough to hold a real crew.

On *The Serendipity*, it had just been her and Irohann. Not a lot to manage. And they'd often been on the same sleep cycle, even though they hadn't had a sentient spaceship looking out for them.

"I'm gonna go catch a nap before all the hustle and bustle hits," Roscoe said. "You might want to check on those flowery fellas and the sick S'rellick that you dragged aboard."

"Is T'resso still not doing well?" Clarity asked.

Roscoe was already at the mouth of the left side corridor out of the cockpit, one of three that ran down Cassie's length from her cockpit to the airlock near the end of her tail. He shook his head and answered without looking back, "Not my department. As long as they don't hurt any of my grandbunnies—and that includes Cassie, Teya, and any misguided critters that she calls friends—I don't care."

Clarity frowned.

Roscoe would be a terrible captain. Maybe that's why he seemed to agree with Clarity that she was in charge—because he was right; she did see herself as the captain. He didn't want the job.

For whatever perverse reason, Clarity kind of did. She'd never seen herself as a captain before. When it had just been her and Irohann, honestly, she'd seen him as being in charge. He'd been older and more experienced than her when they'd met, and that imbalance had stayed in their dynamic for thirty-some years.

Then Clarity had invited all of the chaos into their lives that led to them joining up with Cassie, Roscoe, Mazillion, and now Teya's group of friends. Clarity's choices had made that happen, and she felt responsible for the group that they'd become.

"Hey, Cassie," Clarity said to the empty cockpit. Empty except for her. It was one of the smaller ventricle-like rooms aboard Cassie. The largest room, by far, was the cargo bay with its oversized airlock, large enough to take aboard a smaller vessel. The next largest was the scullery with its tables and benches that swelled up from the floor, fleshy extrusions that almost made Clarity think of mushrooms growing out of a forest floor. But even the six rooms done up as personal bedrooms, featuring actual furniture that wasn't physically part of Cassie, were easily two- to three-times as large as the cockpit on average.

The staticky viewscreens flickered back to life—their gray snowstorms were replaced with bright, cheerful colors showing a dizzying array of snippets of videos that looked like they'd been pulled from children's educational programs, designed to teach Solanese. Put together, they spelled out, "hI ClaRiTy," with a collection of bouncing, jumping, dancing animated letters.

Clarity frowned. "We have got to improve your communication systems."

Four of the screens in the middle of the display reflected Clarity's frown back at her—just her mouth, blown up much, much larger than her actual face. The screens around them played snippets of videos that seemed to be pulled from dark, gritty dramas—all people frowning or crying.

"I'm sorry," Clarity said, putting her hands up, palms out, like she was reaching out to Cassie. "But don't you want to be able to communicate with us more easily?"

Cassie's screens went dark. No static. No stars.

Clarity drew a deep breath, searching for patience. She had come to the cockpit partly because she wanted to communicate with Wisper's roboticist who she needed to visit aboard Crossroads Station. If Cassie were a normal spaceship, that would be easy. Instead, Clarity needed Cassie's cooperation.

Maybe Cassie was picking up on the tension among her inhabitants... Or maybe she was cranky with Clarity because she'd been picking up on Roscoe's feelings toward her. Either way, Clarity didn't really feel like blending her mind with Cassie right now, but that's what she would have to do in order to send an outbound message and receive incoming responses in real time. Her pocket computer wasn't powerful enough to do that.

Clarity climbed into the pilot's chair, crossed her legs inside the bowl-like indentation, and closed her eyes. Then she waited.

She waited for Cassie's curiosity and natural friendliness to overcome whatever hurt feelings the starwhal had. She waited for the feel of sucker disks against her forehead and scalp. She waited for her mind to open up, large enough to encompass an entire starwhal body, floating through space.

She waited and nothing happened.

Clarity opened her eyes and saw that Cassie's screens had changed again. They showed a mosaic view of the space around them—star fields and the bicycle wheel of Crossroads Station directly ahead. "Come on, Cassie," Clarity said. "Won't you talk to me?"

Clarity nearly jumped out of the pilot's bowl chair as she saw spaceships—dozens of them—flying across the view screens. An entire fleet of spaceships, gleaming and metal in every size and shape, were flying in wildly mismatched directions. *Where had they come from? Why were so many ships of different styles suddenly all together at once? Was there a diplomatic summit? Or... a war?*

For a moment, Clarity truly thought the ships were real, and every muscle in her body had tensed, afraid that one of them would crash into Cassie. Or attack them on purpose. Who knew what all those ships would do when there was no explaining how they had all suddenly come to be there? Her body had tensed in preparation for the impact.

But of course, they were just video clips. Cassie communicating something obscure.

"Not cool," Clarity said. This was exactly why she wanted a more normal communication system. "That really scared me."

Dancing, bouncing letters replaced half of the views on half of the screens. The letters spelled out, "nOrMAl ShIps," and then after a moment, "wAt U wAnt rITe?"

Clarity folded forward and clasped her face in her hands, blocking out the madness.

"I don't want a normal ship, Cassie." Clarity said the words loudly, making sure the obstinate starwhal would hear them through her hands, still cradling her face. "I just want to communicate with Maradia's Robot Emporium and tell Maradia that she can buy her robot body back, now that Wisper's done with it."

Wisper's body looked like a blue-and-silver metal skeleton, and it was still tucked away in the cockpit closet. The last time Clarity had looked at it, she'd been fetching back her fuzzy gray Woaoo doll. Wisper had died clutching that doll.

Clarity had given the koala-like Woaoo doll to Wisper to hold shortly before the AI had been killed, wiped clean from the robot body's mechanical brain by the EM distortions in space-time trying to destroy the universe.

Wisper had sacrificed herself nobly in the service of saving the universe. Other instances of Wisper's AI might still exist elsewhere, but the instance that had become Clarity's friend was gone. The blue and silver skeleton was a reminder that she'd rather be rid of. A dead body. Nothing more. But in this case, a dead body worth significant monetary value that a Crossroads Station roboticist probably wanted back.

A voice interrupted Clarity's reverie, and she looked up to see Maradia's face—strangely familiar in its humanity—filling the bank of screens. Each screen showed a portion of her face, adding up to one, large, pixelated view. "Hello? Did you mean to vid message me? Oh! I recognize you. You're the one who mysteriously came in and bought my Orion 23958. Can you tell me what that was all about now?"

Clarity tried not to frown. She needed to pull herself together fast; she hadn't been expecting Cassie to vid message Maradia without warning her. She hadn't expected to find herself suddenly in the middle of a conversation that had started while her face was still cradled in her hands.

"I'm sorry," Clarity said. "I seem to be having some trouble with my communications software..." She bit her own tongue as the words came out. The pain was bright and fresh, reminding her to be careful. Maradia wasn't the only one listening right now, and Clarity was only digging her hole with Cassie deeper. "I mean, yes, yes, thank you, I did want to talk to you. I can't tell you everything—"

Maradia frowned. Her hair was tied back in the same messy knot as the last time Clarity had seen her. "But you can tell me some of it?"

"Also, I can give—well, ideally, sell—your Orion model back." Clarity felt cold describing the body that had cradled Wisper—snarky, acerbic Wisper—with a clinical name like "Orion model."

Maradia looked startled. "What happened to the AI? Did they find a new body? Something specifically suited to them?"

Clarity didn't want to tell Maradia what had happened to Wisper, but she supposed she was going to have to eventually. "Can that conversation... wait... until I'm back aboard Crossroads? My ship is still a few hours out."

Maradia's frown grew deeper. "If you're not telling me, then I guess it's bad." She clearly really cared about her robots—even the ones that were inhabited by rogue AIs that had illegally uploaded themselves into bodies she was still working on. Little did Maradia know that Wisper had actually been an off-shoot of one of the first AI programs she'd ever written... And she wouldn't find out from Clarity. Since Wisper was still out there, meddling with science institutes and research stations, in her larger, more amorphous form, Clarity was compelled to continue keeping her secret. "I guess you're holding out for the free dinner I offered?"

A free dinner sounded nice to Clarity. She was less sure about spending that much time with a woman who wanted information from her that she didn't intend to share. "Actually, I was hoping you could come pick the... body... up. It's kind of... heavy. You know, without an AI controlling it."

"Don't you have a dolly or anti-grav generators you can strap on it?"

"No," Clarity said, feeling foolish. Of course, those were things that a spaceship should be equipped with. But Cassie wasn't a normal spaceship, as she had so recently pointed out. There was going to be a lot of shopping to get done while they were aboard Crossroads. And sure, Clarity could do the shopping before returning Wisper's body, but...

She just wanted the skeleton from the closet gone.

When Clarity didn't elaborate, Maradia sighed deeply. She picked up a pocket computer, typed a few things, and said, "There, I've forwarded a simple sub-sentient AI program to your ship's computer—"

Cassie would love the phrasing, Clarity thought sarcastically to herself.

"—that should upload into the Orion model easily enough. It'll follow simple voice commands and can follow you here."

"Excellent," Clarity said, almost completely certain that Maradia wouldn't be able to hear the bitterness in her tone.

What she was really thinking was: that sounds super creepy. Now, she would get to order her dead friend's body around like some kind of summoned zombie. She should have waited until she'd bought an anti-grav cart. But now it would be weird if she didn't use the program Maradia had sent over.

"I'll see you soon..." Maradia said, voice trailing off like she was already distracted by some other puzzle or problem.

Clarity started to say, "Cassie, can you upload the program she sent over to my pocket computer?" But by the time she'd finished the sentence, her pocket computer had already buzzed, and when she checked, yes, there was the program. "Thanks."

Although Cassie continued to resolutely ignore Clarity, she stayed seated in the pilot's bowl chair, working on her pocket computer, going over the broadcasts from Crossroads Station to see if she could find good prices on any of the supplies they needed to buy while in port.

The money that Wisper had paid Clarity to replace *The Serendipity*, along with the reward from her for saving the universe, was enough to keep a ship with a crew of six or seven (Clarity, Irohann, Roscoe, Teya and her friends, and she wasn't sure how to count Mazillion) in the black for several years, as long as they were thrifty. If Cassie was interested in carrying cargo—which she had the body for, given that massive cargo bay—then they'd be fine indefinitely.

But given Cassie's current mood, and Roscoe's recalcitrance... Clarity didn't want to bet her long-term security too heavily on them. So, she didn't begrudge spending her own money on outfitting Cassie a little better, but she wanted to keep the costs under control. Maybe not to a minimum, but, well, it's always a good idea to have an escape route planned. Maybe she could convince the others that keeping a two-person shuttle in Cassie's cargo bay was a good idea.

Really, for safety reasons, it probably was a good idea. What if Cassie were injured? Drifting in space? A short-range vehicle like a two-person shuttle... Well, it would be totally useless for evacuating a six-person crew, but it might be useful for sending out a party to find help.

Clarity decided it was worth at least checking if there were any cheap shuttles available. Well, not *cheap*. Reasonably priced. No one wants cheap space equipment. That's how you end up dead.

When the beautiful concentric wheels of Crossroads Station filled Cassie's unusual modular viewscreen, Clarity decided that her list of items and postings to check out when they arrived was thorough enough, and it was time for her to check on the big loose end from the Devil's Radio: the S'rellick and two Doraspians.

Once their unwanted visitors were safely on their way, and Cassie was better stocked, they all could put back out to space and start really sorting out what life aboard Cassie would be like for this crew and how they all fit together.

7. LOOSE ENDS UNRAVELING

The Doraspians and S'rellick had stayed almost entirely in the room where they'd been put. The valve-like door firmly shut. Oksana had brought bowls of snailer soup and crickitat rolls for the S'rellick every day—much like she'd been bringing food to the room she shared with Teya and Kwah to feed the wayward avian. Irohann had synthesized the pieces for a simple lamp, constructed it, and set it up for the Doraspians, to make their room brighter.

But that was apparently all of the contact they'd had with Cassie's crew during the short voyage. At least, Cassie's bipedal crew.

Mazillion came and went as they pleased. Clarity had tried asking Mazillion what they'd learned about the Doraspians and S'rellick—and also how Oksana had reacted to meeting them—but they'd been cryptic. They'd called Oksana, "very warm and centered," and the only words that Clarity had dragged out of Mazillion regarding the Doraspians were "rejuvenating," "fast, fast growing," and most cryptically, "eternal."

Mazillion often seemed cryptic to Clarity. They had such different experiences of, well, life itself that it could be hard to connect, even on simple every day topics.

For instance, Mazillion didn't get hungry. Not as an entire

being. Pieces of them could get hungry—individual gnat-like bodies—and if those individual bodies couldn't find anything else to eat, they could eat the smaller, weaker bodies with fewer legs and wings, winnowing Mazillion's self down to their strongest parts.

Clarity had noticed the cluster of five gnat-like bodies that followed her around had been upgraded—more legs, more wings per body. The bodies with the most wings looked almost like little crystalline flowers. She wasn't sure of the reason for the change. Perhaps it merely represented random fluctuations in terms of which bodies were free for which tasks at which times. But Clarity felt like it meant something.

Clarity placed her hand on the sensor beside the valve-like door into the Doraspians' room. She drew a deep breath. She'd spent enough time with Irohann to have absorbed his fear of the plant-based aliens. She didn't want to deal with them. But that's what captains do. They deal with problems aboard their ships.

The door opened and bright light shone out, yellow compared to the pink light in the hall. The Doraspians' branches were silhouetted inside and cast long, tangled shadows.

"May I come in?" Clarity asked. It seemed polite to ask. And yet, she rankled at doing so. Part of her still felt like these Doraspians and their S'rellick-gone-turtle were prisoners of war, not charity cases who simply needed a ride.

T'resso hissed, "Yes, of course." He was lying on the patchwork bed, with his long tail curved in a languorous question mark. His blue-tipped scales glittered in the bright light like sapphires and aquamarine, and the spikes along his back gleamed with the deep galaxy blue of lapis lazuli. He looked a little bit like both a dragon and a dragon's hoard—valuable and shiny.

The older-looking Doraspian, Paurizau, crouched on the floor beside the bed, looking like a tumbleweed, ready to roll away. His leaves continually sprouted, unfurled, spread wide, and then withered, falling off and leaving a layer of litterfall beneath him. He was like an everlasting autumn, all to himself.

The other Doraspian, Genniperri, rose from a knapsack-like contraption full of dirt, sitting beside the pillow at the top of the bed with its straps in disarray. Her emerald leaves and prismatic array of flowers looked so full of the fresh, urgent glow of youth that there was something angelic about her. Like she was too intensely real and alive to exist in only one layer of reality.

She was far and away the most beautiful potted plant that Clarity had ever seen. If she weren't sentient, she'd make an excellent housewarming gift.

Clarity stepped inside the room, and she immediately heard the quiet, subtle, background buzz of Mazillion's presence. There were far more of Mazillion's bodies in this room—hovering near the pinkly glowing ceiling, perched along the edge of the wooden bureau, and even flitting through the Doraspian's branches, nestling naturally among their various and varied flowers—than Clarity would have expected. She'd thought, maybe, a few of Mazillion's bodies would stay here, kind of like spies. Actually... kind of like the cluster of five that followed Clarity around.

Suddenly, the presence that Mazillion kept near Clarity seemed much less significant. A fraction so small that it could be written off as falling within a margin of error. Whereas a full tenth or more of Mazillion was here. In this room. Cavorting among the flowers.

"We'll be reaching Crossroads Station soon," Clarity said. "Will you be needing any help getting off the ship?"

A long silence followed. The longer it lasted, the more that Clarity felt like she was supposed to offer an alternative. That she was supposed to invite them to stay. But surely, she was imagining that feeling of social pressure, based on a childhood among humans where long pauses often were imbued with complex meanings. Subtle communication of that sort was far less common among the diverse populations of Crossroads Station and the wider universe. When dealing with peoples who have entirely different social structures and societal layout, it's generally more effective to simply say what you want.

Dissembling only works with people who know your background well enough to see through the facade.

"We would like to request asylum," Genniperri sang with her purple flowers.

Clarity burst out laughing. When her laughter had subsided, she said, "Are you kidding? We're not a government. We don't do stuff like that." Although, as Clarity thought about it, she and Irohann did have a lot of experience with ducking the Doraspian Empire, specifically. Maybe the request wasn't so ridiculous. However, Genniperri should have no way of knowing that.

Because they'd done a smashing good job of keeping Irohann's secret.

"Look," Clarity said, "if you want to stay here, then I need some answers."

T'resso's tail curled tighter, more the shape of a fish hook than a question mark. "Alright," he said. "Then ask some questions."

"What is happening with your leaves"—Clarity pointed at Paurizau and the pile of dead, crinkly leaves beneath him—"and your roots?" She pointed at Genniperri, potted in a knapsack that looked like it was designed to let T'resso carry her around on his back.

Genniperri's yellow, daisy-like, light-sensing flowers turned away and faced the pinkly glowing wall. Paurizau rustled in his pile of leaves. Neither of them sang a word. Eventually, T'resso said, "Those are still not my answers to give."

Clarity turned back toward the door to the room, saying as she turned, "Fine, I can call Crossroads Station security and have you removed from my ship when we arrive. I'm sure there's a S'rellick emissary on Crossroads who can deal with you."

"No!" T'resso lashed his tail.

Mazillion's buzzing shifted tone.

Clarity stopped. Turned back. "Do you have something to say?" she said, looking at the tiny buzzing bodies, looping and zig-zagging around the curved ceiling.

A collection of the bodies came together, including the five that

Clarity had grown used to having hover near her shoulder. They formed a grapefruit-sized orb—it looked smaller than the orbs Mazillion had used for speaking with before. Could they be getting more skilled, more precise at imitating sapient-style speech?

Mazillion's mouth pulsed, and from their buzzing the words formed: "We will help them."

"Help them do what?" Clarity exclaimed, feeling like a petulant child. "And who are you to choose?"

"We chose," Mazillion answered without answering. "You will agree, or Roscoe will."

Clarity snorted. That seemed unlikely. Roscoe didn't agree with much.

T'resso seemed to read her skepticism and said, "I can offer the lapine man assistance from the S'rellick Mercenary Syndicate in freeing his peoples from the primates who uplifted and enslaved them."

Genniperri added, her yellow flowers still facing away, "And the Doraspian Empire would be a powerful ally to the lapines."

Clarity frowned. "I thought you didn't want anything to do with either the S'rellick or Doraspian governments?"

T'resso rolled his shoulders, imitating a human shrug. "It would be a tempting offer to him, no?"

It would be. Tempting enough for Roscoe to overlook a few inconsistencies along the way. "I could tell him that you're all manipulating him." But Clarity knew he wouldn't believe her. He'd probably close his eyes to the inconsistencies even tighter, just to spite her.

Mazillion's bodies came from every corner of the room, flying away from the Doraspians' flowers, and streaming toward Clarity until they all came together in front of her. They mimicked her human shape in a roiling mass of flittering bodies. "We would rather ally with you."

Clarity did not know what to make of Mazillion. But they had saved her life and sacrificed their selves to help her.

And besides, they had her outmaneuvered. She needed to be on better terms with either Cassie or her pilot—or become her pilot—or else Clarity was going to find herself outmaneuvered a lot on this ship. Or thrown off of it.

"Fine," Clarity said. "You can hide out here."

Mazillion's bodies dissipated, their humanoid form melting back into a cloud spread through the room. T'resso's long tail swayed over the surface of the patchwork quilt like the oscillations of a sine wave, and Paurizau sang with his purple bellflowers. "Thank you and the goodness of your ship."

Clarity smiled. If Cassie was listening, she would like that.

Genniperri continued to look away with her yellow daisy-like flowers, and her other flowers seemed to have drawn in closer to her most central branches.

"As long as we're playing host," Clarity said, trying to get into the spirit, since she didn't have any other choice, "is there anything I can get you while we're at Crossroads Station? I don't expect that we'll be staying long, but I'm already planning to go on a supply run."

"We have everything we need," T'resso said.

Genniperri's purple flowers shook, speaking in a language Clarity didn't know. Her sing-song voice was now filled with hisses and rasps. She was speaking in S'rellick.

T'resso answered her, "You know I'm not well enough to carry you."

"Do you need more medical attention?" Clarity asked, genuinely concerned. She might not want the S'rellick on her ship, but she didn't want him sick either.

"No," T'resso said. "Just rest. But my Genni is restless."

Genniperri's yellow flowers turned back toward the room. "I've never seen a human space station," she said. "And I wish I could see it."

"I could..." Clarity hesitated, feeling strange about the offer. "I could carry you? Actually..." She wondered why Genniperri didn't have a hoverchair, but she looked at the Doraspian's delicate branches and knew the answer.

Genniperri had all of the sensory organs of an adult Doraspian, and she even had the grasping vines for manipulating objects like hands do. But those branches were clearly too delicate and lightweight to handle balancing against the bulky weight of her root ball plus the dirt she needed for it.

"I'm going to visit a talented and skilled roboticist," Clarity said. "I wonder if she could design some kind of... mechanical legs for you? Something that would let you get around on your own. It couldn't hurt to ask, right?"

"You trust her?" T'resso asked.

Clarity chewed her lower lip and thought about what she knew of Maradia, the distracted woman who seemed to have a mind for nothing other than her robots.

Maradia had known there was something strange happening with Wisper—had seemed completely aware that a rogue AI had illegally downloaded itself into the robot body she'd been working on—and yet she let Wisper and Clarity go, no questions asked. It had seemed like there was a complicated bond between Wisper and the woman who had programmed her, and between Maradia and her robots. Almost a motherly one.

"I would trust her," Clarity said.

The room filled with hissing, rasping voices—T'resso and Genniperri seemed to be arguing with each other. Paurizau abstained from the rapid, angry conversation.

Close to Clarity's ear, a buzzing said, "They disagree. They argue."

Clarity turned her head quickly, reaching toward her ear. She had to fight the impulse to brush Mazillion's bodies away from her; they'd been so close, she could feel the movements in the air from their tiny wings.

"We translate," Mazillion buzzed in their tiny voice, meant just for Clarity.

"I could already tell they were arguing. But thank you." Clarity spoke softly, just for Mazillion. "You speak S'rellick?"

"Many languages," Mazillion buzzed. "Very useful. Healthy argument. This is how resolution is found when equally strong bodies disagree."

"You eat your own bodies when they disagree," Clarity pointed out.

Mazillion didn't answer, but she imagined the entire amorphous cloud of buzzing bodies in the room pausing for a moment, considering her point or maybe shrugging.

The argument ended with a choral crescendo from Genniperri that shut down all of T'resso's hissing. She switched to Solanese: "Yes, it cannot hurt to ask. Please, if you will, take me to this roboticist."

Clarity stepped forward and around the bed to where she could reach the straps of Genniperri's potting sack. Gingerly, she lifted the straps, put her arms through, and let the weight of the pack settle on her back.

Vine-like tentacles (or were they tentacle-like vines?) waved disconcertingly in Clarity's peripheral vision, making her feel like she had strange, demonic wings. The pack was designed comfortably with broad straps that spread the weight evenly over her shoulders, but Genniperri weighed as much as a medium-sized watermelon. A substantial, constant weight.

Clarity shifted her shoulders, testing how the pack moved with her, and the tentacle-vines retracted behind her where she couldn't see them, only to creep back into the edges of her vision again a moment later. Clarity barely felt the shift of weight on her back as Genniperri moved and situated. This Doraspian definitely wouldn't have the right distribution of mass to control a hoverboard. The parts of her body that she could consciously control were insubstantial wisps—fluttering leaves and feather-light blades of grass—compared to her thick, tuberous, insensate roots and the support system of nutrient rich dirt they were buried in.

"Be careful," T'resso admonished, his voice the gentlest rasp of air; barely a hiss, more of a sigh.

"You worry too much," Genniperri said from behind Clarity's head. Her chiming voice rang all around the human, like she was standing inside the choir of tiny purple fairies that were Genniperri's voiceboxes. In fact, she was. But they weren't fairies. They were far more real and far stranger. True aliens had entirely outpaced humanity's imagination of them.

"You are my charge; I am the official handler of the Doraspian Diplomatic Envoy to S'rellicka," T'resso answered. "Worrying about you is my job."

"You quit your job when you agreed to help me run away from mine," Genniperri said. "Now you are my traveling companion. Nothing more."

"Nothing less," T'resso said. "But so much more."

Clarity knew that S'rellicks didn't generally form emotional, romantic attachments in quite the same way as humans, Heffen, or most other mammaloid species. Yet, T'resso seemed lovesick for the physically-stunted flower shrub on Clarity's back. "I'll be careful," she assured the lovelorn reptile. She didn't understand the magnetic appeal these plant-aliens seemed to hold for some.

"I'll do what I want," Genniperri said.

Clarity appreciated Genniperri's snarky, independent response. Although, she couldn't help thinking that the Doraspian would be somewhat limited doing only what Clarity felt like helping her do.

Hopefully, Maradia could fix that.

8. DOCKING AT CROSSROADS

Clarity carried Genniperri to Cassie's cockpit, where Roscoe had already settled back into the pilot's bowl chair. His eyelids fluttered, and his ear tips twitched. But his nose and whiskers held stock still, like he was concentrating with all his might.

Teya stood beside the bowl chair, watching her granduncle with as much focus as he was using to pilot Cassie up next to the turning wheels of Crossroads Station.

The beautiful bicycle wheels of the station filled Cassie's array of vid screens now. The half circles and semi-arcs of silver-gray crescents were spinning slowly past, too close now for them to see the entirety of the outer wheels. In the corner, though, the view of Crossroads Station was interrupted by one screen. The single errant screen, taking a rectangular bite out of the bigger picture, showed Teya's face, reflected through the interior video systems that always watched them.

Cassie was watching Teya.

And Teya was watching Roscoe.

Clarity shook her head. She didn't know what to do with these internal politics, but she knew that Wisper's body needed to be returned to Maradia. So, she opened the vesicle-like closet in the back of the cockpit.

Wisper's body stood inside, looking as ready to make a snarky comment as ever. The glassy lenses of her eyes reflected Clarity's face, and for a moment, she had to turn away. She pulled her pocket computer out, called up the program that Maradia had sent over, and uploaded it to Wisper's body.

The metal irises around Wisper's eyes adjusted, narrowing and widening, waking back up. Except, the program inside the body that was waking up was not Wisper. Technically, it wasn't anyone. Sub-sentient. Clarity hated this.

"Whoa, you have a shipboard robot?" Teya's voice caused Clarity to turn around. The young rabbit was watching her bring Wisper's body back online. "What's it for?"

"Nothing," Clarity said. "We have a... borrowed piece of equipment that needs to be returned. That's all. Well, sold back." She did want her money back.

Part of Clarity died inside, calling the corpse of her friend a "piece of equipment." But this body was nothing more than a husk now.

The husk said in the same mechanical hum that Clarity remembered from Wisper's voice, "Orion 23958 online and functioning." The shiny metal skull tilted; the sub-sentient program was looking over its environment, scanning the space for the sentient being it was expected to serve. Its glassy eyes settled on Clarity. "Awaiting orders."

Clarity shuddered, then dragged the words out of her throat: "We'll be docking at Crossroads Station momentarily." In fact, she felt a subtle quiver running through the floor under her feet that suggested Cassie had made contact with the Crossroads Station dock. "I will lead you to Maradia's Robot Emporium. Please, follow me."

"Order understood," the spiritless Orion body said. It looked like a skeleton, and now it was as alive as one.

"I think that was more information than you had to give it," Teya said. "It doesn't sound sentient."

"It's not," Clarity snapped. "Not anymore," she added in a

mutter, under her breath. "I'm sorry," she said, remembering that she might need to be making friends with this young lapine, this potential pilot who Cassie was paying so much attention to. Teya's image still appeared in Cassie's corner screen. "The AI who used to inhabit this body was brave and selfless, and it's tearing me up inside that she's not inside there anymore and someone—I mean, *something*—else is."

Teya's eyes narrowed, and Clarity saw the green fronds in her peripheral vision shift, brushing low, almost against her shoulders. Almost against her cheek. She turned her face, trying instinctively to get some distance, but it didn't work, of course, because Genniperri was rooted to her back.

Clarity didn't want sympathy. She wanted to move on, but she also wanted to connect with the young rabbit who might become Cassie's next pilot. "Teya, do you want to come to the robotics shop with us?"

"I'm going to see if the roboticist can build a mobility aide for me!" Genniperri said cheerfully from Clarity's back.

"That's right," Clarity said. "We're off to see the wizard, the wonderful wizard of Crossroads. She can build Genniperri legs, give the empty Orion model new programming, and maybe she can offer some advice on Cassie's communications systems."

The young rabbit stared at Clarity, nose twitching as if she weren't sure what to make of the human woman and her weird sing-song outburst. Teya was unlikely to be familiar with cultural references from ancient Earth.

"I'm also going to run some supply errands," Clarity said. "Get Cassie stocked up properly before we set out again. So, you want to come along?"

"No," Teya said, slowly, measuredly. "Oksana, Kwah, and I have plans while we're in port. Thanks though."

Clarity felt encouraged by Teya's politeness to her, but also weirdly stung that the younger half of the crew had plans together and she not only wasn't included but hadn't even heard about them until now. "That's fine. Let me know if there's anything you think the ship could use. I don't know where we're heading after this, but we might be out of port for a while. And the next place we stop... Well, you never know what you'll find on some of the more out-there space stations."

Teya tilted her head, and one of her flopped-over ears flicked, standing up. With one ear up and one down, she had a skewed, intrigued look. "I've never been to a space station other than Crossroads," Teya said.

"Would you like to?" Clarity asked.

Teya didn't answer at first. She seemed to expect adults to be trying to trick her, but when Clarity simply waited for a response, not scolding or advising her in any way, Teya finally said, "Yes, I'd like to see Ob'glaung."

Clarity was surprised, but she tried not to show it on her face. "Do you like swimming?" she asked. Ob'glaung was the nearest space station under the rule of the Lintar Oligarchy, a society of fish-like people who had already been well-established, all across the galaxy, by the time humans made it out to the stars at all. Their space stations—and presumably their spaceships—were filled with water. Humans and other similar species needed to use a breathing apparatus to survive on them. Which was only fair—every Lintar on Crossroads Station had to wear a diving helmet at all times to breathe. However, the fish-like aliens were so light-weight that their swim bladders, used to adjust their height underwater, let Lintars practically fly in human-designed spaces.

"I love swimming," Teya said. "We had a watering hole back home where all the young'uns went swimming all the time before Grandpop Roscoe dragged us out to Crossroads."

Interesting. Clarity was pretty sure that Roscoe thought of Crossroads Station as home. Apparently, Teya had grown up back on their home world. And missed it.

Roscoe had never said a kind word about his home world. But then, he didn't say a lot of kind words. He was more likely to give an approving nod than an actual statement of support or agreement.

The rest of the crew crowded into the back of the cockpit—Irohann, Oksana, Kwah, and an amorphous cloud of Mazillion. The five of Mazillion's bodies by Clarity's ear whisper-buzzed, "We'll come with you."

Clarity smiled.

Irohann asked Roscoe, "Are we fully docked then?"

The elder bunny opened his eyes, looking very tired, and said, "Ship shape and battened down." The sucker disks kissed off his head, and the hanging tentacles withdrew, coiling upward. Cassie's screens went dark. "Cassie and I are due for a long nap," Roscoe said. "You young'uns have fun on the station." He hopped down from the pilot's bowl chair, but before leaving, he turned to Clarity and added, "And, please, since you're running errands, pick up some Sagittarian willow bark?"

"Sure," Clarity said, automatically. It was a simple request to fulfill. But her brain started turning fast: Sagittarian willow bark was completely legal, but it was also really strong and mildly addictive. If Roscoe was asking for it, then he had to be in a lot of pain. He was far too sensible and grounded to take something like Sagittarian willow bark without a good reason. "Should you—"

"A nap," Roscoe snapped, not letting Clarity finish asking if he should see a doctor aboard the station. "That's all I need. And some willow bark."

Roscoe shouldered his way past all the others and hopped away down the right-hand hall toward the cluster of quarters. The rest of them filed down the left-hand hall. All three passages leading out of Cassie's cockpit met up on the other side of the scullery. And beyond that, they reached the airlock.

Since they were docked, they entered the airlock without changing into spacesuits, and it was safe to open the outer door without fully cycling the lock.

Back when Clarity and Irohann had lived together aboard *The Serendipity*, they had liked to leave both airlock doors wide open for a while when they were docked at Crossroads Station. Fresh air. Or at least, different air. It had felt good to air their ship out.

Clarity wondered how Cassie felt about having different air inside of her. Did it have a flavor? A feel? Or was it beneath her notice as much as Clarity's own blood, rushing through her veins, was generally beneath hers? She'd have to pay attention to that question next time she piloted Cassie.

Assuming Cassie ever let Clarity pilot her again.

"You're running errands?" Irohann asked Clarity as they stepped into the wide, busy docking bay of Crossroads Station. He seemed to be looking over the sentient tumbleweed on her back and sub-sentient robot at her heels with amusement. "You've got quite the, uh, arrangement there."

"Yes, errands." Clarity was about to launch into a description with more details, but Irohann's ears twisted about, showing he was only half listening and at least half distracted.

"Want to meet up at The All Alien Cafe later?" Irohann asked.

"Uh, sure," Clarity said. Apparently, Irohann wouldn't be coming with her.

"Great!" Irohann said. He skipped away into the crowd of aliens, tail swishing. He seemed to be following Teya's group toward the Refugee Quarter. The big, red wolf caught up with the young lapine, the goat girl, and the feathered avian, who seemed to be carrying her suitcase, strapped to her back between her wings. A stream of Mazillion's buzzing bodies followed them; others dissipated into the cloud. But, as promised, a small cluster continued to hover beside her shoulder, near Genniperri's waving, green tendrils.

Clarity's errands laid in the other direction, in the Merchant Quarter. She set out, wending her way between fuzzy mammaloids, feathery avians, scaly reptiles, and insectoid aliens of every kind—some small enough to skitter along between the ankles of other aliens and others hulkingly large, towering over Clarity; the Orion model clanked along beside her.

"Is it always like this?" Genniperri said with a bellflower nestled disconcertingly close to Clarity's ear.

Mazillion's cluster answered, "Always."

"This busy?" Genniperri sang. "This complicated? So many different species? So much color and noise?"

"Always," Mazillion buzzed again.

Clarity hadn't thought about the noise. The colors were obvious. Compared to the soft pink glow aboard Cassie, the bright station lights—shining on all the booths and stalls, glaring against banners and signs, and simply reflecting off the different alien bodies—were stunningly bright. But the noise...

Yes, there were a profusion of conversations happening all around them, between aliens with wildly different vocal apparatuses, speaking in more languages than Clarity could count, and there were even the occasional stray musicians, claiming a corner of deck space and playing music that sometimes soared with haunting melodies and other times sounded like discordant screeching to Clarity's ears. But it all blended together for Clarity. She knew the sounds here. They felt safe and comforting. A blanketing white noise.

Kind of like the thrumming sound of Cassie's body. A quiet music all its own.

True silence had come to mean a dangerous sense of isolation to Clarity. It only happened when she was floating in space, wearing her space suit. Totally and completely alone; unsure if she'd survive.

Crossroads Station felt much safer to her.

Clarity let Mazillion and Genniperri talk to each other, beside her ear, and focused on making her way to Maradia's Robot Emporium, glancing occasionally at the robot clanking along behind her.

The swarm and plant had a rhythm to their conversation, like they were old friends already, after only a week.

The way small-groups formed within Clarity's shipboard crew left her on the outside, an outcast, or maybe it was just in her head. Listening to the conversation, though inches from her ear, filled her with guilt, like she was eavesdropping on something private.

When Clarity reached the entrance to Maradia's Robot Emporium—a perfectly normal shop door on Crossroads Station—she hesitated, feeling the weight of the moment wash over her. This was the end of a journey that had begun when she entered Maradia's shop. She had come full circle, and it had been a circle large enough to hold the entire universe inside of it. Her life had been forever changed by entering Maradia's Robot Emporium last time. This time... She was simply returning a piece of unneeded equipment.

Clarity took a deep breath and opened the door.

9. ROBOTS, ROBOTS EVERYWHERE

Clarity expected to find the lobby on the other side of the door empty—with Maradia busy in her messy robotics laboratory further inside—or to find Maradia waiting to meet with her, maybe doing administrative work at the front desk. Either way, she expected Maradia's Robot Emporium to be a place of quiet, studious research and reflection.

Clarity did not expect to find two of the most heartbreakingly beautiful humans she'd ever seen arguing passionately with each other while Maradia sat at her front desk, looking bemused with her chin resting on her fist and her elbow on the desktop. Maradia's smile was crooked and impish, like she thought that she was enjoying the other two people's argument far too much and was trying to suppress the unseemly feeling. She looked a little like a woman who had been ignored and then watched her advice—foolishly dismissed—proven right in practice.

After a moment, Clarity realized that the arguing humans weren't human at all. She recognized one of them—Maradia's competitor from Robots 4 Robots who had helped upgrade the Orion model's brain for Wisper. He was a robot named Gerangelo, and based on the argument that he was having with the other heartbreakingly beautiful, simulated human, she was a robot that he'd designed.

Since Maradia had designed Gerangelo, Clarity supposed that made the other robot Maradia's granddaughter. Although, familial relationships between robots and roboticists seemed to be really complicated and deeply messed up. Enough so that Maradia, Gerangelo, and Ronnie—for that seemed to be her name—had no attention to spare for the actual human with photosynthetic green hair and a living tumbleweed in her backpack standing in the open doorway.

Though, eventually, Gerangelo stopped the argument, having noticed the Orion model standing beside Clarity.

"Wait, wait—" Gerangelo raised his hands, palms out. Gods, he was as beautiful as a marble statue from Ancient Earth. "You're back," he said, directly to the Orion model. He walked up and put one of his perfectly formed hands on its skeletal metal shoulder. His human-like hand was full of gentleness and warmth that the Orion model would be unable to feel, even if it had been inhabited by a sentient AI.

"Can I help you?" the Orion model said.

Gerangelo's face darkened, and he turned to Clarity. His dark eyebrows tilted severely, and his eyes glinted angrily; his jaw muscles twitched with tightness. His beautiful face had filled with wrath, enough to wither any human woman who had the misfortune of being attracted to men. Clarity felt fortunate in that moment that she was mostly unafflicted by feelings of sexual attraction.

"What did you do to the AI who left here with you? Because this is clearly a sub-sentient mobility program and not a full AI." Gerangelo had sounded irritable and upset while arguing with the devastatingly gorgeous Ronnie; his tone had been fast-paced and slightly higher pitched than Clarity remembered his voice being. Now his voice was deep, raspy, and slurred with fury.

"Wisper sacrificed herself," Clarity answered. "For her, our trip was always a suicide mission."

Gerangelo frowned, and his eyes continued to glare.

"Oh, give it a rest, Gerangelo," Maradia said. "You aren't the personal savior of every robot ever built and every AI ever to wake up into sentience."

"Most of th—" Gerangelo began to argue, but Ronnie cut him off.

"Your savior complex is the worst thing about you," she said.

"Savior complex!" Gerangelo roared. "You'd still be trapped in a set of family quarters, playing Slappy Cards with organic toddlers if I hadn't told you about the Sentience Tests! That's not a comple—"

"And I would never have been there in the first place if you hadn't designed a sentient robot to do a menial job."

"Would you rather not exist?" Gerangelo snapped.

"Maybe," Ronnie said. "I haven't finished weighing my options."

"Ungrateful," Gerangelo muttered.

"Excuse me?" Ronnie's voice rose in pitch at the end of the phrase. "Are you trying to imply that I should feel grateful because you designed me to start my life as an automated babysitter to be followed by emancipating myself, only to find that you were waiting with open arms, expecting me to come running back and fall in love with you?"

"*Maybe*." Gerangelo twisted the word around to make it sound like he was mocking Ronnie's earlier answer.

"Then you did a terrible job of designing me," Ronnie said. "Because I feel no such thing."

Maradia laughed. She was covering the lower half of her face with both hands now. "I'm sorry," she said, "but that's almost exactly what you told me, Gerry, when you passed the Sentience Tests and sued me for half of my business."

"Don't call me Gerry," Gerangelo said, then threw in an extremely mean-spirited, "*Mom*." He was handsome, but this argument was certainly cutting into his dignity. Pretty, but mean.

Clarity wondered if she should leave, but she couldn't stop staring at the relationship supernova happening in front of her. Besides, she really wanted her money back for the Orion model.

"Should I come back later?" Clarity asked. "Or, you know, you could just wire the credits for the Orion model to me..." But she remembered that Genniperri was on her back, hoping to get a consultation with Maradia. The room was full of roboticists, but it seemed unlikely that either of them was in the mood to do anything that useful right now.

"Look," Gerangelo said. "I wasn't trying to trap you or—"

"Design me for you?" Ronnie asked with a leading tone.

"No—"

Ronnie didn't let Gerangelo get a second word in before spreading her arms wide and asking, "Then why do I look so much like her?"

Gerangelo looked flustered. Maradia turned her face away, trying and failing so hard to stifle her laughter.

Clarity blinked, and then she saw it. Ronnie looked like an airbrushed, perfected version of Maradia physically. Her curves were curvier; her hair—which had to be made of silicon fibers, right?—was fuller and glossier. Her eyes glinted, somehow, with more complex colors. But the basic facial structure, the fundamental physical build... Ronnie was Maradia. But carved out of silicon and electronic guts.

Clarity's jaw dropped, and Ronnie laughed.

"See?" the beautiful robot said. "Even this random human sees it. You were disappointed by the squishy, organic human who created you, so you made a new version for yourself to love."

"I don't love—"

Neither the human mother nor robotic daughter were interested in letting Gerangelo finish a sentence right now. "Like mother, like son, right?" Maradia said, drily. "Get out of here, Gerangelo. Ronnie doesn't want you."

"She's my—"

"Property?" Ronnie asked.

"Responsibility," Gerangelo concluded sullenly.

"She's fine," Maradia said.

"She's sentient and legally independent," Ronnie added

sourly. "Remember, you designed me that way. And she's also standing right here. And, you know what? Before you go, let me give you something."

Gerangelo gawped, clearly off-balance in this whole situation and at a complete loss for what Ronnie might want to give him.

"You have something to give Gerangelo?" Maradia asked, also sounding surprised but intrigued.

"Three things," Ronnie said. "First, my name. I hate it. It's short for robo-nanny, and I'm done with it. Second, my gender. It's awful being saddled with a weird, human gender. And third," the nameless, genderless robot placed its hands—as perfect as Gerangelo's, but more delicate and feminine—on its hips, "this body. You can keep it."

"Your programming is designed to inhabit a body," Gerangelo said. "You'll be miserable in a computer bank."

"What's your name?" Maradia asked.

The beautiful robot closed its eyes, digging deep into the cultural archives stored in its mind. "Zephyr. Impossible to control. But..." The robot's lips curled into a playful smile. "Pleasant. Fun. When I want to be." Its eyes narrowed into a glare pointed at Gerangelo. "I was designed to enjoy playing games."

"And your gender?" Maradia asked. "What pronouns would you like people to use for you, Zephyr?"

"Zhe," zhe answered.

Maradia smiled. "Perfect."

Gerangelo rolled his eyes. "You still won't be happy in a computer bank. Immobile. All intellect, no physicality. It'll make many of the games you like rather hard to play."

Zephyr gestured fluidly, carelessly at the Orion model standing lifelessly beside Clarity. "I'll take that one," zhe said. "I'll trade you this one"—zhe swept zir hands (zir current hands) in a sensuous gesture that encompassed the entire body zhe currently resided inside, then pointed at the body that had once been Wisper's—"for that one."

"Done," Gerangelo said, knowing a good deal when he saw one.

"Hey," Clarity objected. "This Orion model isn't yours."

"I'll give you 30,000 credits for it," Gerangelo offered without hesitation.

Clarity also knew when she saw a good deal, and that was twice what Wisper had had her pay for the body. "It's yours," she said to the handsome but mean robot. She handed him her pocket computer, and he transferred the credits into Clarity's account.

"And now it's yours," Gerangelo said to Zephyr, gesturing at the skeletal, blue robot body.

Clarity realized what she'd actually done—she'd sold her friend's corpse to a new host. She wanted to get out of that robot shop more than ever, yet somehow, her feet stayed rooted to the floor as she watched Maradia pull a length of cable out of a desk drawer and hook Zephyr up to the Orion model. The cable plugged into the backs of each of their heads. It all happened so fast.

Suddenly, the Orion model opened its glassy camera lens-like eyes, nodded its silver skull of a head, and said in Wisper's humming, mechanical voice, "This is much better. So much simpler. Now I can focus on the things that interest me. And ignore the things that don't." The words came out simpler in Zephyr's new voice, less nuanced without the delicate complexity and flexibility of a human face's expressions to accompany them, and yet, zhe managed to convey just as much contempt for Gerangelo.

Wisper's body. Zephyr's mind.

Clarity felt like her own mind had been pulled inside out, watching her friend come back to life—except not her friend at all anymore.

The beautiful humanoid body stood more stiffly now, and its shining eyes gleamed more simply. It followed Gerangelo woodenly out of the shop, like a marionette with invisible strings.

After Gerangelo and his creepy-as-hell, wish-fulfillment

version of Maradia—now entirely empty of sentience and personality—were gone, the whole room relaxed, as if each of them drew a deep breath. A sigh of relief. Or maybe, it was just Clarity. Zephyr, in spite of being named for a breeze, couldn't breathe, and neither Genniperri nor Mazillion breathed in a way that was noticeable to a human eye—their breathing was distributed across the surface area of leaves and hundreds of teeny-tiny bodies. Also, they seemed to still be wound up in whispering to each other behind Clarity's head.

But Maradia sure looked relieved.

"What are you going to do now?" Maradia asked Zephyr.

Zephyr's head turned toward the human woman who had created zir own robotic creator. "You made him to love you?" zhe asked.

"It didn't work out very well, did it?" Maradia said, mouth curling into a sad smile.

"He's a jerk." Zephyr's words were spoken in the simple hum of the Orion model's voice, but they carried the weight of a young, disillusioned human girl. Like Clarity had once been.

Clarity had realized, once upon a time, many years ago, that her father was a jerk. For different reasons. But she remembered the feelings. Outrage. Disappointment. Confusion about what it meant about herself, because she knew, deep inside, that she was similar to both of her parents, even if she never wanted to be like them. She wondered how complex Zephyr's feelings were, and she supposed it depended on what kind of emotional palette zhe'd been programmed to experience.

"Can I—" Maradia started, but Zephyr didn't let her speak any more than zhe'd let Gerangelo speak.

"No, I don't want anything to do with you. You're just like him." Zir glassy eyes stared into space as zhe spoke, reflecting the room and providing no clue as to what kind of roiling turmoil of emotions bubbled beneath.

Zephyr walked away, straight out of zir grandmother's robotics shop.

Maradia looked sad, but no sadder than she'd looked when Gerangelo left. She seemed like she'd grown numb to robots leaving her over the years. "Well, then," she said, moving her attention to Clarity with the strange, leafy passenger on her back. "Is there anything I can do for you? Perhaps the dinner I offered you before? We could talk, and you could tell me about the adventures Zephyr's body went on before becoming Zephyr just now."

"Maybe," Clarity said. "But actually, my friend here"—she gestured toward the leafy fronds rising above her shoulders; it was strange carrying a tiny potted tree around on her back —"Genniperri would like to know if you can build a mobility device for her."

Maradia's eyebrows lifted, intrigued. All the sadness seemed to wash out of her face and the posture of her shoulders at the sudden prospect of a new puzzle. "You're a Doraspian, right?" she asked.

"Yes," Genniperri said. "And not as young as I look."

"Right, your species stays rooted until adulthood." Maradia stood up to get a better angle for peering over Clarity's shoulder. "But you're still rooted, so you don't have the proper limbs for walking, and yet you're saddled with the extra weight of an immobile root bulb... and also nutrient-rich dirt?"

"Exactly!" Genniperri's fronds vibrated in excitement, and Mazillion seemed to buzz along with her.

Clarity shouldered her way out of the backpack's straps, transferring the bulk of the pack onto her arms. She brought the pack forward, trying to see through Genniperri's thick bramble of vines, fronds, leaves, and flowers. She set the pack on the floor, in front of Maradia's desk.

The roboticist came forward, reached a hand toward Genniperri's roots, and asked, "May I?"

Genniperri's branches leaned away, clearing a path for Maradia to lean down and examine the Doraspian's roots. "Do you have feeling in your roots?" she asked.

"No." Genniperri's leaves quivered, and several of her flowers tightened their petals, as if closing for the night.

"But you need the dirt, right?"

"Yes, my roots chafe and my vines grow brittle without it." Genniperri's vines waved languidly. "Sproutlings are extra dependent on their soil right before their final growth spurt. And while I've never experienced the final growth spurt... I seem to have frozen in time, right before it."

Frozen in time. Those words caught in Clarity's mind, reminding her of the Devil's Radio and how she'd feared that she would float in its event horizon forever, frozen in time. The message she'd written to Am-lei, describing the blip of light she'd seen inside the event horizon of the Devil's Radio, still sat in her pocket computer, unsent.

Could Genniperri's condition be connected to the blip of light?

And what about the other Doraspian, Paurizau? The way his leaves kept continually wilting, crumbling, and shedding to the floor around him like an everlasting autumn...

If Genniperri was frozen in adolescence... Could Paurizau be frozen on the edge of death?

Maybe Clarity should send that message to Am-lei. She needed more information, and the Doraspians and their S'rellick keeper hadn't been exactly forthcoming. Although, half of these questions most likely needed analysis from a biologist—not a physicist.

Maradia continued to examine Genniperri, asking questions about her mobility and physical abilities as well as her preferences for the device the roboticist would build for her. After a while, Clarity excused herself, saying she'd check back later, once she'd finished running her errands.

When she stepped outside, Clarity found Zephyr standing like a statue in the crowds of busy aliens. Zir silvery limbs reflected the profusion of colors passing zir by, twisted and distorted to map to zir skeletal shape. Standing stock still, zhe couldn't have seemed less like a zephyr.

But zhe did remind Clarity of Wisper and the way the other AI had pretended to be nothing more than an empty robot body, holding still on the outside while her thoughts had presumably been racing on the inside.

Clarity supposed that if Maradia had programmed Wisper and also programmed Gerangelo, then they were kind of like siblings. And Gerangelo had programmed Zephyr, so in a way, zhe was something akin to Wisper's... niece... or nephew... zephew? Geez, how were humans out here in space, living among the stars, and still constrained by weird quirks of language from hundreds of years ago? At any rate, Zephyr was Wisper's kin, and that compelled Clarity to check on zir.

"You're still here," Clarity said.

"I don't know where to go," Zephyr said.

"You don't have a job as a babysitter?" Clarity asked.

"They didn't want to employ me," Zephyr said. "They wanted to own me. When the robots from the Sentience Board showed up and busted them for illegally detaining a sentient being, they didn't want anything more to do with me. That's why I went to Gerangelo. I guess he does this a lot."

"Does what?" Clarity was having trouble keeping up with all the robot drama aboard Crossroads Station. She'd felt the same when she had first met Wisper too.

"He purposely goads biological clients into overclocking robots they purchase from him, until the robots end up sentient—like me—and then they've basically been tricked into pouring their money into helping Gerangelo reproduce. More sentient robots. I guess," Zephyr said, "most of them are grateful to him. But then, most of them weren't designed to be his perfect woman." If Zephyr had still lived inside the humanoid body, zhe probably would have rolled zir eyes. Instead, the metal irises over zir glassy camera lens eyes narrowed ever so slightly.

Zhe probably didn't look like anyone's idea of a perfect woman now. Take that, Gerangelo!

"Well, I have some errands to run," Clarity said. "You could tag along with me, if you'd like."

The metal irises over Zephyr's glassy eyes widened, and zhe nodded zir shiny, silver head curtly. "Yes, thank you. I would enjoy that."

Clarity wasn't sure why anyone would enjoy running errands, but she wasn't opposed to having some company. Even Mazillion had abandoned her at this point; their tiny cluster that had been her sentinel had stayed behind in Maradia's Robot Emporium with Genniperri.

Zephyr turned out to know Crossroads Station really well. Somehow, Clarity had pictured zir locked up in a tiny set of quarters, playing card games with two toddlers, but apparently zhe'd also been responsible for taking the children around the station, bringing them to the grav-bubble playground, treating them to lunch and confections at bakeries, letting them explore the various shops, and even buying appropriate clothing for them.

Clarity couldn't imagine how anyone could be naive enough to believe a sub-sentient being would be capable of such complex tasks. Sometimes, she simply didn't know what was wrong with other members of her species.

As they wandered together, Zephyr told delightful stories, peppered with relevant anecdotes, and zhe even argued down the prices on several of the items Clarity bought. Zhe turned out to be quite the negotiator. To zir, negotiation was a sort of game, and zhe had been programmed to love games.

Clarity saved more than 10,000 credits from Zephyr's bargaining, and she thought it only fair to offer those savings back to the robot, especially after zhe'd been kind enough to help carry the bundles of supplies back to Cassie's airlock. But Zephyr refused.

"What would I do with the money?" zhe asked. "I don't eat. I don't need somewhere to sleep."

"What about your... batteries?" Clarity asked. "Do they ever need to be recharged?" She didn't remember Wisper needing recharging, but then she'd been distracted by a lot of universe-saving back when Wisper had been alive.

"I ran internal diagnostics as soon as I uploaded into my new body," Zephyr said, "and the battery will last hundreds of years. It's a good body. I'm very happy with my choice."

"So... you're just going to wander around Crossroads Station... for hundreds of years?"

Clarity was already picturing how little space Zephyr would need aboard Cassie. Just a corner of the scullery. Zhe'd be available to chat, tell stories, and play games with anyone who happened to be awake, even if they were on an opposite sleep schedule from everyone else aboard.

Clarity shouldn't offer to take Zephyr aboard Cassie. At least, not without checking with the others. They still hadn't figured out how the current crew fit together. They didn't need to throw a new spanner in the works.

"Why don't you travel with my crew?" Clarity asked, completely undermining her own plans.

"Your crew?" Zephyr asked.

"Well, I mean..." Clarity wasn't officially their captain. Or anything. Really, they were Cassie's crew, and it all depended on what Cassie wanted. Except, Cassie was a persuadable child, and she needed help figuring out what she wanted. "There's a group of us, and we've been traveling together aboard a living spaceship called Cassie."

"A biological spaceship?" Zephyr asked. "A mechanical person traveling aboard a biological vehicle... I like the irony."

"Cassie's more than a vehicle," Clarity said. "She's a person... just a very young, inexperienced one."

"Technically," Zephyr observed, "I'm only three months old. In biological time. My processors run so much faster than biological brains that my age is more equivalent to..." Zhe paused, as if zhe were thinking. Though, it was probably an affectation given how quickly zir mental processors worked. "Twenty Solanese years for a human."

"The age I was, approximately, when I first moved to Crossroads Station," Clarity said. "It's a good age for striking out on your own and going on some adventures."

"Adventures," Zephyr said thoughtfully. "That sounds kind of like... games."

Clarity laughed. "Yes, really big ones with unclear goals."

Zephyr looked so much like Wisper—exactly like Wisper—and yet, they were so different that it was quite jarring. Wisper was serious, deadly serious. Zephyr was all about fun. Clarity felt a little guilty realizing that she liked this new robot better than the one who had upturned her life and goaded her into saving the universe.

Well, maybe that wasn't so odd. Even so, Clarity owed a certain fondness to Wisper through loyalty.

"Alright," Zephyr said. "I have no other plans. I'd love to tag along."

Clarity felt a warm sense of accomplishment inside herself. She'd snagged a new member for the crew that would make their lives more fun and exciting. She couldn't wait for the rest of the crew to meet Zephyr.

10. WESPIRTECH CALLING

The All Alien Cafe was the perfect mix between a popular hotspot and an unknown hole-in-the-wall. Clarity bartended there on and off over the years, when she and Irohann had stayed on Crossroads Station for more than a few days at a time. It was also where Clarity and Irohann had first met.

She'd been a runaway teenager, trying to scrape together enough credits to pay for one of the smallest pairs of shared quarters on the station. Irohann had been a frog-like amphibioid alien on the run from the Doraspians, trying desperately to get up enough courage to buy a complete gene-mod at a black market genie shop and shed her—she'd been a woman back then—green skin for anything that Queen Doripauli wouldn't recognize as her runaway lover.

They'd both been runaways, and the froggy alien who had been Irohann had placed her complete trust in Clarity, not only letting the human girl choose who she would transform into, but trusting her with the secret of his identity.

That trust had bound Clarity and Irohann together through decades of travels. Years and years of adventures. Through all of those years, Irohann had been the greatest constant in Clarity's life. The idea of him changing again—if Queen Doripauli had ever discovered his alias—had been one of her greatest fears. Because he would have had to leave her behind in order to disappear, completely, again.

So, when Clarity walked into The All Alien Cafe and saw Teya and Oksana seated at a table with a big, bushy, red-furred Heffen... with antlers... Her heart nearly stopped. Oksana waved a hoof-hand at her, and Irohann turned his wolfy head. His long muzzle split into a grin at the sight of Clarity, and his tail swished. Clarity loved it when he reacted that way to seeing her.

Her best friend loved her just as much as she loved him, and she could read it in every detail of his posture—the swishy tail, the wide grin, even the tilt of his triangular ears peeking out from his thick, bushy, flowing mane. Yet, she felt cold at the sight of the antlers.

Irohann had gone back to the genie shop without her. His first thought, upon being freed from the fear that Queen Doripauli would track him down, was to change himself. Had he not been happy as the alien wolf that Clarity had picked for him? Had he changed more than by adding antlers?

Clarity stood stock still in the entrance to The All Alien Cafe, afraid to approach closer. Zephyr placed a firm, metal hand on Clarity's shoulder. "Is that the crew?" zhe asked. "Why have we stopped?"

Clarity couldn't explain all of her thoughts and feelings to Zephyr fast enough. If she tried, she'd only get through a broken sentence or two, and it would just confuse the situation. She'd make everything awkward.

If only Zephyr could mind-blend with Clarity like Cassie... then zhe would understand.

In lieu of explanation, Clarity settled for distraction. "Yes, that's them. Some of them," she said, waving and smiling. She wasn't sure why Kwah wasn't with them. Maybe the bird was back at the genie shop, getting her whole body changed. "Let's get drinks first."

Clarity walked toward the bar along the left side of the room, fully expecting Zephyr to stop her with an explanation of how zhe didn't drink. But zhe didn't. Instead, when they got to the bar, the robot placed her metal hands on the wooden surface (it probably wasn't real wood, but it looked like well-worn mahogany), leaned forward, and called out to the bartender, "What is your most popular drink here?"

An alien with a neck so long that it looped up toward the ceiling before swooping back down to hold the creature's knobby head at human height approached them, holding a glass and a rag in its hoof-like hands, aimlessly polishing the one with the other. The alien had short fur, colored with orange and yellow splotches, and its lips were so full and expressive, they were practically prehensile.

"Hmmm," the giraffe-like alien bartender hummed. "Overall? Or non-toxic to a particular species?" The alien's head swooped closer; it was clearly eying Clarity, trying to figure out what kind of drink to suggest for a human as Zephyr was fairly obviously not a creature who would actually be drinking zirself.

"Both," Zephyr said. "Though, we'll probably only order a drink that's non-toxic for humans."

"Wouldn't the most popular drinks here be ones that are ordered by humans and Heffens?" Clarity asked. Those were the most common species aboard Crossroads Station, and they comprised easily half of the customers in the cafe right now. Furthermore, their digestive systems were similar enough that anything toxic to a human would likely be toxic for a Heffen too.

"You'd be surprised," the bartender said. "We host an Avian Night on Thursdays, and those birds order drinks like fish trying not to drown."

"Alright," Zephyr said. "Then what's their favorite drink?"

"Fermented zangle worm juice," the bartender said.

Clarity wrinkled her nose. She'd served fermented zangle worm juice to avian aliens before. It stank like formaldehyde and old feet. She always pictured the zangle worms having been stomped like grapes on Ancient Earth were stomped for making wine. Except, the Bacchanalia she pictured happening afterward was all birds. There were a lot of different species of avian alien on Crossroads Station. None of them had large populations individually, but altogether, they did make up a significant fraction.

"I see you've smelled zangle juice," the bartender said to Clarity, observing her wrinkled nose.

"I used to tend bar here," Clarity said. "So, yeah. I remember Avian Night."

"The most popular drink that's non-toxic to humans is marzicran sherry."

"Do you like that?" Zephyr asked Clarity.

"Yeah, but..." She'd had the sweet and sour, fruity drink many times before. It had been the most popular drink among humans at The All Alien Cafe for decades. Heffen tastes were more whimsical from what Clarity had seen during her stints tending bar. "Why don't you surprise me with something uncommon? But, uh, also non-toxic to humans." Zephyr's sense of fun seemed to be rubbing off on Clarity.

"You got it," the giraffe-like alien said, head already swinging away to peruse the array of brightly colored bottles and canisters on the mirrored shelves behind the bar.

The mirrors weren't standard mirrors that reflected light back instantly. They were slow mirrors that captured and held the light for a while before releasing it back into the world. So, a customer could sit at the bar and stare at the reflection between the shelves of brightly colored bottles and see a different customer who had sat in the same seat as them, but days, months, or years earlier, staring back.

Clarity had never been able to figure out exactly how slow the reflection in the slow mirror was. She'd always figured that if she ever saw herself in the mirror, then she'd have a reference point and could figure out the time offset. Yet, the few times that she had caught glimpses of herself in the mirror, her clothes and behavior hadn't been distinctive enough for her to be sure of exactly when they'd happened.

There was something eerie and, yet, friendly about the slow

mirrors. Clarity, at least, had always enjoyed them. They reminded her of her past and made her feel like she was in a place where she truly belonged.

Right now, the slow mirrors reflected back the same bar, but filled with a different mix of customers—about equally crowded, but many, many more bird aliens. Quite possibly, the mirror was reflecting back one of the Thursday evening Avian Nights. And the bartender, instead of being longnecked and fuzzy in shades of harvest gold seemed to be stout and covered in bare, wrinkly, gray skin. Since the bartender faced the bar, the slow mirror only showed its back, but it looked like it might the same species as Am-lei's wife, Jeko. An elephantine alien. They were uncommon on Crossroads Station, but not unheard of.

While the giraffe-like alien fixed Clarity's drink in the present, she watched the slow mirror, waiting to see the tell-tale reach of the reflected bartender's long, prehensile nose in the past.

"You seem lost in thought," Irohann said, placing a paw on Clarity's shoulder and startling her out of her reverie.

"I was wondering if we should buy a slow mirror for decorating aboard Cassie," Clarity lied. "But... I don't think it would be as much fun if it weren't set up in such a busy place."

Finally, the bartender in the mirror waved its long prehensile nose out to the side where it could be seen. On the far end of the bar, several avian aliens puffed out their feathers comically while staring at the mirror. Clarity smiled. Her smile would be saved for someone else to see and enjoy later, just as the avians' antics had been saved for her.

"Decorating!" Zephyr exclaimed. "Now that sounds like a fun game."

Irohann's eyes widened and his long muzzle fell open, speechless when he noticed Zephyr.

"This is Zephyr," Clarity said. "Zhe bought the... empty robot body that I was returning to Maradia. Then zhe helped me run all my errands, and I've invited zir to join us aboard Cassie."

"Adventuring!" The metal irises around Zephyr's eyes narrowed in a way that suddenly looked like a smile.

Clarity couldn't recall that physical gesture ever looking like a smile when Wisper had performed it.

Irohann continued to stand beside the two of them, speechless. Clarity felt a bit of pride in that she'd managed to overshadow his surprise antlers with an arguably bigger surprise of her own.

"By the way, I like the antlers," Clarity said. Lying again. She really ought to stop doing that. Or maybe, she ought to stop feeling so judgmental of the way that Irohann had chosen to change himself. He hadn't run away from her, discarding his entire identity. He'd simply gotten antlers. A physical embellishment. And truthfully, he did look really handsome with them. His flowing mane always made him look a little dressed up; the antlers branching from behind his pointy ears made him look extra fancy. "They make you look like a jackalope."

"A what?" Irohann said, finally finding a couple of words.

"A mythical creature of Ancient Earth," Zephyr said. "They were desert lagomorphs with branching extensions from their skulls. Like yours! I know lots of entertaining stories about—"

"Thanks," Irohann said. "Maybe later. I guess, we'll have a lot of time for stories if you're traveling with us to Wespirtech."

"Why are we going to..." Clarity started to say.

"Check your messages," Irohann said. "We've been mysteriously summoned. I assume you got the message too."

Clarity pulled out her pocket computer. The message had bypassed all of the other software and popped up on top of everything else. It read, "Friends of Cassiopeia, Starwhal of the Aether Gaia Project: your sub-sentient, organic maintenance creatures are ready and waiting to be picked up at Wespirtech."

The message was unsigned. But a mysterious summons like that had Wisper's name written all over it. Not the Wisper who'd died, but the original, ethereal Wisper whose cold, clinical, controlling personality seemed to crawl surreptitiously, secretively through the electronics of the entire galaxy's worth of human-made computer systems.

Technically, Cassie was stolen property from Wespirtech's Aether Gaia extension base, and Clarity recoiled at the idea of flying her right up to the scientists who thought they owned her as some kind of science experiment. However, Wisper's reach was wide. She could protect Irohann from the Doraspian Empire. And she had already promised to free the rest of the starwhals from Aether Gaia, so presumably, she would protect Cassie from being taken back into the scientists' custody if she flew boldly right up to their front door.

Clarity wondered how.

As soon as Clarity dismissed the intrusive, mysterious message from Wisper, a whole slew of messages appeared in her regular inbox—several from Roscoe, warning that Cassie was feeling restless and impatient to get moving toward Wespirtech. The rest, well, they had to be from Cassie. They were barely coherent strings of babbling words and pictures of bunnies, mixed up together like the archives of Ancient Earth's internet, which Clarity had studied in high school.

"I see that Cassie has figured out how to send messages through the computer system," Clarity observed.

"Yes," Irohann agreed. "I got some of those too. It will be useful being able to communicate with her in a... more traditional way."

"You mean 'more limited,'" Clarity said.

"Well, yeah, I mean, it's nice to be able to keep some privacy inside my own head."

"Is that why you got those antlers?" Clarity asked. "A big ol' defense system for your brain?" They really did look good on him.

"Yes, they're really radio antennae. I'm wired directly into the Crossroads Station computer network now."

"You are not," Zephyr objected. "I would have already invited you to join the game of Starplosions & Spacedroids that I'm running right now if you were."

"Wait—right now?" Clarity asked. "Like, you're playing Starsplosions & Spacedroids in your head right now, while we're talking at this bar?"

"Of course," Zephyr said. "Wouldn't you be, if you could?"

Clarity couldn't argue with that.

"And as it is," Zephyr continued, "I'm going to have to figure out how to adapt the game for non-networked players to invite you and the rest of the crew." Of course, by 'non-networked,' zhe simply meant organic, as opposed to robots whose brains could communicate directly through the computer systems.

Clarity wondered if that felt anything like the squishy, melty, amorphous cloud-like sensation of mind-blending with Cassie... Probably not.

Irohann's tail swished in earnest now. He and Clarity had joined a game of Starplosions & Spacedroids years ago when they'd stayed on Crossroads Station for a full year, grounded by a run of bad luck trades. Come to think of it, the group of chicken-like Renntens that they'd been playing with had been running their game as a kind of after-party to the Thursday evening Avian Nights. Irohann had been desperate to try the game again ever since, but it wasn't well-suited to a team of two plus a sub-sentient spaceship AI. Though, it would be a great way to stay entertained during the long, dark journeys between star systems.

Clarity saw any doubts that Irohann had had about Zephyr joining them aboard Cassie melt completely away. Well... almost. "I suppose, since the S'rellick and Doraspians will be departing us here, there should be room for another new crew member," Irohann said.

"I don't require much space," Zephyr said. "The humans who commissioned my creation as a nanny-bot kept me in their daughters' closet."

Clarity's eyes widened. "That's awful."

Zephyr put zir metal hands out to zir sides in a noncommittal gesture, sort of like a shrug. Zir shoulders weren't really designed for shrugging. Too stiff. "I didn't mind. I spent the nights playing S&S over my wireless connection to the Crossroads Station computer system. The game I've been playing has already lasted the cognitive equivalent of a human decade, and one of the other AI players is planning to convert some of our best adventures into novels."

The giraffe-like bartender casually slid Clarity's drink in front of her, careful to avoid interfering in their conversation. The drink was a rainbow of layers—some creamy and pastel, others brightly colored and as translucent as the glass they were inside of. A twisty straw rose above the drink in complicated spirals. Clarity put her lips to the mouth of the straw and tasted crystalized Aldebaran sugar, strong enough to maintain its structural integrity while she sipped her way through the gorgeous drink, but delicate and brittle enough that it would crunch satisfyingly between her teeth when she was ready to eat it.

The bartender's head swooped close to Clarity's ear and whispered, "That's called a Pau Ceti Prism, and it's my personal favorite."

"Thanks," she said, but the bartender had already swooped away to the far end of the bar to serve a trio of Heffens. When she looked back at her own group, Zephyr had gone over to the table with Teya and Oksana to introduce zirself to the lapine and unguloid. Irohann had stayed by her side and was watching her expectantly.

"So, you really like the antlers?" he asked. His tail swished slowly and tentatively behind him, and his triangular ears flicked, showing his nervousness and uncertainty. Clarity was about to reassure her friend that his antlers were extremely fetching when he added, "Oksana helped me pick them out."

Before she could control her face properly, Clarity frowned.

Irohann's tail stopped swishing, and his ears flicked flat and stayed that way. "That bothers you," he said.

Clarity couldn't sort her thoughts and feelings out fast enough to even know what to say. So, she shrugged and deflected. "I'm tired and confused. A few months ago, my life was sorted out, and now..." Again, shrugging.

Irohann didn't say anything, so after an uncomfortable pause, Clarity continued.

"Roscoe makes me feel young and... difficult? Teya and her friends make me feel old and out of touch. And somehow... you simply fit in anywhere. I guess, I'm a little jealous of that."

Clarity didn't add that Mazillion and their Doraspian and S'rellick visitors made her feel frustrated and outmaneuvered. She didn't need Irohann—or anyone—knowing that the swarm alien had manipulated her latest alliance with them. An alliance that Clarity probably ought to tell Irohann about...

"By the way," she said, "The Doraspians and S'rellick may not be leaving Cassie just yet. They've requested asylum."

Irohann's ears—which had perked back up—flattened again. "Asylum? What do they think we are? A government?"

"That's what I said at first," Clarity agreed. "But if they're on the run from the Doraspian Empire... Well, we have some experience with that. And I have some empathy for that particular plight."

Irohann nodded, causing the pointed tips of his antlers to bob menacingly. Clarity wondered if he'd really thought this newest quirk of a genetic acquisition through.

"I suppose that works," he said. "If Zephyr really doesn't need much space..."

"What do you mean?" Clarity asked. "We have a whole empty room."

"Oksana was planning to move into the empty room," Irohann said. "Since they're planning to stay onboard, possibly for a long time, it seems reasonable for them to each have their own room."

Clarity's brow furrowed. "What about Kwah?"

"Didn't you know?" Irohann asked.

"Apparently not." Clarity tried to keep her answer from sounding acerbic. When she failed, she covered her embarrassment at feeling left out with a long sweet sip of her Pau Ceti Prism. She moved the straw up and down through the layers, sampling each color separately. The creamy pastel layers were smooth and cool on her tongue, tasting like the dream version of fruit—not identifiable as any specific fruit that she'd ever eaten before, but somehow hauntingly familiar. The bright, translucent layers burned on her tongue, spicy and tantalizing in their complexity, unlike anything she'd tasted before. Alternating the warmth of the bright colors and the coolness of the pastel layers was extremely pleasant.

"Well, Kwah is staying here," Irohann said simply. "She's moving in with Oksana's family for a while, I guess. She and Teya had a big falling out, and she tried to convince Oksana to stay here as well. But..." Irohann shrugged. "Oksana likes being aboard Cassie."

Clarity thought: *she likes hanging out with you*. Except, it was a deeply unfair thought. She had no real reason to feel jealous of the young unguloid. Clarity had never been as much of a cook as Irohann, and it was nice that he had someone to share the passion with now, especially since there were so many more people to feed aboard Cassie. Besides, Clarity and Irohann had never really established what their relationship was. They'd traveled together for years, confided in each other, made life decisions together... But they'd never discussed the constraints or parameters of their relationship. It just was. And Oksana didn't change that.

Although, if Oksana was important to Irohann, then Clarity ought to make more of an effort to get to know her.

Irohann's right ear twisted to the side, and his tail started swishing eagerly. "They're figuring out their characters for Star-splosions & Spacedroids!" he said. "Want to..." He trailed off, but his flicking ears and glancing eyes made his intentions clear. He wanted to go play.

"Go ahead," Clarity said. She knew she needed to start connecting with Teya and Oksana, and she did like the idea of a new game of S&S... But she wasn't ready. "I can catch up later.

Right now, I'm going to go check on Genniperri. She's getting a mobility aide built for her at Maradia's Robot Emporium. I'll meet you back aboard Cassie."

Clarity broke off the end of her straw to suck on, like a hard candy, and handed the rest of her drink to Irohann to finish. He went straight over to the table with Zephyr, Teya, and Oksana, and Clarity smiled to see how happy they all looked together. Even Zephyr, whose body was not designed to express emotion, seemed happy. Zir body leaned towards the others, and zir arms gestured regularly, as if zhe were describing an entire universe of adventures for the other three to imagine with zir. Zhe probably was.

Before leaving the bar, Clarity did one last thing: she sent the message to Am-lei that she'd written earlier.

11. HALF PLANT, HALF DROID

Maradia worked fast, and by the time Clarity had returned to her shop, Genniperri was already outfitted with a rough pair of legs, controlled by a pair of her delicate vines. The trunk-like legs copied and amplified the movements of those two vines, and when she stood still, legs together, she looked almost exactly like a tree—branches above, trunk below. Except, the trunk was artificial and could split down the middle into a pair of legs.

Clarity let herself through the lobby for Maradia's Robot Emporium and into the messy lab in the back, strewn with supplies and robot parts.

Genniperri was practicing walking around the room, fine-tuning her control of the legs. If she could manage walking through Maradia's mess without tripping over the half-assembled robot limbs strewn in piles across the floor, she'd do fine anywhere else. And Maradia was at a workstation, perfecting the simulated bark-like pattern for the exterior of the legs. Robotics is half engineering and half programming... but the third half is art.

"We're heading out sooner than expected," Clarity said, drawing attention to her presence. "It looks like your... legs are mostly done?"

Genniperri pirouetted like a ballerina tree, her flower-studded vines twirling colorfully. She was gorgeous, and extremely alien. Somehow, the presence of legs beneath made her plethora of shrubby vines above seems more alien than they had without them. Several of Mazillion's bodies buzzed along, following the twirling ends of her vines, but none of them came flying back to greet Clarity.

Maradia continued staring at the sheaf of fake bark that she'd been carefully, painstakingly etching decorative lines into with a laser scalpel and was now tracing the finished lines with the fingers of one hand, but with the other hand, she gestured for Genniperri to approach her. "Here," Maradia said, finally looking up. "I think they're done. If the balance is working for you, and you're happy with the look of this outer plating, then we can have you ready to go in a matter of minutes."

Genniperri touched the decorative bark-like plating on Maradia's desk, reverentially with the frond-like tips of her vines and laid her leaves delicately over its surface. "It's perfect," she said. "Thank you. This visit has changed my life."

Maradia went to work removing the temporary plating from Genniperri's legs. Once it was removed, and the wiring inside gleamed barely, Maradia began attaching the improved, decorative plating. The removed ones had been smoother, simpler, with noticeably repeating designs in the bark-like patterns. The improved ones looked completely natural and organic, like the trunk of an old-growth tree, deep in a shadowy, wooded dell on an actual planet.

"May I ask," Maradia said, screwing in the final bolts that disappeared seamlessly into the bark pattern, "where you're headed to so suddenly?"

"Wespirtech!" The word burst out of Clarity with more excitement and, weirdly, pride than she'd expected. She'd always wanted to see Wespirtech, and soon, she would get to see it. She'd simply never had an excuse before during her travels, and she didn't imagine that the research institute particularly welcomed random visitors, interrupting their scientists' studies.

In fact, it occurred to Clarity to wonder about how Wespirtech would feel about a visit from Cassie and her crew now. Technically, Cassie was a stolen component from a Wespirtech extension campus research project. They wouldn't try to reclaim her, would they? Surely, Wisper had a plan for how to make it safe for Cassie to visit Wespirtech and collect the gengineered sub-sentient maintenance bunnies that she'd been promised as her reward for helping save the universe.

They wouldn't be flying into a trap.

Definitely.

Definitely not a trap.

"You seem lost in thought," Maradia said to Clarity, jolting her back out of her thoughts.

It troubled Clarity that she'd looked lost in thought to Maradia, who always seemed to have at least half of her brain working on some robotics puzzle in the background. Possibly, more like eighty percent...

Clarity liked to think of herself as more grounded than that. Nonetheless, Maradia was right. She kept drifting into reveries, losing herself in thoughts and worries, and distancing herself from interacting with the actual people in her life. Of course, Maradia had really just meant in that particular moment. But Clarity felt called out at a deeper level.

Part of her really just wanted to go home, and deep down, home still meant her room aboard *The Serendipity*. Clarity had been trying, almost manically, to believe that Cassie was her home now, and that the other individuals who'd been thrown together with her and Irohann aboard Cassie were her family.

But they weren't. Not yet.

Cassie... could be home.

She wasn't yet.

And Clarity was so tired. Not for sleep. But for the universe to stop and let her rest, just for a little while.

"I have a few crates of prototypes for improved joints and other mechanisms," Maradia said. "I've been meaning to hire a cargo ship to take them to Wespirtech for me. Would your ship have room?"

Clarity's eyes widened. Maybe the universe wouldn't give her the chance to rest, but throwing an easy job her way, without having to do any work to scare it up, well, that was something.

"I'll pay, of course," Maradia added. "Whatever your standard rate is."

"Yes," Clarity said. "I believe we should have room." Plenty of room. They hadn't had time to take on any cargo at all, so this would save Cassie from making a run between Crossroads and Wespirtech with a completely empty cargo bay.

There were four crates, each large enough for Irohann to have curled up inside of it, and they were all heavy. However, each of the metal crates had an anti-grav unit built into its base. So, once Maradia hooked the four crates together like a train, they floated several inches above the floor and were easily controlled by one person pulling in the lead, and another bringing up the rear, to make sure the train didn't snake around unexpectedly and knock any innocent passersby over.

Clarity took the lead, and Genniperri took the rear. The Doraspian was thrilled to not only be able to walk herself back to Cassie, but also help with moving the cargo. Clarity couldn't imagine having spent decades of life dependent on others to help her move around. She wondered how Genniperri had managed.

When they entered Cassie's airlock, Clarity was relieved to see that the previous load of supplies had already been moved out of the way. Irohann had probably put everything away and would give her grief later about having left all of it in the airlock for him to handle.

Clarity heard voices deeper down Cassie's corridors. Unsurprisingly, the others had beaten her back, but she and Genniperri went straight to the cargo bay. She could check in with the others once the train of crates was settled.

They arranged the four crates of Maradia's prototypes in the center of the room before turning off their anti-grav boosters and letting the heavy boxes settle onto the fleshy, purple floor.

The large lung-like room only looked emptier having four small crates resting in the middle of it. Their sharp, angular corners looked very out place among the lumpy, curving walls. The uniformly gleaming metal surfaces of the crates looked very artificial next to the mottled, natural coloring of Cassie's fuchsia, orchid, mauve, and glowing pink tones.

Before leaving the cargo bay and rejoining the others, Clarity stopped Genniperri. She wanted a word with the Doraspian without the presence of her fellow travelers, T'resso and Paurizau.

"I don't know why you need asylum," Clarity said, "or what you might be running from. But you should know, we're not an armed vessel. We don't keep weapons, and none of us are fighters. And even if Cassie could fight a ship pursuing her, I wouldn't urge her to—and I don't think her other pilots would either—unless it was to defend herself, not just her passengers. She's a living being—"

Clarity paused a moment, struck viscerally by the memories of *The Serendipity* being ripped apart in front of her eyes, metal twisting and tearing, innards blasting outward with the rush of atmosphere. This young starwhal might not be her home yet, but Clarity would never let that happen to Cassie if there was anything in her power that she could do to stop it.

"I understand," Genniperri said. "You'll give us a place to hide, but you won't defend us."

Clarity nodded curtly. "Not if it comes down to a choice between you—or anyone—and Cassie." Except, maybe, for Irohann. But this Doraspian didn't need to know that. "Do you still want to come with us to Wespirtech?"

"Even as a Doraspian diplomat who's lived among S'rellicks my entire adult life, I'm familiar with Wespirtech," Genniperri said, her frond-like leaves vibrating. "They call them wizards, yes? Wespirtech wizards?"

"Yeah, sometimes," Clarity agreed. She'd called the scientists at Wespirtech "wizards" herself plenty of times. Sometimes reverentially, when *The Serendipity*—with her FTL-drive designed at Wespirtech—had pulled off a particularly fancy maneuver. Sometimes sarcastically, when she was thinking about how they'd decided to mess with the lives of an entire species of space whales without their consent.

"I think, maybe Paurizau and I could use some wizardry." Genniperri hadn't stopped pacing in circles the entire time they'd been talking. It was a little dizzying, following her motion as she circled the cargo bay, one lap after another, practically prancing.

Clarity couldn't blame her though. Genniperri was like a kid with a new toy, but times a thousand. Because the Doraspian had been waiting for this toy most of her life, and her new mobility aid could do so much more for her than simple entertainment.

"Sometimes I think Paurizau and I are under a wizard's spell," Genniperri said, finally slowing a little, as if the words she was saying took more of her focus than what she'd been saying before. She came to a stop in front of Clarity, and all of her flowers turned toward the human woman. "If a wizard put us under a spell, then maybe wizards can lift it."

"What is the spell?" Clarity asked. "It keeps you young, physically at least, and Paurizau... looks like he's on the edge of dying."

"But he doesn't die." Genniperri's flowers turned away, facing toward anything but Clarity. "He'll never die."

"Immortality," Clarity whispered. "Is that it? The whole spell? And that's why the Devil's Radio spat you back out? Because... you can't die?" The implications were too broad, too grand for Clarity to even begin grappling with them.

Genniperri circled again, stepping with a surprising lightness for a tree. Her robotic legs, designed to look like tree trunks, were unsettlingly agile. "I don't know." Her circles grew faster and faster. She was nearly running. "I love these legs," she said, the words blurred by the wind of her running, rustling through her purple bellflowers and frond-like leaves, interfering with their careful vibrations.

"Why were you at the Devil's Radio?" Clarity asked. With a terrifying certainty, Clarity realized that the fracture in space-time caused by the Merlin particle hadn't ended. Not if Genniperri stood in this cargo bay—well, ran through this cargo bay—in front of her, un-aging. Frozen in time.

Genniperri stopped running again. Though, since her legs were robotic, she probably wasn't tired. But Clarity appreciated the stillness.

"When I heard about Paurizau's condition," Genniperri said, "I knew it must be connected to mine. T'resso helped me to... kidnap him. Or rescue him, I suppose, depending on who you ask. The two of us compared the exact times that our conditions changed—when he stopped dying; when I stopped aging." Her vines gestured elegantly, as if placing each concept that she spoke about in the space around her.

"How did you know the exact time?" Clarity asked. "Could you feel the change? What did it feel like?"

"There was a brightness," Genniperri said. "Like the world was a thin veneer, a mere veil over a different reality that was more solid, more real than this one, and the light from that other reality was shining through. It dazzled all of my flower eyes, like sunspots or light reflecting off a stream. Maybe like lightning zigzagging all around me, making the world shimmery and mixing all the colors up? It's hard to describe... and it happened so long ago. I didn't know that anything had changed at the time, but over the years, I've become sure that's when I stopped aging."

The experience sounded beautiful to Clarity, and she found herself feeling a spiritual hunger, like she was longing for something she'd never known and that would always be just out of her reach. Immortality is a tempting prize, and somehow, these two Doraspians had won it without even trying.

"When I described my memories of the brightness to Paurizau," Genniperri continued, "he agreed that he'd had the same experience. And we calculated, based on the times the brightness had come to each of us, that—whatever event had occurred—the next time and place it would happen was... there. Inside that black hole. At that time."

"Except, you were too late," Clarity said. "Your calculations must have been off, because the event happened days earlier, when my crew returned the rogue Merlin particle to its entangled partner inside the Devil's Radio, healing the fracture in space-time forever."

Genniperri's vines writhed in a way that made Clarity's skin crawl uncomfortably, finally ending in a complicated, many-limbed shrug. "Forever? I'm not so sure... If the fracture is healed, why am I still rooted in the pot of dirt at the top of these legs? Why is Paurizau still alive? I think there will be more events. I just don't know how to find them."

Clarity shook her head, trying to deny the truth of what this glorified, cyborg potted plant was saying. She remembered the endless mirrors of reality as space-time had fractured around her. She never wanted to see space-time break apart that way again. Genniperri might have experienced a beautiful glowing light that granted her the gift of immortality—although, perhaps a little earlier in her life than she would have chosen—but for Clarity, the rift had been terrifying. It horrified her that the being in front of her, somehow, represented a failure of the breach to have completely healed.

"No," Clarity said. "It can't work that way. You're remnants."

"Remnants who keep... living? You've seen Paurizau and his shedding leaves. His body is trying as hard as it can to die, but something is keeping him alive, and it must be connected to what happened at the Devil's Radio before we arrived. Our calculations led us there."

"No," Clarity said again. "Maybe your initial condition is connected to the fracture, but something else must be sustaining it. The fracture was healed. The entangled particles were rejoined, and it's as if the fracture never happened." Except Clarity knew that wasn't true. She remembered the fracture. It had affected her, and that meant it had affected the universe. What scared Clarity was not knowing how much.

"Then shouldn't we have died?" Genniperri asked. "If the fracture was keeping us alive, and it's over now, then shouldn't the black hole have crushed us, instead of spitting us back out, against all the laws of physics?"

Clarity didn't like this line of thinking at all.

"I think you're right about one thing," Clarity hedged. She wasn't smart enough to solve this problem on her own, and she knew that. "We should bring you to Wespirtech. There must be scientists there who can help figure this out. Brilliant scientists. Although..."

Clarity thought about what the Wespirtech scientists had done to Cassie, drilling mechanical fixtures into her soft-feeling flesh. She could absolutely picture those same scientists dissecting Genniperri and Paurizau, cutting off their flowers and leaves, slicing them into pieces and staring at those pieces under microscopes, searching for the secrets of immortality hidden inside their cells. Even if that weren't where the secret ended up being hidden. Even if Genniperri and Paurizau suffered unendurable pain during the process.

"I don't think we should tell them that you're... immortal. We should keep that part to ourselves." Assuming it was even true. Immortality was a hard concept to believe in, and the ridiculousness of it all filled Clarity with a sudden desire to shove Genniperri out of an airlock and test how immortal she truly was.

Yet, she had already seen T'resso's metal shell streak like a shooting star, straight out of the event horizon of the Devil's Radio, simply because, apparently, two Doraspians' bodies had become, somehow, incompatible with death...

That was a more powerful test than anything Clarity could do to Genniperri here and now, even if she suddenly decided to become a murderer.

"I fervently agree," Genniperri said with all her bellflowers. "In fact, I'd prefer if you didn't tell the rest of the crew."

"Then why did you tell me?"

"You helped me," Genniperri said with the greatest simplicity. "And Mazillion trusts you."

Shame flared inside Clarity at her previous, murderous thoughts. They contrasted poorly with Mazillion considering her trustworthy. Though, had her thoughts truly been murderous, if Genniperri were incapable of being murdered?

Of all the members of the crew, vying for position with Cassie, squabbling over the power hierarchy inside of the starwhal's belly, it seemed Mazillion had strangely become most powerful. They wielded their power so subtly, so discretely, that none of the others—as far as Clarity could tell—seemed to have even noticed.

One of Mazillion's tiny bodies, like a glittering topaz in flight, wandered dizzily through the air and landed on the back of Clarity's hand with a touch as light as a falling flower petal. She lifted her hand closer to her face, and the body—complex with nearly a dozen legs—fluttered its translucent wings at her, then flitted away.

Moments later, a cluster of Mazillion's bodies drew together in the air, coming from the far corners of the cargo bay, some from hiding places among Genniperri's branches, and still more came flying in from the open doorway into the corridors that ran down Cassie's length like a triply braided spinal column. The cluster buzzed as one and said, "Roscoe cannot pilot. Cassie needs you."

12. HEY HO, HEY HO, TO WESPIRTECH WE GO

Clarity rushed to Cassie's cockpit with Mazillion's bodies swarming and swirling around her, leading the way and following behind her all at once, and somehow urging her on with their insistent buzzing.

Clarity's eyebrows drew together quizzically as she passed Oksana leaning against the glowing wall of the corridor just outside the entrance to the cockpit. The unguloid shrugged, and Clarity's footsteps slowed as she wondered what Oksana knew and why she was lounging so casually in such a suspicious location.

Clarity heard the yelling. It seemed like Teya was always sulking silently and sullenly... or yelling. And right now, it was yelling.

Clarity tilted her head, prompting Oksana to sigh and say, "I can't help. I know, usually, I'm the one who soothes her. But she blames me for Kwah breaking up with her."

Clarity hadn't even known that Teya and Kwah were an item. She fumbled for a useful and appropriate question to ask and settled on, "Why does she blame you?"

"I arranged for my family to take her in." Oksana shrugged again. "Kwah needed a place to be. Somewhere stable." The unguloid quirked a lopsided smile at the end of her long face. "And, I mean, I love it here, but this is not it."

Clarity couldn't argue with that assessment. An adolescent spaceship with an unestablished power hierarchy among her crew was not the most stable environment. Clarity felt a pang of nostalgia for the simplicity of her life aboard *The Serendipity*.

The pang was interrupted by another shout from inside the cockpit. Clarity drew a deep breath and went inside.

Roscoe sat cross-legged in the nightmarish pilot's chair with the straw-colored bone spikes and dangling tentacles above him and the scooped-out shape of Cassie's flesh cradling him underneath. His ears were drooped, and his shoulders hunched. His paws clutched his head, covering his eyes, like he had a pounding headache. And Teya was yelling at him.

Clarity felt bad for the grumpy lapine elder, weathering the full force of the younger lapine's aggression.

In human folklore, bunnies are quiet, timid creatures. Teya was neither of those things. Her fur was a glossy kind of fluffy, and her nose twitched adorably. She was short and had a cuddly, curvy quality. But her eyes shone with rage, and her voice boomed as she yelled, "You can't even hold your head up, and you brought me here to *learn* from you. So, *let* me learn. Let me try. Let me help and be *useful*!"

Roscoe shook his head, and his paws moved to his ears, pulling them down, tugged taut against the sides of his face. "The headache will pass. I'll be fine," he muttered, voice ragged.

Irohann stood between the two bunnies, big and ineffective. The ventricle-like room felt very small with Irohann, Roscoe, Teya, and now Clarity crammed into it. The red wolf's tail swished as if he could wish the situation better by pretending at happiness. Such a canine thought. He looked lost and completely, painfully aware of how useless he was being, simply standing there while the bunnies argued.

Clarity guessed that Irohann felt like he should offer to take over as pilot, but she knew he wouldn't want to. She wondered if

Roscoe had already asked him. He would refuse. Irohann had hated blending his mind with Cassie's.

"I'm here," Clarity said. "I can do it."

Roscoe shook his head harder. "Cassie doesn't want you."

"Cassie wants me," Teya insisted, ears standing tall and nose twitching faster than Clarity had seen a lapine nose twitch before.

"Cassie doesn't know what she wants," Roscoe said.

Although, the bank of vid screens behind him, showing Teya's face in real time, blown up larger than life, belied his words. Cassie knew who she wanted to pilot her. She wanted Teya.

Clarity turned away from the verbally battling bunnies and stepped past Irohann, until she was the one standing closest to the bank of vid screens. She stared at those vid screens, willing Cassie to understand that she was talking to her, and not anyone else. She wasn't talking to anyone inside the room. She was talking to the room: "I know you don't want me right now, but I'm here for you. And I also know, you want to get to Wespirtech. I want to take you there. Let me pilot you, and we can sort this out. You and me. Together."

Teya's face melted off the screens and was replaced with a simple exterior view—the wheels of Crossroads Station, spinning like the bicycle wheel that Clarity had hung from her ceiling as a child. The blackness of space, studded with diamond-like stars spread out beyond the station. Clarity wanted to fly through that space, mind-blended with Cassie, experiencing the feeling of slipping through the gravity-free void.

"You're my home, Cassie," Clarity said. "Let me be your pilot. Maybe not forever." She gestured at Teya, and the angry bunny turned away from her, twitchy nose in the air. "Maybe there's a better pilot for you long-term. But right now, I have the experience and the stability that you need to help you get to Wespirtech."

It was an impassioned plea. Clarity hoped it would work. If she were being honest with herself, she thought it would work.

But it didn't.

A word cloud appeared on Cassie's bank of vid screens—a whole jumble of words in different colors and fonts and orientations. It was confusing and hard to read, but the biggest words were "alone," "independent," and "myself." Upsettingly, the word "independent" was upside down, which didn't exactly inspire confidence.

All of the glowing patches on Cassie's mottled walls shone more brightly for a moment, bright enough to make Clarity's eyes hurt and make her turn her face downward, toward the darker floor. She closed her eyes to block out the light, and when she opened them again, the cockpit had been cast into a murky twilight darkness. The ever-present soft pink glow had dimmed to an eerie, dark red.

Clarity could barely see in the new level of light. Everything around her had become mere shadowy shapes with no discernible features. She knew from experience that Irohann's night vision was better than hers, and she reached automatically toward him. His paw caught hers, clearly prepared for her hand to be reaching toward him. "I've got you," he said.

The word cloud was gone from Cassie's bank of screens already. It had been replaced by the velvety folds of subspace—colors that Clarity couldn't quite describe kept swallowing each other up, like the liquid of a cake batter being mixed or bread dough being kneaded.

Clarity's stomach lurched. She'd never gone into a subspace jump aboard Cassie unprepared before.

Cassie had never gone into a subspace jump with passengers aboard her but no pilot. For all Clarity knew, Cassie had never before gone into a subspace jump without a pilot at all.

Did Cassie even need a pilot?

Clarity wasn't sure. Gravity twisted sickeningly sideways for a moment before settling back into the right direction. Was that an effect of subspace? Or were Cassie's internal, mechanical systems misfiring? Either way, everything seemed like it would get a whole lot better if Cassie would accept one of them as a pilot.

"Get out of the pilot's chair," Clarity said, reaching with her free hand towards where she remembered Roscoe being. She found a paw in the darkness that felt like his, and she halfway-helped, halfway-pulled the elderly rabbit out of the fleshy bowl chair. She let go of both Roscoe's and Irohann's paws and fell forward, fumbling her way into the chair, but another fuzzy body blocked her way. Teya? Probably. The figure felt smaller than her.

Two bright points appeared in the room, and after a moment, Clarity recognized Oksana's eyes from the distinctive, rectangular irises. The unguloid's eyes glowed, like a cat's eyes.

"Come on, Teya," Oksana said in her gruff voice. "I know you want to pilot this beast, but I don't wanna die, and whatever you've been doing in here isn't working."

Teya didn't answer, but she stopped struggling as hard to keep Clarity out of the pilot's chair.

Oksana added, "Kwah can't take you back, if you never make it back to her."

The young bunny climbed out of Clarity's way. As soon as she hopped down from the bowl chair, Clarity climbed in, crossed her own legs, and called out, "Cassie, I'm here for you. I can help."

As if in answer, gravity lurched to the other side, then back down again.

The indescribable colors on the viewscreen disappeared. They were replaced by the bright, shining face of either a supernova or a white dwarf that was far, far too close for comfort.

Clarity hoped fervently for the white dwarf. Even if it were too close, a white dwarf was a much better option than a supernova. Less explodey. Either way, the white brightness filled the room, burning itself into Clarity's eyes, even through her eyelids once she shut them. With a light that bright, she couldn't see any better than she'd been able to in the murky dark.

"Dammit, Cassie!" Clarity yelled. "I get that you're mad at me, but get us away from that star! We're much too close to its gravity well. If you won't let me help, then do a star-crackin' better job of piloting yourself!"

The darkness inside Clarity's eyes turned back to darkness again, and gravity rocked back and forth as if Cassie were a cradle. Falling from a tall tree. Plummeting toward the hard, hard ground, and maybe some dangerous branches along the way.

When Clarity dared to open her eyes, the cockpit was empty except for her and several of Mazillion's stray bodies, droning in lazy circles around the bone spikes and tentacles hanging from the center of the ceiling. Irohann must have helped Roscoe out, and Oksana had managed to get Teya out of the way.

The bank of vid screens had gone dark again. Maybe Cassie had turned them off entirely, sulking and giving her crew the silent treatment. Or maybe they were somewhere without stars.

Except that didn't make sense. Cassie *wanted* to go to Wespirtech. She wanted to go there more than any of the rest of them. And everywhere between Crossroads Station and Wespirtech had stars.

Unless... they were lost somewhere in subspace.

Clarity closed her eyes again, trying to figure out from the feel of her body and mind whether that could be the case. There were tell-tale signals of subspace—time felt different, movement felt different. The differences were so subtle that sometimes Clarity thought she was imagining them. But no matter how hard she tried, she couldn't seem to imagine feeling any of them now. She felt... normal.

Clarity opened her eyes and stared at the blank, black vid screens. No static. Usually, when they weren't showing anything, there was a gentle, white noise, snowstorm of static. But this was sheer, ebon blackness. Like the space between stars.

Like the Devil's Radio.

Clarity's insides turned cold.

"You know," she said in a quavering voice, trying to figure out how to bargain or reason with the space whale who had them in her belly, "you'll need us—some of us, at least—to go inside Wespirtech and pick up your maintenance bunnies for you. Even with Wisper's help, I don't think those scientists will load them aboard you without a few of us, uh"—How should she refer to Cassie's crew as a group?—"planet-dwellers aboard you to bargain with them."

Somehow, Clarity's attempt at bargaining had come out more like a threat. She hadn't meant it that way.

Nonetheless, the tentacles with their kissy sucker discs lowered from among the bone spikes above. They coiled down and the suckers kissed onto Clarity's face, scalp, and neck. Her mind expanded, and with horror, she knew what had happened.

The screens weren't black because there was nothing outside. In fact, there was a perfectly nice blue dwarf star with lovely, icy light glittering off its wide bands of asteroid fields that looked like shimmering rings of crushed and scattered diamonds.

The screens had been black because they were reflecting Cassie's emotions. Bleak, empty, injured, sad.

"Scared, scared, scared." The words chased each other around Clarity's mind.

"I'm so sorry," Clarity said, except her human body felt like it was miles and miles away, and she actually only thought the words. But Cassie was heartbeat-close now, and thinking was all it took to communicate.

The Wespirtech wizards who had—godlike, unasked and unsolicited—turned baby starwhals into prototype spaceships had also done the equivalent of clipping a chicken's wings to keep it from flying away, and Cassie hadn't even known about it until she'd tried to fly to Wespirtech under her own guidance.

Without a pilot hooked into her mind, Cassie couldn't navigate inside subspace at all. The parts of her brain that navigated in subspace had been severed from the rest of her brain, and it took a pilot's mind to bridge the gap.

Cassie needed a pilot.

"Unless I just stay here forever." Cassie's words were cast directly into Clarity's mind, along with a pouting tone and images of the young starwhal wandering, lonely and without the company of other starwhals, through a single, desolate star system for the rest of her life, never migrating farther than she could reach by flying at sub-light speeds through normal space.

"Good plan," Clarity thought at Cassie sarcastically. "Your crew will eventually starve to death inside you, and you won't have any sub-sentient maintenance bunnies to clean up the mess, so you'll be filled with the skeletons of your friends forever."

Clarity's sarcasm punctured Cassie's pout, and the two emotions canceled each other out into amusement on both sides. They laughed at each other while being each other. It was one of those cycles where the laughter builds until neither one of you knows what you're laughing about anymore, if you ever did in the first place, and suddenly, the sensation of the laughter itself is funny.

Doubly, triply so, if the laughter is rippling up and down the belly of a space whale, and you're usually just a simple primate. Or if you're used to being a massive, blubbery space whale, and you can feel your laughter bubbling up inside the strangely isolated torso of a funny little body with strange limbs poking out in every direction and its head balanced precariously on a ridiculously thin neck.

Clarity caught herself wondering whether the others could feel Cassie's laughter in the floors and walls around them, and when she thought of the others, it caused Cassie to remember how worried she was about Roscoe.

His headaches had been blinding. Clarity could remember how they had felt to Cassie through the starwhal's connection to him.

"Did I hurt him?" Cassie wondered.

"I don't know if it was the connection," Clarity answered, "or simply that he's old? Or has some other ailment that I don't know about?"

Cassie thought that she would know if Roscoe had an illness, but then, maybe the elder lapine had been able to hide away parts of his memories from her. Or maybe, she simply hadn't thought to go looking through his memories for traces of unexpected ailing. The starwhal wasn't old enough yet to know how it feels when your body starts to betray you, creaking and cracking, complaining about the slightest mistakes.

But she did know how it felt to have her body betray her because people claiming to be her friends had altered it without her understanding how, and the empathy she felt for Roscoe over his painful headaches was so profound that it washed over Clarity in waves. It was too large of a feeling to experience all at once, at least with her tiny primate body.

Cassie had clearly bonded very deeply with Roscoe, but she was afraid that the elder lapine wasn't strong enough to withstand the bond—or, as she saw it, her love—and so she had become fixated on Teya, who seemed like a younger, stronger version of Roscoe.

Young like Cassie. Strong like Cassie.

Also, Clarity thought, strong-headed like Cassie.

The two of them would be perfect for each other, and once Teya had piloted Cassie, it would probably become impossible for anyone else to ever get between them.

Cassie's emotions shifted, reacting to Clarity's own.

When Clarity thought that Teya and Cassie would be perfect for each other, a wave of longing for Teya washed over her. Her own assessment only strengthened Cassie's desires.

When Clarity reacted to Cassie's desire for Teya with a spark, a mere flicker, of jealousy, she found herself flooded with comforting reassurance from Cassie. Clarity should never feel left out. Clarity was inside. Clarity was home.

Thinking and feeling while mentally bonded to a starwhal was like trying to trudge through the lapping waves at the edge of a beach where the sand was so gloopy, so soggy that her feet sank to her ankles, and the water rushed against her knees, knocking her one way and then pulling her back the other, all while she had to pull her feet, one at a time, out of the sucking, squelching sand, to get even one step forward.

And yet, while her thoughts and feelings flowed as slowly as cold molasses, her body—Cassie's body, actually—was capable of slipping into subspace and jumping lightyears at a time.

Abruptly, Cassie lost patience with Clarity's maudlin reveries and guilt over what her species had done to the starwhals. Cassie didn't want guilt or apologies or even retribution or reparations. She wanted bunnies, and the scientists at Wespirtech had them waiting for her. She just needed to get there.

Cassie's mind squeezed around Clarity's, grabbing hold of the parts of the small primate's consciousness that would let her find her way through subspace without losing track of the trails of where she'd been and where she was going, as if they were nothing more than bread crumbs scattered to a wind filled with voraciously hungry birds.

Wespirtech was three hops through subspace away, and Cassie slipped in and out of subspace like a needle wielded by a professional seamstress who knew how to sew on even the slipperiest, gauziest fabric with edges that frayed and unraveled at the slightest touch. The universe was the fabric, falling apart when single ultra-microscopic particles got separated from their entangled partners. Clarity was the seamstress, except she wasn't controlling the movement of her hand. The needle was.

"We're here!" Cassie announced cheerfully.

Clarity didn't know how the starwhal had enough energy to be cheerful after three successive subspace hops with no discernible break in between them. Clarity felt like she'd been squeezed through the eye of a needle, re-inflated on the other side, and squeezed through the eye of the needle again. Three times. While holding the needle.

"Go get bunnies," Cassie said. "Bunnies, bunnies, bunnies." The words hopped around Clarity and Cassie's shared mindspace as if they were bunnies themselves.

"Oh, that's very distracting, Cassie." Clarity was pretty sure her head hurt, but after three subspace hops in rapid succession, she wasn't entirely sure what a head was anymore. Cassie didn't really have one... The starwhal seemed to sense light with the outer layer of skin over her entire body, and maybe her nervous system was localized into a brain near the base of her long, spiraling, unicorn-like horn. Or maybe her nervous systems and neurons were distributed throughout her body like an octopus's. Clarity didn't know.

"Is it safe to make multiple subspace hops in a row like that?" Clarity asked, feeling kind of woozy.

The starwhal did the mental equivalent of shrugging and continued to think about bunnies as she swam in a happy sine wave toward the small moon that had the buildings of Wespirtech studded into its cratered surface like a particularly unattractive, slate-gray gemstone with a boxy cut, under the glassy bubbles of several atmo-domes.

Cassie didn't care if Clarity was distracted by her bunny-centric thoughts or exhausted from the triple hop. She was too happy about the impending sub-sentient maintenance bunnies to contain her flight pattern into a gravitationally efficient simple curve. Thus, she wagged her way across space like the tail of an exuberant puppy, and Clarity realized with a coldness inside her physical body that she wouldn't know how to extract her conscious mind from Cassie's right now if she wanted to. Or needed to.

"No worries," Cassie thought while the fin along her belly rippled in a contented flutter. "I fly. You just sit."

"While you use my brain to navigate?" With great effort, Clarity located her hands and reached up toward the sucker disks kissed onto her face and scalp. She touched them lightly, but she wouldn't dare tear them off. She didn't know what that would do to herself. Or Cassie.

"This is why I like Roscoe better," Cassie thought. "He doesn't fight." Although, the starwhal immediately felt guilty for her thought when the comparison made Clarity feel bad.

Although, Clarity had to wonder what Cassie meant by, "He doesn't fight." Was Cassie more dominant than Roscoe when they blended minds? With Clarity, the balance had always felt fairly even in the past... right up until the starwhal had squeezed down on her mind and used it to bridge to her navigational abilities without waiting for Clarity to understand.

Yet, had the experience really been that different from when they'd flown together in the past? Clarity had been more off-balance, unsure of what to expect, during their previous experiences of mind-blending and flying together, so maybe she simply hadn't realized how much more in control of their actions Cassie was than her. She'd assumed that the mind-blending had been as overwhelming and confusing for Cassie as it had been for her. Now she wondered.

Suddenly, the sucker discs kissed off of Clarity's face, and the mind-blending was over. The human found herself evicted from the starwhal's mind and unceremoniously dumped back into her own small body and singular brain.

She felt gangly and awkward with all her human arms and legs, and the air against her face felt moist and suffocating compared to the pureness of vacuum.

Wespirtech glittered dully on Cassie's bank of vid screens. It was not beautiful. It looked like warehouse and factory buildings enclosed by greasy, oily bubbles. A bubbling infestation of humans on the surface of an otherwise pristine ball of rock. Sure, the shades of gray that the buildings were made from were in the same color palette as the stony, rocky surface of the moon itself, but there was a gentle shading and natural mottling to the gray tones of the cratered sphere. The buildings were flat shades, uniform and dull, edged in unnaturally straight lines and sharp right angles.

The science institute hadn't looked that ugly through Cassie's eyes. Metaphorical eyes. But Cassie's eyes were full of bunnies. Everything looked better with cute, twitchy-nosed, puffy-tailed bunnies hopping all through it.

A human face appeared on Cassie's bank of screens, replacing the view of Wespirtech. The human woman had short-cropped hair and a crisp collar. She looked very neat and tidy, almost militaristically so. Clarity found herself squaring her shoulders, raising her chin, and trying to match the precision and neatness she saw on the screen. She was keenly aware of her poorly fitted, worn-out clothes. They hadn't felt out of place on Crossroads Station—there were so many different species, each wearing styles suited to their wildly different bodies, that at some level, nothing looked out of place on Crossroads Station.

The woman on the screen said, "Welcome to the system! We've been expecting you here at Wespirtech, and we're so very grateful for your visit!"

Clarity tried not to react to anything the woman had said, although her mind was buzzing with questions. Who did this woman think Clarity was? Why were they grateful? What exactly were they expecting? What was the name of Wespirtech's star system? And did this woman really feel like the universe revolved so thoroughly around Wespirtech that the best way to greet interstellar travelers was by welcoming them to *the* system, without providing the system's name?

The woman stared expectantly at Clarity, and words scrolled across the bottom of the screen in a scripty cursive font: "SAY SOMETHING."

"Um, yes, hello," Clarity managed, while working as hard as she could to control her face and not display her irritation with how Cassie was handling all of this. She wasn't ready to talk to a Wespirtech official. "Thank you for your warm greeting." She felt pleased with herself that the words came out with almost no discernible sarcasm. She needed to save all of her sarcasm for describing this situation and Cassie's impetuous behavior to Irohann later.

"We've prepared a tour of our facilities for you and your associates." The woman smiled primly, but her eyes looked like they wanted something. Clarity had no idea what this woman would want from her.

Maybe this was a trap. Maybe they were going to lure Cassie into docking and then steal her back.

Damn, it had been foolish to decide that Cassie didn't need a short-range shuttle pod. Sure, a short-range shuttle pod would be useless for fetching help if Cassie was ever in serious trouble, but it would free her up from needing to actually dock with space stations, other ships, or places like Wespirtech in order for her crew to leave shipboard.

Feeling her way through the words, Clarity carefully said, "That sounds, uh, delightful. Thank you very much. However, my crew has some business to attend to aboard ship before we'll be ready to dock." She tugged at the loose folds of fabric bunched up around her crossed legs, trying to make her jump-suit lay a little more presentably. She would definitely need to make use of some of the synthesizer programs she'd downloaded while they were at Crossroads Station to print out a better tailored, less threadbare outfit for wearing to this tour of Wespirtech.

"Very well," the woman on the screen said. Words flashed impatiently beneath her in garishly clashing shades of pink and orange: "NOW NOW NOW NOW BUNNIES NOW BUNNIES BUNNIES."

Clarity tried to ignore Cassie's insistent words, but she couldn't ignore the fact that the video connection to the Wespirtech administrator hadn't disconnected. If Cassie were a normal ship, Clarity would have a control panel that allowed her to disconnect the outbound communications. If she were still mind-blended with Cassie through the sucker discs, she could simply think that she wanted to disconnect, and it would happen.

As it was, she had to hope that the woman on the other end would disconnect before this seemingly endless moment of them staring politely at each other became too awkward.

"Was there anything else?" the woman asked, and Clarity

barely kept from swearing. Cassie must have been forcefully keeping the connection open.

"I'm sorry," Clarity said. "I seem to be having some trouble with my shipboard communication systems..."

"We'd be happy to have our scientists look at—"

The woman's face disappeared, replaced by blank blackness. Cassie had finally disconnected the communications.

"Real smooth," Clarity said. "I guess you don't like the idea of their scientists checking out your systems?"

The view of Wespirtech reappeared on the bank of vid screens, but Cassie gave no other answer.

"Are you planning to talk to me?" Clarity asked. "Or just order me around?"

The dangling tentacles began to lower toward Clarity's face again, but she ducked away from their kissy sucker disk ends and said, "Nuh uh, I'm not letting you hijack my brain again until we talk about how you've been acting."

The tentacles kept reaching for Clarity's head and face until she'd climbed all the way out of the fleshy bowl chair. She stood in the cockpit with her fists on her hips, staring at the bank of vid screens. Frowning, really.

Eventually, a word cloud appeared, superimposed over the view of Wespirtech. The biggest word, right in the middle was, predictably, "bunnies." Other notable words were "now," "waiting," "impatient," "uncooperative," and "obey."

"Obey?" Clarity repeated. "How exactly do you think the relationship between a pilot and a starship works?"

The words in the word cloud rearranged themselves, most of them fading into the blackness, until all that was left was: "pIloT geTs buNNies."

"You can talk in full sentences," Clarity said. "I've heard your thoughts when our minds blend together, and you can speak in full, grammatical sentences when you want to."

The bank of screens went blank, and then a single word appeared: "confused." The letters were small and rounded. The font looked a little bit like it had been formed from day old, half-deflated balloons.

Clarity closed her eyes and took a deep breath. Maybe Cassie really couldn't speak in complete sentences. Maybe the coherent voice that Clarity heard when their minds blended was half formed by her own brain giving structure and form to the feelings and thoughts Cassie shared with her. Maybe it was her own voice, and Cassie really did think in word clouds and vid clips from children's programs.

And why wouldn't she? Had anyone taught Cassie to read or write or operate a computer? She'd been trained with positive stimuli to behave like a spaceship. She wasn't a normal planet-dweller hidden inside the body of a space whale. She was a star-whal. It was amazing that she and Clarity could communicate with each other as effectively as they did.

Word clouds would do.

"I'm sorry, Cassie," Clarity said, opening her eyes again. The screens had gone blank while her eyes were closed. "This is new and hard for me, figuring out how our relationship works, and it must be new and hard for you too. But you can't just order your pilot or crew around. We have to work together. And right now, that means I need to go take a break before getting your bunnies for you. Those three subspace jumps completely exhausted me. And I don't know what's going on with Roscoe, whether the headaches were caused by connecting with you, but I can try to find out for you. Would you like that? Would you like me to check on Roscoe?"

Clarity would probably check on Roscoe either way, but it would be good if she could get Cassie engaged and understanding that she was trying to help her, even if it wasn't in the way the starwhal wanted.

Reluctantly, dissolving slowly out of the black blankness, words appeared on the screens in a plain, sans-serif font in bright yellow: "checK on roscoe." A few moments later, Cassie added in smaller letters underneath, in a pale lavender, "say hI teya."

Clarity couldn't help but smile at the ship's shy crush on the young lapine who desperately wanted to be her pilot.

These two were destined for each other, and at some point, Clarity and Roscoe wouldn't be able to keep them apart anymore. Clarity hoped by then that she'd have figured out how to get along with Teya, because she was pretty sure that her future home aboard Cassie would depend upon it.

13. PORTRAITS ON THE SCULLERY WALL

Clarity checked her pocket computer as she walked through the gently wending corridor that ran down Cassie's middle. There was no reply from Am-lei yet. She was probably busy with her family on Leionaia. And no matter how many times Clarity checked the mysterious message that Wisper had sent, summoning them all to Wespirtech, she could figure out no way to send it a reply.

Clarity wanted reassurance from Wisper, but it didn't look like she was going to get it. She would simply have to trust the ethereal, controlling AI.

Clarity stumbled into the scullery after passing the cluster of doors into the quarters—all of them had been closed. Everyone was in the scullery, even the Doraspians and their S'rellick guardian.

The Doraspians were basking beneath a sun lamp, and T'resso seemed to be reading from a pocket computer beside them. Mazillion flitted through the air about them like nothing more than a hive's worth of bees, drunk on flowers and sunlight.

Roscoe was seated at the far end of one of the two long tables that protruded from the floor, clutching his head in his paws and looking generally ill, but he did have a bowl of some sort of steaming broth or tea in front of him.

Teya, Oksana, and Irohann were clustered eagerly around Zephyr whose shiny metal hands were raised and expressively gesturing as zhe spoke in a surprisingly fluid, musical lilt considering that zir voice had always sounded a little like a muffled buzz saw when Wisper had used it. Zhe seemed to be verbally guiding the three fuzzy mammaloids through a Starsplosions & Spacedroids game scenario. Zhe had a large sheet of actual, physical paper spread in front of zir with a scattering of colored pencils beside it, and every so often, zhe interrupted zir storytelling to scribble in details on what seemed to be a beautifully illustrated map of the imaginary terrain in their game.

Zephyr was quite the artist. The fantastical landscape of stars, gravity wells, and space stations spread out in front of zir was gorgeous enough to frame and hang on a wall. In fact, Clarity noticed that Zephyr must have done some decorating while she'd been busy letting Cassie use her brain to navigate subspace.

Silken streamers hung from the ceiling in scalloped trails, held in place by glittering clumps of irregularly shaped crystals. A few silken streamers were wrapped cheerfully around Irohann's new antlers as well, and a single silvery bow had been tied neatly onto Oksana's left horn.

Zephyr must have found a way to affix the clumps of crystals that held the streamers to the scullery ceiling painlessly to Cassie's flesh. Clarity knew the process must have been painless, because she would have felt it while mind-blended with Cassie otherwise. Maybe suction discs or some kind of non-toxic glue.

The memories of having the vid screens and computer systems embedded into her flesh still haunted Cassie, and by extension, Clarity. Searing, drilling pain that had continued to ache dully for months afterward.

Clarity shuddered at the visceral quality of the memory, and she actually flinched when she noticed the view of Wespirtech on the scullery's large vid screen. She couldn't let the Wespirtech scientists take Cassie back. It would be unconscionable.

But there was also no way that she could convince Cassie to

leave Wespirtech without at least trying to get those sub-sentient maintenance bunnies. She'd simply have to trust Wisper.

Clarity went over to the synthesizer and punched the codes into its control panel to print out a simple bread bowl filled with fruit goulash. Once the steaming meal was ready, she entered in the codes for a couple of simple synth-cotton shirts and pants. Each with lots of pockets and soothing pastel rainbow colors. They'd look simple but elegant. Much more appropriate for touring a top-notch science institute than her tattered jumpsuit.

After finishing with the synthesizer and cupping the warm bread bowl in her hands, Clarity noticed another set of decorations on the curved scullery walls: pencil sketch portraits of every member of Cassie's crew. The portraits were stylized, but not quite caricatures. Each sketch was monochrome, but also, each one was in a different color. The sketch of Clarity showed her face turned slightly upward, looking at a sky or maybe just an abstract future, and was drawn entirely in the same emerald green as her hair. Irohann's portrait was sketched in the orange shade of his fluffy fur and strangely, to Clarity's eye, included his new antlers. She still couldn't see the elegantly branching appendages as actually being part of him and not simply an affectation, like a fancy bowtie that he might take off at any time.

Oksana was sketched in tawny brown; Teya in nut brown; and Roscoe in shades of gray. The color matched his fur, but it also made him look, in his portrait, like he was about to fade away. A ghost walking, not realizing yet that he was already gone.

Interestingly, Genniperri, Paurizau, and T'resso had been included in the portraits, as well as Cassie herself. Cassie's tail flipped joyfully in her drawing, and the shade of dark purple that Zephyr had used for her conjured the darkness of space and the velvety mystery of nebulas. Unsurprisingly, T'resso had been sketched in a blue that matched his scales.

What surprised Clarity was that neither of the Doraspians had been sketched in green. A monochromatic sketch of a Doraspian was a stretch in the first place, given their riotous array of colorful flowers, but it was even stranger to sketch them each in gold, as if they were glowing. Bursting with an energy that their bodies could barely contain. Sunlight, reformed in the body of a plant, straining against the physical nature of their vines and flowers.

Clarity brought her bread bowl over to the table where the others were playing Starsplosions & Spacedroids. She sat down beside Irohann, and he wrapped a friendly, fuzzy arm around her back. She wanted to sink into his fluffiness and forget everything else forever, but she needed to eat her meal, get dressed more appropriately, and deal with the Wespirtech hurdle.

It's sad how something that you're excited about can turn into something that you're afraid of when it gets too close.

When Zephyr finished describing the space battle scenario that the others had been playing through, the robot turned to Clarity and said, "Would you like to design a character and join the game?"

Irohann gave her shoulder a squeeze, clearly excited by the idea of Clarity joining them. Clarity did want to play, but she didn't think she could concentrate on a game right now. She swallowed the mushy, sweet bite of fruit goulash that had been searing her tongue and said, "Maybe later. May I ask, why didn't you include a portrait of yourself? Or Mazillion?"

Clarity gestured toward the row of portraits on the wall. From her perspective, Zephyr was more a part of the crew than Genniperri, Paurizau, and T'resso. They were passengers. Zephyr was... Well, Clarity wasn't entirely sure of anyone's long term position aboard a temperamental, teenaged space whale, but she liked the idea of Zephyr being something akin to the ship's entertainment officer. A kind of homemaker in space.

Clarity liked the way that the portraits looked down at her. She liked their eyes. And she liked the way that they made all of them into a group who belonged here. Not just her with Irohann's arm around her; Teya and Oksana being young together; the political refugees in a corner; and Roscoe alone. But all of them together.

"I included Mazillion," Zephyr said. "There are several of Mazillion's bodies in the background of each of the other portraits. Well, except the portraits of the Doraspians. I tried to include Mazillion in those, but... It did not feel right."

Clarity was startled by that answer. Mazillion was as stealthy and mysterious in Zephyr's portraits as they were in real life. Zhe really had captured something of their essence, and that made Clarity want to go over and look at the portraits more closely to see what other details and insights she'd missed in them. But later. For now, she said, "Okay, but what about yourself?"

"I'm not sure who I am yet," Zephyr said. "So I can't draw myself."

Clarity wanted to quip, "But you know who all of us are?"

She didn't though.

She just nodded. Seriously. Trying to understand exactly what Zephyr meant. It was still so strange to Clarity that Zephyr wore Wisper's body. Like a costume. Like a hand-me-down, too small for its original owner, discarded and pawned off on someone younger, someone who might grow into it or might not. "When you're ready," Clarity said, "I'd love to see your portrait added to the others."

"You like them?" Zephyr asked. Zir body wasn't designed to convey uncertainty or nervousness or much of anything. Yet zhe seemed nervous, like zhe cared very much whether the portraits had pleased Clarity.

And they had. "I do," she said. "They make this room feel... less like a station run cafeteria and more like a family dining room."

Zephyr nodded curtly with zir metal skull. "Thank you."

"So, what're we going to do now that we're at this Wespirtech place?" Teya asked. She'd been fidgeting restlessly with the colored pencils, lining them up in rows and arranging them by color. "I don't want to be left out of the loop on this ship like I was on the last one."

"Teya," Oksana brayed, her voice quiet and cautioning.

"I've made my intentions clear," Teya said. "I want to be a pilot."

"Yeah," Clarity said, spooning more of the piping hot goulash into her mouth, tempered by a piece of the bread bowl scraped off from its interior. "Cassie wants that too. I feel like I'm some kind of Shakespearean villain getting between the two of you, keeping apart star-crossed lovers."

Teya sniffed. "Don't be dramatic."

Clarity raised her eyebrows, subtly turning the dramatic young lapine's accusation of drama back at herself. Oksana laughed.

Irohann rearranged himself, taking his fluffy arm back from around Clarity's shoulders and inadvertently tangling some of the silken streamers decorating his antlers around her head. She managed to get the streamers off her without dragging them through her fruit goulash or yanking too hard on ribbons attached indirectly to Irohann's head. He grinned sheepishly—a real trick with his wolfish muzzle—then swept the remaining streamers back behind his own shoulders to keep them out of the way.

Clarity felt colder without Irohann's arm around her, but she loved that he'd been feeling affectionate enough to initiate an embrace like that.

Clarity felt ridiculous for having been jealous of Oksana back on Crossroads Station. They weren't rivals. There was plenty of room for Clarity in this group. In fact, they probably needed someone like her—older and steadier than Teya and Oksana, and well, also older than Zephyr—although robot ages were hard to understand—but younger and more optimistic than either Irohann or Roscoe.

She still needed to check on Roscoe. Clarity glanced over at the older lapine. His head was still clasped in his paws, worrisomely.

"What is the plan?" Irohann asked. "We jumped here awfully fast."

"Yeah, about that," Clarity said. "Cassie is..." She frowned. She didn't want to say anything bad about Cassie, but she was also deeply troubled by the way that Cassie had commandeered and controlled her mind. "I don't know, but she..."

When it came down to it, was Clarity even sure that Cassie had controlled her mind? She had mind-blended with Cassie on purpose to help pilot her here. Maybe Cassie's own eagerness for getting here had overwhelmed Clarity as well. Maybe she was as much responsible for the triple jump as Cassie had been. She shook her head. It was too much to sort out. But she did know the plan.

"Whatever; we can deal with questions about Cassie later. Right now, Wespirtech is expecting us to dock and to give us a tour."

"A tour?" Irohann asked. "Why?"

"No idea," Clarity said. "But a very fancy looking administrator was being extremely solicitous and saying how glad they were to have us here."

"Glittery as stardust!" Teya exclaimed. "That's great. I'm coming. My second-aunt wanted me to apply to Wespirtech, now I can check out what kind of overly organized nonsense she had in mind for my future."

Clarity wasn't sure that was a good idea, but she wasn't sure it was a bad idea either. If the Wespirtech people gave them trouble on the tour—if it turned out to be some kind of trap—then it might not hurt to have a larger group of them all together.

"Anyone else want to come?" Clarity asked.

Oksana nodded.

Irohann shrugged. "I'll come if you think I should," he said to Clarity.

"What about you?" Clarity asked Zephyr.

The robot shook zir head vigorously. "I have access to more than enough knowledge regarding Wespirtech from hacking into Maradia's data banks while I was still an AI in Gerangelo's workshop."

Clarity narrowed her eyes at the robot. "You guys are a strange family. You sure you don't want to visit Grandma Maradia's old stomping grounds? See where your earlier robot cousins were programmed?"

Zephyr narrowed zir eyes back at Clarity. "No."

Definitely a different person from Wisper. Completely different.

Then again, Wisper—Clarity's Wisper—had existed for one purpose and one purpose only: to assemble a team who had a chance of saving the universe from an entangled particle destroying the universe, and sacrifice herself in the process. She had been a suicide mission incarnate. Self-sacrificing was her primary personality trait.

Zephyr was more complicated, more confusing.

"What I will do," Zephyr said, "is unload the cargo crates once we're docked while the rest of you are on your tour. I want to earn my keep here."

Clarity looked at the decorations all around the scullery and the game board spread in front of them all. "I think you're more than doing that already," she said. "But thank you. That would be helpful."

Clarity finished spooning the soggy, sweet fruit goulash out of her bread bowl and switched to gnawing on the nectar-soaked bread while listening to the others resume their game. When she'd finished with her meal, she slipped away from the group now busy fighting an imaginary space dragon that Zephyr was gracefully sketching for them. Its wings looked like navy blue nebulas; its spine was a string of yellow stars; and their imaginary characters circled it in their imaginary spaceships, like Mazillion buzzing around Genniperri and Paurizau.

Clarity checked the synthesizer had properly produced the clothes she'd ordered, and once they were draped over her arm, ready to be carried back to her quarters, she steeled herself and went over to sit down beside Roscoe.

The elderly rabbit sighed. "What do you want?"

"Cassie's worried about you," Clarity said. "And I'm worried about... well, both of you. Both you and Cassie."

Roscoe grunted and kneaded the paws that were covering his face into his eyes. "We're both fine," he said through gritted teeth. "We don't need you worrying about us." His paws dropped from his face, and he tilted his head toward the group playing Starsplosions & Spacedroids. "We need *you* to worry about *them*."

"Them?" Clarity asked, honestly bewildered. "They're fine. They're all getting along and bonding, doing exactly what they should be doing right now. *You* are slumped over this table like an invisible axe is buried in the back of your skull, and Cassie is terrified that she's the one who put the axe there."

Roscoe sneered and muttered something unintelligible and grumpy.

"What?" Clarity asked, raising her voice a little, just enough to show her impatience with the lapine elder's behavior.

"I'll be fine," Roscoe said. "I just need to give the Sagittarian willow bark more time to take effect."

"How much have you taken?"

"Enough," he grumbled, then frowned, his whiskers turning downward. "Well, maybe not enough."

"Do you need a doctor?" Clarity asked. "Is this something that started before you began piloting Cassie? Or... Is it something that I should be looking forward to, as a consequence of mind-blending with her?"

"Mind-blending," Roscoe repeated with a laugh. "Is that how it seems to you?"

Clarity hesitated before answering. "I had thought so," she said. "But I'm less and less sure."

Roscoe stared at her with tired, hollow eyes, and his long ears drooped back behind his head. He glanced to the side, toward the big vid screen on the wall. It still showed a view of Wespirtech with all its boxy buildings clinging to the stark, rocky surface of the silver-gray moon. Clarity didn't think that Cassie's ability to sense and see the comings and goings of the crew inside her depended on anything so crude as a video camera embedded in the vid screen. She had started to feel like maybe Cassie simply felt them with her skin and saw them through the glowing patches of pink. Yet, she understood how Roscoe could feel like the vid screen in some way represented Cassie and the fact that she was almost certainly watching them, listening to Clarity and Roscoe's conversation as best as she could.

Although, it was not at all clear that Cassie understood them very well when she wasn't mind-blended with a pilot.

"Puppetry," Roscoe muttered.

When Clarity looked him inquisitively, he shook his head and looked away, unwilling to say more than the single word.

He looked haunted.

Clarity felt a reflection of his frown mirror itself on her face. She put a hand, gently, gingerly on his shoulder. He startled at first, but then he relaxed into the touch. "Cassie doesn't want to hurt you."

"I know," he said. "She's a good grandbunny."

"But a big one," Clarity said.

"Yes."

"And sometimes... She doesn't realize her own power..."

He agreed grimly, "Yes," but quickly added, "She'll learn."

Clarity tilted her head to the side, taking in the measure of this old man's devotion to Cassie, unwillingness to betray her, and yet clear terror of the harm she might be doing to him. "Maybe, but only if we hold her accountable."

"She needs love," he said. "She needs... gentleness."

"Unlike Teya?" Clarity asked archly.

Roscoe grumbled, "Different people. Different situations. Teya has a family and a home. Cassie has... me."

"Cassie has all of us," Clarity said, holding her hands up to indicate everyone else in the room. "She is not your sole responsibility. She isn't a responsibility at all. You don't have to let her use you up, just because someone else snipped the connections in her brain that would let her navigate without a pilot."

Roscoe's ears perked up a little. He looked surprised. Clarity supposed that since Cassie hadn't realized her navigational limitations before their most recent subspace hops, Roscoe hadn't known about them either.

"Anyway," Clarity said, "Wespirtech has offered to give us a tour of their facilities when we go down to pick up Cassie's maintenance animals."

Roscoe nodded. The movement looked like it hurt his head.

"I'm guessing you don't want to come?"

"That's right," Roscoe said. "But bring Teya. Her second-aunt has been pushing her to apply to Wespirtech. It would be a wonderful experience for her, I'm sure. Very focused. Very grounding. And it would open up marvelous opportunities."

Clarity was glad that Teya hadn't heard any of that. She was also glad that Teya had already expressed a desire to go on the tour. Clarity didn't think she could make that young lapine do much of anything against her will, no matter how much her granduncle Roscoe thought it would be good for her.

Finally, Clarity went over to the two Doraspians, the S'rellick, and the buzzing cloud of Mazillion to tell them about the tour. She didn't really intend to invite the Doraspians or S'rellick along—they were guests, hiding away aboard Cassie from both of their governments, after all—but the tips of Genniperri's fronds twirled, and her flowers spread their petals, blooming even wider as she listened. And T'resso, long spiny tail swishing sinuously behind him, insisted on accompanying her.

In the end, only Roscoe, Paurizau, Zephyr, and an unmeasurable percentage of Mazillion stayed behind aboard Cassie.

14. THE EMERALD CITY IN SHADES OF GRAY

Clarity felt overdressed the moment she stepped out of the airlock and into Wespirtech proper. She had changed into her simple, elegant, pastel rainbow clothes, thinking that she'd look more presentable for that intimidating administrator. But they weren't met by an administrator.

They were met by a small human woman with holes ripped into the knees of her faded denim jeans and ashy smears on her oversized, lopsided shirt. Her hair looked like it hadn't been brushed in days, or maybe just like it was thick and unruly, and the woman didn't know how to handle it, even though the touches of gray suggested she'd had plenty of time to learn.

The vista behind the woman wasn't a shining, glittering facility but a rundown-looking hallway, full of hatchways to docked shuttles, alternated with windows that looked out on the stark, desolate surface of the moon. Of course, they were still outside of the atmo-bubbles that curved over most of Wespirtech's buildings. Maybe the institute would look more impressive once they'd walked all the way down the hall and were truly inside.

Regardless, Clarity immediately wished that she hadn't changed clothes to dress up for this. She wanted to be back in her familiar, worn-out jumpsuit. Instead, she was wearing brand new clothes, including an elegant powder-blue-fading-to-sunshine-yellow blazer, and she felt horribly conspicuous. None of the others had changed clothes.

Clarity tried to take comfort in the wide range of body types among them as the others stepped out of the airlock around her—scintillating blues scales, fluffy orange fur, dusky brown fur, and brightly zebra-striped fur. Not to mention Genniperri's rainbow bouquet of flower organs. So, sure, Clarity was wearing a pastel rainbow pantsuit, but she hardly stood out compared to the others.

Irohann even had to duck his head to get through the airlock door now. Between his usual height and the added height of the new antlers, he was ridiculously tall, and on his first try, he caught the topmost points of those branching appendages noisily on the metal doorframe. She hoped he hadn't been jabbing Cassie too badly with them while walking around aboard her.

Mazillion, however, was conspicuously inconspicuous. Clarity knew that many of their bodies had been buzzing inside Cassie's airlock when the valve-like door had sealed shut. But by the time that Wespirtech's airlock had opened, all of their buzzing, flitting bodies had seemingly all disappeared into Genniperri's foliage, silently perched on her vines with their wings held perfectly still.

Mazillion never held still like that.

Clarity could only assume that the swarm alien was specifically hiding from the Wespirtech people's notice. She didn't mind the idea of a spy amongst them. A spy on her side.

Although, in retrospect, it seemed strange to Clarity that Zephyr had included Mazillion in all of zir drawings on the scullery walls except those of the Doraspians. Mazillion seemed drawn to the Doraspian foliage, constantly swarming among their leaves and flowers, and Clarity couldn't imagine why it would have seemed wrong to Zephyr to have included them. Perhaps that was something to ask zir about later.

The human woman who had been waiting to greet them stepped forward, rubbed a hand nervously against her thigh, and held it out, straight and awkward, toward Clarity. "I'm Anna

Karlingoff," she said. "Tenured research physicist. They asked me to give you a tour?"

Clarity wasn't sure if Anna was actually asking her a question or just expressing the anxiety that seemed to overflow her small body. She reached out and took the physicist's hand, shook gently, and said, "Yeah, that's what I was told too."

Anna laughed and looked a little more at ease. She looked even more comfortable after shaking hands with Irohann's warm, fuzzy paw, Teya's less-warm-but-also-fuzzy paw, Oksana's pleasantly rough hoof-hand, and finally a trio of vines from Genniperri that wrapped themselves all the way up the human woman's arm in the Doraspian's attempt at mimicking the others.

Clarity noticed a few of Mazillion's bodies flitted off of the vines that shook Anna's hand, rearranging themselves inside Genniperri's foliage. However, anyone who hadn't met Mazillion would never guess that those tiny flickering buzzes were indicative of the presence of an entire extra sentient being in the room that had gone otherwise unnoticed.

When Anna turned around to lead them all away from the airlock, Clarity noticed several of Mazillion's bodies take flight and subtly disperse. They flew high and close to the ceiling or low and close to the floor, but either way, they went on ahead, not waiting for a guided tour. Anna didn't seem to notice any of them.

Clarity wondered what secrets Mazillion would learn and if they'd share them with her.

Anna led the group down a hallway with a series of hatches that seemed to lead to more airlocks. Large windows between and above the hatches showed that small shuttles were docked at many of them. More excitingly, as they got some distance from the original hatch that they'd entered through, Clarity saw Cassie's fleshy bulk through the windows as well.

The airlock that Cassie had sealed herself to was at the end of the long hallway that was lined with shuttles on either side. Each shuttle looked approximately large enough for two to four people, and Clarity was pretty sure that she could fit two to four of the shuttles inside Cassie's cargo bay.

Cassie dwarfed the little metal shuttles.

Clarity had never seen Cassie laying on her side, like a beached whale on the surface of a small moon. Or really, on the surface of any type of planet. She wondered how the rocky surface felt against Cassie's skin that was usually so free of encumbrances. She knew from memory what gravity wells were like when they tugged on Cassie, and she wasn't sure if lying there beside Wespirtech's buildings felt like an amusing novelty or a terrible strain, an uncomfortable burden to be tolerated only because there would be a reward at the end.

Clarity was curious about Wespirtech, but that curiosity was nothing compared to her desire to protect Cassie and get her back into the soothing vacuum of space, safely away from these Wespirtech wizards and their dark magic that passed for science.

At the end of the hall of airlocks, Anna stopped and turned back to the group. She said, "The administrators have a fancy brunch planned for you, and they want to tell you all about the marketable products that they're able to extract from the research we do here."

"Okay," Clarity said, unsure of what was happening. Why did they rate a fancy brunch?

"But most of the administrators are asleep, because you happened to show up during the middle of the simulated night cycle that they're always trying to impose on us." Anna's smile took on a mischievous, impish quality that Clarity quite liked. It felt like she was being included in a secret, even if she wasn't sure yet what the secret was. "Basically, they like your money, and they want more of it, so they want to give you a boring old sales pitch."

Clarity blinked, but other than that one subtle expression of confusion, she worked hard to control her face and keep herself from revealing the surprise she felt at the phrase "your money."

She was extremely glad and grateful that the rest of her group seemed to know enough to hold their tongues as well.

Anna continued: "And of course, we scientists love what we can do with the funding that you've sent our way." Anna paused, twisting her hands together nervously. "Thank you very much, in fact. However, I don't think a good way to thank you is with a sales pitch. I think—and the other scientists too—that it'd be much better to thank you by letting you see all of the messy, complicated, fascinating, and just plain fun things that we're able to do with funds like that."

Clarity risked glancing at the others. Irohann's tail had gone stock still behind him, and Oksana was staring at Teya, as if waiting to follow her lead. Teya looked downright gleeful. And of course, Clarity couldn't read Genniperri's expression, but most of her flowers were open wide, looking alert if not especially revealing of the Doraspian's inner thoughts.

"Well," Clarity started, fumbling her way through this strange interaction, "that sounds... wonderful?"

Anna's face lit up. "I'm so glad!" She clapped her hands together, more like a happy child than a lead researcher at the foremost knowledge institute in this corner of the galaxy. "I knew it was the right choice to hack into Prefect Osterio's alarms and disable them. Here, follow me!"

Anna practically skipped her way down the hall, glancing over her shoulder every few feet to check that the group of aliens —fat-pocketed donors, apparently—were still following her. Every time she turned back, a big grin spread across her face. The group followed along, but clearly slower than Anna would like them to. She was so eager to show Wespirtech off to them.

Clarity stepped close to Irohann and spoke under her breath, "So, we're generous philanthropists, I guess."

"Wisper's work," he said softly. "Has to be."

"I guess it's as good of a cover story for us as any," Clarity replied, matching the softness of his voice. "Maybe we don't have to worry about them kidnapping Cassie back from us after all."

"Maybe," Irohann said. He sounded skeptical. He often sounded skeptical. For all of his big, orange fluffiness and the wolfish grin that could melt the coldest heart, Irohann could be a reticent, withdrawn, and sometimes cynical fellow. It made Clarity want to give him a big hug. But this was not the time.

Teya and Oksana skipped ahead, their youthful exuberance seemingly engaged by Anna's enthusiasm. Long feet and keratinous hooves bounced along the nondescript floor tiling, decorated with strangely ugly rectangular patterns in clashing shades of burnt umber and bubblegum blue. Their footsteps echoed badly down the hall, suggesting the architect hadn't bothered with any sound-dampening materials.

Genniperri walked slowly and lagged behind. Each step looked precise and careful as she swung her tree trunk-like legs into a rhythm. She was still learning to control them and couldn't skip quite as freely as the young ungulatoid and lapine.

Once they made it to the end of the corridor, Clarity expected a shift in the decor. It seemed reasonable to assume that Wespirtech-proper would look more urbane, more polished than the row of shuttle docks. But no. The maze of corridors that Anna led them through no longer had airlock hatches clunkily disrupting the flow every twenty feet, but instead, angular protuberances bulged out of the walls. They didn't seem to serve any purpose and thus must have been decorative, but they weren't at all visually pleasing.

Clarity had imagined that a bastion of science would be beautiful. A blending of the arts and sciences. But Wespirtech seemed to be as boxy, plain, and service-oriented on the inside as its rectangular buildings had looked to be on the outside. Almost hostile to the very idea of beauty.

Eventually, Anna came to a closed door and turned her back to it, spreading her arms just a little bit away from her body. She blocked the door as if she were an elven creature barring the entrance to fairy land.

"Are you ready?" she asked when the group had all caught

up. Behind her, the door was covered with scraps of paper and strange notes, taped onto its wide surface. Many of the notes seemed to be hand-drawn cartoons with punchlines that must have depended on understanding high-level physics or being privy to in-jokes, because Clarity couldn't make any sense of them. The drawings were cute though.

The whole top of the door was covered with a mosaic of empty packets of High Caff Tea in a wide variety of flavors—mango, melon, matcha; blueberry, greenberry, red sage; lemon, lime, creamy coffee. Apparently, the scientists who worked in this lab wanted to brag about how much caffeine they needed.

The mosaic of packets was strangely pretty—each flavor packet was a different color, and they added up to a lovely, pixelated rainbow.

A rainbow of caffeine packets, curving over the door to fairy land.

Anna opened the door, and the inside of the room instantly made Clarity think of Maradia's lab, filled with detached robot limbs, arcane tools, and piles of random materials and supplies. Nothing in this lab looked like robot arms or legs—none of it was that recognizable to Clarity—but otherwise, the effect was very, very similar. It was a chaotic whirlwind of technology, and Anna began running from one lumpy, clumpy, clunky-looking machine to the next, calling them "Analyzers" or "Ultrascopes" or "Anglometers."

Clarity didn't know what any of it meant and couldn't keep track. "So, this is your lab?" she asked, trying to participate.

Anna stopped up short. She'd been bending over a boxy machine with a telescopic tube pointed at a glassy plate. Some kind of microscope, presumably. "Yes," she said. "Well, I'm the primary researcher in this lab."

"Hey!" The voice came from the door behind them, and Clarity turned back to see a human man with a dark, scraggly beard and short but unkempt hair.

"That's Jon Einray," Anna said. "He works here too. At least, he did until he started mixing his pure physics up with squishy biology."

"I still work here," he snorted, stomping past them all to another one of the machines. This particular machine was humming, and he worked several controls at its base until the humming noise rose in pitch into a painful squeal, then stopped abruptly. "Well, those are weird readings," he mumbled to the machine. "Hey, did any of you touch this?"

Anna assured him that none of her visitors had touched anything. He grumbled that something was messing with his readings. He stuck a pocket computer into a cradle on the side of the machine, seemed to download whatever data he'd been gathering, and finally stomped back out of the lab.

But he poked his head back in to say, "When Anna lets you see the bio lab, make sure that she shows you my trees. They're the best project here." Then, he disappeared again enigmatically.

Scientists have a lot in common with elven dwellers of a fairy realm: arcane interests, arcane rules, and always making deals that border on selling their souls.

Design a faster spaceship!

But enslave a species of peaceful space whale to do so...

Create robots that can do all of our work for us!

But end up recklessly birthing a whole new sentient race who doesn't necessarily want anything to do with our expectations for them...

Discover a source of boundless energy!

But accidentally unleash that energy in a way that threatens to destroy the universe...

Deals with the devil.

Clarity didn't believe in devils, but she sure did believe in deals made with them. And she believed those deals were sometimes—maybe often—necessary, but they should always be entered into with caution. And she didn't see any caution here.

Teya and Oksana oohed and ahhed appropriately as Anna showed them all devices that she'd invented that could bend the properties of space in small, contained ways to make the air itself rush into a space and pack itself densely into near-invisible walls or flip around the properties of light so that prisms cast rainbows with an entirely different arrangement of colors than usual.

Anna used the dense air to make invisible mazes that Teya and Oksana chased each other through around the lab. Genniperri tried to play with them, but she was still too new to her legs and couldn't keep up. Although, the dense air didn't seem to affect her the way it did the lapine and ungulatoid; Genniperri walked right through invisible walls that stopped the two of them up short. Clarity wondered how that worked, but she decided not to ask Anna about it. The physicist hadn't noticed, and Clarity didn't want to draw undo attention to her immortal companion.

When Teya and Oksana were out of breath, too busy laughing to run through the invisible mazes any more, Anna turned on a different machine to amuse them: this one could flip around the properties of light, and she hung a simple, teardrop-shaped prism in the light it cast.

Rainbows danced all over the room, but their colors bled together in hauntingly different way than with usual rainbows. Clarity wasn't sure that she'd even seen all of those colors before —some of them seemed to be entirely new, and their brilliance, their reality, their uniqueness took her breath away. She couldn't have described them if she tried, but the closest her brain could come was: the taste of yellow, sewn into a blanket, draped over you during a cold night, and the resulting warmth spun into a sugary confection that was then melted down into a tea... that got spilled over a blank sheet of blue paper.

The stain on the paper would be a color exactly like and yet completely and utterly unlike green. Clarity thought she'd never before seen anything so beautiful, and she desperately wanted to reach out and pocket the prism that had cast the rainbow with that beautiful not-green color.

She wanted to hang teardrop prisms off of all the branching tips of Irohann's antlers, as if he were a raincloud, and watch the prisms cast impossible rainbows everywhere he walked, and maybe even tinkle and chime as he jostled them with his movements. His antlers already cast funny shadows; they'd look even better casting rainbows-worth of new colors too. He was already so good at surprising her; the idea of his antlers summoning new colors into existence every time that he did something unexpected seemed almost appropriate.

Except, Clarity suspected the prism wouldn't work outside of this magical laboratory. The color hadn't come from the prism, which was really only a cleverly cut piece of faceted glass; it had come from whatever forces the machine around the prism had exerted on the space and the air where Anna had dangled it.

Irohann caught sight of Clarity looking at him, and said, "What?"

She knew the expression on her own face—a lopsided half-smile, bemused, amused, and a little off-balance. "Nothing," she said. "I just want to hang prisms all over your antlers and watch you light up rooms like you're a disco ball."

Teya laughed and Oksana smirked, an amusing expression on her long, horsey face. The lapine had been laughing a lot since they'd arrived, and it was good to see her so happy.

Even T'resso seemed to hiss out a reptilian version of a giggle at the idea of dressing Irohann up in prisms.

Genniperri sang with her flowers to Irohann. "You would look very pretty. I like rainbows."

The Doraspian waved her branches through the spangled array of rainbows, dancing around the prism like a moth drawn to lamplight. The colors swirled around Genniperri, painting her own colorful petals with an even wider palette of hues, even more new shades than had been there a moment ago.

Anna frowned, suddenly all seriousness, and said, "That's never happened before..." She checked the machine, still frowning. Had Genniperri's presence affected the way light was bending? Was her immortality somehow interfering with all of the experiments here?

Clarity hoped they would get through this tour without the scientists here realizing there was anything stranger about Genniperri than that she looked like a houseplant with robotic legs.

After a few moments of frustrated mumbling to herself, Anna shut the machine down, ending the rainbows, and locked the prism away in a drawer. She actually locked it, punching in a complicated keycode to make sure the drawer was secure. "I'll have to check on that later."

Maybe the prism had been more than mere cut glass. Clarity wanted to pocket it all the more. She felt like a child on a tour of that fantastical, historically fictional chocolate factory. Treats everywhere. Touch nothing.

After Anna finished showing them all around the physics lab, she led the motley group—passing for exceedingly rich philanthropists—into a chemistry lab next door.

There the treats became literal as a scientist named Ivan handed them each a bright pink blob that he called an Exo-Candy. He said that it would undergo an exothermic reaction when their teeth bit into it.

Clarity popped the blob into her mouth, and when the candy coating broke, the filling heated up, growing all warm and melty as it slid sweetly over her tongue. The taste was tangy and familiar. Citrus. Grapefruit, maybe.

Ivan handed out purple ones that he called Endo-Candies, explaining that these ones would undergo endothermic reactions as they were eaten.

This time, the candy coating cracked between Clarity's teeth, and the insides cooled to the perfect, refreshingly cold chill of ice cream. Lavender ice cream. "Those are lovely," Clarity said.

Teya and Oksana were already taking seconds. The lapine even experimented with eating both kinds at once, tucking them into opposite sides of her mouth so that they made her cheeks pouch out like a chipmunk's. The lapine ended up breaking out in laughter at the confusion of temperatures in her mouth, as pink and purple sugar dribbled out and matted the fur on her lips.

T'resso took seconds too, but only of the Exo-Candies; he said he liked the warm feeling against his forked tongue.

Next, Ivan dazzled them with a chemical reaction that flickered like fire but was cold to the touch. The cold flames burst and popped with tiny, crackling explosions of icy sparks in brilliant gemstone colors like a fireworks display.

The firecracker lights in the air reflected dazzlingly off T'resso's shiny blue scales, and the reptilian alien flexed the muscles in his shoulders, causing the brilliant reflections to ripple aesthetically. He was a very handsome lizard, and he seemed to be showing off for his floral paramour who had looked so enamored with the idea of Irohann dripping in rainbows.

Genniperri had seemed nonplussed by the endo- and exo-candies, since she had no real way to eat them, but her leaves shivered with delight at the shining brilliance of the cold-fire pyrotechnics, and her daisy-like eye-flowers spread their petals as wide as they went.

Clarity watched the bursts of light closely, but she couldn't tell for sure if the sparks exploded a little more complicatedly—perhaps tracing tiny fractals in the air—when Genniperri was near.

"I suppose you'd like to hang this fireworks display off of my antlers too?" Irohann asked.

Clarity grinned, glad of the distraction from worrying about Genniperri's secrets, but didn't answer. Irohann knew he would look good with sparklers fountaining from the tips of his branching antlers. She didn't need to say it for him.

Clarity noticed a trio of Mazillion's bodies flitting above the dish of endo-candies when Ivan and Anna were looking away. She didn't see how the swarm alien could successfully eat the candies, especially with only a scattered handful of their bodies, but she didn't want them to be left out of the fun. And maybe when their bodies were all together, back aboard Cassie, Mazillion would be able to crack the candy coating properly and get the full effect. So, Clarity went over and grabbed seconds of each candy and pocketed them. It wasn't as thrilling as stealing a prism, given that the whole group had been invited to take seconds when Teya had asked.

Clarity whispered to the trio of Mazillion's bodies, "These are for you. You can have them when we get back to Cassie."

The trio of bodies flitted away from the candy, flew over to Genniperri where they rejoined many of their other bodies, still hiding among her foliage, and then returned to Clarity in a slightly larger group. The tiny clump of buzzing bodies flew close to Clarity's ear and whispered back, "Thank you. We look forward to them and will share information in return."

"Would you not have shared information anyway?" Clarity whispered archly.

Mazillion's bodies dispersed without answering, enigmatic as always.

Ivan showed them a crystal seed that could be placed on a plant leaf—there was one, single potted plant in the entire chemistry laboratory—and that would catalyze a crystallization response throughout the poor potted fern's cells, propagating through its entire body, until the whole fern was a glittering, green, crystalline mimic of a fern.

Genniperri stepped away and continued backing away from the crystallized fern until she was on the far side of the lab. Clarity thought that was probably a good idea. In general, Genniperri staying away from the experiments seemed wise.

T'resso stood protectively between her and the crystallized fern. He looked like a character out of an ancient Earth fairytale—both dragon and knight, hybridized into one.

"Oh, don't worry," Ivan said, "I wouldn't use this method on a sentient being."

Suddenly, Clarity found herself wondering how exactly Ivan defined sentience. If he wouldn't crystallize a sentient creature, would he do it to one of the sub-sentient maintenance bunnies that they'd come to pick up for Cassie? Tiny, fuzzy things that Cassie already loved before she'd even seen them...

Would he do it to Cassie herself?

"Besides," Ivan continued, nonchalantly, "the whole point is that this effect is completely reversible." He grabbed a wand that looked like a cross between a curling iron and a high-tech thermometer, pressed a few buttons, and it emitted an indigo light. As the light shone over the fern's crystalline fronds, the glittering crystal aspect melted away, leaving the fern seemingly-unharmed, and returned to its original condition.

"It's for putting creatures into stasis," Anna said, clearly believing that her comment was helpful.

It was not.

Clarity was still horrified. "But..." She didn't even know what to say.

"Is the fern really unharmed," Oksana said, reaching out to gently, gingerly touch the tip of one of the green fronds with her keratinous fingertip, "after being crystallized and... uncrystallized?"

"Completely," Ivan answered with the kind of confidence that Clarity was sure had gone into the Aether Gaia project that had done so much damage to and caused so much pain for Cassie.

"What about brain cells?" Irohann said pointedly.

"Well..." Ivan hedged, fidgeting with the indigo-light wand.

"There's a reason that he doesn't use it on sentient beings yet," Anna said, trying to rescue Ivan.

Clarity was not impressed. In fact, she was horrified.

Anna smiled warmly. Condescendingly. She clearly thought her tone was reassuring.

It was not.

Clarity wanted to get those bunnies and get out of here.

"I think that makes it time for our tour to move onto the biology lab," Anna said with a big, big grin.

Ivan still looked discombobulated, or miffed, over Irohann's skepticism. He'd clearly expected adulation and amazement from the rich rubes. Not questions and skewed ears. The chemist put his research supplies away, less carefully than Anna had been with that prism, and then he stomped out of the chem lab, leaving them all with Anna.

Bewilderingly, Anna knelt down to the floor and slid aside a large, square tile from underneath one of the desks. "The fastest way from here to the bio lab is through an underground tunnel," she said. "The admin wouldn't have shown you this, right?"

Teya and Oksana lost no time climbing past Anna into the dark tunnel. Genniperri followed them, quickly enough that Clarity suspected she was glad to get away from the poor, abused fern and the chemistry lab that had crystallized it. T'resso followed her, ever loyal.

Irohann kept throwing troubled glances at the fern, but when he saw his friends disappear into a dark, hidden, secret tunnel, he couldn't keep his tail from wagging. It looked like too much fun, and he clambered eagerly after them.

There was something that seemed right about an alien who looked a little like a red fox disappearing into an underground tunnel; the same held for the bunny-girl and lizard-man. Less so for the ungulatoid and walking tree...

Though Clarity was unexpectedly relieved to have Genniperri leave the chemistry laboratory. Whether Clarity had been imagining all the effects she'd been seeing or not, it seemed better to have Genniperri farther away from the delicate, sensitive physics and chemistry equipment in here; she hoped the biology lab would prove to be less weirdly responsive to the Doraspian's presence.

Clarity was about to follow the others into the dark tunnel, when she caught sight of Zephyr's face on one of the laboratory computer screens. Clarity blinked, unsure of what she was seeing. Was Zephyr trying to contact her from the ship? Zir metal hand rose up, one metal finger out, until the finger was over zir mouth, signalizing silence.

Clarity pulled her pocket computer out and checked for

messages from the ship. There was one message, but it was unsigned, and didn't seem to have come from aboard Cassie: "Stay behind. Don't tell Anna about me. Tell her you'll catch up."

"Uh..." Clarity stared at the message on her pocket computer's screen; then she glanced at the image of Zephyr on the chem lab computer. And suddenly she got it: that wasn't Zephyr. This was Wisper, using a face that she thought Clarity would recognize as hers.

Damned robots with their hand-me-down faces.

"Hey, I, uh, have a message from my ship that I need to deal with," Clarity said. "Is it okay if I catch up with you?"

Anna shrugged and climbed into the tunnel herself. "Pull the tile back into place when you do, okay?"

"Sure. Am I... gonna get lost in there?"

"Naw," Anna said. "The path is pretty straightforward—only one way out, and that's into the bio lab." With that, the small human woman disappeared into the dark tunnel under the desk.

15. THE GHOST IN THE RESEARCH INSTITUTE

Alone in a Wespirtech chemistry laboratory, Clarity stepped up close to the computer screen with Wisper's old robot face pictured on it. She said aloud, "I assume you can hear me?" She glanced around the lab, trying to figure out where there might be speakers or microphones to pick up her voice or possibly broadcast Wisper's voice back to her.

There was machinery everywhere. Clarity had no idea how much of it could be listening to her. Or which parts could talk to her.

But instead of speaking aloud, the image of Wisper's old, robotic face—now Zephyr's face—disappeared from the computer screen and was replaced with scrolling text: "It's nice to meet you in person, Clarity."

"This is 'in person'?" Clarity asked, before realizing that it might be an insensitive thing to say. She knew that Wisper—this Wisper, anyway—thought of Wespirtech itself as her body. And was it really so different, talking to Wisper like this than talking to Cassie from inside of her?

"Yes," Wisper answered in text. "I'm here, all around you." Machines around the room beeped, blinked, whirred, and hummed, just enough to call attention to themselves. Then they stopped. And the text began scrolling again: "If you were in the robotics lab, I could use arms and legs and heads with faces to communicate non-verbally with you."

Clarity tried to imagine an entire laboratory of disembodied robot parts—like in Maradia's workspace—emoting at her, somehow believing that it was a helpful way for them to communicate. Suddenly, Cassie's collection of video clips and word clouds seemed extremely familiar and friendly... and a great deal less like a horror movie than what Wisper was suggesting.

"That's fine," Clarity said. "I mean, this is fine. I'm used to talking to Cassie this way. Except, she's more likely to use word clouds than complete sentences... Complete sentences are nice."

"Yes, I agree," Wisper wrote on the screen. "My consciousness was trained originally on a large databank of academic papers, followed by novels and other fictional works, and eventually entertainment videos and free-form conversational forums. But I learned from academic papers and novels first, and in those formats, clearly structured, grammatical sentences compose the majority of the content. As such, complete sentences are my native language."

Clarity didn't know what to say to that. She didn't know what to say to Wisper at all. The AI had arranged for them to come here safely and had paid them all handsomely for participating in her plans for saving the universe; she was even playing the role of Irohann's digital patron saint, making sure his current identity would never become connected to his old identity that was known as a traitor to the Queen of the Doraspians.

But...

Clarity had more in common with Cassie—another organic lifeform with a single, mortal body—than an AI who could inhabit a robotics laboratory, or a moon full of laboratories, or copy herself onto the computers of a research extension base, or prune herself down to become small enough to fit into a single maintenance robot.

Wisper could consume entire databanks of academic papers and novels. Clarity had to read books one at a time, because she got lost and confused sometimes if she tried to switch between two novels at once. Clarity's brain had a certain linearity that Wisper's code didn't seem to require.

Clarity didn't know why Wisper wanted to talk to her. She wasn't sure if she and Wisper had anything in common at all. Except, apparently, for believing it was better if the universe didn't get destroyed.

Clarity supposed that she could work with that common interest, and she said, "So, how goes your mission of keeping the scientists here from destroying the universe?"

"It is challenging," Wisper typed onto the screen matter-of-factly.

Clarity drew a deep breath, startled by Wisper's answer.

Clarity remembered Anna locking that prism securely in a drawer and the way the physicist had turned ultra-serious when the colors it cast had changed in response to Genniperri.

The prism had altered light waves, converting them into different forms. Could light waves be entangled... and then dangerously unentangled... like particles could?

"I don't like that answer," Clarity said. "In fact, I dislike it very much." She wondered—to herself; she knew better than to say it out loud—whether the whole facility, all of Wespirtech and all of its extension basses—should be shut down.

"Humans are good at disliking things," Wisper observed. "Liking and disliking things seems to be one of their most basic functions. However, rarely does the fact that humans dislike something affect whether that thing is true, and it only affects whether something will happen if time, effort, and research are devoted to stopping it."

Of course, a research institute's inhabiting spirit would believe in the importance of research.

Of course.

"For instance," Wisper continued, "humans dislike dying, and so they put a lot of research into expanding their life spans, and they've had a moderate amount of success—"

Clarity shifted uncomfortably, moving her weight from one foot to the other as she read the words on the screen. It troubled her that Wisper was, essentially, talking about the search for immortality, and Clarity was harboring a secret about actual immortality. But there was no way for Wisper to know her secret. The AI could not read minds; she could barely read facial expressions.

Unless... Wisper had picked up on the subtle effects that Genniperri's presence had on the various physics and chemistry experiments. But then, maybe Clarity had only imagined them. She hoped she'd been imagining them.

Wisper forged on: "Despite their best research attempts though, after a couple of hundred years, humans do still die. Similarly, the sun in this star system will die and expand into a red giant in three billion years, destroying everything of value to humans in this system. Unless, that is, my researchers find a way to stop it. Three billion years may sound like a long time to you, but I fully intend to still be alive then, in some form, and I would like to be able to keep the descendants of the organic lifeforms that I've taken an interest in alive as well. Sometimes, this means I must allow them to take their research in dangerous directions. Only with risk comes great payoff."

Clarity tilted her head, trying to process all of Wisper's words that had streamed a little too rapidly across the computer screen. She felt a bit like a pet dog trying to understand an ancient gramophone playing a human's voice. Wisper was thinking on time scales that hadn't even occurred to her, making plans to protect descendants that Clarity had never even imagined. "I'm... sorry?" she offered. "I didn't mean to suggest you were being short-sighted or cavalier." Although, that was actually exactly what she had meant.

"Apology accepted," Wisper typed. "Also, unnecessary."

"Because... I didn't hurt your feelings?" Clarity asked. After all of the time she'd spent with the other incarnation of Wisper, and now Zephyr, she was pretty sure that Wisper—even this Wisper—

had feelings, even if those feelings were too amorphous and arcane for Clarity to understand them. Or hurt them.

"Because I am out of practice talking to humans," Wisper said. "Usually I only observe them and alter their environment in ways that will indirectly affect and manipulate them. I should have known better than to be completely honest. I should have known that my answer would disturb and frighten you. I will do better."

Was the AI that inhabited the most powerful research institute in this corner of the galaxy admitting, straight-forwardly to Clarity that she was going to start lying to her? Ostensibly for her own good?

Clarity stared at the screen, waiting for Wisper to realize that she had done it again, already. Been too honest. Too forthright.

Instead, the previous words disappeared from the screen and were replaced with a simple sentence: "It is nice to have someone to talk to who knows what I am." A few beats later, Wisper added, "You organic lifeforms always undervalue the complexity of the skills required for interacting with you socially."

This was getting awkward. As far as Clarity could tell, Wisper was talking to her merely out of loneliness. She wanted to be nice to this AI who had the power to erase all of her money from the digital systems where it existed and flag her entire crew as criminals for the rest of their lives. Instead, she poked it: "Why can't you talk to the scientists here and have them know what you are?"

This time, Wisper seemed to have learned her lesson about being too open and honest. She didn't answer. She changed the subject. "I observed your message to your friend Am-lei," she said, "and I hope you don't mind that I took the liberty of directing some of the scientists here to work on the problem you posed. Indirectly, of course. It wouldn't do for any of the scientists to know why they were studying the phenomenon. In fact, I also took the precaution of removing your message from Am-lei's account before she had the chance to access it. It's safer that way."

Well, maybe Wisper had answered Clarity's question after all.

If the AI was intercepting private messages and moving money around—making Cassie's crew look like philanthropists and manipulating scientists to work on different projects with the lure of grant money—then she probably wouldn't enjoy the kind of oversight and limitations that would be placed on her if any of the scientists here actually knew about her.

Huh, Clarity had more power over Wisper than she'd realized. One word from her about Wisper's illicit behaviors—or rather, mere existence—and the AI might find herself firewalled out of her usual playgrounds.

That is, assuming anyone believed Clarity, and she was pretty sure that Wisper could flag all of the philanthropic donations that had supposedly been made in Clarity's name as illegal and stolen before... well, anything. Wisper could probably do it in the blink of a human's eye.

Yeah, Clarity still didn't want to cross Wisper. She wanted to be nice to the big, scary AI. "Thank you for setting us up as philanthropists," she said, avoiding the new topic that Wisper had brought up. She wanted to be nice, but she still couldn't quite bring herself to pretend to sound happy about Wisper intercepting and snooping through her private messages.

At least, now Clarity knew why she hadn't heard back from Am-lei.

"Yes, yes, of course," Wisper typed out on the screen, managing to convey her impatience with Clarity's dodge through pure-text. "It was the easiest way to fulfill my promise of delivering sub-sentient maintenance creatures to *Cassiopeia* that are designed to match the aesthetic qualities of Earth-dwelling rabbits. A frivolous request. But don't you want to know what my scientists have learned regarding the blip of light that bounced back out of the Devil's Radio?"

Clarity's fingertips and toes went numb, and her head felt light. Her vision wobbled a little, as if it had come unhinged from reality. She most certainly did not want Wisper to talk to her about physics irregularities involving the Devil's Radio. The last time that had happened, she'd found herself in charge of a near-suicide mission to save the universe by watching it crack apart around her.

"That message was private," Clarity mumbled.

Several machines around the room blinked green lights or suddenly hummed for a beat. It was eerie. Like Wisper was trying to imitate a human rolling her eyes or shrugging or who-knows-what, because humans don't have piles of machinery with blinking lights and humming mechanisms to communicate with. They just have faces. And shoulders. And an ability to exist entirely in one body, at one time, without copying themselves into other bodies or taking over research institutes from the inside of the computers.

"Fine," Clarity said, wrapping her arms tightly around her middle, trying to subdue the waves of anxiety that she felt washing over her. "Tell me what you found out and then send me on some terrifying mission to the unraveling edge of the universe."

"What?" Wisper said. "Humans can be so dramatic. The universe is fine. But it does seem to have become entangled with another universe."

"A-another universe?" Clarity dug her fingertips into her sides, tightening her own grip around herself and trying to ground herself to reality with the pain of her fingernails biting through the soft fabric of her pastel blazer. She wished her fingernails were claws like Irohann's or had keratinous tips like Oksana's so that they would hurt more, and thus distract her more from the idea of dealing with an entire other universe having become entangled with her own. "What does that even mean?" she asked, voice faltering. "*Entangled universes*? How can two universes—it's only two, right?—how can two universes become entangled with each other?"

"Most likely, the Merlin Particle that was originally placed in the Devil's Radio traveled through the black hole from our universe to another one, and it got snagged, such that when its matching entangled particle was returned to it—by being placed in the Devil's Radio as well—the tears in space-time that the two of them had ripped open connected the two universes, and the tears in the fabric remain, even though the needle that ripped them has been removed."

This was literally Clarity's worst fear realized. Wisper was telling her that the horror of the universe cracking around her hadn't ended yet. Events that had seemed to be over were continuing, ongoing, hidden in the fabric of the universe all around her. Clarity shivered.

"Of course, obviously, the metaphor about ripping fabric and entangled particles being a needle is merely a way to describe incredibly complicated physics concepts to a layperson who lacks the mathematical training to understand the actual situation."

Apparently, Wisper was still struggling with how honest she should be.

"So, what do we do?" Clarity asked in a small voice. "How do we... sew it back together? Do we need another pair of entangled particles, or would that make it worse?"

Clarity wished that there was somewhere she could go to avoid this problem. A safe place in the universe, where she could live out her life without being forced to remember that the fabric of existence itself could come apart at the seams all around her.

But that was the problem.

The whole universe, all of it, was far less stable and permanent than she had imagined. Blissfully imagined. She missed the ignorance.

"Nothing," Wisper said. The word hung on the screen. Just the one word. "Nothing." Wisper's previous explanation of how Clarity wasn't smart enough to understand the situation without metaphors had already scrolled away, and that single word hung in the black space of the screen like a benediction.

Whatever was happening to the universe, Wisper didn't think that it was Clarity's problem to solve. "So... you have your scientists working on it?" she hazarded. "And they'll fix it without Cassie's crew this time?

"No," Wisper said. "I didn't say that you'd do nothing. We all do nothing. The universe will heal. Give it time."

"That... is a huge relief," Clarity said, ready to fall over from the weight of the entire universe having been lifted off of her shoulders. She reached out to the nearest work table and laid a hand on its surface, steadying herself. "It will really heal on its own?"

Clarity jumped, startled as all of the machines around the room blinked, beeped, and buzzed again. Wisper shrugging at her, Clarity supposed.

The next words on the computer screen were: "Time will tell, but I'm not worried. There is no reason that I know of to worry."

Clarity might know a reason to worry. Wisper was the smartest being she knew, so it seemed unwise to keep pertinent secrets from the AI. But then Clarity didn't know how much she could trust Wisper.

The AI clearly had a completely different sense of time scale and danger than any human could. Wisper was willing and able to copy a subset of herself into being the living incarnation of a suicide mission. She was able to look at a mission that involved a half dozen lives and make decisions based on slim probabilities, weighing those half dozen lives against an entire universe. Clarity didn't think that she could do something like that, even if the whole existence of the universe—and every life inside it—was being weighed in the balance.

Yet Genniperri's life truly was tangled up in the knotty jumble that the universe had become when it entangled with another universe. How could she weigh the balance between an abstract universe full of sentient peoples and the individual life of one person that she knew? And would betraying Genniperri's confidence and revealing her secret make a difference? Could it save lives? Or only endanger hers and Paurizau's?

How do you look at someone you know and choose to sacrifice them—right then and there, in front of you—in order to save abstract millions of billions?

How do you even understand the idea of millions of billions?

But Wisper could understand those concepts, and the AI couldn't make informed decisions if she weren't fully informed.

"I know something that didn't make it into my letter to Amlei," Clarity said. She still wasn't sure that she should tell Wisper about Genniperri and her seeming immortality. She had sworn that they shouldn't tell the Wespirtech scientists. Was it better or worse to tell Wespirtech herself?

Clarity couldn't risk the possibility that Genniperri's condition was indicative of a larger problem, something in the ripped fabric of the universe that meant it wouldn't heal. Or would stop it from healing.

Clarity explained everything that she knew about Genniperri and Paurizau—how each of them had stopped aging, how they'd come together and pinpointed the Devil's Radio as the source of their strange circumstances, and how the Devil's Radio had spat them back out, defying everything that Clarity knew about physics.

When Clarity had finished talking, she watched the computer screen, hoping for reassuring words. Words that meant she didn't need to worry. Words that meant Genniperri's condition didn't imply a catastrophic failure in the universe. Even a few blinks or beeps from the machines around the room would have been welcome to her now. Instead, the screen stayed dark, and the machines stayed damningly quiet.

AIs think faster than humans; especially an AI like Wisper who had access to every research computer in the entirety of Wespirtech to do her processing for her. Clarity had only her one, squishy, lumpy, fleshy brain. When an AI like Wisper paused long enough for a human like Clarity to notice it, they must be thinking really hard.

The longer the pause went on, the more Clarity's thoughts turned inward on themselves, imagining the universe breaking into pieces around the fulcrum of two sentient shrubberies who had the audacity to become immortal.

To stop the universe from breaking apart, Clarity would have murdered those shrubberies herself.

Maybe, maybe she could balance an individual life against the weight of all the lives in the universe after all.

Or maybe, she was just really selfish and didn't want to experience existential pain again, and she'd trade whole lives to protect herself.

Eventually, words appeared, haltingly, on the computer screen: "This explains the anomalous readings that have been occurring in every laboratory Genniperri enters. More study will be required."

Ah, so Clarity hadn't been imaging the strange effects that Genniperri had been having on the physics and chemistry equipment. "I'm not turning Genniperri and Paurizau over to your scientists," Clarity said, contradicting all of her own thoughts from only moments ago. She was glad that Wisper couldn't see into her head and observe how much of a mess it was in there. "I've seen what the Aether Gaia base has done to Cassie and her kin. I've experienced the pain first hand through sharing my mind with that sweet, innocent starwhal." Sweet and innocent, yes, but also a pain in the brain when she got stubborn.

"I could mark your donations as stolen and alert my scientists to the oddity of their Dorsaspian guest," Wisper threatened.

"And I could tell them that you exist," Clarity countered.

"A stand-off," Wisper typed.

"Yes."

"Perhaps a smaller threat would be more effective," Wisper suggested. "I could alter the atmosphere in the sub-sentient maintenance rabbits' hutch and suffocate them. You would not get what you came here for."

Clarity was shocked, though maybe she shouldn't have been. "Are you... threatening to murder innocent, harmless bunnies? Seriously?"

"I can't protect the universe from problems that I don't understand," Wisper said.

"Would cutting off Genniperri's leaves and dissecting them really help you to protect the universe?" Clarity asked.

"Maybe," Wisper answered. Notably, she didn't deny that cutting off leaves and dissecting them was what her scientists would do. "I won't know for sure until my scientists try."

"Isn't there anything else—anything less... invasive and painful—that you could try instead?" Clarity asked.

This time, Wisper's answer came back more quickly than Clarity expected, given its content: "Your point is fair. Having reached out and accessed all of the historical and biographical archives I could find related to Genniperri and Paurizau, including all of their private messages and journals"—she really didn't know when to keep information to herself—" I've ascertained the most likely points in space-time when each of them underwent their transformation. It is unfortunate that they must have miscalculated the proper time for them to enter the Devil's Radio. If they had flown into its event horizon at precisely the same time as you successfully returned the Merlin Particle to its partner, then they most likely would have been crushed to death, and we wouldn't have to deal with the uncertainties surrounding this problem."

"Life is full of uncertainties," Clarity observed wryly.

"Yes," Wisper agreed. "It is. And you are correct: I am uncertain that examining the affected Doraspians would make a difference in the outcome of these circumstances. There is a 95% chance that regardless of the outcome of the research, that the best course of action would be for the affected individuals to return to the site of their original entanglement."

"What do you mean?" Clarity asked. "They can't travel back in time, c-can they? Is time travel possible?" The universe made no sense to Clarity anymore.

"Time travel is irrelevant," Wisper said, which didn't address the question of whether it was possible at all. "The damage that the Merlin Particles wrought on our universe—and whichever universe had the misfortune of becoming entangled with ours—exists outside the space-time continuum that we live inside of. It supersedes our entire experience of space and time."

"What does that *mean* though?" Clarity missed the sewing metaphors. She didn't like that she wasn't smart enough to get by talking to Wisper without them. But dang, a good sewing metaphor really makes high-level physics easier to understand. And Clarity didn't even know how to sew. She'd seen her dad mend a few pieces of favorite clothing and stitch up some simple pieces of doll clothes for her collection of plushies when she'd been a child, but that was about it.

All of those pieces of doll clothes had been destroyed, along with the plush animals wearing them, when *The Serendipity* had been ripped to pieces. Clarity hadn't expected a discussion of physics with the AI inhabiting Wespirtech to remind her of everything she'd lost when she'd lost her ship—those pieces of doll clothes had been some of her last connections to the world and family where she'd grown up. She didn't need or want to be thinking about them now.

Grief was weird, how it could creep up on you, pouncing at the most unexpected times.

"The phenomenon that Genniperri experienced in her youth, the similar phenomenon that Paurizau experienced on his deathbed, and the various cracks in space-time that you've encountered, Clarity, are all different protrusions of the same extra-universal event, encroaching into our space-time."

"You mean, they all happened at the same time?"

"No. In no way do I mean that."

Clarity stared at the screen. The screen stared back at her, stubbornly failing to add any words that might actually be helpful.

"The same space-time?" Clarity hazarded.

"Quite the opposite, actually."

Clarity frowned.

"They're all the same event, but that event is occurring simultaneously at a range of different space-time locations in our universe."

Well, that was almost helpful.

"So, will there be more of them?" Clarity wished the answer would be "no," but she didn't think they'd be having this conversation if that were the case.

"Yes," Wisper said. "And I believe you and *Cassiopeia* should take the two affected Doraspians to the nearest possible space-time occurrence."

"Meaning one in the future."

"Yes, unless you have a time travel device that I'm not aware of," Wisper said, possibly in an attempt at humor. There was no way for Clarity to tell for sure. At any rate, the AI's attempt at levity failed to lighten the weight of the situation. "I can provide you with the most likely coordinates. I'm already in the process of calculating its location, and the calculations should be finished before your crew is ready to depart from this system."

Clarity nodded. She didn't trust herself to speak. Words felt so far away right now. All she had was a deep well of feelings, telling her that cracks in the universe were meant to be ran from, not traveled toward.

But she'd taken on the responsibility of healing the damage done to the universe by the Merlin Particles, although she'd played no part in creating them, and that work, apparently, wasn't done.

Finally, she pulled herself together enough to say, "Send the coordinates to Cassie when you have them. Is there anything else you wanted to say or tell me? Because I should probably be catching up with my group, before that physicist gets suspicious."

"Don't worry about Anna," Wisper said. "I've distracted her from your disappearance with several minor, unimportant, but irritating equipment failures with the systems that she's trying to show off to your friends. Most recently, I opened the door to the sub-sentient maintenance rabbits' hutch, and the whole group has been chasing the animals around the biology lab atmo-dome, trying to re-catch them all. Your disappearance is the last thing on any of their minds."

"Oh, well, thank you," Clarity said.

Research institute-sized AIs certainly kept one on their toes—Wisper could oscillate between saving the universe, threatening to destroy Clarity personally, and hassling a scientist by releasing the bunnies from their science project in a single human heartbeat. At least, that's how it seemed to the human whose heart was beating.

Clarity took a step toward the open panel in the floor, but a final sentence appeared on the computer screen, catching her eye right before she turned away.

"Thank you for talking with me," Wisper said, a strangely simple and touching thing to say in response to such a fraught conversation.

The two of them had threatened each other with mutual destruction and brainstormed how to save the universe. Clarity had found the whole ordeal exhausting. But Wisper... was simply happy to have had a conversation with someone.

"You're welcome," Clarity said, remembering her manners. "Thank you for... everything you've done for us."

16. DOWN THE RABBIT HOLE, BACK WITH RABBITS

Once Clarity had climbed into the tunnel between the chemistry lab and the bio lab atmo-dome, she didn't want to leave. It was dark and cramped after she pulled the tile back into its place over her head, barely enough space to stand. Irohann must have had to hunch over, especially with those new antlers.

Clarity felt safe in the dark, tight space, whether or not she actually was. After a few minutes of breathing deeply in the musty, dusty air of the tunnel, she convinced herself to creep forward through the narrow passage, taking small careful steps, so she wouldn't trip over anything in the dark.

A buzzing in the air beside Clarity let her know that Mazillion was with her. They'd probably been there for her entire conversation with Wisper. She wondered what the swarm alien had thought of it.

Only a few footsteps ahead, Clarity noticed twinkling lights strung along the edges of the corridor ahead. The ground was smooth and flat, so she could take larger, less cautious steps.

The walls were covered in graffiti—scrawls of mathematical equations, notes addressed to people she didn't know, and more in-jokes, like on the door to the physics lab pressed close to her on both sides. Every inch was packed with scrawled messages, incomprehensible to Clarity but clearly dripping with meaning to the scientists who lived and worked here.

Clarity felt like she'd left Willy Wonka's chocolate factory and gone down the rabbit hole to Wonderland.

The effect was magnified when she walked out of the tunnel and found she'd emerged from a doorway set into the gently sloping side of hill. Green grass stretched out all around her, and the night sky, filled with stars, stretched out above, behind the tessellated, triangular windows of an atmo-dome.

Adorable, hoppy bunnies in all shades of brown, gray, and white gamboled over the grassy hillside, doing their best to escape the grasping hands of Anna, another human woman who Clarity hadn't met yet, and all of her crewmates that had come down to Wespirtech for the tour.

Irohann looked hilarious chasing after the little bunnies with his hulking size and incongruous antlers. The bunnies didn't seem especially fond of the idea of a giant wolf man catching them and scattered wherever he ran; they had a similar reaction to T'resso, seemingly not interested in being caught in the talons of a giant, blue reptile either.

Teya looked a little too much like the bunnies, and that made her look like an ancient Earth cartoon character somehow—Goofy chasing after Pluto. Genniperri was especially bizarre, running around on her robotic legs and trying to wrap twisty vines around the bunnies, many of whom managed to slip away from her plant-like machinations, but the others wiggled, wrapped in her vines, like strange, fluffy balls of fruit.

Oksana was having the most luck. She wasn't chasing the bunnies. She'd merely sat down on the hillside and spread out her digitigrade legs, hooves together and knees wide, like a corral for the bunnies. Every time a bunny hopped by her, she grabbed it around the middle, lifted it up, and put the fuzzy bundle with the growing collection of other bunnies between her knees. Once trapped, the bunnies seemed content to groom their ears and wiggle their noses. The ungulate seemed to have a calming presence on the sub-sentient creatures.

Goodness, Cassie was gonna love these things.

Clarity got into the spirit and sat down on the hill beside Oksana. She wasn't as good at catching the bunnies as the ungulate was, but she managed to catch a few. They were warm, wiggly puffs, fur as smooth as silk. Once Clarity had a trio of them trapped, she picked up a spotted brown-and-white one, and she held it up in front of her face. Nose to nose with a sub-sentient maintenance bunny. She couldn't help but smile at the bunny's charmingly twitchy nose, and its glossy brown eyes reflected the stretch of green hillside and black sky.

"You're going to be perfect for Cassie," Clarity said to the bunny.

The bunny twitched an ear, but it didn't offer any other response.

Sub-sentient. Clarity wondered how complex their minds were —would they be able to bond emotionally with people who cared for them? How much caretaking would they need? Hopefully not much, given that the idea was that these bunnies would be maintenance creatures and help keep Cassie's internal organs clean and healthy.

Eventually, Anna and the other human woman gave up on chasing the bunnies around themselves and carried a large crate over to where Oksana and Clarity sat. They set the crate down and then took the bunnies that were nestled around Oksana and Clarity, one by one, and placed them back in their hutch.

Genniperri brought over her collection of wiggling bunnies, who looked much less happy about being wrapped in vines and carried around than the rabbits who'd been caught by Oksana. T'resso had given up catching bunnies of his own and stood beside his Doraspian ward; the bunnies wrapped in her branches nearest to him wriggled the most.

In contrast, the ungulate's collection of bunnies looked like they'd be perfectly happy to stay with her forever and consider the goat-horned girl to be their surrogate mother and permanent caretaker.

Irohann brought over the one lone bunny that he'd managed to snatch, clasped firmly in his big paws—it had glossy, ebony fur and looked like it had given up on life when the giant red wolf had caught it. When it got close to the hutch filled with other bunnies, the black bunny struggled and practically leapt out of Irohann's paws, back into the safety of its cage and the company of the others.

Irohann sat down on the hillside, beside Clarity. His tail was swishing, suggesting he'd had fun chasing the bunnies, even if he'd been remarkably ineffective at catching them. "You missed out on seeing the tabby cats—an Earth animal, apparently—that had their fur programmed to change colors and bioluminesce. Apparently, T'resso's scales can change color a little, because the S'rellick seemed to get into some sort of visual conversation with the cat, each of them changing their colors in reaction to the other." He tilted his head, looking at Clarity, making his antlers list dangerously to the side. "You know, I bet it's possible to get a gene-mod like that. You'd look good with glowing rainbow hair."

Clarity reached up automatically to touch the photosynthetic hair that fell around her shoulders. "I'm happy with green, thank you."

Irohann shrugged.

Oksana said, "You also missed out on a machine that lets you mind meld with a slug."

The ungulate sounded excited about that, but all Clarity could think of was how exhausting it had been lately to deal with piloting Cassie and sharing her mind with the giant, emotionally complicated starwhal. She didn't feel the need share her mind with a creature in the other direction—small, simple. She shuddered and noticed that Irohann looked equally discomfited by the idea. "Did you try that machine?" Clarity asked

Irohann shook his head. "No, I don't need to share my mind with anyone, let alone a slug."

"It was really relaxing," Oksana said. "So simple. No words. Few worries. Just... existing." Her long face went all dreamy and soft; she looked peaceful just remembering it.

Clarity still shuddered.

Oksana saw that her description wasn't landing, so she added, "You know, like floating in space—nothing weighing you down."

"Gah," Clarity said, actual words not being enough to express her distaste and discomfort at that idea. "Apparently, floating at the edge of a black hole didn't faze you nearly enough," she said. "Because, as I recall, that's where I first met you, and floating in space is freakin' *dangerous*."

Oksana shrugged and continued petting the bunnies on her lap that hadn't been dumped into their hutch yet. Tough keratinous fingertips stroked gently over silky, downy fur. She lifted one of the bunnies up, and as the ungulate stared deep into the sub-sentient rabbit's eyes, she said, "I wouldn't mind using that machine on you—knowing what it feels like to twitch your nose and cuddle up beside all your friends. You have a pretty good life, don't you?"

The sub-sentient maintenance rabbit didn't answer.

Oksansa continued, "And I know you don't understand this, but we're going to take you to live inside a giant animal who flies through space, and you're going to help take care of her! Her name is Cassie, and even though she hasn't met you yet, I'm told that she already loves you—and all of your friends—very, very much. She's a really kind and generous creature, and you're going to need to take good care of her, because she's going to take good care of you, and keep you safe from the dangerous vacuum of space that Clarity here fears so much."

Clarity sniffed. She wasn't afraid of the vacuum of space. She was afraid of being trapped in that vacuum forever.

She was afraid of... forever.

Clarity looked at Genniperri, relieved of her burden of wiggling bunny-fruits now, and thought about how frightening and upsetting it must be to live with the weight of eternity resting on your... well, not shoulders. Branches.

Clarity thought she would crack under that weight, but then, she supposed, eventually she'd have to pull herself back together and keep moving on. What other choice would there be?

She was glad it was Genniperri and Paurizau facing the burden, and not her. She was standing outside the vortex of cracks that the Merlin Particle had wrought on the universe, but the two Doraspians were already sucked in. She didn't know if she could pull them out and save them when, hopefully, she saved the rest of the universe from following after them.

But maybe it would be a relief to them... to die. Clarity wasn't sure how old Genniperri was by now, but apparently Paurizau had already been on his deathbed when this happened. Was he relieved to become suddenly immortal? Or would he be relieved to have the immortality come to an end?

Was immortality a reprieve? Or an endless nightmare?

Irohann leaned against Clarity, jostling her shoulder with his fuzzy orange one. "Hey," he said, "you look like you disappeared somewhere deep."

"I did," Clarity agreed.

"Is something going on?" He sounded worried, and his tail had stopped swishing from the fun of bunny-chasing.

"Yeah," Clarity said. "I can't tell you about it now. Here. But... yeah."

He nodded. His orange-furred muzzle had tautened into a serious expression. "Whatever it is," he said, "we'll take care of it. We've already faced the end of the universe. What could be worse than that?" He smiled, but Clarity couldn't smile back at him. He'd put his paw directly on the problem, and he saw that in her face. He must have, because he said, "Oh, okay. Well..."

What can you say to learning that the universe hasn't finished breaking apart? He looked scared. Clarity certainly was.

Anna and the other scientist, presumably a biologist, finished putting the bunnies in their hutch, leaving Clarity and Oksana's laps bereft of the warm, cuddly presences. The universe might be quaking, out there in the reaches of space, tangled up with another universe, and threatening to fall apart or smash together, or whatever two universes do when they get entangled... but right now, right here, Clarity was really looking forward to giving this hutch full of bunnies to Cassie. They would make the big, young-hearted starwhal happy, and sometimes, making someone else happy—even for a minute—is enough.

Enough to hold on to.

Enough to look forward to.

Enough to keep you going, keep you fighting, keep you doing what needs to be done.

Anna introduced Clarity to the other scientist, Keida, who was indeed a biologist and who had designed Cassie's sub-sentient maintenance bunnies. Keida talked about the many changes she'd had to make to the underlying design—which hadn't evolved to live inside a starwhal and apparently had looked more like a guinea pig by default.

Since guinea pigs are basically round lumps of fuzz, Keida had needed to extrude their ears and enlarge their hind legs. Keida seemed to have a lot of thoughts about how these changes had actually benefited the functionality of the sub-sentient maintenance creatures in ways that she hadn't expected, and she thanked Clarity profusely for the—apparently—insightful suggestion to make them look like bunnies.

When Keida got to asking about what had inspired the suggestion, Clarity was saved from answering the awkward question by a chime from her pocket computer. She didn't really want to talk to a Wespirtech biologist about Cassie and how the other Wespirtech scientists at the Aether Gaia extension base had trained an impressionable young starwhal to love bunnies, using cute videos as positive reinforcement during training; Clarity thought she might get very mad, very fast if she did so, and probably say more than she meant to or should.

Clarity asked for a minute, to check if the message was important, and stepped a few feet away on the grassy hillside to look at the message with a modicum of privacy. When she looked at the screen and saw Zephyr's face, she wasn't sure if the call was from Zephyr zirself calling from onboard Cassie, or Wisper again, using Zepyhr's hand-me-down face.

Then the robot face spoke, and Clarity could immediately tell the difference.

"I hope all y'all are having fun on your tour of the big ol' science factory, but Cassie received a weird message just now and thought I should pass it along to you. Although, the old bunny man with a headache didn't think I should bother you all. He seems very concerned with Teya making a good impression over there and doesn't want me to mess anything up for her, but I don't think she wants to be a scientist. Or would be a very good one... That girl is way too reckless for a research lab."

Clarity couldn't argue with that.

"I think her boldness might make her a good pilot though," Zephyr added, apparently having already picked a side in the political schisms happening within Cassie's crew.

"Hi, Zephyr," Clarity said. "What's the message?"

"Well, it's basically just a set of space-time coordinates—deep in Doraspian space, approximately two weeks from now."

Clarity's head pounded. Two weeks. That was soon. And Doraspian space was somewhere they didn't want to go. She and Irohann had been avoiding it for decades.

"Can we... get there in time?" she asked. *And could they get back out safely?*

"Roscoe says we could, but he doesn't think it's a good idea." Zephyr's expression was blank. Zir face wasn't built to communicate expressively, but Clarity suspected the robot would have looked noncommittal right now anyway. "I don't know what the coordinates are for, but I'm up for whatever you think is best."

Wow, that was a pretty clear expression of loyalty. Clarity wasn't used to the kind of trust that the other members of Cassie's crew—other than Roscoe—had been placing in her lately. She wasn't exactly sure what she'd done to earn it. As far as she could tell, any reasonable person who'd found themselves in the situations she'd been in would have done the same, or maybe better. Regardless, she hoped she was worthy of the others' trust and loyalty. She would try to be.

"Thanks, Zephyr," Clarity said. "Did you get all of the cargo off-loaded yet?"

"Ages ago," Zephyr said. "Eons really. It's like you've all been gone for several lifetimes, and my Starsplosions & Spacedroids game is just *waiting* for you to bring my players back."

Clarity smiled at the pocket computer. "I'll do what I can to wrap this up and get your players back to you."

Zephyr tilted zir head slightly, causing the pink light aboard Cassie to gleam off different parts of her metal face and glassy eyes. Zhe said, "Acknowledged, Captain Clarity. Over and out."

Well, that was new. Clarity hadn't asked anyone to call her captain. She liked it better from Zephyr, voluntarily given, than when Roscoe had told her that she seemed to see herself that way.

Clarity put her pocket computer away and rejoined the others, who were mostly gathered around the hutch, cooing and oohing and ahhing over the adorable animals.

"Is there anything that we need to know about these animals before we take them?" Clarity asked, directing the question to Keida, since she was the biologist who had designed them.

"They're designed to be self-sufficient when living aboard the inside of a cybernetically adapted starwhal," Keida said. "Like gut flora and other micro-organisms that live inside of human and other"—Keida gestured at the other aliens who'd come into Wespirtech from Cassie—"macrobiotic lifeforms."

That description of Cassie—"cybernetically adapted"—made Clarity's jaw tighten. She wanted to show this scientist exactly what Cassie had felt when she'd been *adapted*, but she also wanted to get out of here, quickly and without breaking the cover story of being eccentric philanthropists that Wisper had so helpfully woven for them.

Clarity didn't especially like the way that Keida had lumped all non-human aliens into the category of "other" either. She wouldn't be sorry to leave this place, in spite of all its wonders.

"Thank you," Clarity said tightly. "I think it's time for us to take them back to our *ship* then." It was so hard for her to not lecture this woman who looked about her own age, on the effects that her research was having on real, living, feeling individuals like Cassie. But then, Wisper knew. And Wisper was directing the research here.

It was definitely time to go. Maybe, once the universe was saved—again, this time from entangling itself with another universe—there would be time and attention to spare for problems like how Wespirtech and its extension bases were treating Cassie's kin.

Because Clarity had no confidence that Wisper had followed through with their arrangement and released all of the *cybernetically adapted* starwhals. If she had, then why would Keida still be working on designing self-sufficient, sub-sentient maintenance creatures for them?

At her most optimistic, Clarity could hope that now that the sub-sentient maintenance bunnies were nearly in Cassie's possession, Wisper would start the process of ending all of the exploitative research concerning the transformation of starwhals into spaceships without their consent.

Clarity wasn't really feeling that optimistic though. Not after learning that the universe was still trying to destroy itself, in spite of her previous best efforts to stop it.

"Wait," Anna said, closing the lid on the bunnies' hutch. "Are you saying that you're ready to leave? Because there's a whole fancy brunch and spiel that the administrators wanted to give you, and they're not going to be happy with me if I let you leave before they've even woken up."

Somehow, that didn't bother Clarity much. Maybe her anger was misplaced on these specific human scientists. It had been different scientists who had hurt Cassie. But she was still angry, and she didn't need to waste time on some kind of fancy brunch, even if she did find herself disturbingly curious about what they'd be serving... Food is always more exciting when it's free.

Besides, it was safer to get Genniperri far, far away from Wespirtech before the scientists noticed the strange, subtle effects of her presence. Wisper had already noticed them. The scientists couldn't be too far behind.

"I'm terribly sorry," Clarity said, "but yes, we must go." What would an eccentric philanthropist say? What kind of emergencies called them suddenly away from their fancy brunches? "I got a message from my ship, and there's a, uh, financial crisis with... some of our... investments. We need to check on them. Immediately."

Anna and Keida looked nonplussed by Clarity's vague excuse. She wondered if it would have played better or worse to the administrators. She got the sense that the administrators did more in terms of actually handling the money, so they'd probably care more about a supposed financial crisis, but that meant they'd also be more likely to ask uncomfortable questions.

Keida just shrugged and said, "I wouldn't want to waste time at one of the fundraiser brunches either, if I had a choice."

Anna frowned, but she didn't really have a way to keep Clarity and the others here. So, she acquiesced and helped them figure out the operating controls on the bunnies' hutch. Once the hutch was floating on its anti-grav skis, she guided them back toward the passageway of airlocks where Cassie was still docked. They took the long way, though, staying in the normal halls and corridors of Wespirtech instead of delving into the darkness of the secret passage again.

As they walked through the halls, Clarity noticed tiny buzzing bodies—Mazillion's scouts—returning and subtly hiding among Genniperri's leaves and flowers. She wondered what Mazillion had learned during their unguided tour of the facility. She wondered if Mazillion would share what they'd learned.

Wait. Had all of Mazillion's scout bodies returned? Or would a fraction of them—possibly even a self-sustaining fraction of them —stay here, split off into essentially a new being?

Mazillion had divided in half before. At the time, it had seemed like a horrible, traumatic transition for them. But what if it didn't have to be? What if it wasn't always like that?

Clarity wanted to ask Mazillion; she thought it might be useful to have a fraction of them stay here. Though, she wasn't sure why. If Cassie never came back to Wespirtech—and Clarity didn't really think they would come back—then the fraction of Mazillion who stayed behind would be stranded forever. Not so useful. Or at least, until they could escape, maybe steal a shuttle and rejoin Cassie and her crew on their own.

Unfortunately, Anna spent the entire walk back to the airlock trying to convince Clarity to stay longer and see more of what Wespirtech had been doing with the money that Wisper had claimed came from them. There wasn't a chance to step aside and have a private few words with a clump of Mazillion.

Clarity was profoundly relieved when she stepped from the metal floor of Wespirtech's airlock and onto the forgiving fleshy surface of Cassie's vesicle-like airlock. The pink glow of Cassie's walls felt like home. The slightly coppery tang in the air smelled like home.

Cassie was Clarity's home.

17. STAR-CROSSED LOVE

As soon as the inner valve of Cassie's airlock opened, sliding to the side like a nictitating membrane, Roscoe greeted them all, looking more enthused and energetic than he had in weeks.

"How did it go!" The lapine man was practically bouncing with eagerness. His question came out as more of an exclamation, and he was fidgeting with the walking stick in his front paws so much that Clarity was afraid he'd fumble it and hit someone.

Teya dropped back behind the others, waiting until she could be the absolute last of the group to exit the airlock and face her overeager Grand Uncle's interrogation.

As soon as Genniperri set robotic foot inside Cassie, safely returned from the foray into a human science wonderland, T'resso declared in a hissing voice that he should go check on how Paurizau was doing and get back to work on fine-tuning his mostly repaired mechanical shell. He set off for the quarters he'd been sharing with the Doraspians, tail swaying behind him like sine wave.

Clarity and Irohann steered the rabbit hutch together through the airlock valve and into the hallway. It was a large, awkward object, even with anti-grav skis to make it slide easily a few inches above the fleshy floor. "Let's take this hutch to the cargo bay," Clarity said to Irohann.

Oksana and Genniperri lingered in the hall outside the airlock, seemingly interested in following the hutch of bunnies wherever Clarity and Irohann took it.

"Are you sure you don't want to just store it here? In the hallway?" Irohann asked. "We could climb over it every time we go in or out of the airlock. It would be almost like a security measure. A sort of blockade, if you will."

Clarity grumbled. "I don't leave stuff stacked up in front of the airlock that much."

Oksana seemingly missed Irohann's sarcasm and said, "I don't think that would be a good idea. Clarity's right—the bunnies will be much happier if their home is in the cargo bay where there's more space for them to hop around than in this narrow passage."

Clarity pushed against the hutch and got it floating down the hall again; Irohann scurried up in front of it and helped guide the hutch away from bumping into the curved wall.

Behind them, Roscoe was too busy grilling Teya about his imaginary future for her as a scientist to care about the new hutch of bunnies, and Teya was too busy dodging his expectations for her to do anything else. Clarity was not at all sorry to leave their familial argument behind as she helped guide the hutch down the hall.

Once they were almost around the nearest bend, Roscoe exclaimed, "What do you mean you came back early?" in response to something Teya had mumbled. The elder came hopping down the hall, following the Clarity, Irohann, and the hutch of bunnies. He elbowed past Oksana and Genniperri who had been following down the hall as well, but more slowly.

Once Roscoe caught up with Clarity, he said, "I told Zephyr not to bother you with that message. I really don't know how much we can trust that robot."

"I trust zir," Clarity said wryly.

Roscoe wrinkled his fuzzy nose in perturbation, but he didn't pursue the question of Zephyr and zir loyalties. There was nothing for him to do about the fact that the new robotic crew member was loyal to Clarity. "You know that we can't make it to those space-time coordinates safely, don't you?" he said, still hopping alongside Clarity. "And why would we want to anyway? What's there that we'd want to fly towards?"

"Loose ends," Clarity mumbled. She didn't want to be having this conversation. She didn't want to have it ever, but she especially didn't want to have it right now; she was busy with more important concerns.

Clarity had noticed that the soft pink bioluminescent patches in Cassie's walls glowed brighter as she and Irohann passed by them with the hutch of bunnies.

Cassie was watching the hutch, eagerly awaiting her bunnies. The starwhal was probably losing her mind waiting for them to be released and start hopping about inside her.

Clarity didn't want to think about flying towards the unraveling ends of a tangled-up universe. She wanted to think about Cassie finally getting her bunnies.

But Roscoe didn't want to wait. He kept hopping after her and kept pressing at things he didn't want to know about and she didn't want to think about. "Loose ends? What loose ends?"

Clarity ignored him and continued steering the hutch down the gently curving hallway. The only hard part to navigate came when they arrived at the valve-like entrance to the cargo bay. The valve-like door was one of the largest inside of Cassie, but the hutch was awkwardly bulky, and it needed to be angled just right to avoid catching its square corners on Cassie's curved edges. Before Irohann and Clarity could finish perfecting the positioning, the vaguely oval shaped doorway suddenly widened; the entire hallways seemed to stretch around them like Cassie had drawn a deep, deep breath, expanding the passageways inside of her as though they were lungs.

Clarity hadn't known Cassie could do that.

Once inside the cargo bay, Clarity and Irohann positioned the hutch at one end of the vaguely lung-shaped space. When Clarity knelt down and opened the hatch to let the bunnies out, the pink glowing patches on the walls around them burst with light more brightly than Clarity have ever seen before. The pink light was almost white with its brightness.

One of the bunnies, paw on the edge of the hutch's hatch, looked ready to hop out and explore. Its nose twitched nervously, excitedly, smelling its new surroundings. But the sudden burst of light scared the bunny back inside.

"Settle down, Cassie," Clarity said, looking up at the ceiling of the cargo bay, as if that would make any difference in Cassie's ability to hear her. It wouldn't, but it made Clarity feel more like she was talking to Cassie. "The bunnies are here. They're yours. There are several dozen of them, and they're going to live inside of you. But if you flash lights at them like that, you're going to keep them too scared to explore."

The lights in the cargo bay dimmed sadly. Okay, maybe not sadly. Just practically. But the dimmed lights felt like they held sadness to Clarity. She knew exactly how excited Cassie was about this shipment of sub-sentient maintenance bunnies. She'd experienced the feeling herself, and although she wasn't mind-blended with Cassie now, she was still half-giddy with the thrill of vicariously sharing this experience with the big, excited starwhal.

The boldest of the bunnies cautiously returned to the hatch and, after an excruciatingly long moment, placed a brown-and-white paw on the cargo bay floor.

Clarity half expected the walls around her to explode in light again, but Cassie managed to restrain herself.

After a few more nose twitches, the bold bunny hopped out onto the cargo bay floor. All four fuzzy feet rested on Cassie's dark purple flesh. Usually, the floors didn't bioluminesce like the walls, but a gentle, soft pink pawprint appeared in each position where the bunny placed its paws. As it hopped away from the hutch, a trail lit up behind it.

Clarity was learning a lot about Cassie's abilities today. For a being who had blended minds with her, Cassie was full of surprises.

Another bunny followed the first one out of the hutch, then another. The brown, gray, and white puffballs explored the space around the hutch, and the floor lit up with trails and tracks of pink pawprints following them. Like kisses on Cassie's cargo bay floor. The young starwhal was so happy to have the bunnies inside her that she was literally glowing.

Clarity smiled, closed her eyes, and felt at peace. She had made Cassie happy, and for this moment, that was enough. She would hold onto that. This moment in time—she wanted to remember this moment forever.

Irohann stepped close to her, and his fluffy bulk leaned into her side. "This was a good wish," he whispered.

But like every good moment, it had to end.

Roscoe exclaimed once again, "What loose ends!"

Clarity gritted her teeth, and when she opened her eyes, she saw that Roscoe's frustrated exclamation had scared many of the sub-sentient bunnies back into their hutch. Their pawprint tracks on the floor were already fading.

"We're not done saving the universe," Clarity said. "Somehow, the whole thing—the whole universe, apparently—got tangled with a whole *other* universe, and we need to untangle them."

"Why?" Roscoe asked obstinately. "We saved the universe last month. Isn't it somebody else's turn now?"

Clarity had trouble arguing with that. "You'd think," she conceded. "But no, it's on us. We're the ones who know about it. We're the ones who..." She glanced over at Genniperri who had followed them into the cargo bay to watch the release of the bunnies. "Well, let's just say, we're the ones who have found ourselves holding onto the loose end of the tangle. If we don't pull the tangle loose, no one will."

Genniperri was the loose end.

But Roscoe didn't know about Genniperri's immortality, and

much like when Clarity had asked T'resso about Genniperri and Paurizau's situation, it wasn't her secret to tell.

Or was it?

If Cassie and her crew were flying into the breach, yet again, then anyone aboard had the right to be informed about what they were facing. Didn't they?

Fortunately, Genniperri saved Clarity from wrestling with the moral quandary of revealing another's secret any longer by singing softly with her flowers, "Does this mean... Is it possible... You've found the coordinates for another phenomenon? Like the ones that froze Paurizau and me in time?"

"Froze in time?" Oksana's braying voice tore through the quiet tone of Genniperri's singing. But there was a quaver in her bray. "What does that mean?"

"Immortality," Genniperri said, her choral voice taking on a minor tone. "Whether we want it or not."

Teya blurted, with the exasperation of youth facing age, "Why wouldn't you want it??"

Oksana repeated the question, but she didn't sound exasperated, merely wide-eyed with open, honest curiosity: "Yeah, why wouldn't you?"

Neither of them had been fazed one bit by floating on the edge of a black hole's event horizon. Clarity could hardly believe the naivety that it took for the lapine and ungulate child to look out at the universe from such an unsullied, hopeful view.

They had never truly faced the horrifying, daunting, unending prospect of *forever*. Instead, all they saw was *more*.

Doripauli's branches sagged; her shrubby body above the solid, tree trunk legs seemed to wilt. She didn't answer the young ones' question. How could she? It was too heavy, and the distance between their experiences and hers too vast. Instead, she turned her rose and daisy-like flowers toward Clarity and said, "We have to go there—Paurizau and I. If there's a chance that we can end this, we have to try."

"Agreed," Clarity said. "But it's not just about you, apparently."

"Two whole universes, you say?" Genniperri's sing-song voice had taken on the doleful tone of a dirge, appropriate to the enormity of the danger, but a mirthful note entered the song as she added, "Paurizau and I had thought this was our problem, and our problem alone. And before I met him... just mine."

Roscoe stamped his long foot. "It is, you selfish plant! Get your own doggarned ship if you want to fly off after bamboozly brambles of broken edges of the universe! Whatever's happening to you and the universe, I do not care, and you are NOT dragging my grandbunnies into any kind of danger."

Clarity muttered something under her breath about Roscoe's grandbunnies tending to fly into danger of their own accord from what she'd seen. Irohann chuckled, and Roscoe glared at her.

"Grandbunnies?" Teya asked her granduncle. "Plural?"

"Yes," Roscoe said. "You, Oksana"—he nodded at the ungulate—"and Cassie." He waved his walking stick menacingly, but he was probably just trying to gesture at the all-encompassing girth of the starwhal surrounding them.

"I am not your grandbunny," Oksana said, crossing her angular arms across her narrow chest. "And if the whole universe is involved—two universes, even—then it kind of is our problem, whether we want it to be or not, isn't it?"

"And I don't need you trying to run my life, old man," Teya said, stamping her foot in exactly the same way that her granduncle had. "If you want to get off the ship and stay here, then stay here. I'm with Clarity and Genniperri on this. Let's go find the, uh, space-time phenomenon."

Roscoe's glance flicked to Oksana, as if he had expected support from that quarter. Oksana had sided with him against his actual grandniece before, but the ungulate stepped closer to her lapine friend and said, "I'm with Teya. And the universe. Both of them."

Roscoe turned his gaze to Irohann, but the tall, fluffy red wolf man shrugged. Of course, he would support Clarity.

Roscoe stomped a foot again. "I won't do it. I won't pilot Cassie into danger."

"I'm not sure you have as much control over Cassie and her choices as you think you do," Clarity said.

"Let's ask her." Teya's voice trembled as she said the words. Like she was speaking of a long-separated love. Someone that she held in her heart but hadn't seen in years.

More accurately: someone she hadn't truly met. Not yet.

"Yes," Clarity agreed, already heading toward the valve-like door out of the cargo bay. "Let's ask Cassie where she wants to fly."

"Yes," Roscoe agreed. "Let's ask."

The others followed Clarity and Roscoe down the gently curved hallway that ran along Cassie's length, from the airlock in her tail up to the cockpit that was nestled next to where Clarity imagined the starwhal's brain must be. Starting at the cargo bay, they were already halfway to the cockpit.

Clarity entered the cockpit to find Zephyr, wired up to a panel beside the bank of vid screens. Several black and gray electrical cords were plugged into the base of Zephyr's skull and then draped down to where their other ends plugged into the panel. The robot must have synthesized the cords, since Clarity was pretty sure they hadn't had any cords like that aboard. In order to synthesize electrical cords, either Zephyr had downloaded patterns for them before leaving Crossroads Station—entirely likely—or zhe was simply really good at programming the synthesizer. Much more skilled than Clarity. Honestly, that was also really likely.

Either way, Zephyr's skills—in downloading and storing patterns or writing them zirself—were going to be really useful. They probably already were being useful. Although, Clarity wasn't entirely sure what Zephyr was up to here. She tilted her head, questioningly, and the robot said, "I've been experimenting with ways that Cassie and I could communicate more directly. We know that my brain won't function for letting her pilot herself, but it seemed like there might be times when a more direct communication would still be useful."

"How's it working?" Clarity asked, genuinely curious.

Beside her, Roscoe huffed and shuffled restlessly, seemingly impatient for them to get to the point but unwilling to press the conversation to the point himself. He was going to lose this argument, and he probably knew that. If he didn't, he would soon.

Zephyr raised zir metal claw-like hands in a so-so gesture to answer to Clarity's question. "Our minds are so very different," zhe said. The mechanical buzz of zir voice sounded especially robotic when contrasted with the idea of Cassie's squishy biological existence.

"I bet." Clarity stepped forward, closer to the bank of screens, but side-stepped the pilot's bowl chair.

"It does make it faster to respond to incoming messages," Zephyr observed. "The administrators on Wespirtech have been pinging us with a lot of questions about whether you're coming back and something about brunch."

Clarity frowned. "Yeah, they were keen on the brunch thing."

"Well, it's a lot easier for me to answer them this way." Zephyr gestured at the cords running between her head and Cassie's console. "I've basically just been giving them the runaround to keep them from figuring out that we're leaving, until it's too late for them to do anything."

Clarity nodded. "Sounds about right. Thank you." It would definitely be useful to have Zephyr filter incoming messages rather than have Cassie simply throw them on the bank of screens with no warning. Although, Zephyr probably wouldn't stay plugged in like that all the time... Still, it was an improvement, and they could figure out the details of improving Cassie's communications systems later. Right now, they had more important questions to address.

Clarity shifted nervously on her feet, not ready to ask. The cockpit felt small with Roscoe beside her, and Teya, Irohann, and Genniperri crowded behind them. Clarity narrowed her eyes at the group that had followed them in and asked, "Oksana didn't come?"

Teya shrugged. "She said she was staying behind to make sure the bunnies settled in well. I don't think she cares very much where we go—mostly, she's happy to be here."

As soon as Teya said the word "bunnies," the same word appeared all over Cassie's bank of vid screens, raining down from the top, sliding across from the sides, and rotating round and round like the word itself was doing backflips.

All of the instances of the word "bunnies" disappeared from the screens and were replaced with one, clear, large statement: "THANK YOU."

Clarity smiled.

Roscoe grumbled and rolled his eyes, which didn't seem especially supportive to Clarity given that he claimed to have Cassie's best interests at heart. And more than anything, Cassie had wanted those sub-sentient maintenance rabbits.

"We have to ask you something," Irohann said, speaking toward the bank of screens.

"Let me," Roscoe grumbled, trying to clamber up into the pilot's bowl chair. He had to awkwardly drop his walking stick to the side. Once he was settled in the scoop of a chair, looking upward expectantly, the tentacles and sucker discs failed to descend. He looked surprised, hurt, and confused.

Maybe he truly hadn't known that Cassie would side with him.

Zephyr said, "Cassie doesn't want you to pilot her anymore, Roscoe. She says that the willow bark you've been taking makes her feel muddled—"

Roscoe started to object, but Zephyr continued on, without letting him take over the conversation.

"—and whether mind-blending with her is hurting you or not,

you're not well and need more rest than you can get while connected to her."

Even though Cassie hadn't answered their question yet—or even been asked it—Roscoe slumped in the pilot's chair, knowing he'd already been defeated. He couldn't manipulate Cassie into following him if he couldn't mind-blend with her. He couldn't control her into making the choices that he thought were safe.

Roscoe clambered back out of the chair, picked up his walking stick, and looked like he was seriously considering just giving up on them all and leaving. Staying at Wespirtech until he could get another ride, or maybe *The Warren* could come for him. He glanced toward the three valve-like doors that led into the three main corridors away from the cockpit. But he didn't leave. He turned back toward the bank of screens and said, "Cassie, you don't have to do this. You don't have to fly towards danger, just because that's what you've been made to do before now. You can leave. You can do what you want."

Words appeared on Cassie's bank of screens in different fonts and colors and sizes, at different angles, and some of them moving. It was a bewildering and strangely beautiful display—all of the words were formed into phrases: "Want help," "want *to* help," "want save," "want *be* saved," "want Teya," "want to please Clarity," "want Irohann to like me," "want Roscoe feel better," "want Teya," "want Teya," "want do what's right," "want other starwhals," "want be good," "want Teya."

The word cloud was so deep and primal—a view directly into the morass of conflicting desires inside a giant, loving heart. Clearly, more than anything, Cassie wanted to be piloted by Teya.

And Clarity and Roscoe had been keeping them apart.

Hell, if they were flying into the apocalypse, trying to stop the apocalypse from happening by throwing themselves bodily into it, then the least they could do was let these two young lovers finally know each other.

"Climb into the pilot's chair, Teya," Clarity said.

"What?" Teya looked startled, like she hadn't expected her pleas to pilot Cassie to ever actually work.

"We asked Cassie, and she answered." Clarity gestured at the word cloud where all of the instances of Teya's name had turned a burning shade of burgundy, like the embers of a long burning fire. "She wants to try to fix the tangles in the universe, and she wants *you* to pilot her there."

Teya's long ears flattened behind her head, trailing down her back. Her expression was complicated—scared? hopeful? excited? Clarity couldn't read it all, but before she could worry about Teya's reaction too much, the young lapine stepped past the others, toward the pilot's chair. As she climbed in, well before she was settled, the tentacles with their sucker disc ends lowered toward her.

Teya closed her eyes as the sucker discs kissed onto her, attaching to her head at the temples, beside her long ears that were laid back behind her head, and at the base of her skull.

The bank of vid screens went dark, as if Cassie had closed her eyes too. Zephyr unplugged zirself, yanking the cords out from the base of zir own mechanical skull. Zhe didn't say anything, but it looked like she was giving Teya and Cassie a moment of privacy, the chance to blend their minds together organically without another mind—electronic and different from theirs—participating or watching from too close inside.

Slowly, Teya's ears rose up until they were standing tall, and when she opened her eyes, they shone brighter than Clarity had seen them shine before. "We're ready," Teya said. She didn't seem to fumble over finding her tongue like Clarity always did. She didn't look lost or confused. The young lapine looked centered. Grounded. Perfectly at peace. At home.

Teya had found her calling.

Roscoe looked totally defeated and hopped past the others, out of the cockpit.

"Wait," Clarity said. "Are you leaving, Roscoe? Or coming with us?"

"I'll stay with my grandbunnies," he said without looking back. "No matter how foolish they are. I'll be in my quarters if anyone cares." The valve-like door to the cockpit closed behind him.

The bank of vid screens flickered back to life, filled with the image of Wespirtech sprawling gray and boxy in front of them, under a cluster of atmo-domes like bubbles in dingy dishwater. The whole institute looked a poorly healing scar on the surface of the silver moon.

"If everyone else is ready," Teya said, glancing around the room, "we'll start with one subspace hop towards the coordinates. But if it goes well, we plan to jump directly into the next two."

Clarity's mouth opened to speak—she wanted to ask, "How do you feel? Is Cassie okay?" But she didn't want to be condescending or motherly. Teya was a grown lapine. Cassie was... well, she was perfectly capable of living her life as a starwhal without them. She didn't need a crew. And yet, she'd consented to have one, and she'd chosen a pilot for herself from among them. It wasn't Clarity's place to interfere.

Many of them seemed to have accepted Clarity as captain, and captain is a different role than pilot. But just because she'd blended her mind with Cassie several times before didn't mean that she was an expert. She had no particularly special knowledge to share with Teya.

Clarity hoped that Teya and Cassie would come to a more comfortable, equitable arrangement in sharing their minds than Roscoe, Irohann, or herself had.

"Do you have maps of Doraspian space to work with?" Clarity asked, having successfully held her tongue when it came to the more patronizing questions. "Those should be easier to download here, where you can relay download requests through the Wespirtech computers, than they will be once we're in deep space."

Irohann startled. "Doraspian space?" His ears flattened against his head, and his muzzle tightened, jaw clenching.

"Yes," Clarity said. "We'll get in; we'll get out. It'll be like we were never there."

Irohann didn't say anything, so Clarity went over and took his paw. "You know the stakes," she said. "We have to do this, but... you could stay here. I'm sure Wespirtech could arrange passage for you down to the planet below. I understand there are some beautiful cities on Da Vinci, and we'd come back..."

They'd come back if they succeeded, and they survived.

Irohann shook his head, but he looked uncertain. "I'm part of this crew. I'll come."

Clarity couldn't tell if he was coming to stay by her side, or if there was still a part of him longing to be closer to Queen Doripauli, even if it took him into danger. Even if it was a terrible idea. Half of her was glad he was coming, but half of her wished that he'd asked to stay behind.

Teya closed her eyes for a moment, and when she opened them again, the bank of vid screens also changed their scene: the boxy gray buildings of Wespirtech were replaced with a star map, complete with dotted lines and swooping curves outlining the imaginary borders of political empires. "We do now," Teya said. "Thank you, that was a good suggestion."

"Great," Clarity said. "Then when we get to Doraspian space, can you and Cassie try to keep us hidden until we've managed to assess the situation? I'd much rather get the lay of the land from hiding behind a nice safe asteroid than from the middle of a bunch of Doraspian warships pointing laser weapons our way."

Teya laughed, and when she spoke, her voice was light and airy, "Cassie says that she's grateful to still have you looking out for me. I mean, her." The lapine looked bewildered at her own words for a moment, and then said, "Us, I guess." So, maybe Teya didn't have the balance between her and Cassie totally figured out yet. That said, pronouns can be confusing in the best of situations.

Irohann said, "I'm going to go warn the others that we're about to fly through subspace."

"Good idea," Clarity agreed.

Irohann, Genniperri, and Zephyr left the cockpit, each taking a different one of the hallways. Irohann headed back towards the cargo bay, where Oksana would be. Genniperri followed in Roscoe's footsteps, toward the crew quarters, where she would most likely find Paurizau and T'resso. Zephyr took the path towards the scullery which seemed to have become her home.

A cluster of Mazillion that had been silently clinging to the ceiling of the cockpit during their conflict took flight, dispersed, and followed the others down all three of the hallways at once.

"Happy flying," Clarity said to Teya and Cassie, and then she left them to it.

18. HEY HO, HEY HO, TO DORASPIAN SPACE WE GO

Clarity paced the halls that ran up and down Cassie's spine, stretching out her legs and working off her restless energy. There was nothing she could do to prepare for where they were going—even Wisper hadn't known what to expect. The AI whose code crawled through one research base after another, reaching across the galaxy with hidden tendrils inside of who-knows-how-many computers hadn't even known there were loose ends left to tie up from the whole Merlin Particle debacle.

One step after another, one foot and then the next, drawing breaths until they became labored, Clarity paced the cave-like tunnels through Cassie's innards that had somehow become her home. She remembered walking on the dirt ground of the planet where she'd grown up—taking long strides with legs that seemed to confuse her by being a little longer every day. The sky had stretched out above her, teasing her, calling her. Taunting her with how trapped she felt, even though an entire sphere of a world stretched out around her, and the sky above was infinite.

Cassie's innards didn't usually feel small to Clarity. But right now, she wanted to turn her face upward and feel wind caress her skin while she stared into an atmosphere that tried to swaddle its world from the depth of the void of the universe... but failed, stretched too thin every night, and the stars would come out to twinkle.

Clarity couldn't even see the stars, not for real, while inside Cassie. Sure, she was floating among them, away from any gravity field, even those as strong as the paltry pull on her home world's smallest moon. But she felt like she was deep in a burrow. A rabbit warren.

Clarity stopped pacing. Sighed. Closed her eyes and turned her face upward anyway, pretending the gentle breathing movement of air inside Cassie was a real breeze, caused by miles and miles of atmosphere stretching above her, filled with clouds and currents, castles of vapor and eddies of aether. When Clarity opened her eyes, with her face still turned upward, she was surprised to see one of the bunnies... on the ceiling.

The sub-sentient maintenance rabbit with its long, snow-white fur was hopping gently along the curved, pinkly glowing ceiling. Its hops were funny and stilted because it never took more than one paw off the ceiling at a time, and its long ears dangled downward amusingly.

Clarity tilted her head, trying to see the bunny from a better angle. "How are you doing that, little one?" Clarity asked the bunny.

Of course, it didn't answer. Instead, Clarity reached up and gently grabbed the fluffy puffball. The rabbit didn't object, and its nose twitched curiously at her as she held it, cradled in her arms so that she could inspect its paws.

Clarity didn't have any experience to speak of with normal Earth bunnies—most of what she knew, sadly, came from the clips of videos that seemed to run constantly through Cassie's thoughts when they were mind-blended. Hopping, twitching, wearing fancy clothes to tea parties... Yeah, it wasn't helpful.

Regardless, this bunny's paws seemed different to her—it had large, scaly pads on the bottoms of each paw. Under the fluffy fur running down the leg, the rabbit's paws actually seemed more like gecko toes than mammalian paw pads.

"I suppose this is one of the ways you were altered to suit life aboard a starwhal, huh?" Clarity played with the bunny's toes, smoothing her finger along the scaly ridges. The bunny didn't seem to mind.

Eventually, Clarity took the bunny out of the crook of her arm where she'd been cradling it and raised it toward the ceiling, upside down. It reached out its paws and clung onto the fleshy, glowing surface, and floated there like a strange cloud in the weird, close sky above Clarity's head. She reached up and gave its silky-soft fur one more pat before leaving the bunny to its business of nibbling on bits of moss or fungi growing on Cassie's flesh, tiny flora that Clarity hadn't even noticed before.

"Self-sustaining," Clarity mused. That's what the biologist, Keida, had said about the sub-sentient maintenance rabbits. They would even calibrate their breeding, automatically, to suit the needs of their environment. Keida had told them that the bunnies could even be slaughtered and cooked, used for food for the crew, and they'd simply increase their breeding levels to keep up their population.

However, Cassie would never forgive anyone who killed and ate her bunnies. Clarity didn't have to think twice to know that. She knew it gut-deep.

Yet, an evil part, even deeper inside her, wondered how good the bunnies would taste, properly roasted, maybe with some mint jelly or apricot stuffing on the side.

Not that there'd be a good way to safely roast raw meat inside a spaceship of any sort, let alone one whose floor and walls were living flesh. And killing rabbits? Ugh. Clarity didn't want to think about that. No thank you. She was happy to have her food synthesized from a slurry of basic proteins in a machine and served to her ready to eat.

Speaking of food, Clarity decided that it was time to make up for missing the fancy brunch at Wespirtech. She finished a final loop up and down Cassie's halls and walked herself into the scullery.

Zephyr was at one of the tables, sketching on a large sheet of paper with colored pencils. Zir metal hand moved so rapidly over the sheet, it looked like a silver blur.

Mazillion swarmed en masse, filling the scullery's ceiling with complicated shapes. When Clarity stepped close enough to see the shape emerging in bright hues on Zephyr's white sheet, she realized that Mazillion was posing for zir. The drawing on the page was a two-dimensional, multi-colored rendering of their monochromatic, three-dimensional shape. Color became the third dimension.

Glancing between the roiling shape in the air and the rainbow sketch on the table, Clarity started noticing patterns in the positions of Mazillion's plethora of pinpoint bodies, especially around the edges of their swarm. Recurring, fractal patterns.

There were swirling, paisley shapes in the chaos that reminded Clarity of the Mandelbrot or Julia Set.

"Very pretty," Clarity observed.

"Thank you," Zephyr said, not bothering to look away from zir sketch which continued growing more detailed with every second.

"We'll need to start hanging your art on the walls in the hallways too. We'll run out of room in here." Clarity went over to the synthesizer and punched in the codes to summon a variety of breakfast foods and waited while the machine composed them.

Clarity still wanted that fancy brunch that was probably happening back on Wespirtech right now, but without her. Just a bunch of administrators and scientists, complaining about the ungrateful philanthropist, running off without their free food, while nomming up all the food themselves.

"This one was commissioned," Zephyr said. "So, after it's finished, I'll digitize it, send the file to the purchaser, and destroy the original. As they've requested."

Clarity blinked. "What?"

"They want me to destroy the original."

"No, I heard that," Clarity said, removing the steaming platter of food from the synthesizer. "What do you mean commissioned?"

Zephyr sighed dramatically. Since zhe didn't need to breath, and in fact, couldn't breathe, the sigh was entirely an affectation to show impatience with Clarity's question. "I mean that I received a request to make this particular drawing, and in exchange for payment, I'm doing so. That's how commissioned art works."

Clarity placed her tray of basic breakfast foods—a cube of yellow protein with a slightly more rubbery consistency than scrambled eggs, a rectangle of sweet brown carbohydrates, and a smaller rectangle of dark brown protein that almost passed for sausage—on the table, carefully far enough away from Zephyr's drawing to make it clear that she wouldn't spill anything on the impressively detailed, beautiful artwork.

"I know how commissions work," Clarity said, mashing up the egg-like substance with a fork so that it'd look less like a gelatin cube and more like the scrambled eggs that it would taste like. "I'm just surprised..." She paused, realizing what she was about to say could sound like an insult. "I didn't know that you received commissions for artwork."

"I've been keeping a virtual gallery available on the Crossroads Station network," Zephyr said, returning to zir drawing. "I upload digitized copies of my physical work, and various digital-only works every time that Cassie's in range to bounce a data packet back to the station by relays. My gallery has a substantial following."

If Zephyr weren't a robot, zhe would have sounded quite proud saying that. Scratch that. Zephyr sounded quite proud.

After eating a bite of the eggy yellow protein, Clarity said, "That's really awesome." She hadn't expected Zephyr to become an artist in residence. "So, why does someone want a drawing of Mazillion?"

"Huh?" Zephyr stared blankly with her glassy camera lens-like eyes at Clarity for several moments before following Clarity's own gaze and looking up at Mazillion, swarming around in the shape of zir drawing. "Oh, I'm not drawing Mazillion. They're imitating my piece."

Clarity stared up at the roiling mass of tiny, winged bodies. They glittered, even in the soft pink light aboard Cassie.

A melon-sized sphere's worth of bodies extruded from the fractal cloud, broke away from the rest, and came to hover above the table, near Clarity and Wisper, and about at the same height as their heads. The sphere pulsed and spoke: "We have never been a fractal before."

As Clarity ate the sweet, spongy carbohydrates with their aftertaste of maple, she remembered how Mazillion had used to regularly mirror the shapes of herself and the other bipedal, one-bodied members of Cassie's crew. They'd tended to mirror whoever they were speaking to, but she hadn't seen Mazillion do that as much lately. Now, Mazillion broke into spheres and ribbons, abstract shapes, more often than imitations of one-bodies.

Clarity wondered if Mazillion had simply lost interest in those sorts of shapes. Perhaps, they'd only been interested in mimicking the others' shapes while it was still novel to them, and it hadn't been a communication tactic after all, even though that's what Clarity had always assumed.

"How do you like being a fractal?" Clarity asked Mazillion.

Seemingly in answer—though Clarity was learning that she shouldn't assume too much about the intentions and emotional interiority of lifeforms as different from her as Mazillion, Zephyr, Genniperri... really, all of the rest of her crew—Mazillion's roiling, fractal shape smoothed into a simple torus, spinning lopsidedly around Clarity, Zephyr, and the separate orb of Mazillion's bodies who'd done the speaking. The torus tightened around them, evened out its lopsided spinning, and stretched upward, forming a cone over their heads. Clarity's heart skipped a beat, uncomfortable with all of the tiny insectile bodies surrounding her. Claustrophobia hit and reminded her of sharing a spacesuit with

Mazillion, all of their tiny bodies crawling over her skin, through her hair...

She shuddered. She loved Mazillion, but she wanted her own space.

Before Clarity had time to speak up, asking for more space, the cone of Mazillion over their heads dissipated and dispersed into the room, spreading out enough that they no longer seemed like a single organism, simply a diaspora of tiny, disconnected bodies.

"What was that about?" Clarity asked, feeling a little shaken.

"A... hug?" Mazillion's mouth said, still floating, head-sized and at head-height, beside them. "We did not think you wanted us to actually touch you."

Clarity didn't know what to say to that. Fortunately, Mazillion continued on, answering the question she'd asked them: "Being a fractal is exciting and interesting—every piece of myself must be engaged, focused, playing its part. Every body. But it is also tiring. Much of myself is used to... coasting, following along with the more highly developed parts. Simpler bodies follow the lead of more complicated bodies. That cannot be the case when every body is called for equally to play a role."

"It's like a whole-body workout," Clarity said. "You stretch and exercise muscles that aren't used to being used."

"Yes," the orb of Mazillion pulsed, wobbling a little in the air.

"May I ask," Clarity said, holding her fork awkwardly perched above her half-finished tray of food, "why did you stop imitating our shapes? When we first met, you copied the shapes of bipedal, one-bodied aliens all the time."

The orb flattened into a disc before rounding back into a sphere shape and answering, "We are not bipedal. Not one-bodied."

"I know," Clarity said. "But you used to... pretend?"

"Don't need to now. Not anymore." The orb wobbled wildly, not actually moving anywhere, but vibrating. Almost, nervously.

"Did you 'need to' before?" Clarity asked.

"Didn't know," the orb answered. "Didn't know you. Didn't

know if we could trust one-bodies to listen to us, unless we pretended to be like you."

Clarity nodded slowly.

Zephyr, who had gone back to sketching, looked up from zir drawing. "I hear you there," zhe said. "Organics aren't so good about listening to digitally brained sentients either, unless we pretend to be like them and think at a fraction of our usual speed. The crew here seems to be unusually good about it though." Zhe held out a fisted metal hand toward the orb of Mazillion and said, "Fist bump?"

The orb extruded into a snake-like shape, and the spade-like head composed of tiny, winged bodies brushed gently against the curled metal fingers of Zephyr's fist before the whole snake deformed, floating away to join the diaphanous cloud of Mazillion that filled the whole scullery, and arguably, the whole ship.

As long as Mazillion's bodies continued to reproduce, one generation after the next continuing on as the same individual collective, the swarm was as immortal as any species could be.

And, Zephyr's digital brain could be downloaded from one aging metal body into the next, and even live disembodied inside a computer network, like Wisper, if zhe chose to do so. Another form of immortality.

Clarity felt very small and finite, sharing the scullery with two beings who were so much more flexible and long-lived than she was with her human brain in a human body.

One squishy human brain inside of one breakable human body. Sure, humans lived into their second century these days, but they still died.

Clarity couldn't regrow body parts the way that Paurizau could, regenerating leaves as fast as he shed them on Cassie's floor in his eternal autumn. She couldn't download her brain into a computer like Zephyr. If she ever chose to have an actual offspring—hah, not likely—it would be an entirely separate person from herself, not a continuation like Mazillion's ever self-replicating bodies.

Someday, Clarity would end. She would die, and she'd never learn what happened next in the story of the universe. For a moment, she felt the pull of the offer of immortality. She understood how Teya and Oksana could stare at Genniperri, aghast at the idea that she found immortality to be a burden.

Clarity was old enough to understand that immortality was a frightening yoke, but young and breakable enough to feel the draw of its siren call.

Zephyr slid a piece of paper and a few colored pencils in front of Clarity, next to her mostly empty tray of food. "Draw something," zhe said. "You look like you need an activity to put your mind at rest."

Clarity started to object, "I'm no good at drawing—"

But Zephyr said, "It doesn't matter. Just scribble in different colors. Or one color. Whatever's happening inside your head, the physical motion and emotional expression of drawing will make you feel better."

Clarity nodded. "Thank you." She liked having a robot with nannying skills aboard Cassie. Even adults need nannies sometimes.

As Teya jumped Cassie across massive sectors of the galaxy, threading the starwhal through subspace like a giant needle, Clarity sat in the scullery and drew a very poor picture of a fluffy bunny.

And it made her feel a little better.

After Clarity finished her drawing, she retired to her room where a blackberry-sized cluster of Mazillion hummed her to sleep, and several of the sub-sentient maintenance bunnies hopped onto her bed and curled up around her. She awoke hours later, disoriented, and covered in fluffy, warm bunnies. She didn't remember her dreams, but she felt off-balance, making her wonder if they'd been nightmares.

Deep, dark nightmares without any content—the equivalent of the existential horror of floating in the emptiness of space forever as the universe dies around you, unable to die, unable to be a part of it, only to watch and be drawn into an eternal isolation.

Floating at the edge of the Devil's Radio's event horizon still haunted her.

Abruptly, the valve-like door to Clarity's quarters slid open, and Irohann stood outside, ears flattened. He made an imposing silhouette in the opened door, large and wolfy. "You're awake?" he asked.

Clarity nodded. "I think so." She felt like a character in a fairy tale, a strange hybrid of Little Red Riding Hood and Sleeping Beauty—instead of a girl eaten by a wolf or a princess awoken by a prince, she was the Starship Captain Awoken by the Space Wolf.

"We're here," Irohann said, ears still flattened. He looked stricken. "We've arrived."

"At the coordinates?" Clarity asked, shoving the various rabbits who had settled around her away and climbed out of the soft bed.

"We're in Doraspian space," he said. "Hidden in an asteroid belt, like you recommended to Teya. She and Cassie jumped straight through, one subspace hop after another."

"Just like they said they would," Clarity mused. Teya must be exhausted from jumping three times consecutively.

Clarity glanced up at her shelf of dolls, taking a moment, especially to look at the shiny glass bead eyes on her hand-me-down lapine doll. "From one rip in the universe to the next..." she muttered.

"The coordinates correspond with a planet," Irohann said. "It's habitable, but I don't think it's inhabited."

"That's convenient," Clarity said, following Irohann as he backed out of her quarters and into the hallway.

"There's also a fleet of Doraspian warships surrounding the planet."

Now Irohann's flattened ears and stricken expression made sense.

"That's less convenient," Clarity said grimly. "Any chance we can just blast the two sentient flower bushes out of the airlock, hope they fall into the planet's gravity well, and then turn tail and get out of here without the warships seeing us?"

Irohann shrugged as they walked. He seemed to be leading her toward the cockpit. "I guess it depends on if we want to take the chance that the Doraspian warships will pick them up before they get to the exact coordinates and keep them from reaching the phenomenon. Whatever this phenomenon is."

Clarity grimaced at his words as she remembered the universe fracturing around her like a broken mirror. She didn't want to see the phenomenon up close, whatever it looked like. But she also didn't want to bet on the Doraspian empire making a *good* choice when it came to sewing up rips in space time.

The Doraspians had tried to pry the universe open with the Merlin Particle for their own purposes the last time Cassie and a Doraspian warship had crossed paths. No one in their right mind would have considered the Merlin Particle a good weapon, since it would take the rest of the universe down with whoever it targeted. Yet, they'd tried to buy the Merlin Particle from Mazillion's evil half like a rip in space-time was nothing more than a hand grenade.

To hell with hand grenades. Clarity hated weapons. And warships. And war.

When Clarity stumbled, still only half awake, into the cockpit, she was surprised to find nobody else there—only Cassie's bank of vid screens, showing a close-up of a blue-green world with stars sparkling brightly around it. Too brightly. Clarity squinted, peering more closely at the scene and realized that the bright points of light that looked like twinkling stars were in fact the Doraspian warships Irohann had warned her about.

Doraspian vessels bled light into space; they overflowed with light, and their insides were blindingly bright for a human who didn't subsist on light like it was a banquet. When Clarity had been taken captive aboard the last Doraspian warship, the brightness aboard had soaked into her photosynthetic hair, leaving her giddy and jittery, like she'd drunk a dozen cups of extremely strong coffee.

"Hi Cassie," Clarity said.

The word 'HI' flashed, translucent and large, over the scene of the planet.

"I bet you're thrilled to see more Doraspian warships," Clarity added, and then a different, large, translucent word flashed over the screen in answer: "NO."

Clarity smiled, amused. "Yeah, I know; I was being sarcastic. I'm not happy to see a fleet of Doraspian warships either." Changing gears, she said, "But did you and Teya have a good time flying together?"

This time the word wasn't translucent; it was bright yellow, like a daffodil, and blocked out the scene behind it: "BEST."

"Well, I hope you didn't tire her out too badly," Clarity said.

A voice interrupted her from behind, before she could say anymore. "Tired out?" Teya stood in the mouth of the hall to the scullery, holding some sort of sweet-smelling pastry in her paws. "I've never felt this rested before. Blending with Cassie feels a little like dreaming, so I think it actually takes the place of sleep for me."

Clarity was skeptical but said, "That's great."

"I'm a bit hungry, I'll admit. Though, less hungry than I felt when Cassie and I were blended. Feeling hungry as a starwhal is a far bigger feeling than as a lapine!"

Teya climbed back into the pilot seat, as though she lived there now, and nibbled on the pastry. Crumbs gathered in the fur around her mouth, but she brushed them off with a paw.

Clarity shook her head. "I thought you'd sleep for a week after a triple subspace hop."

Teya shrugged. "You did, but I guess blending with Cassie doesn't wear me out like it does you and Uncle Roscoe."

"No headache?" Clarity asked.

Teya shook her head, causing her long ears to flop. She looked so relaxed, sitting cross-legged in bowl chair of a pilot's seat. She actually laughed, even. Clarity had never seen the young lapine look this happy. "I think my head feels *better* than before." Teya smiled, and her shoulders slumped in a comfortable way, releasing a tension she'd been carrying since before Clarity had met her.

"That's great," Irohann said, sounding far less positive in tone than in words. "But we need to figure out what we're doing here."

"Where exactly are the coordinates?" Clarity asked. "On the planet's surface? In what, like, twelve days?"

"TEN" flashed across Cassie's bank of vid screens in pale lavender.

"And yet a fleet of warships is already guarding the planet?" Clarity frowned at the glittering points of light on the screen. "I wonder if they're here for a different reason, or if they got here early."

"Like we did!" Teya said, straightening her back and looking proud of how fast she and Cassie had flown here.

Clarity glanced up at the sucker disc tipped tentacles. They were still coiled up around the end of the straw-colored stalactite horns that poked down from the ceiling, showing no interest in kissing onto Teya's skull again just now. Clarity supposed that even new lovers need a little time to themselves.

Irohann approached the control console at the base of the bank of vid screens, and after doing a few calculations, he said, "From what I can tell, yes, the focal point of the coordinates is on the surface of the planet. Well, more exactly, about a mile under the ocean on the southern hemisphere."

Clarity rolled her eyes, saying, "Well, that's convenient. We just need to find a submarine..."

"ME... SUBMARINE!" flashed across the bank of vid screens in bubble letters with a cartoony yellow submarine bouncing behind them.

Clarity blinked. "Seriously? You can, uh, fly underwater? Wouldn't the pressure on your skin... I mean, you're used to flying through a *vacuum*. This sounds like a bad idea."

Irohann's tail swished, and he said, "Actually, the one time that I piloted Cassie, she shared a memory with me of another, older starwhal telling her about how they'd used to subspace hop down into planetary oceans and swim sometimes. Kind of as an extreme sport, I think."

Clarity realized she was shaking her head. This just really seemed like a bad idea. "So, what, we hop through subspace past those warships ringing the planet, appear out of subspace in the middle of an *ocean,* a mile underwater, and then shove Genniperri and Paurizau out of the airlock... into an ocean."

"You seem really hung up on this ocean thing," Teya said. "Do you have a problem with oceans?"

Clarity dimly remembered the dauntless young lapine telling her how much she loved swimming, back when she and her friends had first joined the crew. And here, Teya was being presented with the opportunity to swim while sharing the body of a starwhal. That must seem like an experience not to be missed.

"What the hell," Clarity said. "Maybe it's not such a bad plan. Sometimes, I can't tell the difference between the worst idea in the world... and the only idea that will work."

"Sometimes they're the same idea," Irohann said gently.

"I hate it when that happens." Clarity frowned. "But it seems to happen a lot lately."

"So... what?" Teya said. "We wait ten days in this asteroid field and then hop down to the ocean at the right time?" The lapine pilot looked bored already.

"No," Clarity said. She faced Cassie's bank of screens and asked, "Have you ever swum in an ocean before? Or is it just tales you've heard?"

"TALES" flashed across the screen in wibbly pink letters, as if Cassie didn't want to admit that she'd never swum before.

Clarity nodded. "That's what it sounded like." She turned back to Teya. "We find a nearby planet with a comparable ocean—hopefully—and you two practice short-hopping into the ocean and swimming. You train. Without warships watching you. Then, when you're ready and the time is right—which hopefully happen at the same time..." Clarity paused, listening to herself. "Geez, there's a lot more 'hopefully' in this plan than I'd like..."

Teya shrugged. "We'll be ready."

The closeup of their target planet on the bank of vid screens was replaced with a different mostly-blue world. Irohann looked down at the control console he'd been working and said, "I think Cassie's showing us the sixth planet in this system. The one that lines up with the coordinates is the fifth."

"And it's all ocean?" Clarity asked, amazed that something was going right. "That's perfect. Now get swimming. And make sure to stay on the far side of the planet, so that its gravity field and shadow block us from those Doraspian vessels, in case they decide to scan around the rest of the solar system for anyone else chasing after the same phenomenon."

Teya brought a paw to her brow and said, "Aye, aye, Captain!"

Cassie covered her bank of vid screen with image and video clips of dolphins and orcas, jumping out of the ocean with impressive splashes, and some larger, larger whales—possibly blue whales—swimming peacefully through the blue watery deeps.

"Exactly," Clarity said. Now she just had to inform the rest of the crew of the plan...

19. TRAINING MONTAGE

For days, Teya piloted Cassie as the starwhal hopped from orbit down to lavender-blue ocean of the sixth planet, where they swam, dove, flipped, and generally had far too much fun considering they were training for racing Doraspian warships into the fraying, tangled ends of the universe.

Clarity, with Irohann backing her up, told the plan to every other member of the crew. Mazillion had no comment; Zephyr began drawing ocean scenes and tacking them up in the hallways.

Oksana expressed concern at first about Cassie's health, but when the starwhal showed no ill effects from the squeezing pressure of being underwater, the ungulate turned her attention toward Roscoe.

With each subspace hop, the elder lapine's headaches grew worse. His ears were held low all the time now, trailing down his back, and the muscles in his face never relaxed. He was always flinching and grimacing. He could barely function well enough to feed himself and seemed to be in too much pain to sleep well.

Oksana tended to Roscoe, bringing him food, helping him eat, and trying him out on different medications in addition to the willow bark. The ungulate had seemingly made herself the unofficial ship's doctor. She had limited formal training, but apparently, the ungulate had taken a few first aid and basic alien anatomy classes back on Crossroads Station so that she'd be better equipped to help her mother care for her large number of siblings of disparate species.

Clarity couldn't help feeling as she learned more about the family Oksana had grown up in that the ungulate's mother must be a member of some sort of cult. But Oksana was so kind and gentle; whatever her background, she was a wonderful individual, and they were lucky to have her as a member of Cassie's crew.

Clarity watched Cassie and Teya's progress on the large vid screen in the scullery. Cassie transmitted her view to the screen, and Clarity watched on the edge of her seat as the curve of the planet, as seen from space, with the distant sun cresting over its horizon would suddenly become swallowed up by the murky depths of the inside of its oceans, light streaming down from above in the strange, flowing curtains caused by waves and tides above. And then, as she swam downward, the light would disappear entirely, leaving the screen to show grayscale shadows, all in shades of dark and darker blue.

In the shallower waters, Cassie swam past underwater creatures that lived on this alien world which looked like mutated sea turtles, lantern fish, balloon-like jellies, and schools of guppies that glittered like golden coins, flitting through the sea together. All of them dispersed, fleeing at the sight of Cassie, but the starwhal seemed to delight in them anyway, sometimes chasing after the larger creatures before diving deeper and then subspace-hopping back up into the atmosphere to begin the strange process of diving from vacuum into ocean and back to vacuum over again.

While Clarity watched space and ocean alternate on Cassie's scullery vid screen, T'resso the self-appointed S'rellick guardian of the Doraspians pleaded with Clarity to let him pack them back in his mechanical turtle shell, which he had fixed with Zephyr's help, and fly the immortal shrubberies to the coordinates himself, leaving Cassie and her crew behind. Leaving them out of saving the universe entirely.

Just a lizard with a mechanical turtle-shell filled with flowering shrubs, off to save the universe, like some kind of heroic gardener.

Clarity loved that idea. She desperately wanted to drop T'resso, Genniperri, and Paurizau off in orbit of the fifth planet and abandon them to save the universe on their own. But there was a fleet of Doraspian warships between them and the coordinates underneath the planet's ocean, and she didn't believe that T'resso could sneak past them in his mechanical turtle shell.

But Cassie could hop past them in subspace. If she wanted the universe to be saved, she still needed to play her part in it. She couldn't pass it off to T'resso.

And although Genniperri and Paurizau demurred, telling T'resso to argue with Clarity, they clearly knew his mechanical turtle shell wouldn't be enough to deliver them to the coordinates just as well as Clarity did. They were simply leaving her to be the bad guy.

Clarity supposed that being the bad guy was part of the captain's job, standing behind and backing up the hard decisions, like refusing to give crew members what they wanted.

With two days to spare before the space-time coordinates occurred, Cassie and Teya stopped training. The lapine pilot explained that they had practiced swimming and short-hopping through subspace enough and that while blending with Cassie felt sort of like dreaming, she should get some real sleep, and a full meal instead of some nibbled snacks, before facing off with a Doraspian war fleet.

And Cassie wanted to spend some time skimming through the upper atmosphere of the closest gas giant, filling her belly with its nutrient rich gasses, and relaxing her body, worn out from all the strain on her muscles caused by swimming through an actual fluid.

Clarity sat in the scullery, watching waves of creamsicle-colored atmosphere wash past Cassie, as shown on the viewscreen, and felt like she was about to ride off a cliff on an antique, archaic bicycle without any anti-grav hover abilities. Half of her wanted to wake up Irohann—who had somehow ended up on an opposite sleep cycle from her again—and cajole him into helping her fix a giant feast for the crew to share together, the night before their big battle. Big heist. Whatever it was they were doing. Possibly the last night of their lives—hopefully the last night of Genniperri's and Paurizau's immortality. But most of her felt sick at the idea of eating. She was too nervous.

The universe might fracture in front of her again.

Two universes might fracture in front of her.

Would that be worse? Two universes, twice as bad?

Is it possible for something to be worse than infinitely horrifying?

Clarity supposed, based on her knowledge of math, that it must be possible. Certainly, infinities came in different sizes. So, it could simply be a larger infinity of terror.

Besides, Clarity was in no mood to invite T'resso to pester her more about parting ways; Roscoe was in no condition for a party, and Oksana had tired herself out with caring for him. Teya needed her rest. Zephyr and the theoretical guests of honor at this imaginary meal—the Doraspians—didn't really eat.

Mazillion ate sugar juice. But sharing a sugary drink and toasting to the unentangling of two entangled universes with a swarm alien didn't really appeal to Clarity. So, she let Irohann sleep, and spent the last night before they planned on diving past a war fleet and into a rip in space-time with Zephyr in the scullery, not eating, but simply creating a character for the game of Starsplosions & Spacedroids that the others had been playing.

Clarity started out by making her character just like herself—human, with clorophyllically modded hair, who escaped from a backward Expansionist Colony with little more than a duffle bag of clothes to her name. But Zephyr pushed at Clarity to find alterations and differences, prodding her to experiment and have fun. By the end of the session, her imaginary character had modded her entire skin to be lime green and photosynthetic; she had antlers kind of like Irohann's recent mod, except hers glowed in the dark when she wanted them to. She also got herself—well, her character—butterfly-like wings that could fold demurely against her back most of the time, but would let her actually fly on low gravity worlds.

Once Clarity was done designing her character, Zephyr had her play through the sectors of space in the game that the others had already played through, chasing after a trail they'd left behind.

For a while, Paurizau sat beside Clarity, shedding leaves while watching her and Zephyr play. When he did, somehow every dice roll came up maxed out, and Clarity's character progressed far faster. Zephyr seemed displeased, but Clarity was delighted and called the autumnal Doraspian her good luck charm.

By the time they quit for the night, Clarity's invented character was all caught up, and she'd be ready to play with the others next time.

If there was a next time.

Clarity had trouble seeing past the metaphorical event horizon of the space-time coordinates of the entanglement phenomenon they were chasing.

It was nice to play a game where she could choose to stop, and the universe would fold up and wait—possibly forever, if she never played again—as opposed to living in the real universe, where the future crept toward her at its steady pace, whether she wanted it to or not. There was no off button. No pause. No way to slam the game shut, rip up the beautiful maps Zephyr had drawn (which she would never do; they were truly beautiful drawings), and switch to watching a nice, simple sitcom saved in her pocket computer's databanks... Maybe some kind of dramedy about an interspecies couple settling down in an asteroid colony.

But if Clarity wanted to watch sitcoms about interspecies couples or play Starsplosions & Spacedroids with the rest of Cassie's crew, first she had to walk through the time between now and the space-time coordinates of the phenomenon that had immortalized Genniperri and Paurizau. The only way out was through. Clarity hated that.

She remembered, dimly, deep in her brain, what it had been like to live on a planet and have the beginning of the day marked by the rising of the sun. She'd never been good at matching her sleep schedule to the implacable, unalterable, interminable turning of her home planet, as marked by the apparent rising and setting of its sun. She felt much more comfortable in the soft, changeable, pink twilight aboard Cassie—or back before the Serendipity had been destroyed, the silvery yellow artificial twilight there—where lights could be turned up or down or off to suit the needs and wakefulness of the crew. Here, her environment responded to her needs, instead of being too big to care about her.

Like the universe was. Cold and uncaring.

Well, if the universe was too big to care about any of them individually, then Cassie's crew would just have to do the work of caring about each other themselves.

That meant Clarity needed to tell the others about what they might be facing. They deserved to be prepared for the possibilities, even if it made Clarity's hands start shaking when she thought about putting words to her experiences aboard the fracturing Wespirtech Extension Base or the Doraspian warship that Cassie had torn in half with her horn and Clarity had watched fall into the maw of the Devil's Radio.

Nervously, Clarity rounded up the other members of Cassie's crew from wherever they'd hidden themselves—mostly in their own quarters. Roscoe was curled up on his bed, quivering unhappily instead of sleeping. Irohann was reading in his own quarters. And Teya—who probably needed rest more than anyone else aboard Cassie, except for Cassie herself—was animatedly describing to Oksana what it felt like to suck water through Cassie's tube organ and flip the starwhal's tail to steer her way through the depths of an ocean. The ungulate looked riveted, and possibly a little in love with the storytelling lapine. The Doraspians were allowing T'resso to tend to them, trimming withered and dying leaves from Paurizua; spritzing Genniperri's fronds and buds with a fine mist of nutrient-laced water; and gently oiling the joints of her mechanical legs. The blue reptile looked like a dyed-in-the-wool, lifelong gardener, rather than the political attendant he had apparently been.

Mazillion was everywhere. But especially clustered on Genniperri's branches.

Clarity had never seen a stranger love triangle than a swarm alien and a reptilian alien doting after a pretty, planted shrubbery with robot legs. An immortal one, no less.

All of them agreed to join Clarity in the scullery. Though, it took T'resso a while to pack up and carry all of his supplies, since the blue, lizard-like alien seemed unwilling to quit fawning over the immortal plants who he'd taken on as his charges and who would likely soon leave him behind.

Once they were mostly all seated on various benches in the scullery—T'resso still trimming and spritzing and oiling the Doraspians; Zephyr continuing to draw; Roscoe grumbling to himself; and Irohann synthesizing some bowls of snacks to pass around—Clarity stood in front of them, hands clutched tightly together to keep them from shaking, and said, "Cassie? Can you hear us in here?"

The viewscreen flashed a simple, lowercase "yes."

Clarity nodded. "Good." She looked down at her feet. One of the sub-sentient maintenance bunnies had hopped up to sniff her toe. She smiled at it, then forced herself to start speaking in earnest, although she couldn't seem to force herself to look up at the crew, most of whom were barely paying attention to her, but Teya and Oksana were watching her far too raptly.

"None of us know what we're going to find at the space-time

coordinates that we're chasing," Clarity said. "But some of us have encountered related phenomenon. From what Genniperri described to me"—Clarity glanced up at the cyborg shrubbery with technicolor flowers watching her like daisies following the sun—"well, it sounds like the phenomenon that she and Paurizau encountered was much more... gentle... and... pleasant than the version I encountered with Mazillion when we infiltrated the Wespirtech extension base that started this whole problem. And I think you all deserve to know what we might be facing."

A gentle rustling came from the direction of Paurizau as he shifted his tangle of shrubby limbs, withered leaves falling to the floor around him. Mazillion's buzzing, coming from every direction, seemed to increase in volume just subtly, just enough to notice.

Clarity cleared her throat and continued. "The space around me... the very fabric of space fractured, like time and physical space were nothing more than a mirror, and when it broke, every piece reflected every other piece..." She frowned, struggling with the memory, let alone putting words to it. "It's hard to describe, but it was wrong. Very wrong, and it felt like everything was breaking down, right down to the atoms that make up my body. I couldn't trust anything anymore. I could... see myself, moving ahead of and behind me... I..." Her voice broke off in a strangled sound.

"It was scary," Teya said, ears straight back behind her head. "Got it."

"But that might not happen here," Irohann said. "And if it does, we'll be better prepared for the possibility. Last time, we were sent into a dangerous situation with no guidance about what to expect. Knowing might make a difference."

Clarity couldn't help thinking, bitterly, *How would you know? You weren't there.* He had been safely aboard Cassie while she and Mazillion had faced the horror of the universe breaking apart around them. And the terror hadn't had anything to do with a lack of preparation or surprise. It had been bone deep. It had been an animal, survival response to the fundamental fabric of her environment melting into tattered shreds around her.

But that was unfair... Irohann had been aboard the Doraspian warship with her when it was ripped apart. He'd had a taste.

"From what Wisper told me when I slipped away at Wespirtech," Clarity said, "our universe has become entangled with another universe. So, it isn't just ripped open... it's... snagged? So, no, the same thing might not happen. Probably won't happen. But what does happen... We don't know what it will be. And..." She hesitated before saying this, but she had to be honest here. "It could be much, much worse."

Clarity stared down at the bunny. It had no voice, no words, no say in this matter. But the sentient beings aboard Cassie did. She said, "There's no good option for anyone who wants to back out now, but... this is it. This is your last chance to back out before Cassie nosedives into a tangled tear in the universe. And... Well, I just wanted to make sure that you all took a moment to consider your options and, well, I wouldn't think less of anyone who wanted us to drop them off on a nearby planet with a radio transmitter and some basic supplies. I don't think anyone would."

No one spoke. The weight on Clarity's shoulders and the lump in her throat grew. "But, uh, I couldn't promise that we'd ever manage to come back for you."

Irohann barked, a sudden and surprising sound that took Clarity several moments to recognize as laughter.

"Well, you're certainly feeling bleak today, aren't you?" Irohann asked. He put the latest bowl of snacks that he'd fixed down on one of the tables and then came up to Clarity and wrapped her in a big, tight hug. He whispered into her ear, "Didn't anyone ever tell you that part of the role of a captain is to inspire their crew?"

Clarity glowered. "No," she whispered back. "And I'm not entirely sure why people keep calling me captain."

"Oh, I can answer that," Oksana said, holding up a hoof-hand.

"We voted on it while playing Starsplosions & Spacedroids. And you weren't there to object, so, yeah, now you're the captain."

Teya giggled, and her grumpy uncle harrumphed.

"I didn't vote," Roscoe grumbled.

"Too bad," Teya said. "Cassie's with us, and her vote should count for like ten of the rest of ours."

Mazillion's omnipresent buzzing changed tone, as if switching from a minor chord to a major one. A happy sound. The swarm seemed to be weighing in, agreeing that they saw Clarity as the captain. Apparently, they felt that they had voted too.

Clarity wondered whether Oksana was speaking literally or metaphorically. Had they actually voted? Had Oksana raised her hoof to vote for her, the way that she'd raised it to tell Clarity about the vote?

"Fine," Clarity said. "You want a captain, and you want her to be inspirational? I'll try." She drew a deep breath, squared her shoulders, and looked straight at the assembled crew, catching each of their eyes in turn, or, well, the closest equivalent in the case of the Doraspians and Mazillion. "Let's go save the universe. Again. Maybe this time it will stick."

"Good try," Irohann said, condescendingly. "It's a good thing we didn't pick you to be captain for your ability to be inspirational."

"I have no idea why you all seem to have agreed that I'm the captain."

Zephyr pointed at Clarity with her metal claw hand. "That," zhe said. "That's why we picked you. You do the work and don't waste time seeking recognition or power."

"Besides, if it's inspiration that we wanted..." Oksana trailed off, staring at her best lapine friend expectantly.

Teya grinned lopsidedly and then shouted, "Time to swim!" She raised a fisted paw in the air exultantly.

To match her pilot's excitement, Cassie made swimming dolphins appear on the scullery's viewscreen, coupled with the word "swim" repeated over and over again in rippling lines like waves. Yes, Cassie and Teya didn't need any more inspiration. They were plenty capable of rushing headlong toward danger without a pep talk to work them up.

"You guys are fools," Clarity muttered under her breath. She wasn't sure if she meant they were fools for voting to make her their captain or that they were fools for being excited about jumping to the face of danger. Either way, she noticed a gleam in Roscoe's eyes that suggested he agreed with her, at least on that one point.

Genniperri stood up on her mechanical legs, brushed T'resso and his fawning blue-scaled talons away from herself, and stepped toward Clarity. A pallor flushed over T'resso's scales, dimming their azure, turquoise, and sapphire hues, as if all of them had been painted over with a fine mist of gray. The lizard man looked sad. Paurizau twined a vine-like appendage around one of his scaly arms comfortingly, dropping ever more autumn colored leaves to the floor with every move he made.

To gain the others' attention, Genniperri stretched out her branches, making herself larger, more tree like and less of a shrubbery. Her dainty, colorful flowers vibrated, singing the words, "Thank you, all of you, for helping me and Paurizau. You all have a choice, but we don't. We need to end our immortality, one way or another. And this seems to be the only chance we have." She paused, branches waving gently, as if there were a breeze through the scullery. "How ever our quest turns out, we are extremely grateful."

A murmur of acknowledgment passed through the rest of the group, muted and uncomfortable since they were essentially being thanked for taking the Doraspians to their deaths. Helping them commit assisted suicide. Teya, disturbingly eager as ever, announced that she was going to go blend with Cassie and everyone should prepare for the flight to begin in a matter of minutes. Oksana walked beside her bounding friend, as Teya bounced her way toward the door.

Clarity was troubled to overhear the lapine pilot say to her ungulate friend, "I wonder... If this phenomenon made Genni and Pauri immortal when they encountered it before, could it make the rest of us immortal this time?"

But Teya and Oksana were out of the scullery, and the valve-like door slid shut behind them before Clarity could react. None of the others seemed to have heard.

20. ONCE MORE INTO THE BREACH

At Clarity's request, most of the crew stayed in the scullery to watch their flight on the big screen. There was more room in the scullery than in the cockpit, and apparently, if Clarity told the other crew members where they should be, they listened to her. Being a captain was strange.

However, Clarity asked Zephyr to come with her to the cockpit. Zir ability to plug into Cassie's mind electronically seemed like a useful failsafe in case anything went wrong during their mission.

When Zephyr and Clarity arrived in the cockpit, having walked down the winding corridor much more leisurely than the young lapine and ungulate, Teya was already seated in the pilot's bowl chair with sucker discs kissed onto her face and scalp and base of her neck. Her eyes were closed, and Oksana held one of the lapine's paws in her hoof-hands, lightly stroking her gray fur with keratinous finger tips.

Clarity considered asking Oksana to join the others in the scullery, to make the small ventricle-like cockpit less crowded. But the way that Teya's gray-furred paw curled tightly, possessively around one of Oksana's hooves stayed Clarity, leaving the words unspoken. If Teya took comfort from her friend's presence, then maybe it was better if Oksana stayed. Clarity wanted Cassie—and that meant her pilot too—in her best form for this dangerous mission.

Teya opened her eyes, looked first at Oksana and smiled, then over to Zephyr, hooking zirself into Cassie's control panel. "Oh, that's a good idea," the lapine said.

Clarity was relieved. She didn't want to argue with Teya and Cassie about Zephyr intruding on their communion, but since they'd elected her captain she would have.

Finally, Teya looked over at Clarity, and her smile faded into a determined expression. "We're ready, Captain. Shall we... begin?"

Clarity nodded. It took a moment longer to force the words out: "Yes, please, take us to the coordinates."

Teya closed her eyes again and gently withdrew her paw from Oksana's hooves, presumably needing to focus. At the same time, Zephyr's glassy camera lens-like eyes unfocused.

Oksana stepped back, nervously away from the pilot's chair, like she no longer knew if she belonged in the cockpit.

Clarity stepped up to Oksana's side and took one of her hooves in her human hand. "Do you want to stay?" she asked, squeezing the hoof lightly. The keratinous tips of Oksana's fingers felt rough against Clarity's skin. "Or do you want to join the others in the scullery?"

Oksana glanced at Teya again. The lapine's eyes were closed tightly, but they could open again at any time. When they did, maybe Teya would be comforted, kept stronger, if she could see her close friend beside her. "I'll stay," Oksana said, although Clarity could see it was a sacrifice. The young ungulate would have been more comfortable in the scullery with Irohann, Roscoe, T'resso, and the Doraspians who were at the center of this all.

Clarity could sympathize. She'd rather be sitting beside Irohann, pretending that he was in charge instead of her, as well.

But Clarity was the captain, making the decisions, and Oksana was Teya's greatest emotional support aboard Cassie. And Cassie was their ship.

None of them could escape their roles or the responsibilities that came with those roles.

Cassie's screen showed the castle-like clouds of the upper atmosphere of the gas giant where she had been frolicking. Orange, red, yellow, and all of the hues in between were piled upon each other in ice cream towers, stretched and skewed by the wind that she swam through. Inside of Cassie, all was still. But outside, creamsicle waves of mist brushed and rolled over her like waves as she swam upward through them.

The starwhal's long, twisting horn broke through the top layer of clouds, and all was blackness, studded with stars. The frothy orange ocean of gas fell away behind them, first a wide field that stretched from horizon to horizon, then shrunk to the sphere it had always been.

Cassie flew past the gas giant's collection of moons—balls of ice and rock in different shades of gray, both sparkling and dull—and skimmed her way past the asteroid belt where they'd first hidden upon arriving in the system.

There it was: the planet they had spent a week training to infiltrate. Green, blue, and ominously normal. Just a perfectly plain, habitable world. Surrounded by the glowing army of Doraspian warships.

Clarity didn't know what those warships wanted. She didn't know what they were up to. But it wouldn't matter if they could slip past them, return Genniperri and Paurizau to the rip in space-time that they'd become tangled with, untangle two universes from each other, and seal the tear in their own universe for once and for all.

Nothing much. Not a tall order. No, there was nothing to worry about. That's what Clarity told herself anyway as her stomach clenched at Cassie's sub-space hop. The view of the planet disappeared, and Clarity held her breath, waiting, in the moment of darkness in between that usually went by too fast to be noticed. Then, suddenly, her breath escaped in a gasp: the darkness burst into aquamarine brilliance. Blue, it was the blue of water. Water all around.

Clarity wanted to jump and scream with joy. They'd hopped right past an entire fleet of warships! They could offload the Doraspians and leave them floating in the ocean—they couldn't drown right? That was the problem, wasn't it? Immortality? Or could Doraspians drown anyway? They were plants. Maybe they'd be just fine underwater.

Of course, it wasn't that easy. Nothing is ever that easy. Clarity knew that. Which was why she dampened and contained her own burst of joy, waiting to see if it had actually been warranted.

The ocean around Cassie was a deep shade of steel gray with only the slightest note of navy blue. Clarity felt like they'd jumped into a movie from the ancient Earth archives—black and white, deep under the sea in a submarine, waiting to see if enemy submarines would attack.

Lights flickered in the dim gray distance. Ephemeral sparkles in the sea, uncertain enough that Clarity wondered at first if she'd imagined them.

But the lights grew stronger. Brighter. Clearer.

The lights flashed now, instead of flickering. Instead of mere sparkles in the water, they coalesced into coherent beams.

"Can you tell what those lights are?" Clarity asked, apprehension rising.

Zephyr was the one to answer: "I have visual enhancement algorithms in my neural code... Give me a sec, and I can run them on what Cassie's seeing out there."

"ENHANCE ME" appeared on the viewscreen, in fancy scrolly, rainbowy letters, over the oceanic scene in shades of gray.

"Zooming in..." Zephyr said.

The view zoomed in, and the beams of light became closer. They emanated from headlamps... Well, that was the wrong word... But still, lamps strapped onto several dozen different writhing balls of Doraspian limbs. Clarity supposed that answered her earlier question. Doraspians could indeed survive deep underwater. Although, these ones seemed to have something that looked a little like oxygen tanks strapped onto them, making their middles clunky and awkward. The lamps were strapped onto branches, perhaps more like wrist-lamps than headlamps.

So, the Doraspian warships in orbit had sent down a fleet of scouts to the space-time coordinates under the ocean.

The Doraspian scouts were swimming around the featureless gray depths of the ocean. And now, Cassie was the most interesting feature here. One by one, more and more of the beams of light began to point her way.

"Oh gods," Clarity said. "Doraspian scouts from those warships."

They couldn't simply drop Genniperri and Paurizau off in the ocean. They'd get captured by their own people. Their own ruthless, short-sighted people who would sell out the structural integrity of the universe for a militaristic advantage.

Cassie and her crew were going to have to stay and defend the immortal Doraspians until the problem of their immortality was entirely sorted out.

"Do you think those scouts have any weapons with them?" Teya asked. The lapine's eyes were shut. She didn't need to see anything happening inside Cassie's cockpit. What was happening outside of Cassie was much more interesting and important right now.

"My spectral analysis suggests that they don't," Zephyr offered.

"Yeah," Clarity said. "But they have a whole fleet of weapons in orbit that they can call down, and they probably have a surface-to-orbit ship around here somewhere. Who knows if it's armed?"

"Okay," Teya said. "But it'll take them time to summon those ships, and the space-time coordinates are, well, they're for any minute now. So, we just need to figure out if it's safe for Cassie to swim around here a little longer or if those scouts are going to hurt us."

Clarity bit her lip, trying to figure out what they should do. Eventually she said, "If Zephyr says they're not armed, I believe zir. I mean, they're Doraspian scouts on an uninhabited planet in Doraspian space. They had no reason to expect anyone else to show up here. So, yeah, let's risk it. Can you, I don't know, whack them out of the way with your tail, Cassie?"

Teya snickered. "It's fun having a tail that's good for something. My own cottontail isn't good for much more than being cute and making jumpsuits not quite fit right."

Well, that answered the question of whether lapines had bunny tails. Clarity had discouraged Cassie from pestering Roscoe about that question, back before the two of them had ever melded. She supposed Cassie had gotten her answer when the starwhal and grumpy old lapine man had mind-blended for the first time. But this was the first Clarity had heard the answer.

The ground lurched under Clarity's feet as Cassie contorted and flailed, swatting any Doraspian scout who dared swim too close with the full breadth of her whale-like tail. Clarity leaned against the pilot's bowl chair and grabbed its lip firmly with her hands to brace herself against the violent surges one way and then the other.

Teya's eyes were still shut, and she sat cross-legged, looking peaceful and zen in the bowl chair, except for a growing grin spreading widely beneath her whiskers. She was having far too much fun playing whack-a-mole with sentient swimming shrubberies.

This situation couldn't last. Clarity lifted a hand to her head. She could feel her panic rising with each passing minute, waiting for the water to fracture around them like a broken mirror.

"How long is left?" Clarity asked.

"I don't know how precise the coordinates that we were given are," Zephyr said, entirely failing to answer the question. "Also... We have a problem."

Clarity's jaw tightened. They didn't need a problem. "Let me guess," she said. "The surface-to-orbit vessel that I theorized existed before?"

"Probably," Zephyr said. "Cassie's picking up a significant EM-presence approaching us from high in the ocean. We have... I'd say, ten minutes until it gets here."

A line-drawing of a shuttle appeared superimposed over the scene on Cassie's bank of vid screens. It looked like an arrowhead, angular and fierce, pointed directly toward them.

"Is that the vessel?" Clarity asked.

"It's a visual rendering," Zephyr said, "based on Cassie's somewhat... subjective sensory impression of it."

Clarity had never wished for the universe to crack open around her before. But right then, she swore to any gods that existed that she'd be eternally grateful if they'd finish up tarrying and smash that other universe into this one, cracking both of them open like eggs RIGHT NOW, so that she didn't have to deal with a probably-armed surface-to-orbit Doraspian vessel in addition to everything else.

Whatever gods existed—or didn't exist—answered Clarity's unspoken prayer.

The water around Cassie filled with bubbles, fizzing and frothing, turning golden instead of gray. Clarity felt warm, and the hairs on her arms—limited as they were—stood on end. Goosebumps, and a tingly fizzy sensation in the air. The air was bubbling and golden too. Like everything had turned sweet and fizzy—ocean and air transubstantiated into champagne.

The bubbles melted away, and Clarity was left feeling lightheaded. Dizzy. The view on the bank of vid screens cleared—the golden fizz was still there, but further away. Many of the Doraspians in their diving gear were swimming toward that.

"What was that?" Clarity asked.

Zephyr said, "That is a space-time phenomenon that's making all of Cassie's electronic hardware go haywire."

"Can you open up two-way communication between the scullery and the cockpit?" Clarity asked. She wasn't sure if she was asking Cassie, Teya, or Zephyr. Either way, the answer was apparently, "yes."

The steel gray underwater scene on the bank of vid screens disappeared and was immediately replaced by the much more cheerful, comforting view of everyone in the scullery, watching their own vid screen, which presumably now showed them the scene in the cockpit.

Irohann waved, triangular ears perked high. Roscoe's long ears drooped over his hunched shoulders. A series of spines had stood up along T'resso's scaly back; the reptilian man looked very much on edge.

The pair of immortal Doraspians looked as placid as ever—two shrubberies.

Clarity said, "Genniperri, Paurizau, was that anything like the phenomenon you encountered before?" Maybe that brush with the space-time tangle was enough. Maybe their immortality had already gone away, and Cassie could fly them all out of here.

Or maybe...

With a prickly sensation of fear all over her body, Clarity realized the alternative: What if all of them were immortal now? What if that brief brush of fizzy golden light was enough to have changed the fundamental nature of their existence forever? To have given them *forever*? How would they even know?

Genniperri hadn't known the true nature and effects of her encounter with the phenomenon for years.

Hell. They should have stayed out of this. Universe be damned. Let the universe tangle itself up and watch the wreckage from a sandy beach somewhere. She watched Paurizau on the screen, narrowing her eyes to peer as closely at him as she could. He was still shedding leaves. More importantly, he seemed to still be re-growing them.

Genniperri sang with her flowers. "It felt like... returning to childhood. It felt like I remember. But it was over so soon."

Clarity nodded grimly and turned to Teya, who had opened her eyes and was holding Oksana's hoof-hand tightly. "I think

Cassie needs to swim directly into that weird golden field of bubbles. Can you do that?"

"She wants to," Teya said. "She liked how it felt, and I've been struggling to stop her, to convince her to wait until you told us what to do."

"Right," Clarity said. "Because I'm the captain."

All of them were watching her—Irohann, Roscoe, T'resso, and the Doraspians in the scullery; as well as Teya, Oksana, Zephyr, and Cassie herself.

Probably Mazillion too.

Clarity glanced around the cockpit until she spotted a cluster of Mazillion flying in lazy swoops around the ceiling. She stared at the cluster long enough for Mazillion to notice her gaze; a blackberry-sized clump flew down and hovered an inch below her ear, where Mazillion could easily whisper to her, or hear her own whispers to them.

For a being without a unified bipedal body or anything resembling a face, Mazillion was shockingly good at understanding human nonverbal communication. Clarity supposed that had been a survival skill on a human run space station.

Clarity said, decisively, "Give me a moment to think," and turned away from the screen. She didn't know if Cassie could still hear her. The starwhal probably could, but none of the others would be able to, and from what Clarity had experienced, Cassie wasn't great at interpreting whispered speech between bipeds inside of her, even if she could technically hear it.

"What if it doesn't cure them?" Clarity whispered in words that were barely more than a breath. "What if it makes all the rest of us immortal, like them instead?" With a catch in her throat, she added, "What if we already are?" She brushed a hand along her arm, where the hair still stood up on goosebumps from the fizzy feel of the bubbles of space-time in the air.

The cluster of Mazillion buzzed and flew from beside her jaw, up to where it hovered in the middle of her sight. All of the tiny insects making up the cluster turned on each other. No, they all turned, as one, on a single one of them. They tore the wings and legs off of the sacrifice, and Clarity put her hand up barely in time to catch the broken body as it fell.

"Not immortal," Mazillion buzzed.

"But Paurizau loses leaves..." Clarity objected.

"All part of one," Mazillion's cluster hummed. "Not the same. Not immortal."

"Are you sure?" Clarity asked.

"Certain."

Clarity felt relief, mostly, except for a tiny, deep, animal part of her brain, responsible for protecting her from imminent physical danger. Deep inside, in a place past rationality, she felt a sharp stab of disappointment.

The cluster of Mazillion flattened into a disc and spiraled into a corkscrew before flying back into a spherical formation. "Besides... no choice. Must proceed."

They were right, of course. There was no choice but to proceed. And yet... Clarity wondered. Could Mazillion be lying to her? She didn't know the swarm alien's motives in this situation.

Clarity whispered to the cluster of insectile bodies, "Do you *want* to be immortal?"

"No," Mazillion answered without hesitation, a feat that most singular beings would find difficult when faced with such a question. "You've seen me evolve."

"You mean, when you split in half?" Clarity asked, remembering how half of Mazillion had betrayed them all to the Doraspians and ended up dying when the Doraspian warship fell into the Devil's Radio.

"The most dramatic example," Mazillion buzzed. "But yes, without the death of individual bodies, there is no change, no growth. That means stagnation. And death of meaning."

Immortality is death, Clarity thought.

Underwater is above the sky.

Up is down.

Over is just starting.

Nothing makes sense.

"Will you be able to tell if it changes?" Clarity whispered. "If you become immortal?"

"Instantly," Mazillion buzzed.

"And you will let me know if that happens?" she asked.

"Instantly," they repeated.

Clarity turned back to the others, all still watching her. The conversation with Mazillion couldn't have taken more than a few moments, but they all looked terribly expectant. She said, "Genniperri and Paurizau, I need you to be ready, inside the airlock, in case we need you to leave the ship."

"I will accompany them," T'resso said. He lifted something from behind the scullery table where he was seated. It was the shiny dome of his mechanical, metal turtle shell. He'd brought it with him into the scullery, and he climbed inside it, head first. Once his head emerged, clothed in a translucent fabric bubble from the other end, he said, voice amplified by whatever spacesuit speaker he had inside the shell, "I might be useful in guarding them, if they need to leave the ship."

Clarity nodded. "Good idea. And now—" She turned toward Teya. The lapine woman looked ready for the order that was about to come. She'd been born to be a starwhal pilot, as much as anyone ever could have been. "Fly Cassie directly into the heart of the space-time distortion."

21. UPSIDE DOWN AND INSIDE OUT

The bank of vid screens in Cassie's cockpit showed the steel gray underwater world again, but this time, there was a fizzy cluster of bubbles, a golden heart in the distance. Sprays of bubbles foamed outward in frothy waves, then contracted. All of it grew larger on the vid screen as Cassie flew through the water, swimming inexorably toward the tangled mess where two universes had come to meet and snagged upon each other.

A spray of bubbles washed through the steel gray water, thick and foamy, as gold as honey, and summertime, and yellow starlight. When the spray brushed over Cassie, the fizzing bubbles —points of space-time, curled into infinitesimally small pockets of extra dimensions, rolled up like pill bugs—passed right through her flesh, as if the starwhal's body were nothing.

Cassie was a part of a fabric of the universe. As were all of the passengers aboard her. Whereas, the bubbles of space-time transcended any singular universe.

Clarity felt lightheaded again, and her skin prickled all over. But then, instead of fragmenting, like she had at the ruined Wespirtech research base or on the lip of the Devil's Radio, she felt a heaviness, a sense of being centered and complete. Every organ inside of her beat and pulsed with solidity, and she looked down to see her own heart, red and smooth, beating in a rhythm that defined her life, pushing crimson blood outward in strands and filaments, defined by the insides of her veins, and pulling cobalt blue blood back.

Except, the blood wasn't the inside of her veins; the veins were the inside of the space defined by the flowing of her blood, and her heart wasn't an organ inside of her, with the rest of her body around it. Her heart was the universe, and her body the center.

Everything was inside out.

Even deeper inside herself, Clarity saw the others in the cockpit. Teya and Oksana, with furry paw clasped tightly in keratinous hoof-hand, were wonders of muscles, bones, and filamented networks of blood flowing throughout; all the pieces working together in an astounding feat of organic clockwork. They should have looked horrifying, seeing them in their entirety, with their skin and fur nothing but a shallow layer deep inside, but instead, they were deeply beautiful. Working as intended.

Clarity was overcome.

She looked at Zephyr, and the literal clockwork of the robot's mechanical body was laid plain to see—every piston, every motor, every circuit board with shining lines of gold and silver solder. Zephyr was so beautiful that the sight almost made Clarity cry.

Further inward, deeper inside, Clarity finally saw Cassie. The young starwhal who surrounded them had been flipped through the dimensions, and for once, instead of seeing her from the inside, Clarity looked on her home, her spaceship, her Cassie, as a complete, whole being. She was shaped like an ancient Earth narwhal, with a spiraling horn emerging from her head, and her orchid-purple body narrowing down to a flippy tail at the other. She had a tube organ for sucking up space dust, a large dorsal fin, and smaller fins on either side of her belly. She noticed Clarity looking at her, somehow, and flipped her tail in delight.

The shape of Cassie's exterior, being inside out in this transcendent confusion of dimensions, was surrounded by all of her internal organs, some filled with muscles and blubber, and others empty—the scullery and cargo bay like twin lungs; the smaller quarters; the two airlocks; and various vesicle-like closets throughout—they were all open to each other now, because the fleshy walls between them had become the inside instead of out.

Clarity grinned at Irohann, directly through the empty space between them, and when the beautiful sculpture of shining white bones, glistening red muscles, and flowing blood grinned back at her, she realized that she could see his past and future selves rolled up in him as well—the amphibian woman with slick green skin and bulbous eyes who he'd been when they'd met, and also forward in time... He would shed the antlers, and return to being the red wolf who had traveled with her for so long, antler-free. She laughed. She didn't know if the future she saw for Irohann was fixed, or if she was understanding what she was seeing properly, but before she could think any harder about it, Clarity's thoughts turned inward. She felt her past and future selves inside of her, superimposed upon each other, each version of her at every different age, all of them taking up the same position in the string of space-time that was her life.

Clarity wrapped her arms around herself, and in doing so, it was as if she reached outward and embraced the entire universe... but also, and more importantly to herself—more intimately, more personally—it was as if she was reaching backward through time and embracing her younger self, reassuring and promising her that her future would be bigger and brighter than the days she'd known on the dirtball where she had been born. She would fly among the stars.

She would brush against the tangled strands of another universe.

Clarity's younger self returned the embrace, and she felt more complete than she ever had before. Her past, future, and present were all at one. All at peace. She could never be alone, because she would always be there for herself.

Cassie flipped her tail and swam in a circle through the golden rush of bubbles, and it made all of the rooms distort and stretch.

"This is the strangest experience I've ever had," Clarity said.

The words felt like she'd said them before, or had been saying them for a long time, or maybe she'd never said them at all.

But then Teya answered, saying, "Try it while blended with a starwhal."

And Cassie flipped her tail again, happy, joyful. The purple starwhal swam up to Clarity, as if she meant to gently rest the side of her blubbery body against the human woman's cheek. Except Clarity's skin—her external self—was buried deep inside of her now, and it was her heart that opened outward.

"This is dizzying," Oksana said. With her curled horns inside out, Clarity could see that a fine braiding of nerves extended through their core, nearly all the way to the pointed tips.

"Is this how you remember it feeling?" T'resso's hissing voice carried from the far end of Cassie's central corridor, cutting through the folded, flipped-around, rolled-up space between them like a knife. "When you were a sproutling?"

Clarity looked over at the reptilian alien and saw that his blood was green—bright emerald cords that traced out his shape, winding through his muscles, and tying themselves around his bright white bones. His flowing blood looked like vines.

Whereas the Doraspians beside him, who usually looked like vines, were now bursting with golden light, nearly too bright for Clarity to look at them. She turned away, and their shapes stayed traced as an afterimage in her eyes.

Genniperri sang, and more than ever her voice sounded like a choir of fairies: "Yes, this is the same, except also, so much more."

Paurizau sang too, and his voice, like a choir of pixies, provided harmony to Genniperri's fairies: "What I felt before was only dewdrops on my leaves; this is a tidal wave, washing over me, slaking whatever thirst my roots have ever felt."

Zephyr said in zir mechanical hum, "Near and far have stopped holding the same meaning... but regardless, I think the Doraspian vessel is approaching us."

Clarity opened her eyes, saw Zephyr pointing with zir blue-

and-chrome arm towards what could have been the sky, if space hadn't become all twisted up.

The Doraspian vessel no longer looked like an arrowhead; maybe that shape was deep inside of it, but now, its primary shape was defined by all of the rooms inside of it, with Doraspians working at control panels, laid open for Clarity to see. Though, these Doraspians didn't look like Genniperri and Paurizau. They didn't burst with golden light. Their bodies flowed with beautifully translucent sap. They looked like delicate sculptures made from glass.

Clarity's attention was drawn away from the approaching ship by Irohann, whispering in a deep, soft woof, "My Queen."

Clarity's eyes widened in surprise. Was Queen Doripauli here?

With even more surprise, Clarity realized that her own eyes could see themselves now. Her eyes had never looked beautiful or remarkable to her before. She'd seen them in mirrors and pictures. They were perfectly normal human eyes. But now they looked remarkable, turned inward on themselves—they weren't mere windows between her and the world; they were entire tiny worlds within themselves, globes of color and light.

Yet she tuned that out.

Clarity tuned out everything that she could, focusing on the surfaces of things, no matter how deeply inside they were hidden now, instead of allowing herself to be taken in by the complexity of their whole realities. There was no way to function, drowning in that much information.

Fortunately, her brain seemed to be adjusting and editing out the information she didn't need. The profusion of layers to every object around her had started to coalesce into more readily understandable forms.

Clarity followed Irohann's gaze toward the arrowhead vessel and saw the Doraspian he was raptly watching. Her branches were wound with gold and silver wires, dripping with diamond and gemstone ornaments to supplement her own crayon-box-colored flowers and petals. The ornaments were on her outside, of course, but with everything turned inside out, they had become her center. Her crown was buried deep inside her, a gold and gilt core, barely even visible beneath the layers of translucent xylem, phloem, and flowing sap that turned her into a piece of blown glass art.

The difference between a queen and a commoner hardly matters when you look at them from deep inside.

Clarity stepped across the space between the cockpit and the scullery, now strangely passable without bothering with following the winding path of the central corridor. Space had folded up, and she could walk right through solid walls, without touching them. She reached out and took Irohann's paw. He had gone disturbingly still, staring at his ex-beloved Queen Doripauli. He didn't object to Clarity taking his paw, but he didn't react either, letting his arm fall limply. She squeezed his paw tight.

Clarity hoped the queen wouldn't recognize him. She could see his past self—green skin, bulbous eyes—inside of him as clearly as she could see Queen Doripauli's glittering ornamentation, her equivalent of a crown. That didn't mean anyone else would notice, not if they weren't looking closely.

And why should the queen look closely at a random mammalian crewmember on a ship that was nothing more to her than an impediment as she chased immortality? For surely, that must be why the queen had come here.

"Don't draw attention to yourself," Clarity whispered, leaning in close to Irohann's ear. Usually, she would have felt his orange fur, slightly frizzy beneath his ears, brush against her face when she leaned in so close. Instead, she felt the whispering rush of blood in his veins as his heart sped up. It was painfully intimate, leaning in so close when they were both laid out flat in this higher dimensional plane.

Finally, Irohann seemed to find himself again, and he squeezed her hand with his paw. "I won't," he whispered. "But... I want to. I want her to know me, to recognize, and have to look me in the eyes."

"I know," Clarity said. She didn't need to say that they couldn't afford the distraction of Queen Doripauli trying to arrest him as a traitor to the crown. Not before they'd sorted out these tangled-together universes. And for her own sake, Clarity hoped that Irohann wouldn't reveal himself to Queen Doripauli afterward either. She didn't want to see him dragged away to be executed or imprisoned.

Clarity would fight with every breath in her body to stop that from happening, but surrounded by Queen Doripauli's warships? Deep in Doraspian space? Her determination to defend Irohann wouldn't count for much, and she couldn't expect Cassie or the rest of the crew to throw their own lives away to defend him with her, not if he chose to be a fool.

The arrowhead ship had nearly drawn close enough to Cassie that with the new rules for how space-time worked, Queen Doripauli would be able to send her soldiers to board the starwhal, and they would be able to comply simply by tumbling—as fully grown Doraspians without robot legs do—from one vessel to the other.

Clarity was tempted to order Cassie to pull away from the oncoming vessel, but playing games of chase through higher dimensional space seemed like a losing proposition in the long run. What they needed to do was unentangle two universes from each other, and Clarity realized that she had absolutely no idea how to do that. She wished Am-lei were still with them. "An expert on ultra-dimensional physics would be really useful right now..." Clarity muttered to herself.

A voice echoed through Clarity's mind and body, much in the way that Cassie's voice did when they were blended, except even more profoundly. The voice shook her, as if she were a crystal, and it oscillated at her perfect resonant frequency: "You came to an ultra-dimensional, multi-universal space-time event without any experts on physics?"

Another voice spoke, and Clarity felt that this one was different, although she could never have explained how: "Their universe is total chaos. We cannot staunch this flow of entropy across the membrane between our universes soon enough. They are bleeding chaos on us."

A third voice spoke, except this time, it felt like the locus of the voice had withdrawn from Clarity's body, receding into a glowing shape that took the loose form of a bipedal being, floating somehow above and between Cassie and the Doraspian vessel: "They're so small... with their mere five dimensions... I don't think these beings are smart enough for the entropy fountain they've created to be an intentional, malicious attack."

Five dimensions? Clarity thought there were only four—three spatial dimensions, and one dimension of time. Did the universe have a fifth?

Also, as she listened to the third voice speak, Clarity was no longer sure that it wasn't the same as the second voice. She couldn't tell how many speakers there were here. Maybe the voice had only sounded different because it was moving away from her, locating itself in the strange, amorphous, glowing stick figure of a bipedal body that now stood in front of her.

"Who are you?" Clarity asked. "And how many of you are here?"

"And how do you know lapine?" Roscoe asked in astonishment. He had left the scullery, and walked right through the non-existent space in between to join Clarity and the others in the cockpit.

"Lapine?" Irohann said. "I heard Solanese..."

"Me too," Oksana brayed.

"We're not here at all," the glowing figure answered. Its voice sounded to Clarity like raindrops on the roof of the house she'd grown up in as a child. She hadn't heard that sound in decades, and she wasn't really hearing it now, but somehow, the sound of this glowing figure's voice tapped into the deep sense of safety and security that she'd felt when she snuggled up under the covers of her childhood bed, reading and listening to rain patter on the roof.

That made Clarity nervous. An alien from another universe probably shouldn't be able to make her feel safe like that, simply by speaking. And yet, the droning, soothing quality of its voice was hard to avoid or ignore.

"We exist in a 9-dimensional universe," the glowing stick figure continued, "and we can't fully fold ourselves down into your... more limited space. So, what you're experiencing—"

As the voice said, "experiencing," Clarity realized that she could smell the burnt sugar and stewed rosebuds from a dessert her grandmother had made—once, only once—when she was five years old. She hadn't thought of that dessert since, well, probably before she'd left her home world.

"—is partially a lower-dimensional projection of ourselves, but mostly direct stimulation of your brains, which are very pretty by the way, in order to trigger the appropriate memories, sensations, feelings, and thoughts necessary to communicate with you."

The other voice, which sounded more like the mechanical thrum of *The Serendipity*'s engine before it had been destroyed, perhaps mixed with the cheerful clatter of dishes as Irohann experimented in the kitchen, said, "That's why each of you hears us in your own language." By the time the voice had finished speaking, it moved away from Clarity's mind and located itself in another glowing figure, this one shaped more like a Doraspian—lots of limbs, tumbled and tangling, but all of them bursting with light, like Genniperri and Paurizau.

Between the higher dimensions of this other universe turning everything inside out and the heavily laden emotional connotations of every sound and move made by these new aliens, Clarity could hardly think. She was drowning in too much information.

"Please, make it simpler," Clarity said. "No more memories from my childhood; no more sounds and smells that I'll never get to experience again."

The glowing beings multiplied—two became hundreds, half of them bipedal stick figures and the other half line drawings of Doraspians—all of them glowing too brightly. The glow suffused into a cloud, bursting through all of the space around and inside of them. Clarity heard the crowd cheering during her high school graduation, combined with the roar of the engines on the ship that had taken her into space for the very first time.

The glow dimmed, coalescing into a single form, spherical like one of Mazillion's orbs, and the sound quieted. If Clarity stared too hard at the glowing sphere, she saw shapes in its brightness: fractal patterns and faces of people she'd known, like her parents, grandmother, Irohann, and even aliens she'd only seen once in passing as they'd walked by each other on Crossroads Station. She felt like she could fall into the sphere forever.

But when she didn't stare too hard... The brightness coalesced into the simple warm glow of sunlight reflecting off a lake on a lazy afternoon.

"Is this better?" This time, the voice sounded like the voice of the giraffe-like bartender who had been at The All Alien Cafe during her last visit. Unsettlingly comforting, given that it was coming from a higher dimensional alien—or perhaps several—but much less overwhelming than the clashing pieces of her memories drawn from her early childhood and sewn together into a Frankenstein's monster of a patchwork quilt, then wrapped around her like a spacesuit before dropping her into an ocean of haiku and sonnets.

"What the hell is happening?!" exclaimed a voice like an elven choir, accompanied by satyrs playing panpipes.

Clarity blinked, surprised to realize that the exclamation had come from Queen Doripauli herself. The Doraspian monarch was here; all of her soldiers were here, including the ones who had been swimming around in diving gear. With everything inside out, they'd been able to tumble right on-board Cassie without anything as mundane as walls giving them any trouble.

Queen Doripauli's arrowhead-shaped vessel had pulled up alongside Cassie too, since during the chaos the starwhal hadn't managed to flee, and they were all mixed up together now, like mangos and raspberries bouncing around inside of a blender, well on their way to becoming a fruit smoothie.

And somehow, the strangest thing was: Queen Doripauli had spoken Solanese.

"No, no, no, I can't do this," the glowing sphere said in the giraffe bartender's voice still. At least, that was how Clarity heard it.

Roscoe heard his mother's voice, although she was long gone; she had died before his family had even escaped their home world.

Teya heard Kwah's squawking voice, although her avian friend was still back on Crossroads Station.

Oksana heard her own voice, and Irohann heard Queen Doripauli's, which he was finding very confusing.

How did Clarity know all of that?

"Your universe has fewer dimensions than ours," the glowing sphere said. "But a much higher level of entropy. The membrane that's opened between our universes—we thought you'd opened it, possibly as an attack, but now we see that it must have been a mistake—is draining entropy from your world into ours."

"Like osmosis," Oksana said, "when molecules cross over a membrane, trying to balance out their concentration on either side."

"Yes," the voice answered. "But since your universe is so chaotic, the entropy is bursting out into ours, spraying us with chaos."

"An entropy fountain," Clarity said.

"And for you," the voice continued, "the energy flowing into your universe is creating order, structure... bringing meaning. Putting pieces together. My goodness, it's hard to even describe what the opposite of chaos is in your minds. Each of you sees it differently, and each of you experiences life separately, although your experiences may be starting to bleed together now, with your proximity to our universe."

Ah, Clarity thought, with a profound sense of realization that echoed through all of them—Cassie, her crew, and all of the Doraspians. That's what was happening. Their minds were bleeding together.

Oh gods, Clarity thought, she hoped Queen Doripauli wouldn't...

She clamped her mind down, shutting out all the thoughts she could, and when she still couldn't seem to keep from worrying about whether the queen would recognize Irohann, she tried the opposite solution and cluttered her mind up, stuffing it full of noisy, useless memories—a time that she'd tripped while tending the bar at The All Alien Cafe and embarrassed herself in front of a S'rellick popstar; the time that she'd turned off the gravity in *The Serendipity* and simply floated, listening to the music of that same popstar, a singer who went by the stage name Starshaker, until she'd fallen asleep; every lyric she could remember from every song by Starshaker that she'd ever heard...

The glowing sphere's voice broke through Clarity's forceful reverie, and said, "It will add a deep poignancy to our universe forever that we are unable to help you, without injuring ourselves. But we must—*we must*—sever the connection."

"Wait," Clarity said, trying to shove her mind back into a useful space. "I mean, yes, yes, that's what we want. We want to sever the connection."

"You want to be abandoned in chaos?" the glowing sphere sounded horrified.

Clarity had never felt judged by a higher dimensional being before. She suddenly saw herself, and everyone else aboard Cassie and the arrowhead-shaped vessel, as bright orange salamanders, squirming around in the muddy muck beside a creek she remembered from her childhood. Creatures of mud. Creatures of chaos. It was a new experience. Along with everything else that seemed to be happening today...

"No!" Queen Doripauli exclaimed, sounding like the choir of elves had been startled in the middle of their song when their satyr accompanists suddenly snapped all of their panpipes in half across shaggy, knobby goat knees. Oh gods, metaphors had begun to feel much too concrete in this confluence of more highly ordered dimensions. "Touching your universe makes my people immortal! You cannot leave until you've bestowed this gift on the only Doraspian truly worthy of it!"

Irohann turned away, seemingly embarrassed by the tenacious egocentricity of the royal shrubbery he had once—and possibly still—loved.

"Soldiers," Queen Doripauli commanded, totally unaware of Irohann or his complicated feelings. "Seize that higher dimensional being!"

The glowing sphere rippled slightly as various Doraspian soldiers, some still wearing diving gear, threw themselves at the higher dimensional patch of light, wielding thorn-like metal daggers, grasped in their twisting vines. But daggers aren't sharp when they're inside out. Clarity couldn't actually imagine the topology of an object that would be necessary for it to be sharp when it was inside out.

One after another, the Doraspian soldiers with their tangles of vines, leaves, and flowers tumbled through the glowing sphere as if it were no more substantial than a sunspot shining on a lake. A mere reflection of something in another universe.

A voice buzzed beside Clarity's ear, or maybe inside her head, those two places felt like the same thing now. The buzzing voice said: "They're doing it wrong; all they have to do is twist."

Clarity turned to see a blackberry-sized cluster of Mazillion; turned inside out, they were larger than an entire multi-star star-system.

"What do you mean?" Clarity asked, breathing the words so softly that she wasn't sure Mazillion could have heard them if the proximity of the other universe weren't causing their minds to subtly bleed together.

Oh, gods, no, Clarity made the mistake of wondering what the world must look like through Mazillion's gagillion multi-faceted eyes, and the extra dimensions of space around them complied by letting her mind-blend into theirs, for only a brief moment, but she thought the vision she saw in that moment was complicated enough that she could spend the entirety of a human life studying it, and never figure out what Mazillion saw.

Clarity felt profound respect for the swarm being—able to process all that information, from all of those different eyes, every moment of every day.

"The queen's soldiers are trying to grab the higher dimensional being inside our universe's space," Mazillion buzzed. "What they should do is... turn."

"Turn?"

"Yes, turn." Mazillion seemed frustrated when Clarity didn't immediately understand. "You shared my sight. Now let yourself do the same with the higher dimensional being. Then you'll see."

Clarity didn't know how she had bled her mind into Mazillion's, so she didn't know how to repeat the action, let alone direct it toward a higher dimensional being who probably didn't want to have its mind probed.

Yet the more Clarity thought about the glowing sphere in front of her, the more she felt her mind drawn toward it, like soapy bubbles circling the drain in a bathtub. Until all at once, space opened up around her. It was as if she'd been living in a house all of her life, and suddenly the roof pulled away, and above it, she saw sky for the first time. Blue and clear, bright and stretching from horizon to horizon, wider than anything she'd ever seen before.

Clarity felt an openness and freedom that was analogous to stepping into water and floating for the first time, after a lifetime living on land. Or your first spacewalk, when your feet leave the ground and the bonds of gravity are too weak to pull you back, so nothing tethers you to the rest of the physical universe anymore, except for your eventual desire to return to it, and the jetpack on your back that will let you steer your way home.

Except, Clarity had been required to attend a safety training aboard Crossroads Station, have her spacesuit and jetpack checked out, and provide proof of both before she'd been allowed step out of the station airlock and float into the vast emptiness around the wheel station.

Here, Clarity wasn't sure how she'd get back to her own universe if she stepped into one of the new dimensions around her and floated away.

22. THE POINT OF NO RETURN

"You can't return."

The words reverberated unpleasantly through Clarity's body, making her organs vibrate. They came from the higher dimensional being, and Clarity realized that the being was answering a question she hadn't asked out loud, and it was answering the question for all of them—the rest of Cassie's crew, all of the Doraspians, everyone who was near enough to have had their minds begin bleeding into each other. What she'd done in reaching into the higher dimensional being's mind had caught its attention and also the attention of everyone around her.

"If you step into our universe," the voice said flatly, "there's no coming back."

"Why?" Clarity asked. "If we're close enough to step in one direction, why can't we step back in the other?"

"You are chaotic, and entropy only passes in one direction through the membrane torn between our universes."

"Then how will you get back?" Clarity asked the question herself, or she thought she did, but she could hear everyone else's voices joined with her own. Their minds were getting too close to each other, and Clarity desperately wanted to pull away, but she was afraid to move at all. Every direction felt either freeing, and she knew she could never return from it, or cramped and stifling...

But she didn't want to leave her entire universe behind. She had put so much work and self into saving it.

The higher being answered, "I told you, we are not really here. And that is why. None of us wish to be exiled into your universe forever. But we suppose, since you are here, if any of you wish to leave your universe for ours, we will offer you asylum."

"What is your universe like?" the question came, more than from anyone else, from Genniperri. Her flowers had curled up tightly, closing their blooms, and most of her leaves had folded in closely to her vines. She didn't speak her concerns with words, but Clarity could feel her fear. She had barely experienced what this universe had to offer, having been kept confined to a diplomatic office like a potted plant in the corner. Now that she had robotic legs, and she could move through the universe under her own power, she wanted to explore.

But...

If she had already halfway crossed into the higher order universe, having been bestowed with immortality by touching it in her youth, perhaps she couldn't shed the immortality without leaving. If chaos only traveled in one direction between the universes, and death was a piece of chaos, perhaps her death in this universe had been permanently stolen from her, drained through the osmotic membrane into the other one.

"You are worrying about whether you have a choice," the higher dimensional being said to Genniperri and Paurizau. "But you have not truly passed into our universe, merely become snagged on the ragged edge of the wound between our universes."

To Genniperri, that sounded worse. T'resso rushed to comfort her, gently petting her leafy vines with his scaly talons. "What will happen to them?" the S'rellick hissed. "To Genniperri and Paurizau?"

Clarity sympathized with the reptilian alien's fear for his beloved, but she was more worried about the universe itself. A ragged edged wound did not sound good, and Clarity had no idea how to heal it. She could see why the beings from the other universe—or one being? it was hard to tell how many there were —had laughed at them for not bringing a team of research physicists. Why hadn't Wisper sent Wespirtech physicists with them?

Had Cassie and her crew risked everything for no reason at all?

"Goodness," the glowing sphere said. "You chaotic beings do worry a lot. I suppose there must be a lot more to worry about in a universe so thoroughly overflowing with entropy."

"Why shouldn't we worry?" Clarity asked. "Our universes are tangled together. Aren't you worried about what our entropy will do to you?"

"You have already brought the anomalous beings to us," the higher dimensional being said. "We will unsnag them, and the wound torn between our universes will heal. The tangle will untangle. And as order stops flowing into your universe, while bleeding entropy back into ours, the order that has clung to each of the anomalous beings—Genniperri and Paurizau, as you called them—will dissipate. The immortality will fade. Like all the others, they can choose."

Genniperri's flowers and leaves shook with emotion, somewhere between heaving sobs of relief and delighted laughter. "The curse will end!" she said. "And I can live again... for real this time."

"But, in answer to your earlier question," the glowing sphere admonished, "we cannot explain our universe or what it will be like for you here. You must choose without knowing. Without understanding. That is the limitation of your own five dimensions. You cannot understand the sixth through ninth."

"That sounds like suicide!" Roscoe shouted. His mind was overflowing with a desire to protect his grandbunnies, and with his mind opened to all of them, Clarity could see that—although when asked, he only listed Teya, Cassie, and Oksana as his grandbunnies—in his heart of hearts, he counted all of them—including Clarity, Irohann, Mazillion, and even Zephyr.

"It's suicide with the promise of an afterlife," Genniperri corrected. "That's more than most mortals get." But she didn't sound tempted. All of her flowers had opened again; their wide-open petals—yellow daisies, purple roses, and pink camelias—faced toward T'resso, measuring what their reptilian companion would do, now that the secret of immortality was available to him directly, and no longer hidden inside of her. Had he loved her for the glow that she'd carried from brushing past this other universe?

Or had he loved her?

"I'm staying," Genniperri said with her flowers. "If you stay too, we can travel through this universe together."

T'resso didn't answer, and his mind felt uncharacteristically closed to the rest of them. Whatever thoughts were passing through his mind, he had clamped them down tightly. He had, emotionally, closed himself off in a turtle's shell.

A thought echoed through all of their blurring consciousnesses—a feeling, really—as Cassie communicated directly, mind to mind, with Genniperri to tell her: "You would be welcome to keep traveling with me."

While Genniperri flared the glowing petals of her flowers, showing gratitude for the sentiment, they could all feel that she'd rather travel the universe in a mechanical turtle shell, entwined around her blue dragon knight, T'resso.

"What about you, Mazillion?" Clarity asked, trying to draw attention away from Genniperri and T'resso's deeply personal and far too public confrontation.

The blackberry-sized cluster of Mazillion no longer hovered near her jaw, but a different orb of Mazillion formed, near to the glowing sphere and buzzed. "We have lost half our mass to scouts passing into the other universe already. We cannot understand what they've tried to tell us about the other universe, but we seem very happy there. All that's left of us will stay."

Mazillion shared a glimpse of what they'd experienced through their link to their other self—it tasted like music and sounded like rock candy; it was the sensation of satisfaction and revelation that you feel as you reach the surprising twist at the end of a good book, except experienced over and over again. Vast meadows of sunflowers encircled a star that shone with rainbow-colored light, but every petal of every sunflower was another sunflower itself, and every rainbow was composed of countless new shades of every hue.

Everything was as colorful and structured as a stained glass window but as fluid and flowing as a crystal clear stream, tied into the most complicated knot imaginable.

Paurizau reached out his branches, still glowing with immortality, toward the higher dimensional being. His leaves continued falling from him in his eternal autumn, losing their glow as they fell away. "Take me," he said. "I was dying before, and when the entropy takes over here, I would finish dying for sure. I would rather take my chances on another universe."

Paurizua's glowing branches touched the glowing sphere, and in the blink of an eye, he was gone. With a single step, a simple turn, he had twisted into a dimension the rest of them couldn't see.

Paurizau had traded the certainty of winter for a new, albeit unfamiliar, spring. That was an easy trade to make.

For the rest of them, they faced a much harder choice: untold wonders in return for every shred of familiarity, anything or anyone they'd ever loved, all of it left behind in a universe closed to them forever.

With a queasy sickness, Clarity recognized the feel of Cassie's mind, mulling over the exciting glimpse they'd all shared of the other universe. Only minutes ago, Cassie had encouraged Genniperri, who had already decided quite firmly to stay in this universe, that she should stay aboard her. But young starwhals can change their minds...

Clarity cast her mind toward Cassie's, trying to get a stronger feel for the starwhal's plans. She needed to know what Cassie was thinking, and she needed to know now, because she realized: the impetuous, risk-loving starwhal and her pilot could make the choice for all the rest of them in a moment, without giving them a chance to object. If Cassie flew through the membrane, they'd all go with her. And the mind most closely blended with hers right now was Teya's.

The young lapine was not known for her restraint.

But when Clarity's mind finally felt the familiar shape of Cassie's mind responding, the answer she felt was: "You don't need to worry; I can't leave the other starwhals behind."

With relief, Clarity's mind relaxed, and she began to sense more of the thoughts and feelings of the others.

Teya and Oksana's positions were clear enough that they didn't even have to say what they were planning. They missed their friend Kwah, and wanted to see how their siblings and cousins were doing back on Crossroads Station and *The Warren*; they were attached to their lives here. They would stay.

Irohann's mind was more closed, so Clarity asked him outright, "What about you? You love exploration."

He held out a paw to her, and when Clarity took hold of his paw, she felt the deep devotion that he felt to her, first-hand. "There is enough to explore here," he said.

Clarity agreed. "Then we stay." She would have stayed either way—she had a home here with Cassie—but it was better to stay together. The other universe was tempting, but she didn't want to leave her new home and family behind, whether Irohann chose to be a part of that family or not.

"What about you, Zephyr?" Oksana asked.

"Yeah," Teya said, "We need to know if you'll stay and continue leading our game of Starsplosions & Spacedroids. It wouldn't be the same without you."

Zephyr laughed, a mechanical sound, but there was real feeling behind it. "I don't find order tempting. Did any of you notice what happened every time that either Genniperri or Paurizau came too close to the gameboard?"

Clarity remembered the string of good luck she'd had when

Paurizau had watched her play. Apparently, it hadn't been luck at all, but order seeping into their universe from another.

"All the randomness leaked away," Zephyr said, "and every roll came out perfect—as high or low as possible. Every plan worked out the way it was supposed to. Nothing surprising or interesting happened at all."

As Zephyr spoke, zir thoughts and feelings leaked into the others' minds, and Clarity was surprised to find the robot's thoughts didn't feel all that different from the thoughts bleeding into her mind from the other sentient beings around her. Less different, certainly, than Mazillion's mind had felt.

Fragments of visual and auditory memories, showing the Starsplosions & Spacedroids game from Zephyr's perspective—perhaps flashing by at a slightly faster pace and better organized—were mixed with urges and desires, such as to surprise zir players and see them have fun.

Mechanical life didn't feel that different from organic life on the inside. Maybe a little more orderly, but fundamentally, still built from the same components as other sentience: memories, thoughts, and feelings.

"No, I'm not interested in order," Zephyr concluded, walling off zir mind from the others again. That was one difference: zhe seemed to have much better control of zirself. "Chaos is much more fun."

And with that revelation—all the rest of Cassie's core crew was staying—Roscoe's true fear was laid bare, because there were no more excuses to obscure it; no more grandbunnies to pretend to worry about.

Roscoe was afraid that he would choose to cross into the other universe himself.

While Cassie's crew had been discussing and deciding their fates—all decided now except for Roscoe—Queen Doripauli's soldiers had begun defecting from her crew, and following Paurizau into the higher dimensional universe, one shrubby, flower-encrusted being tumbling after another.

"You could go with them," Genniperri suggested to the royal tumbler who had once been her own queen, before she had, herself, defected.

"Into another universe?" Doripauli asked, her leaves fluttering mockingly. The mere existence of Genniperri, glowing with an immortality that Doripauli coveted, even if that immortality would soon fade away, clearly infuriated her. "I rule an entire quadrant of the galaxy here, warships at my command, and soldiers..."

Well, fewer soldiers than before, but surely, the crew of a small surface-to-orbit vessel was nothing compared to the legions of Doraspians who had sworn fealty to her, and who were not being given the choice of trading their lives as her subjects for the freedom of a higher dimensional universe.

Queen Doripauli wouldn't be a queen in another universe, just another refugee from chaos like the others. No, she was staying behind.

Although, apparently, she was staying behind on an otherwise empty surface-to-orbit vessel.

After the last soldier tumbled away into the other universe, Irohann said gently, "Can you pilot that ship on your own, Your Majesty?" He knew that she hadn't known how to pilot a ship before, back when he'd run away from her, and it seemed unlikely that the royal Doraspian had taken piloting lessons since then.

Queen Doripauli's vines furled tightly inward, and she didn't answer, but she radiated pride and fear. Too much pride to admit a failing, and fear that if she did admit her failing, her remaining subjects would see it as weakness. And possibly opportunity. No, she wouldn't want to admit to her soldiers in orbit that she'd been abandoned by her soldiers down here, left helpless and foolish under an alien ocean, rejected by beings from another dimension and her own crew.

"I can pilot your vessel into orbit for you," Irohann said. He had experience with Doraspian vessels. He'd stolen one once, just a small footnote in the list of the crimes that Queen Doripauli had hanging over his head. "In return, you will not interfere when I return to my own vessel, nor will you interfere with my vessel leaving Doraspian space, nor with any other members of my crew, regardless of their possible previous status as diplomats in your government. Agreed?"

Clarity wasn't sure that Irohann's offer was wise. She wanted to ask, "But what if the queen recognizes you?" Surely, Irohann's previous betrayal of the queen would trump any last-minute agreement that she'd made here. An agreement that she probably felt strong-armed into, and would certainly feel tricked by if she realized who Irohann was. But any question Clarity asked would only increase the likelihood of Queen Doripauli recognizing her estranged lover.

"Agreed," the queen said. "We should leave as soon as possible. I am more than finished here."

"I'll join you soon," Irohann said. "First... I have to say goodbye."

The queen didn't care about Irohann's goodbyes and tumbled away to the far end of her ship, as far as away from the glowing sphere of the higher dimensional being as she could get.

Clarity felt the queen's mind recede from the bloody mess of shared consciousness that the rest of them had become. And as soon as she was gone, Clarity's mind flooded with thoughts about Queen Doripauli—every story that Irohann had ever told her about their affair; every word of loss and praise he'd ever said about her. The image of her emerald vines wrapped around him, and her flowers staring into his eyes—an amphibioid woman's eyes—so deeply, so contentedly that he couldn't understand how the love between them had ever died, how anything had ever managed to kill it.

At first, Clarity thought that the flood of images and memories were her own, cascading out now that it was safe to remember them. But then she realized: these thoughts were Irohann's. He had been blocking his mind as hard as he could to protect himself from being recognized, and now, his loss and love was flowing out of him, raw and painful, shared with everyone aboard Cassie.

Clarity opened her arms, and the giant red wolf, nearly a head taller than her, collapsed into her embrace, fluffy and sobbing. "I miss her so much. And I hate her so much. And I wish I'd never seen her again."

"I'm sorry she doesn't recognize you," Clarity said, although they both knew that wasn't true. But it also was true, in a deeper way. Practically, it would have been a disaster for Queen Doripauli to recognize Irohann, but Clarity could still feel sorrowful for her friend that he felt forgotten, overlooked, and as if he'd never been as important to his ex-beloved as she had been to him.

"Wait," Clarity said, pulling away from Irohann's embrace enough to look him in his face. The fur around his eyes was damp, matted with tears. "Who do you need to say goodbye to? You're coming back to us..."

"Roscoe," Irohann answered, wiping the back of a paw against the wet, tear-stained fur of his long, canine cheeks. "We all need to say goodbye to Roscoe."

"Uncle?" Teya's voice quavered, filled with too many feelings and questions to put into words. She wanted to rush straight to her granduncle, but she was still, in spite of all the bizarre chaos of merged minds and inside out spatial dimensions, sitting in the pilot's bowl chair with Cassie's sucker disks kissed onto her head.

"Is this true?" Oksana asked Roscoe. "You're going to the other universe?"

Roscoe stepped forward and took one of Teya's paws in his own; with his other paw, he took hold of one of Oksana's hoof-hands. He smiled sadly, and they could all feel the complex emotions behind both the smile and the sadness: years of protecting grandbunnies, sheltering them, nurturing them, and then watching them outgrow him.

Roscoe had rescued his extended family from their lives of servitude on their home world, helped them build lives on Crossroads Station, and watched them flourish. His children, nieces, nephews, and niblings had grown into a flourishing lapine community. The first lapine community in space. And they no longer needed him; they saw him as an amusing old man, good for an entertaining yarn and watching the kids sometimes.

Then he'd joined Cassie's crew, and he'd gone through the same process in miniature: the group had gone from needing him to outgrowing him. And he no longer fit there.

"I want new adventures," Roscoe said. "And unlike the rest of you young whippersnappers, I've already seen enough of what's going on around this old universe."

Clarity had doubts that Roscoe—with all of his familial commitments—had traveled as far and wide as she and Irohann had, even if he did have a couple extra decades on them. But she locked those feelings down deep inside. She didn't need to be one upping an old man while he was saying his final goodbyes.

"Well, you're snarky to the end, ain't ya?" Roscoe said, ribbing at Clarity. She felt mortified that he'd heard her thoughts.

"I don't know how you did it, Irohann," Clarity said. "Keeping your memories and feelings secret until Queen Doripauli tumbled away. I can hardly even tell the difference between thinking and speaking right now... and I'm not sure at all if I'm in love with Genniperri, or heartbroken that T'resso might be leaving me... Or just sad that my uncle is leaving?"

Roscoe smiled again, less sadly now. "Yes, it is chaotic here, my grandbunny." He let go of Oksana's paw and gave an awkward sideways hug to Teya in the pilot's chair. He came up and offered a hug to Clarity. She had to lean down to receive it. "You'll be okay, Captain," he whispered into her ear. His own ears stood tall. He was not scared. Only excited to leave his headaches, aging body, and endless string of responsibilities behind. He was ready for something new.

Roscoe gave a hug to Irohann too; a giant red wolf, leaning down to embrace a frail, old rabbit. But the rabbit was the strong one right now, and he told Irohann, "The snooty royal bush with gold twined all over her doesn't deserve you. So, don't let her have you."

Irohann nodded, but that wasn't enough for Roscoe. "I'm serious," the old lapine said. "You play your game of chicken, driving her home to her fleet of warships if you must. But don't give her the gift of knowing who's doing it. Because the rest of my grandbunnies here need you. And you need them."

This time, Irohann nodded more certainly, and they could all feel his resolve to do as Uncle Roscoe asked. He had, apparently, been wavering before. Half tempted to risk his life and freedom, simply to see his ex-beloved realize who he had become.

Having said his goodbye, Irohann grabbed his spacesuit from the vesicle-like closet beside Cassie's airlock—which was easier than usual with everything still inside out—and stepped from Cassie's fleshy hallways to the metal corridors of the inside out arrowhead vessel. "I'll meet you in orbit soon. You'd better be there to pick me up."

"We will," Clarity said. She didn't think they'd be here much longer. Almost everyone had left for the other universe, or sworn they were staying here. In fact, only T'resso was yet to declare his intentions, and they could all feel Genniperri's leaves and petals, still glowing with immortality, fluttering with breathless hope while fearing crushing heartbreak. Clarity was glad that Irohann wouldn't be present for the resolution of their conflict; either way —declaration of love or heartbreaking rejection—it would resonate much too deeply with his own feelings, and it was better for him to be away, on the arrowhead vessel now.

Even if he was there with Queen Doripauli, the star in his own story of heartbreak.

The arrowhead vessel pulled away, from Cassie and from the wound in space-time. As it withdrew, flying out of the tangle of dimensions and back into the steel gray ocean, the vessel flipped outside in again, closing away Irohann and Doripauli in their own, private environment with metal walls around it, walls that couldn't be seen or walked through.

Clarity wouldn't feel right again until Irohann was back aboard Cassie. She hugged herself tightly, wishing this waking dream of rolled-up, spread-out, twisted-around dimensions would end, and her mind could be its own again. Private and alone, inside a body that kept its heart stored safely inside.

Finally, Roscoe finished his goodbyes by offering a salute to Zephyr and a wave to Cassie. There was too much to say, and too few words to capture the meaning between the two of them. He had been her first beloved pilot, and she had been the biggest of his grandbunnies.

Roscoe didn't need to say goodbye to Mazillion; they would be exploring nine-dimensional space together, momentarily.

Then with a nod, wink, and turn, like Santa Claus in the old poem from Ancient Earth, Roscoe was gone. All it took was one step toward those higher dimensions, and all that was left of him here, in this universe, was the memories shared by the people who had known him.

"The membrane is closing soon." The voice of the glowing sphere spoke in Roscoe's voice now. They all heard it that way. Clarity thought she could even see a shadow, shaped like his face, pass over the glowing light like a sunspot, before it dissolved into fractals. "And one of you has yet to decide."

"No, I've decided," T'resso said.

23. THE LOOSE ENDS

Clarity had never fallen in love.

She'd read books and watched shows; she had listened to Irohann's stories of love and loss over the years. She knew what it looked like, and it looked like a lot of work. All the feelings, both good and bad.

The relationship she had with Irohann seemed better. They loved each other, ardently, loyally, completely. But it wasn't messy and intense. It was stable. And calm. And comforting.

So, when T'resso let down the emotional walls he'd built up around his feelings—partly broken down by the force of Irohann's heartbreak that had been shared with them all—the passion and intensity that washed over Clarity was entirely new to her.

The S'rellick man had tended to Genniperri as her aide and assistant for many years, bringing her things and serving as her legs while she'd been bound to a pot of dirt. Their affection had steadily grown as he'd come to admire her tenacity, cleverness, and diplomatic acumen, not to mention her soft petals and brilliant colors; she had come to see the deep loyalty and kindness in his soul.

But Genniperri's frustration with her dependence on T'resso—and the joy he took in helping her—had always been between them. How can you tell if you love someone, when it would destroy your entire life if you didn't? When love becomes a matter of survival, then the passion can become tainted with resentment.

And T'resso had been deeply hurt when the bleeding together of dimensions had allowed him to feel the resentment that Genniperri had harbored toward him for years, at the same time as her love. He'd seen her frustration with her limitations, in subtle actions over the years, sure, but that wasn't the same as feeling it first hand. He'd never realized how much she blamed him for a situation that had never been his fault.

Even if the resentment that T'resso had felt was the echo of an emotion that Genniperri had finally been freed from—she had her legs and would soon shed the burden of her immortality—he was still hurt by it. And he'd wondered, briefly, whether he actually loved her, or whether he had simply loved being needed.

Emotions get so complicated. So tangled up.

"I'm staying," T'resso said.

Genniperri wrapped her glowing vines around the scaly blue S'rellick. Relief radiated from both of them. "You will have to modify your shell to fit my new legs inside," Genniperri said.

"I don't think that will be a problem."

T'resso and Irohann had built walls of sand around themselves, and the romantic love each of them felt for a sentient flowering shrubbery was an ocean that swept it all away. Swept them away.

Clarity liked keeping her feet on the ground.

She was deeply relieved when the higher dimensional being—or beings—spoke in Roscoe's voice to say, "We have begun the process of healing the wound between our universes. Goodbye beings of chaos, and best of luck to you in your universe where entropy is so high that luck is required."

The glowing sphere faded, and the fractal patterns that moved over its surface like shadows on water simplified, collapsing in on themselves until they were no more. The color of the glowing light melted through shades of butter yellow to the pink-orange of a sunset and finally the blue at the heart of a candle flame, before finally flickering out.

Clarity's heart beat inside her chest again, instead of all around her, and her mind steadied, remembering what it felt like to be singular again. Now that the normal five dimensions of this universe were straightening back out to their usual rigidity, the whole experience felt unreal, like a dream or a drug trip.

Cassie's fleshy corridors enclosed Clarity, and her friends—well, the ones who had stayed—were around her, but she could no longer see their hearts and minds as plainly as if they'd been laid out on paper in painstaking detail with multi-colored diagrams and helpful notations.

Teya still sat in the pilot's bowl chair with her legs crossed, and Oksana stood beside her, holding a paw with a hoof-hand. They both looked dazed, staring glassily at nothing.

Genniperri and T'resso were apparently still at the far end of Cassie, now that space had stretched back out into its usual shape. And while a few stray, buzzing bodies of Mazillion's flitted around the ceiling above Clarity, most of them seemed to be at the far end too.

But Zephyr was in the cockpit. The robot was standing in the front corner of the small rounded room, beside the bank of vid screens showing the steel gray ocean outside, but zhe had already ripped out the cords connecting zirself to Cassie, seemingly unwilling to share zir mind with anyone at all anymore.

Clarity could understand that.

She was actually kind of surprised that Teya and Cassie were still connected by the sucker disc-tipped tentacles danging from the spikes in the ceiling. But then, Cassie had a profound emotional need to blend with a pilot; she couldn't communicate as easily with her crew when she was disconnected. She couldn't wander around inside her own corridors, chatting and playing Starsplosions & Spacedroids like the rest of them, and Clarity knew that made the starwhal lonely.

"We should jump through subspace back into orbit," Clarity

said. "Irohann should be finished flying Queen Doripauli back to her fleet of warships soon, and we don't want to leave him floating out there in his spacesuit waiting for us to pick him up for too long. Besides, I'm done with this dreary ocean."

Except, as Clarity complained about the ocean, creatures swam into view on the bank of vid screens, bringing color to the scene. A jellyfish pulsed with lines of pink light radiating outward over its diaphanous mantle, and mossy green shadows with fins and strands of something like kelp clinging to them swam past. A school of tiny fish like bright copper pennies darted together in formation, seemingly running away from an aquamarine tangle of tentacles jetting after them.

Perhaps this patch of ocean had only seemed lifeless and dismal before, because all of the Doraspian soldiers and the wound in space-time had scared everything away.

Clarity wondered whether it had been more the Doraspian soldiers or the messed up, mixed up, upside down and backwards space-time draining away all the chaos that had scared off the local fauna. As Zephyr had pointed out, life thrives on chaos, and without it, this patch of sea might have become too perfect, too organized for the raggedy ecosystem of a fish-eat-fish world.

Then again, a bunch of Doraspian soldiers in diving gear had probably been pretty scary for all of these deep-sea fish too. They didn't know the shrubberies weren't interested in eating them. The idea of subsisting on sunlight must seem pretty strange this far under the ocean.

"So, can we jump into orbit?" Clarity repeated, trying to jar all of them out of staring wordlessly at the undersea jungle scene enfolding in front of them.

Teya said, "I think we can, but..." The lapine woman broke off, whiskers turned down in a frown.

"What's wrong?" Clarity asked.

"Cassie says that something feels different, but neither of us can figure out what the weird feeling is."

"Before I unplugged," Zephyr offered, "all of Cassie's mechanical components were showing perfectly normal readings."

The fur around Oksana's eyes crinkled in concern, and the ungulatoid said, "I think I've had as much excitement as I can handle. So, I'm going to trust these big questions to the captain and the pilot. I'm going to go check on how the maintenance bunnies handled all of the excitement, okay?"

Oh gods, Clarity suddenly imagined how horrible and distracting it would have been if the fluffy, little, beloved maintenance rabbits had decided to hop around, possibly hopping into the other universe, during the situation with the higher dimensional beings. Cassie would have been devastated.

Maybe the rabbits had been scared away into their hutch, like all of those fish had been scared away.

"Checking on the maintenance rabbits is a really good idea," Clarity said. "Thank you." She waited until Oksana had left the cockpit and the valve-like door into the corridor had sealed behind her before pursuing the conversation she'd been having with Teya. Gods, it was nice to have doors. And walls. Barriers that could enforce privacy.

Clarity asked Teya, "Does it feel to you like it would be safe for Cassie to jump through subspace right now?" She hoped so. Cassie wasn't evolved to spend this much time with her skin in constant contact with a dense fluid. And she really didn't like the idea of Irohann floating around in space, with nothing but a spacesuit and a flimsy promise between him and a bunch of Doraspian warships.

"Yeah..." Teya said, carefully. "I think so." Before Clarity could object to the uncertainty in her answer, Teya upgraded her response, showing that she took the heavy responsibility of being Cassie's pilot more seriously. "I'm confident it will be safe to make a short jump. But then we should probably fly through normal space for a while until we figure out what feels different and why."

"Great," Clarity said.

The words were no sooner spoken than Clarity felt a flip in her stomach and a lightness in her head. The sensation passed nearly as quickly as the ocean scene on the bank of vid screens was replaced by a view divided into two halves: the curving horizon of a blue-green world and a field of black space, speckled with stars and Doraspian warships twinkling with artificial sunlight from all of their windows.

"Do you see Irohann?" Clarity asked.

"No..." Teya said. "Oh! But wait, we're receiving a message. It's not from a spacesuit radio though." Teya sounded confused, and the view on the bank of vid screens zoomed in on a small vessel, similar to the arrowhead vessel that Irohann had piloted back into orbit but smaller. "It seems to be coming from this short distance shuttle craft. And it's a... docking request?"

"That vessel should fit inside the large airlock on the side of Cassie's cargo bay," Clarity said. Had Queen Doripauli decided to give Irohann a ride home? Or had he slipped up, revealed himself, and been tossed in a warship brig? If so, this shuttle craft could be full of Doraspian soldiers, hoping to board Cassie and take the rest of them prisoner.

Well, okay, even if the shuttle were full of Doraspian soldiers, it was really only large enough to hold two of them. At full capacity, crammed in tightly, maybe three.

"Open the outer airlock valve, and let them dock," Clarity said. "I'll meet the shuttle's occupants in the cargo bay."

"Are you sure?" Teya asked. She was staring intently at the image of the shuttle craft on the bank of vid screens, looking puzzled and uncertain.

Clarity tilted her head in a way that asked, are you questioning my orders?

The lapine woman nodded, uncertainty melting away. "Aye aye, Captain."

Clarity really could get used to that.

Zephyr offered to accompany Clarity to the cargo bay, as zhe was likely the strongest individual on the ship, now that Mazillion's mass had been diminished by them splitting in half once again. Clarity accepted the backup, but she wasn't worried. She had a plan for dealing with Doraspian soldiers.

Clarity stopped by her quarters on her way to the cargo bay and dug through the drawers in her bureau until she found the light emitter, still set to emit UV light, that they'd used as insurance against Genniperri and Paurizau attacking them when they'd first woken up.

A couple of flashes of UV light and any Doraspian soldiers in that shuttle would be too sleepy to attack anyone. Then Clarity could take them hostage, and she'd have a bargaining chip for getting Irohann back. Maybe not a very valuable bargaining chip, since Queen Doripauli likely didn't care too much about any two or three individual soldiers. But better than nothing.

As Clarity slid her bureau drawer shut, she thought something seemed different in her quarters. But she didn't have time to worry about that now.

Walking down the corridor to the cargo bay, Clarity and Zephyr passed by the quarters that the Doraspians and S'rellick had been sharing. The door was open, and inside, they could hear T'resso and Genniperri already working together to modify his shell. Mazillion buzzed around them, and their voice asked, "May a third of myself join you on your journeys?"

Genniperri sang in response, "We were hoping you would."

Clarity smiled. Mazillion would see more of this universe—and the other—than any of the rest of them with singular consciousness would ever have a chance to experience.

Another, different cluster of Mazillion flew close to Clarity's ear and buzzed, "We have your back."

Even with Mazillion and Zephyr by her side, Clarity worried that she was being overconfident and would find herself out of her depth when faced with a Doraspian boarding crew, no matter how minimal. For what it was worth though, those worries stayed contained safely inside of her own head, and she didn't have to feel anyone else's worries on top of her own. That was nice. It was nice to live in a universe with well-defined dimensions that weren't being all topsy-turvy.

In the cargo bay, Oksana was sitting cross-legged in the corner by the hutch, with sub-sentient maintenance rabbits all around in her. Several were nestled in her lap like birds in a nest; one had managed to crawl up on the ungulatoid's shoulder and was nibbling at the tip of her curved horn.

Clarity was tempted to try to herd all the rabbits into their hutch to keep them safe from whatever confrontation was about to happen, but she remembered how hard it had been to gather them up at Wespirtech. And how long it had taken. She'd simply have to trust that she and Zephyr would be able to get any Doraspian soldiers under control quickly, and the rabbits would know to stay away from a fight.

Clarity did not need collateral damage in the form of Cassie's beloved bunnies.

Between the shiny silver robot standing beside her, strong as steel, and the light emitter wielded in her hands like some kind of ray gun, ready to flash UV light, Clarity felt like a badass, ready to face a whole shuttle craft full of Doraspian soldiers.

The light beside the airlock valve flashed green, indicating that the outer door had closed behind the docking shuttle, and the air pressure inside the airlock had returned to normal. The wide valve-like door into the airlock slid open like a nictitating membrane.

Irohann stood in front of the shuttle, parked inside the airlock. Just Irohann. With a wide, wolfy grin. And strangely, no antlers. "Look what I got us!" he said. "Good work, huh?"

Clarity went from feeling like a badass ready to fight off Doraspian soldiers to a complete fool who'd worked herself up over nothing. She glanced around the airlock suspiciously, just to be sure. But, no, there were no Doraspians lurking about with thorn like metal daggers.

Clarity surreptitiously slipped the light emitter into one of her pockets. She wanted to ask Irohann about what had happened to his antlers, but the new shuttle craft seemed more important. "This is ours?" she asked.

"Stem to stern," he said, fluffy tail wagging behind him. He looked very proud, like a big dog who had fetched the biggest stick.

"Awesome," Zephyr said.

"How did you manage that?" Clarity asked.

"Well, I knew you wanted one," Irohann said. He looked so much less ridiculous without those antlers. But what could have happened to them? Had Queen Doripauli sawed them off? As some kind of torture? "So, I just explained to the queen that I could either tell her soldiers when we got back that she'd sent the missing soldiers on a reconnaissance mission into the other universe. Or I could tell the truth, that they'd abandoned her."

"And she gave you a shuttle?" Clarity was dumbfounded. "Instead of, you know, throwing you in the brig?"

Irohann shrugged. He looked uncomfortable now. "I know her pretty well, and she was really shaken by everything that happened. So, I made the right pitch at the right time. Mostly, I think that a single two-person shuttle craft doesn't mean much to her, and getting rid of me meant a lot."

"She didn't know who you were though?" Clarity asked, confused and a little worried.

"No, other than a witness to her humiliation." Irohann didn't sound devastated when he said it, but Clarity knew him well enough that she could tell the queen's obliviousness to their past together had to sting. He was taking it really well.

For a moment, Clarity almost missed the way that the dimensions of the universe going sideways had let her tap into exactly what Irohann was feeling. There had been something beautiful—albeit confusing—about the way all of their minds had communed and commingled.

Then she heard the buzz of Mazillion's bodies, converging on the airlock, flying around the shuttle, and checking their new acquisition out from every angle. The sound reminded her of the glimpse Mazillion had shared from the other universe: fields of impossibly perfect fractal sunflowers.

Chaos was more interesting than order, but it was also exhausting. She thought the glimpse of that perfectly ordered universe, hidden behind a veil that could only be passed through in one direction, would haunt her for a long time. Probably the rest of her life.

Anytime anything in this universe was too hard, she would wonder: what if I'd followed Roscoe through the veil?

Untold wonders. Unseen visages. Unheard music.

But there were wonders here, and now that the weight of the universe was off of their shoulders, Cassie and her crew could go find them.

"Let's get out of here," Irohann said. "I don't want to be in Doraspian space for one more minute."

"Well..." Clarity hedged, but she had to say it. "There might be a problem with that. Teya said that Cassie was feeling... different, and we probably shouldn't do a big subspace hop until we've figured out how."

In the corner by the rabbit hutch, Oksana exclaimed with inarticulate surprise, but also happiness. A sudden whinnying bray. The sound startled both Clarity and Irohann. Zephyr simply asked, "Did something good happen?"

Oksana was holding a bunny with both of her hoof-hands clasped around its middle, and she looked embarrassed by the attention they were all giving her. "It's silly," she said. "But... This bunny has the exact same color pattern as the pet Algolan hamster I had as a kid."

They all stared blankly, and Okasna tilted the bunny to show the spotted stripes running down each of its sides. Gray stripes on a brown bunny. It was unusual coloring.

"I'm almost certain none of the bunnies were colored like this before," Oksana said. "I would have noticed."

"That's a fun coincidence," Irohann said.

Clarity lifted an eyebrow.

Zephyr observed, "A happy coincidence. Very lucky."

Clarity was reminded of the way her quarters had felt different when she was in them. "I need to go check something," she said, and excused herself from the cargo bay. When she got to her quarters, the change was immediately obvious to her. She was surprised she'd missed it before.

Next to her Lapine, Lepidopteran, and Woaoo dolls on the shelf above her bureau was a new doll. This one had a porcelain head and hands, long green hair, and looked like a perfect, tiny caricature of Clarity herself. She picked it up off the shelf reverentially. The arms and legs were jointed, and the practical jumpsuit the doll wore looked like it had been hand-stitched.

And it had not been in her quarters before they'd dove into the tangled-up rip in space-time between their own universe and one that was more highly ordered.

Irohann stood in the doorway to Clarity's quarters, watching her with the doll curiously.

"Another gift from you?" Clarity asked.

"No," he said, simply.

"Maybe Zephyr? Or Oksana? Teya?"

"Maybe." He sounded skeptical. "I don't know when any of them would have had time to buy or synthesize something that... perfect?"

Clarity put the doll back on the shelf. A little human, leaned companionably against her plush Lapine, fuzzy Woaoo, and twiggy Lepidopteran friends. "Well, it's beautiful."

The pocket computer in Clarity's jumpsuit pants buzzed, and she pulled it out to see Teya's face on the screen. "We figured out what changed," Teya said. The lapine's eyes were shining, and her face could barely contain her grin. "Cassie feels different because she doesn't need a pilot to navigate subspace anymore!"

"That's amazing," Clarity said. And also impossible, she thought. "The severed part of her brain just... healed?"

Teya nodded a little too vigorously, jerking the tentacles that dangled down and clung to her head with sucker disks. "It gets better though: check your messages."

Clarity thumbed through the information on her pocket computer and found a message from Wisper: "Cassiopeia's wish is granted: non-consensual research on starwhals has been banned in all outposts in the human expansion. My debt is paid."

"That's wonderful," Irohann said, looking over her shoulder.

"It looks like Wisper sent the message to all of us," Clarity said. Then switching the screen back to communicate with Teya, she said, "I think we should go visit the freed starwhals at the Aether Gaia base. Would Cassie like that?"

Teya beamed. "We were just waiting for word from our captain! It'll take a couple of hops, and we should stop by a gas giant or thick nebula for Cassie to get a good meal in her belly along the way."

"Sounds good to me," Clarity said. "Keep me informed, but otherwise, yeah, go for it." The screen darkened, and she put the pocket computer away.

Irohann put a paw gently, fondly on Clarity's shoulder. "That was a good idea," he said.

She leaned into him. Fluffy, bulky, tall, and stable. And he ran his other paw through her photosynthetic green hair.

"Did I ever tell you that I like your hair?" he asked.

"No," she said. "But I didn't mod it for you." Except, she kind of had. At least, a little bit. Still, she loved the way her hair looked and felt.

Mashed against Irohann's chest, feeling warm and safe in his fluffy arms, Clarity asked, "Do you miss your relationship with Doripauli? The intensity... the..." She was afraid to ask, but she had to know. "The physical side."

"No," Irohann said, without hesitation. He squeezed Clarity tight. "I miss who I thought she was. That's all. What you and I have is better."

Clarity squeezed her best friend back.

"I think I'm going to get rid of these antlers," Irohann said. "Next time we're at Crossroads Station."

Clarity laughed. "They did seem like a lot of work. But wait... Did you say you're going to get rid of them?" She pushed away from him and looked up. No, the antlers were definitely gone. "Have you not noticed? They're gone."

"What?" Now Irohann stepped away, stumbling in his surprise as he reached over his head and felt the empty air with his paws. "Oh gods, my head feels lighter. How did I not notice this?"

"Well, a lot has been going on..." Clarity said.

Minds blending together.

Spatial dimensions flipping inside out.

Long lost loves breaking hearts all over again.

"True," Irohann said. He sighed in relief. "They were terrible, weren't they? Always catching on things. I think, I was just trying to prove to myself that I could change if I wanted to. But I don't really want to."

"Do you think," Clarity asked, "that all of these coincidences... Could they be the work of Roscoe... or Mazillion, in the other universe?"

"The wound between the universes healed," Irohann said, cautiously, as if he were trying to avoid telling Clarity that she was being ridiculous. "Right?"

"Yeah," Clarity said, "but for the few moments before it healed... Roscoe and Mazillion were living in a higher dimensional universe, and order was still leaking into our universe from theirs. What if they, kind of, sent back all of these coincidences... as gifts. A doll for me; a pet for Oksana; healing Cassie; and getting rid of antlers you didn't really want."

"What about Zephyr?" Irohann asked.

"Zhe wouldn't want a gift of order."

Irohann nodded. "Hmm. Maybe. But how would they have known what to give each of us?"

"Are you kidding?" Clarity said. "With our hearts spread out and blended together like that? We were all open books to read."

"That's true."

"And what is a string of happy coincidences other than... structure. Order. Things working out the way you want them to. The right way."

Clarity thought this adventure had worked out in exactly the right way. And she was excited to start another one.

ALSO IN SERIES

ENTANGLEMENT BOUND

THE ENTROPY FOUNTAIN

STARWHAL IN FLIGHT

FROM THE PUBLISHER

Thank you for reading *The Entropy Fountain,* book two of *The Entangled Universe*.

We hope you enjoyed it as much as we enjoyed bringing it to you. We just wanted to take a moment to encourage you to review the book on Amazon and Goodreads. Every review helps further the author's reach and, ultimately, helps them continue writing fantastic books for us all to enjoy.

If you liked this book, check out the rest of our catalogue at www.aethonbooks.com. To sign up to receive a FREE collection from some of our best authors as well as updates regarding all new releases, visit www.aethonbooks.com/sign-up.

Made in the USA
Las Vegas, NV
30 September 2021